SEEK THE TRAITOR'S SON

SEEK THE TRAITOR'S SON

VERONICA ROTH

TOR

First published 2026 by Tom Doherty Associates / Tor Publishing Group

First published in the UK 2026 by Tor
an imprint of Pan Macmillan
The Smithson, 6 Briset Street, London EC1M 5NR
EU representative: Macmillan Publishers Ireland Ltd, 1st Floor,
The Liffey Trust Centre, 117–126 Sheriff Street Upper,
Dublin 1 D01 YC43
Associated companies throughout the world

ISBN 978-1-0374-0117-6 HB
ISBN 978-1-0374-0127-5 TPB

1 3 5 7 9 8 6 4 2

A CIP catalogue record for this book is available from the British Library.

Map by Virginia Allyn

Printed and bound in the UK using 100% Renewable Electricity by CPI Group (UK) Ltd

Visit **www.panmacmillan.com** to read more about
all our books and to buy them.

To the second ones

Cedre is not a place, it's the idea that something beautiful can be made out of ruins.

—IRYNA ROSYK,
THE FIRST SWORD OF CEDRE

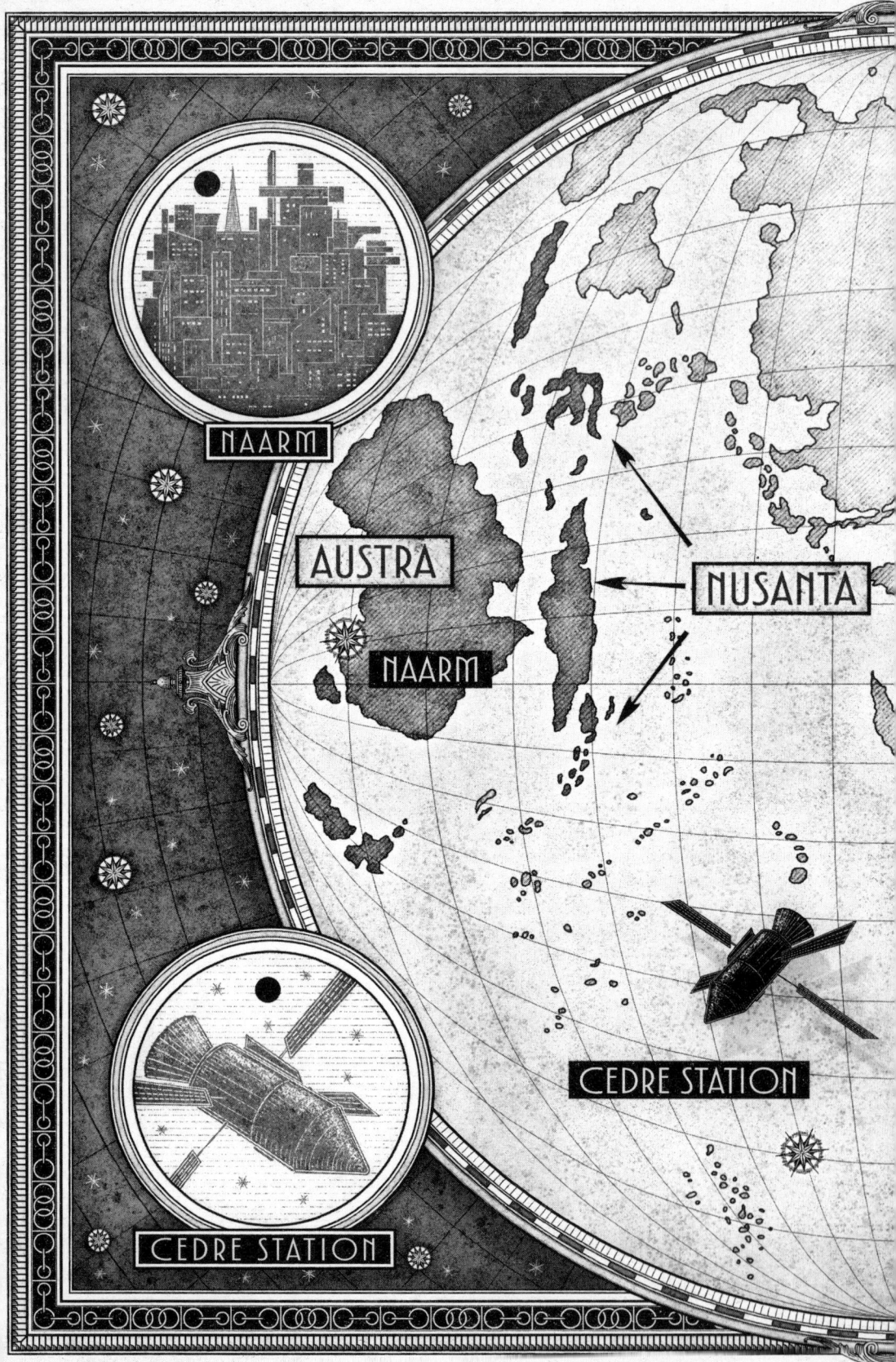

NAARM

AUSTRA

NAARM

NUSANTA

CEDRE STATION

CEDRE STATION

HENZOL

CEDRE
TALUSAR EMPIRE

VALLA

NORAM

THE CENOBIUM
THE MONASTERY
VALLA
HOUSE VIDAR
TWENTYNINE

LOSAN

LOSAN

SEEK THE TRAITOR'S SON

BEFORE

The man kneels in the dark and waits.

The plant before him, suspended in water by a delicate metal lattice, is a cluster of dark purple leaves drawn up and in, like a teardrop. It isn't moving, but the exarch told him to be patient, so he is. He waits until his knees ache.

Then: a creak. The sound of a bent stem.

And a shiver, right through the middle of the teardrop.

The man suppresses a gasp as the plant splits open and peels apart, the leaves unfurling all at once. Then in the center of each one, a vein of light. Of color.

It's only a plant, but the gentle pulse of its light is almost like a heartbeat.

"Are you ready for the hardest part of our journey?" he says to it, his voice gentle.

He reaches into the water to run a fingertip along one of the leaves. He checks that the lattice is secured to the tank. Then he replaces the lid, locks it down, and steps out of the room and into the main deck of the ship.

There, looming huge in the front windows, is a gate. The sight fills him with dread. He's passed through so many gates, spent more time in the Manifold than most people ever will, but still: that dread. It's primal.

A gate is a strange-looking thing. A spherical warping, almost like a soap bubble. At the edges of it he can see pieces of other universes—a streak of starlight, the sliver of a planet, or a moon, or a planetary ring. As his ship draws closer, all those pieces swirl together, as if he's going down a drain.

He wishes he'd taken a sedative.

He sits and straps himself in.

The ship passes through the threshold, and the gate in front of it splits in two. Two identical soap bubbles. Then three. Then four. The sight makes him dizzy, so he closes his eyes. The ship chimes at him when the array is complete: twelve universes, each with an identical yet distinct gate.

He's already programmed the ship for the correct one, the second from the left. Passing through that gate is punishable by execution without a trial. It leads to the Cloistered Planet, the one that once refused the offer to join the greater order.

The Cloistered Planet is also the only safe place left. The only place where they won't look for him.

So he watches as that gate draws closer—or rather, as he draws closer to it, his ship creeping across the vast space that separates them.

When the gate is so large it seems to engulf him, he sees it: the edge of a massive planet with a bright red eye swirling along its belly. It's not his destination, just a waypoint, but still, his body trembles at its size.

The gate swallows him, and in the instant before the wormhole rips him to shreds, he screams.

1

W ait." The Sword stops her before she can descend the steps.
Elegy stares at the hand on her shoulder. The Sword removes it.
"This place has been neutral ground for hundreds of years," the Sword says. "I need your assurance that you will tread lightly."

"'Tread lightly'?" Elegy repeats. "I'm unarmed. What do you think I'm going to do, throw a boot at them?"

They're about to meet their enemies, the Talusar, under a temporary ceasefire. But even if the ceasefire didn't compel Elegy to restrain herself, she's seen enough battlegrounds to know how foolish it is to engage with Talusar soldiers on foot. Especially when outnumbered—and the Talusar always outnumber them.

The Sword presses her already thin mouth into an even thinner line. "Six years in the army have made you rough around the edges, at best. But this is a delicate situation. So I want your word."

The door at the bottom of the steps opens, and warmth rushes into the Sparrow. Elegy tastes dust and salt on the air. Wind kisses her cheeks, soft and prickling with particles of earth.

"You have it," she says to the Sword.

The Sword nods, and walks on.

Elegy stretches her hand behind her, and her husband's calloused fingers catch it. For a moment he stands at her back, and she can feel the heat of him.

"Wow, you can really feel the love between you and your mom," Shir says into her ear. "I don't understand why you waited so long to introduce us."

Elegy's laugh surprises her.

Shir's eyes crinkle at the corners. When she first met him, she noted—with disdain—that he looked like he'd walked straight out of an old-fashioned romance designed to appeal to as many people as possible. Thick, wavy hair. Easy smile. Long eyelashes.

But she fell for him anyway. Annoying.

"Are you ready?" he asks, his thumb tracing a circle on the back of her hand.

She isn't—how can a person be "ready" to hear a prophecy?—but she nods, and together they descend to the salt flat, where the Sword waits for them.

She doesn't think of the Sword as her mother, though that's who she is. Elegy is the result of a transaction. The Sword was required to have two children, one to inherit her title and the other as a spare. Elegy is that spare. Her father applied for the privilege of contributing his genes to her, and once he was approved, he was given the lifelong job of protecting and instructing her. Growing up, she visited her mother and half sister once a year to learn what her father couldn't teach her, but otherwise, she only had one parent . . . and it wasn't the woman in front of her.

Her hand trails behind her to keep hold of Shir's. The salt flat is wide and white and surrounded by mountains. It's patterned with hexagons the size of dinner plates, like the scaly skin of a mythical creature. She understands why the Cenobium is here—it feels like a holy place.

She lets go of Shir's hand and crouches to press her palms to the earth. The salt is hard but fragile, cracking under pressure. It flakes onto her palms and stings the little cuts on her cuticles.

Behind the Sword is a lonely building of flat, circular stone with a vaulted wooden roof: the Cenobium, which houses the augurs. The ones who summoned her here.

Elegy's first reaction to the summons was a snort. *I'm not a dog*, she said to Shir. *They can't just call my name and expect me to come running.*

But the augurs' foretellings are something even she can't ignore. That they perceive the future isn't a matter of faith; it's a biological reality produced by the Fever in their blood. And they don't issue a summons for anything less than world-shaking prophecy.

Movement catches Elegy's attention in the land behind the Cenobium. Approaching the structure from the north is a line of people on horseback, shimmering in the desert heat. Even from here, she can tell their clothes are too heavy for the hot sun. They're not used to the desert.

Fear and rage war inside her at the sight of them. They're Talusar. The augurs summoned them, too.

"Did the augurs say anything else about what to expect?" she asks the Sword.

"No." The Sword sighs. "As usual, they were irritatingly vague."

"And we're sure they're trustworthy? This isn't an ambush?"

"They've never given us a reason not to trust them, in over a hundred years."

She touches the mask that covers her nose and mouth, a standard precaution for anyone confronting the Talusar. "They're Fevered. Isn't that enough of a reason?"

The Talusar empire stretches across the entire planet—the temperate regions, anyway—and what unites its people is Fever. The Fever is highly infectious, and it kills everyone who contracts it—every single person.

Half of them stay dead.

The other half come back to life, two or three days later. Their bodies regenerated. Possessing special gifts.

As a result, they've come to worship the Fever as a god, and it's hard to blame them. But Elegy's people, the people of Cedre, view the Fever as what it is: a virus that devastated their planet's population; a virus whose fifty-fifty survival rate isn't worth the risk, regardless of the power it offers. So from the start, Cedre sealed itself off from the Fever. To the Talusar, this is denial of God, the height of blasphemy. To Cedre, it's simply survival.

Shir's hand is steady between Elegy's shoulders as they walk to the Cenobium's front doors. It's larger up close than it looked from afar. The biggest part of the building, which she assumes is the sanctuary, is spool-shaped, with walls of interlocking stones and a slatted roof made of wood. Another part extends east, a line in the salt—living quarters, if she had to guess. Even augurs need sleep and food.

Waiting at the set of double doors in the sanctuary is a pale older woman with her gray hair in a tight knot. She's dressed in black robes that are stained gray at the bottom from the salt. Her feet are bare.

"Hello," she says, once they're close enough to hear her. "Welcome to the Cenobium. My name is Nerina, head attendant to the augurs."

Elegy wonders, as she often does when confronted with the Talusar, what this woman's gift is. Most of the infected have the gift of retrocognition, which means they perceive the past, not the future—as near in the past as a few seconds ago, and as distant as a millennium. Elegy's even heard talk of Fevered people who can erase memories, seal them off, or warp them. But the rarest gift of all that the Fever produces is the opposite: precognition, the ability to see the future. Only ten people alive have it, and she's about to meet them.

"This is your daughter?" Nerina asks the Sword. She's speaking Talusar. Her voice makes the language sound as delicate as a song.

"Yes," the Sword replies.

Elegy tenses at the description of herself as "daughter," but she's not petty enough to argue. Nerina looks right through Shir without greeting him. If he's bothered, he doesn't let on.

"She looks nothing like you," Nerina says, after looking Elegy over. "Her name is Elegy? Was her arrival in the world a lament?"

"Maybe," Elegy replies, also in Talusar. "I've never asked."

Nerina looks surprised, and then laughs. Elegy can feel the Sword staring at her.

"Forgive my rudeness," Nerina says. "Not many Cedrae speak Talusar. I just assumed you wouldn't."

She leads them into a dim, plain antechamber. Lanterns hang from the walls, and Elegy stares at the flame flickering behind the glass. No electricity here. The energy fields emitted by Fever-changed people tend to interfere with it.

"Wait here a moment. I'll find out if they're ready." Nerina points to a line of slippers near the door. "There are no shoes allowed in the sanctuary. Only the two of you are permitted inside."

Elegy glances at the Sword, who kneels to untie her boots. They're fine shoes, polished, not sensible for walking across salt. The Sword is from Cedre Station, so unlike Elegy, she's not used to walking on the ground.

"I'll just wait out here," Shir says. Elegy didn't really expect him to be able to come into the sanctuary with her. But it's better to have him close.

"Obviously," the Sword replies, without looking at him.

Elegy makes a face at Shir, who makes an identical one back. Stifling a laugh, she undoes her own shoelaces and strips off her mismatched socks, one striped and the other covered in little hearts. She stuffs them into the toes of her boots and stands. The stone is cold under her heels. She ignores the shiver that moves through her at the thought of what waits past the sanctuary doors.

The Sword is staring at her. She opens her mouth to speak, then hesitates, and then does.

"You weren't a lament," she says.

Elegy stiffens.

"We thought we might lose you, your father and I. So. When you came, and you were healthy and strong . . . you brought joy with you, and relief."

It seems like she's going to say more, but Nerina returns with an ornate gold thurible at the end of a long golden chain. Smoke spills from its decorative openings.

"Stand together, please," Nerina says. "I need to prepare you."

"Prepare us for what, exactly?" Elegy says.

"To receive the future." Nerina gives her the gentle smile of an adult being patient with a child. "It requires fortitude. You'll see."

Elegy is about to object when the Sword pinches her arm.

The Sword stands beside Elegy so their shoulders are together, their arms brushing. They're the same height. Nerina swings the ball so the smoke spills out of it in long, jagged lines that wrap around Elegy and the Sword. It smells like sage and something greener, like eucalyptus.

Nerina finishes, and opens one of the doors to the sanctuary with her shoulder. Just before following her, Elegy looks back at Shir. He gives her a lopsided smile.

"I'll be right here," he says.

Elegy's mouth is dry. She follows the Sword through the sanctuary door.

Her steps falter. The room is bigger than she expected, and circular, the outer wall made of thousands of small stones arranged in a spiral from bottom to top. The ceiling is wooden, hundreds of narrow planks converging in the center at a round window that lets in a shaft of light. The floor is white-dusted stone, as cold as the antechamber, and in the center of the room is a mirror with the light from the skylight sparkling on its surface.

It's as big as a pond, and fragmented, so it reflects bits and pieces rather than whole images: a wisp of cloud, a wink of sunlight, a sliver of blue.

Standing in a semicircle around that mirror are ten people in dove-gray robes with bands of white across their throats. The augurs.

The Sword ushers Elegy forward, toward the augurs and the future she doesn't want to know.

The augurs are all different ages, the oldest a straight-backed elderly woman, the youngest a teenager with soft, pink cheeks. All their eyes lock on her the moment she walks in, and the effect is unsettling. Those eyes see more than hers ever will.

"Go to the center of the mirror," Nerina says to her.

Elegy glances at the Sword. She may not like the woman whose body formed hers, but in this strange place, she's Elegy's only ally. The Sword nods, and Elegy walks past Nerina to the edge of the mirror. It looks fragile, like her weight will break it, but when she steps on it, it feels solid. She can see herself reflected upward at a dozen different angles, in one a downturned mouth, in another a fidgeting hand. She walks to what looks like the center, the window showing blue sky above her. Sunlight stretches across her body. At once, all the augurs step forward and look at the reflections of her in the glass.

"You see," the youngest one says, pointing at one of them. "It *is* her."

"That's the faulty logic of the young," one of the others replies. "One piece of evidence and you say it's certain."

"Enough," the oldest augur says. "We've decided on a course of action, and no debate will change it."

The other augurs nod, and fall silent again.

The oldest augur goes on: "Elegy Rosyk. Welcome."

"That's not my name," Elegy says, before she can stop herself. "Rosyk" is the Sword's name—Elegy goes by her father's, which is "Ahn."

"It's not your name yet," the oldest augur says. "But we can hardly be expected to keep track of 'yet.'"

"'Yet' is meaningless," one of the others says, rolling his eyes. "Everything is *was*."

Elegy doesn't get a chance to puzzle over this bit of nonsense. A heavy door closes somewhere deep in the building. There are voices. Scuffling. A moment later another black-robed attendant, like Nerina, comes into the room from the door behind the augurs, identical to the one Elegy used to come in. She's followed by a Talusar woman.

The woman is tall. The tallest woman Elegy has ever seen. Her feet are bare, but she wears armor in the pattern of a thousand tiny copper plates layered over each other to look like feathers. Her dirty-blond hair is braided into a crown around her pale face, which has an aristocratic look to it, her nose hooked and her mouth pinched.

"Stand beside her," the woman's attendant says to her, gesturing toward Elegy.

The woman looks Elegy over with a mixture of contempt and curiosity. She steps onto the mirror, and Elegy shifts to put more space between them.

"Rava Vidar," the oldest augur says. "Welcome."

Elegy chokes, and tries to disguise it by coughing. The Sword told her the Talusar would be here, but she didn't mention one of them would be *Rava Vidar*, the Butcher of Calgara.

The Talusar empire spans their planet under the headship of the emperor, Icar Talus. Rava is his grandniece. Her mother, Icar's niece, is the most famous of the family members the emperor has installed to reign over his territories, known for her exacting standards and her fatalistic acceptance of brutality.

Rava is her mother's enforcer and her right hand. It's a job she's had from a young age, young enough that all of Cedre made jokes about the child general. (*What does the Talusar general say to her first in command?* someone would ask. And the answer: *Nothing, she just learned her first word last week!*) But Rava attained early victories against Fever-changed rebels from the north, and then—Calgara. She invaded Cedre's colony there, infected its residents with Fever, and turned the cold war between the Talusar and the Cedrae boiling hot.

The jokes about Rava Vidar's age didn't sound so funny after that.

"It's only right that you should be introduced," one of the augurs, a bearded man with round spectacles, says. "Rava Vidar, daughter of Ileth Vidar, this is Elegy Rosyk, daughter of the Sword of Cedre."

Elegy sees herself through Rava's eyes: a woman not much younger than she is, who stands a head shorter than her, in worn black pants and a rumpled shirt, her face covered to protect against Fever. Compared to this blond titan in febra armor, she's nothing and no one. Daughter of the Sword, what a joke.

"I'm sure you're both wondering why you're here," the oldest augur says. "Or perhaps . . . why the other is here."

Rava and Elegy don't look at each other.

"There is a prophecy," the youngest augur says, his pink cheeks even pinker than before. "It might concern you—" He gestures to Rava. "And it might concern you—" He gestures to Elegy. "It will decide the fate of one of your nations, or the other."

"It . . . *might* concern me?" Elegy says, her voice muffled by the mask.

"Show some respect," Rava says to her. "Cedre swine."

It doesn't occur to Elegy to be angry. She just looks at Rava with interest. She's never been called "swine" before.

"Some augurs deal in words, and some in images," the oldest augur says, as if neither of them spoke. "Some see few visions, and see them clearly, and some see many, and see them vaguely. We work together to arrive at the path we believe to be the most likely, but it's not an exact science. And in this situation, we have reached an impasse. That is partly because of the relationship between you."

The oldest augur steps onto the mirror. Her skin is freckled across her nose. There are creases around her mouth, as if she's spent a lifetime keeping words in. The end of her robe trails on the glass. She stops in front of Elegy and Rava.

"The two of you share a two-pronged lineage, of which each of you is the last living descendant," she says. "This prophecy trickles down that bloodline—all the way down to Ileth Vidar, and her many-generations-removed cousin: Keen Ahn."

Elegy thinks of her father, Keen Ahn, slouched over his morning coffee, his hair sticking straight up as he checks her math homework. The memory aches. The thought of him being related to Rava Vidar even distantly is laughable. But the augur doesn't appear to be joking.

"What does this prophecy say?" Rava asks.

The augur smiles.

"That is where our solution to this problem comes in," she says. "This prophecy concerns the future of your respective people. It assures victory for one of you over the other—and through you, victory for your people over the other's."

Elegy feels a laugh bubbling up inside her, but it's not a mirthful one. It's all panic, all confusion. *Victory for one of you over the other.* She can't look at Rava Vidar, the titan, the warrior, the legend. Elegy and her mismatched socks are no match for her. *Victory for your people over the other's.* Victory for the Cedrae over the Talusar isn't something she's ever imagined. She thought they were fighting to survive, fighting to maintain the little corners of this planet that they occupy—not fighting to *win.*

The augur goes on: "But this prophecy is . . . a storm. Chaos and confusion. Tumult and rupture. And we have devised a way to make it settle." She looks back at the other augurs, her body angling away from Elegy so she can't see the woman's face. "Half of us believe it speaks of one of you, and half of us believe it speaks of the other. So we will divide and reveal it to you separately. The questions you ask, and the guidance you receive, will force the prophecy in one direction or the other. But you will not know which—not until it's too late to change anything. By the time you leave this place in peace, the wheels of fate will already be in motion. One of you will triumph, and the other will not. The Cedrae will be victorious . . . or the Talusar."

The augur looks from Rava to Elegy.

"We will proceed immediately. Yes?"

"Yes," Rava says.

And though all Elegy wants to do is refuse, run out the double doors to the salt flat, and leave this place far behind her, she knows that's not an option.

"Yes," she answers.

2

Elegy sits with the Sword in the antechamber, on a bench that makes her back ache. Salt prickles on her palms. At the Sword's request, Shir stands just outside. The shadow of his boots interrupts the line of light under the door.

When Elegy was a child, a blast from a nearby furnace blew a hole in one of the buildings in the market. Chaos erupted in the street and she lost track of her father. So she crawled to the nearest market stall, climbed it, and stood on top of the awning to look for him in the crowd. He spotted her crouched there over a row of paper umbrellas.

She remembers that now, and she tries to find that feeling—to climb *above* this somehow for a better vantage point. Instead the words of the augur rattle in her head. *This prophecy is a storm.* Standing within reach of Rava Vidar, more legend than woman, more monster than Talusar. *One of you will triumph, and the other will not.*

"I never wanted children," the Sword—her *mother*—says, and Elegy chokes a little.

"The fun never stops when you're around, you know that?" she says.

"I don't say this to wound you." The Sword rubs beneath her eye socket where the mask digs into her cheekbone. "I say it to explain. I was destined from birth to be the Sword; the Cedre founders believed that having the role of protector be inherited would serve us better than leaving the office of Sword vulnerable to eager campaigners. And I was suited for it, this guardianship of my people, but I wasn't suited for every part of it."

Elegy doesn't want to hear this. She's comfortable with what she is and who she is: her work with the search and rescue team, her rank as primary, her marriage, their little apartment in Losan that they barely spend any time in, and a specter of a mother she never has to deal with. She doesn't want the Sword to come any closer to that life.

"I was told to produce at least two children. I chose Larke's father as a clever bit of social maneuvering, and I chose your father because I believed he would be a capable teacher and protector, and so I had two daughters, just as I was told to." The Sword clears her throat a little. "No one expected me to struggle with it, because despite all the progress we've made toward equality, people still view women as naturally maternal and I am a woman. Yet I did struggle with it. I did."

The Sword's mouth twists, and Elegy feels sympathy, despite herself. Cedre encourages its citizens to have children, if they can, but it's not compulsory. She never thought about the fact that her mother didn't have another option.

"But despite my various failures," the Sword goes on, "both my daughters have grown up capable. So it all turned out well, somehow. My point in telling you this is to explain that fate doesn't require us to be well-suited to our roles . . . it simply requires us to fill them."

Cedre is supposed to be a nation of choices. The choice of Quorum leaders. The choice to quarantine from Fever rather than surrender to it. The choice to speak whatever language you wish. "Fate" isn't something Elegy has ever thought about . . . but now it's a hand wrapped around her throat.

"I'm supposed to ask them questions," Elegy says, and there's a note of panic in her voice that she wishes she could get rid of. "And the questions I choose will affect the future of Cedre. How am I supposed to know which ones to ask?"

"That's my point, I suppose," the Sword says. "Simply ask the questions that occur to you. Trust that you will be what you're required to be, in this role you didn't choose."

Elegy laughs again. "You make it sound so easy."

"It's the only wisdom I can offer you," the Sword says, a little gruff.

Elegy leans her head back against the stone. "Well . . . I guess I'll take it."

+ + +

When Nerina invites her back into the sanctuary, it's empty. The augurs have disappeared into some rear chamber, and Rava Vidar is gone.

Elegy walks to the edge of the mirror and looks at her reflection in one of the larger facets. It's strange that all her life, she thought that if some important role were to fall in her lap, it would come through her mother, not her father. But if the augur is to be believed, it's her father's bloodline that brought her here. Some fine, breakable thread connects her to Rava Vidar.

Keen's eyes stare back at her, Keen's downturned mouth.

She steps onto the mirror again, disrupting her reflection, and walks to its center. With the sky reflected back at her, it almost looks like she's floating. She tips her head back to look at the window above.

The door opposite her opens for the augurs. She's curious to see which ones will come in—which ones believe in her, and not Rava. The oldest is the first to enter; the youngest, with his bright cheeks, is last. There are three others: one with a shaved head, one who's at least a head shorter than any of the others, and one with black hair down to her waist. They stand in a semicircle around the edge of the mirror, fanned out so she can't look at them all at once.

The oldest augur clears her throat.

"I saw a vision." She takes a piece of what appears to be chalk from the pocket of her robes, then bends down to draw a horizontal line on the stone floor in front of her.

—————————

"I saw a great lever, with the Cedrae on one side and the Talusar on the other," she says. Beneath the horizontal line, right at its center, she draws a triangle.

"And beneath it, a fulcrum that determines which side rises and which side falls."

The augur tucks the chalk back into her pocket. Elegy recognizes the drawing from her brief study of physics. It's a seesaw, basically, and it balances on a single support. In this case, that support is a triangle the augur called a fulcrum.

"She who moves the fulcrum," the oldest augur says, "controls the outcome."

Before Elegy can process that statement, the youngest augur steps forward.

"When I saw the great lever, I received words," he says. "I heard that the three points of the fulcrum are three voices in harmony." He kneels before the drawing the oldest augur made, and touches a finger to each point of the fulcrum's triangle as he speaks. *Three voices in harmony.* "She who moves the fulcrum controls the outcome."

Elegy's mind is blank. She doesn't understand this image, this abstraction. Moving a fulcrum that's made up of three voices—it's nonsense. It's meaningless.

The augur with the shaved head steps forward. "I saw a vision of a sign that will precede the outcome. I saw a great storm quenching the thirst of the dusty streets of Losan, flooding its streets with water."

"I saw," the augur with the long hair says. Her voice is low and clear as a bell. "I saw a man."

Questions rage in Elegy like the bubbles in a boiling pot, about to spill over. She forces herself to think of what the Sword said. Ask what occurs to her. Trust that it will be enough. She thinks of the youngest augur's finger touching each point of the triangle. If the triangle is this *fulcrum* they're talking about, she has to get them to be more specific about it.

"What do you mean when you say the fulcrum is 'three voices in harmony'?" she asks.

The youngest augur leans forward to smile, almost smugly, at the one with the shaved head.

"In this case," he says, "I mean the fulcrum is a meeting of three specific people."

Elegy nods. Her hands tremble as she goes over the words in her mind. The fulcrum is a meeting of three people—so all she has to do is assemble the right three people?

"These people," she says. "How will I know who they are?"

"You already know them," the smallest augur says, and the one with the shaved head makes a scoffing sound.

"She doesn't know them all yet," the augur says. "She is aware of them; there's a difference."

Elegy wants to spit curses. She wishes they were speaking her native language; Talusar is confusing enough without augurs debating its fine points. She forces herself to focus on what she's heard. These people, the fulcrum. The meeting she needs to facilitate.

"How will I recognize them?" she asks. She feels like she's repeating herself, but if she can just get them to be more specific—

"One will bear the Vidari name," the oldest augur says.

"One knows the taste of Cenobium salt," the youngest augur says.

"And one," the augur with the long hair says, "you will know by other means."

One will bear the Vidari name. It turns her stomach, but at least it's specific. *One knows the taste of Cenobium salt*—well, that sounds like an augur.

But what about the third person?

"The third one," Elegy says. "I'll know them by *what* other means?"

"You have never said his name," the oldest augur says.

"He will bring you death," says the one with the shaved head.

And the black-haired one: "You will fall in love with him."

Elegy's first thought is of the shadow of Shir's boots under the door to the Cenobium. His rough fingers curled around hers as she descended the steps to the salt flat.

She's said Shir's name so many times. Admonishing him for leaving suds on the dishes when he puts them on the drying rack. Calling for him when she gets home from the corner store. Whispering in his ear when they're tangled together in bed. She can feel his name in her mouth right now, as familiar as her own. Elegy's throat feels so tight she can barely breathe.

They aren't talking about Shir.

"I'm already in love," she says. "And how can I love someone who *brings me death*, anyway? What the hell does that mean—he's going to kill me?"

"Kill you?" the youngest augur says. "Doubtful."

And the oldest: "Though . . . perhaps the transformation forced by love *is* a kind of death."

"That's not an answer! I'm married. I'm *happy*. I'm . . ." She takes a slow, tremulous breath, and begins again: "That's not an answer."

"It's the last one we'll give," the oldest augur says. "The prophecy has settled. The paths are laid. It's time for you to leave, Elegy Rosyk."

"Are you fucking kidding me?" Elegy says. "You unload this . . . *thing* on me, and that's it, those are the only questions I can ask?"

"Rava Vidar asked as many, we're told," the youngest augur says. "Different questions, with different answers, perhaps—but she left unworried."

"Good for her," Elegy says. "But I don't worship you just because a virus stuffed your head with the future."

The youngest augur's cheeks get impossibly redder. The oldest augur only shrugs.

"Tumult and rupture," she says, as if that's an explanation.

+ + +

Elegy sees Rava Vidar only once more.

She marches out of the sanctuary, startling the Sword, and stuffs her feet into her boots without taking out the socks that are rolled up in the toes.

"Slow down," the Sword says, and Elegy shrugs off the woman's hand, yanks her shoelaces tight, and walks out of the antechamber, into the hot afternoon sun.

The salt flat is blinding. She squints into it: the white, shimmering hexagons of salt; the hazy mountains beyond them; the pale blue sky; the glow of Cedre Station, a small white barrel above them even during the day, with the *Sundial* just a speck at its side. When she turns back to the Cenobium, toward Shir, she feels the wind on her cheeks and realizes she's crying.

"What is it?" he asks, and she remembers the first time she saw him, how annoyed she was with how charming he was, how desperately she wanted to hate him.

And then, years later, in the forest just outside of Nusanta, how his dark, gentle eyes called her back to herself.

She hears the hollow strike of horse hooves. Waiting at the edge of the Cenobium is a line of Talusar soldiers with Rava Vidar at their head. The wind tosses her black cloak to the side and blows her blond hair over her face. Their eyes meet, and it occurs to Elegy that the fate she just heard— that she's the hope of her people, and that she heralds the destruction of her enemies—might belong to Rava, instead.

Whatever the outcome of their twin destiny, their collision is inevitable.

"We have to wait for them to leave," the Sword says to her. "Part of the deal we both made with the augurs."

Elegy's enemies have always been Talusar. The Talusar have taken over most of the planet. Talusar soldiers killed her father for helping a child flee Talusar country, and then, after Elegy joined the military, they killed her friends and colleagues, too. She's picked through the aftermaths of a dozen skirmishes in search of survivors; she's seen, up close, just how deadly their army can be. And Rava Vidar is the worst of them, a monster that lurks in the dark, a mythical thing.

Rava Vidar points at her, her arm straight even as she nudges her horse into motion with her heels. Her body twists as she rides away, her finger still locked on Elegy, until she can't hold the posture anymore, or until she's too far away to see.

The message is clear: Rava Vidar wants her dead.

"I need help," Elegy says, into the wind.

"You'll get it," the Sword replies.

✦ ✦ ✦

Later that night, Elegy and Shir lie side by side in the double bed of their small apartment in Losan. The air smells like pancakes from the dinner Shir pieced together for them with pantry staples and a pat of butter from their next-door neighbor.

Every time Elegy opened her mouth to tell him what the augurs told her, she felt so choked she couldn't breathe.

Finally Shir told her, *Tomorrow.* They would talk about it tomorrow.

In the semidarkness of their second-floor apartment, she stares at the back of his neck, at the chain he wears there. On the end of it is a silver ring—his wedding ring. She touches her own ring, which hangs in the hollow of her throat, sticky with sweat. Outside, the late-night patrons of the tavern below break out into a chorus of laughter.

They got married in the courthouse. Shir wore white, because it glowed against his skin. Elegy wore a red dress. Their reception was in the hangukskie diner around the corner from his parents' house, and all their friends and neighbors came, as well as every last one of Shir's cousins. Elegy had only her adopted sister, Hela, and an old photograph of her father.

They ate until they were about to burst, and drank twice as much, and then spilled out into the street, laughing. Hela sang an old folk song at the top of her lungs just to give them something to dance to. Then they stumbled home, stumbled out of their shoes, stumbled into bed. Shir woke up a few hours later to vomit and make oatmeal. *Worth it*, he said to her in the morning, with a sleepy smile.

She touches the chain that stretches across the back of his neck with just her fingertips. She's loved him for five years, ever since he stopped her from killing a young Talusar soldier in the forests north of Nusanta. *How we fight them matters, Elegy. I know you believe that.* She wasn't sure, at the time, that she did. But she came to.

And now, the hope of Cedre's victory—not just survival, but *victory*— will be preceded by a betrayal she can't even imagine. *I saw a man. You have never said his name. You will fall in love with him.* It's a reminder that she's never touched a rose without being pricked by a thorn.

"Shir," she says. "Are you awake?"

He turns, and she can see the freckles dusting his nose, the curl of his eyelashes, the lines in his forehead that weren't there when they first met. And *oh* . . . she loves him.

She loves him, so she tells him the truth.

3

Theren is late.

It's not his fault. He had to cross all of Cedre Station to get here from the university library where he works as a custodian, and there was some problem on the train tracks, a busted signal, that took ten minutes to resolve. As soon as the shuttle doors open, he breaks into a run, dodging people in line for the food carts—the woman selling dumplings is particularly popular—and children playing marbles *right in the middle of the walkway*, for some reason, and the grassy edges of the birch grove before he skids to a stop right outside the temple.

He's a little sweaty and a little disheveled, but he smooths down his hair and strolls in like this chaotic arrival was all part of the plan. The priestess standing in the temple antechamber looks startled. She's dressed in green ceremonial robes, with a glowing headdress that looks like the halos from ancient religious art. The gilded, embroidered, and embellished robes are so elaborate that he doesn't recognize her at first.

Not until she says, "Theren?"

He chokes a little as he replies, "Zuza?" But that's a stupid question—he knew Zuza worked in the temple. He just didn't know she would be working *today*, the day of his brother's Imbuing.

"Not that I'm not glad to see you," she says quietly, looking left and right like she expects to be discovered, "but I thought we agreed 'no defiling of sacred spaces'?"

Theren laughs. "I thought this wasn't a religious thing. Besides, I'm not here to . . . *defile* anything."

Zuza rolls her eyes. "Semantics."

"No, no." He shakes his head. "My brother is about to be Imbued. Isre Din?"

Understanding dawns on Zuza's face. "*Oh.*" She adjusts her headdress, which is dipping a little on the left side. "Well, in my defense, I would have known that if you'd ever told me your last name."

"I still haven't." Theren's grin widens. "He's my stepbrother. Different name."

He and Zuza met in the university library, when Theren was supposed to be reorganizing a bookshelf but was actually taking an illicit reading break. The book was a volume of Talusar poetry that Zuza needed for her thesis. She mistook him for a fellow grad student—and he nearly convinced her that he was, given how fluent he was in Talusar—and ten minutes later they were pressed up against the shelf, hands all over each other. They've been chasing stolen moments ever since then, but they hardly know anything about each other.

Or rather, she hardly knows anything about *him*, which is by design. It's become a kind of joke between them.

"I'll just have to get better at sleuthing," Zuza says. "Later? After the ceremony?"

"Yes," he says.

She smiles. She has the kind of smile that always looks a little bit mischievous. "Your brother's already in the vestibule. You should just go into the hall."

"Right." Theren looks at the door behind her, which is sealed with light. "I can't actually open that."

She raises her eyebrows. Theren is twenty years old, which means that if he was normal, he would have elixir running through his veins like every other person over the age of sixteen on Cedre Station. And elixir is all that's required to open doors to rooms where children aren't allowed . . . like the one that leads to the temple sanctuary.

But he's not normal. So he can't open it.

Zuza doesn't ask, though he can see how badly she wants to. She turns away from him, and sweeps her fingers over the panel on the heavy metal door. It lights up at her touch, and the door opens. His face warm, he walks past her and into the sanctuary.

He was right, before—this place isn't a religious space, though it's still sacred to the Cedrae, and it looks the part. The ceiling is so high it's shrouded in darkness, and the walls are as elaborately decorated as Zuza's ceremonial robes. They're a mosaic of gleaming metal and green glass, sparkling like the scales of a fish caught in sunlight. There are friezes above them depicting the ritual Isre is about to perform: a figure walking into the pool, diving beneath its water, swallowing one of the gems at the bottom, surfacing with elixir suffusing their body.

At the center of the room is the pool itself, deep and green and crystalline. Theren takes a position at the edge of the water, careful to keep his feet dry.

It's his mother's fault that he hasn't been Imbued, that he can't use most Cedrae technology. After quite a few arguments, he agreed to delay the ritual, in accordance with her religious beliefs, until after he took his oath. It's a cold sort of comfort to know that in a year, when he becomes a Knight and loses most of his freedom, he'll at least be able to send messages and walk into adults-only spaces unaccompanied.

He's only been standing there for a few seconds when the vestibule door opens across from Theren, and Isre walks in. He's dressed in simple garments, the same deep green as Zuza's robes, and his feet are bare. His riotously curly hair is already springing away from his head, despite whatever he did to tame it. He sees Theren and grins, but when his eyes search the room for their mother, his face falls a little. Theren isn't sure why—she's made her position on this ritual very clear, ever since they were young. Maybe Isre thought his stepmother would bend for him eventually. But Theren could have told him that Kesia Forint bends for no one, even when it arouses the suspicions of the Cedre government.

Still, Isre looks happy enough. He goes to the steps at the far end of the pool so he can descend, and Zuza takes her position across from him. Most of the time, a person's entire family comes to their Imbuing. But Isre's father—Theren's stepfather—died years ago, and his aunts, uncles, and cousins live planetside, thousands of miles below them, on the Cedrae continent of Austra. So Theren is all he has.

"Welcome, Isre Din," Zuza says, in a deep, serious voice Theren has never heard from her before. "Here on Cedre Station, we know better than most Cedrae just how much we have inherited from our ancestors. After all, we live in a place we didn't build, using technology we didn't develop. Our very existence is a testament to our predecessors' care for us."

Zuza gestures wide, to encompass the room around them, the station that holds two million people suspended over the planet like a thunderhead.

"The Imbuing Pool is another gift we receive with open hands, aware of the great benefits it offers us," Zuza says. "But with those benefits comes the responsibility to leave this world better than we found it, and to care for those who come after us. This is the work that, regardless of religious tradition, every Cedrae holds to be sacred. Do you accept that responsibility, Isre?"

"I do." Isre flashes a smile at Theren. He's bouncing on his toes a little. Isre never was any good at staying still.

"Then please." Zuza gestures to the pool. "Go ahead."

Isre steps into the pool, wetting his feet first, and then stepping down so the water covers his calves, his thighs, his stomach. When he's in as far as his chest, he sinks beneath the surface. Theren studies the ripples he leaves behind, wishing he could see what it looked like at the bottom of the pool. He only knows from what he's read: the bottom of the pool is covered in stones no bigger than a fingernail. Isre will choose one—the one that calls to him, if he's superstitious, or any random stone, if he's not—and then swallow it while he's still underwater. He'll surface, breathless, with elixir in his veins.

It only takes a few seconds for Isre's face to break through the surface of the water. He stands, soaked, and waits. Theren waits, too. And then a line of light climbs up from beneath the collar of Isre's shirt and sprawls across his throat like a glowing white vein. It spreads quickly down both of his arms and up into his face, creeping over his scalp. Suddenly Theren's brother is a shining, brilliant thing, like a fallen star. Bright with elixir.

The light spots Theren's eyes, but he doesn't look away. He feels, instead, a pang of longing for a thing he can't yet be—a thing he'll never quite be, whether he gets elixir or not:

Cedrae.

✦ ✦ ✦

They celebrate at the noodle place in the Grasslands District, Isre's favorite restaurant. It's casual and easy, just a group of his friends and Theren slurping noodles as someone sings the blues next door in Lugha—which Isre understands, because his late mother taught him, but Theren doesn't. Isre is in the middle of translating the song for Theren when Zuza appears in the doorway.

"Is that . . . my priestess?" Isre says, interrupting himself to squint at her.

"No, it's my date," Theren replies. He pauses, and then amends, "Who is also a part-time priestess, yes."

Even though Zuza's not any kind of religious figure, Isre still looks a little scandalized as Theren waves Zuza over and wraps an arm around her waist.

"I told you I'd get better at sleuthing," she says, right up against his mouth. She kisses him, then looks up and says, "Hey, Din. What's your brother's surname?"

Theren doesn't have to give Isre a warning look, because Isre is a good brother.

"He doesn't have one," Isre says casually. "It's just 'Theren.' Like a famous artist."

"Oh, so the entire family is in on the bit, huh?" Zuza says, smiling down at Theren.

"Want some noodles?" Isre asks her.

"No," Theren and Zuza say, in unison.

Theren slides his hand into hers and stands. "Happy Imbuing, Isre. See you on Friday?"

Friday is the day of their weekly family dinner. Isre gives him a clumsy salute, and Theren and Zuza make their way out of the noodle shop and into the market.

The Grasslands District market is a chaotic place, and a beautiful one. The ceiling's ductwork and pipes are shrouded by huge swaths of yellow fabric, which gives everything beneath a warm glow. The space itself is a maze of restaurants and shops. The signs are in every language of Cedre— hundreds of them, though their number dwindles by the year—and every shade of neon. The smell of spices washes over Theren; a woman nearby flips a savory pancake. He dodges a rack of plush toys shaped like extinct animals and then they're outside of the market, walking into the quiet beyond it.

He doesn't live far from here. They wander down the starboard hallway, taking their time. They pass a case of emergency oxygen masks—*break seal in case of sudden oxygen loss*—and a row of launch seats tucked into the wall. He realizes the "On This Day in History" display is just ahead of them, and he tries to tug Zuza down a side path. She tugs right back.

"No, I love this display, come on—" She drags him toward the pavilion. In the center of it there's a holographic projection hovering over a large sheet of obsidian, older Cedrae technology that doesn't use elixir.

The projection is a spaceship. Theren recognizes it, and his mouth goes dry. Text scrolls across the top of the hologram.

> On this day in history . . . twenty years ago, a ship called the *Hoatzin* entered Cedre Station's airspace carrying twenty Talusar self-exiles who fled their homes after several of them spoke out against the Talusar government. They claimed to be seeking safe harbor in Cedre. A month of tension ensued as the Sword of Cedre, fearing that the exiles had been sent to contaminate Cedre Station with the Fever, contemplated eliminating the *Hoatzin* for the good of all. Ultimately, though, the exiles' story of political persecution was confirmed, and they were able to come to terms with the Sword of Cedre.

"Oh, my parents were just talking about this the other day," Zuza says. "They said everyone basically camped out in their news pavilions for weeks. I don't remember how the crisis ended."

"The exiles promised their firstborn children in service to Cedre,"

Theren replies. "They had to become Knights or their citizenship would be revoked and they would all be deported back to Talusar country."

He speaks without thinking about how it will sound. He can feel Zuza staring at him, but he doesn't want to acknowledge it. He tugs her away from the pavilion, toward his apartment, and she goes without argument.

His apartment is in a column of sixteen single-resident dwellings, arranged around a small central courtyard. There's a garden in the courtyard tended by all the column's residents, where they've managed to grow radishes, peas, and lettuce.

He brushes a finger over one of the radish leaves on his way to the stairs. And then he stops, so abruptly that Zuza runs right into him.

He can see through the grate floor that there are two people standing outside his apartment. One of them is his mother. And the other has the seal of Cedre on their jacket.

This can't be good.

His mother, Kesia Forint, is Theren's height—almost 183 centimeters, by his last measurement—and wiry, with a square jaw she didn't pass along to him, and a stern brow she did. She isn't beautiful, but wherever she goes, people flow around her, like she's a rock in a stream.

The man with her is shorter, but broader, with black hair and a tic in his jaw that suggests irritation. His name is Fenn Kovek, and he's a Knight.

"Mom," Theren says, in greeting, when he reaches the top of the stairs. "Fenn. What's going on?"

"Fucking finally," Fenn says irritably. "If you had elixir like an *adult*, I could have sent you a message instead of waiting here for an entire hour." He looks at Zuza. "Tell your girlfriend to go home, Forint."

Theren's too busy taking in his mother's troubled expression to respond. She just shakes her head a little.

"Your name is 'Forint'?" Zuza says.

The reason he never gave her his surname is that he wanted to avoid precisely *this* moment, when she realizes who he is and how he knows so much about the Talusar exiles on the *Hoatzin*:

Because his mother was one of them.

Theren releases her hand. "I'm sorry. I have to deal with this."

She's frowning at him; not like she's unhappy, but like she's sorting through what she knows about him in her mind. He's fluent in Talusar, despite being a humble library custodian. He refused to give her his last name. He doesn't have elixir. He knew too much about the *Hoatzin*.

He's the son of a Talusar exile.

"Yeah, all right," she says. She's stiff, like clay drying in the sun.

And just like that, he realizes this is the last time he'll ever see her. It doesn't matter that he's lived in Cedre his whole life, that he's not infected with the Fever, that he's never even set foot in Talusar country. He's enough like Cedre's enemies to have scared her. And Theren's not interested in pursuing someone who's afraid of him.

Zuza descends the stairs again. Heavy with disappointment, Theren unlocks his apartment door, and holds it open for his mother and Fenn.

Space is a precious commodity on Cedre Station, so his apartment is only large enough for one person. It's a single room with a bed built into one wall like a shelf and a kitchen on the other. The bathroom is down the hall, shared among the four people who live on this floor. There's a kitchen table with attached stools that folds down from the wall, and he unfolds it for them.

Kesia lingers by the door, looking at the practice sword he keeps there, leaning up against the shelves. She takes it in hand.

"Have you been practicing?" she says to him, in careful English. She doesn't speak to him in Talusar when anyone else is around, especially not the son of another exile, like Fenn. She has to maintain the appearance of total compliance with Cedrae culture and customs. The only thing she's ever publicly insisted on was Theren not getting Imbued yet—and even that was enough to raise a few eyebrows.

"Of course," Theren replies. "I promised you I would."

She smiles at him. Theren can feel Fenn's eyes on him.

"You taught him the sword?" Fenn asks her.

"I did," Kesia says. "Is that not allowed?"

"No, it's just . . ." Fenn trails off, then clears his throat. "I'm given to understand the Sword of Cedre doesn't care if her Knights are trained or not."

"Because she's content for you to be human shields but doesn't want you to be competent fighters," Kesia supplies. "In case you decide to turn on her. Is that right?"

Fenn shifts in his seat, obviously uncomfortable. It's as much of a "yes" as he'll give.

Kesia leans the sword against the wall again. She sits on the stool opposite Fenn, but Theren's too antsy to sit. He leans against the kitchen counter, instead.

"Tell him what you came here for," Kesia says to Fenn.

"The Sword sent me," Fenn says. "It seems your oath is required sooner rather than later."

Theren feels even heavier.

This was the bargain the Sword struck with the Talusar exiles on the

Hoatzin: at twenty-one years old, their firstborn children would become Knights of Cedre, oathsworn to protect the Sword with their lives. In exchange, they could be Cedrae citizens. If any of them refused, they and their family would be deported.

It was a good bargain, he reminds himself. He's a Cedre citizen. If his mother had stayed with the Talusar, he would have to be infected with Fever with a fifty-fifty chance of survival; he would likely have to join the army; he would have to live under the emperor's tyranny. To remain here, safe and uninfected, all he has to do is act as one of five "human shields"—as his mother calls them—for the Sword and her heir. He'll get paid for his time. He can still get married, if he wants, or have children. And because the Sword and her firstborn live here, he'll even spend most of his time on Cedre Station, not far from his friends and family. This is the life his mother bought for him, and he's grateful for it, even if it doesn't offer him any choices.

I'm grateful for it, he reminds himself.

"How soon?" he asks Fenn.

"Why?" Kesia demands, at the same time.

Fenn looks them both over, as if deciding who to answer first. He folds his hands on the table—perpetually tacky, no matter what Theren does—and looks at Kesia.

"What I tell you must remain here for the time being," Fenn says. "Yesterday the Sword and her secondborn, Elegy Rosyk, went to see the augurs at the Cenobium. So did Rava Vidar."

At the mention of the augurs, Kesia's hand twitches, and he knows why. She usually makes the sign of the Fever—three circles—over her mouth every time the augurs are mentioned. But not in front of Fenn.

The most religious Talusar worship the Fever like a god. His mother is among them. That's why she insisted he not get Imbued yet—because *those who worship the Fever despise what it despises*, she once told him, and the Fever burns elixir from a person's blood. That's why most Cedrae technology requires elixir—so that the Talusar can't use it.

"The Sword's youngest daughter is the focal point of a prophecy that predicts Cedre's triumph," Fenn goes on. "It's not a guaranteed outcome—it could very well apply to Rava and the Talusar, instead."

"Cedre's *triumph*," Kesia repeats. "What does that mean?"

"I don't know." Fenn glances at the wall clock that hangs over the small refrigerator in the corner. It's shaped like a walrus, with whiskers that tremble with each second. Isre bought it for him. "Regardless of what it means, Elegy Rosyk is now in considerable danger from the Talusar—and from Rava Vidar, specifically. The Sword believes it's best for her to have as much protection as she can."

Fenn's dark eyes fix on Theren's, and Theren understands. The Sword wants Elegy Rosyk to have her own Knight. There's no protection quite like someone who's sworn to give their life for yours, after all.

"An oath, once made, can't be changed. And you're the only one of us who hasn't taken his oath yet. The Sword would like you to swear it, not to her, but to Elegy, who those in the know are now calling the Hope of Cedre."

"When?" Theren asks softly.

"This is an urgent matter," Fenn says. "You're to come with me back to Losan tonight, and swear your oath tomorrow afternoon."

Theren wants to scream.

Tonight.

"He has a *year* left," Kesia says hotly. She brings her hand down hard on the table, making Fenn jump a little. "The Sword wants to take that time from him? When she didn't take it from any of the others?"

"Yes, and what a critical year it would have been," Fenn says dryly. He looks Theren over. "Judging by that hickey, you were engaged in something *very* important this evening."

Theren doesn't react. He's learned not to take anything Fenn says personally—one of the other Knights, Maeve, insists that he doesn't like anyone except his own parents.

But he's surprised when Kesia rises to his defense.

"You will not shame my son for savoring what little time he has before signing his life over to the state," she snaps. "Particularly when your own twentieth year was replete with mischief."

Fenn looks away. But Theren can't help but stare at her. Her eyes are sparkling—with tears, he thinks, and he's never seen his mother cry, not even five years ago when his stepfather died and they flew to the planet, to Austra, to scatter his ashes. But it's anger, not sorrow, that burns in her stare now. For the first time, he wonders if she regrets the bargain she made with his future. If she hates it.

"I'll call your brother," she says to him. "Is there anyone else you'd like to say goodbye to?"

He thinks of his friends in the library, who he's kept at a distance, knowing his life as a Knight would take him far away from them; his old friends from school, who he only gets to see every few months, now that everyone is so busy. He thinks of the expression on Zuza's face when she said his name. He wants to walk back to the rare books room and breathe in its familiar smell, wants to steal one last kiss in the stacks, wants to watch a film in his next-door neighbor's apartment, projected on the wall, wants to try one of the dumplings near the temple. He wants to remember what this life *feels* like, before it's gone.

But there's no time, no choice, no path other than this one.

"No," he says. "Just Isre."

+ + +

Fenn leaves soon after that, to arrange transport back to Losan. Kesia leaves, too, to find Isre at the noodle shop and to grab a few things for Theren to pack. Theren stands in his kitchen for a long time, watching the seconds pass.

Then he picks up the practice sword by the door, and moves into the center of the apartment. There's not enough space to practice in here, not really. There are fourteen postures for the longsword, according to the Talusar; they practice them in a fluid sequence, as a warm-up or a meditation. He steps into the middle of that sequence almost without meaning to, the sword held out from his chest, his legs staggered.

The other Knights went through a mere month of training, just enough to keep up the charade that they're actually bodyguards. But while the Sword wants to showcase the children of Talusar exiles as a kind of triumph over their enemies, she doesn't actually trust them to fight for her. She has her own cadre of soldiers for that.

But Kesia wanted to pass along the knowledge she suffered so much for, and Theren was happy to learn, even if he had to keep the lessons quiet so no one thought he was becoming dangerous.

He shifts the sword up to high guard—over his head, the blade angled down. Then he swings the sword down, narrowly missing the bed frame, to low guard.

He's gone through the sequence twice by the time she comes back, tapping on the door to open it. She carries a garment bag by the hanger at the top. Theren has seen it before, in her closet, but he doesn't know what's inside it.

She looks at the sword in his hand—his left hand, always, since he's almost useless with his right—and offers him a grim smile.

"I had this made for you," she says, holding up the garment bag. "It's modeled after something my father used to wear. I thought you could wear it to swear your oath, to send a message . . . but I'll understand if you don't want to be provocative."

Theren isn't sure how a suit jacket can be provocative, but he unzips the bag.

Talusar formalwear is like armor. Strict, almost bulky shoulders, a sturdy collar. The design is only provocative in combination with the color: a deep blue with copper detailing at the collar and buttons. Talusar colors.

Theren warms at that, his mother surprising him, thinking of him. He puts the jacket on, and though it's a little loose in the shoulders—she always insists he has one last growth spurt left in him, and she won't be dissuaded—the rest of it fits.

Kesia sucks in a breath at the sight of him.

"You look so much like your father," she says.

Theren's father died long before he was born. Also a soldier, Kesia told him, his body buried under a tree outside of Valla. Most of the time, her grief seems to keep her from speaking about him, so Theren doesn't know much more.

He hears footsteps on the stairs outside. "Isre's here."

"I'll fill him in," she says. "Start packing."

He does, running a fingertip over the framed picture of his stepbrother and stepfather that he keeps on a shelf. His mother married Harun when Theren was a child, and it took a while to think of him and Isre—four years younger than Theren and twice as obnoxious—as his family. But now it's hard to imagine a family without them.

He's just zipping up his bag when Isre walks into the apartment, a troubled set to his mouth.

He's almost Theren's height, but narrower through the shoulders. In the last year, he's settled into his face, learning to shave the scraggly hairs on his upper lip, to put gel in his hair when it's wet so the curls don't turn to frizz. He's starting to fill out a little. He's becoming something, and Theren wishes he could be around to watch it happen.

"Nice jacket," Isre says. Theren forgot he was wearing it. He looks at himself in the wall mirror, blue-clad, his face wan.

He can't come up with a response. Isre comes to stand behind him.

"I hate them," Isre says.

Theren shakes his head. "You don't hate the Sword of Cedre. And it's not Fenn's fault."

"Solidarity in hatred is one of my jobs as your brother," Isre says sternly. "You can be mature and above it, but I'm sure as hell not going to be."

Theren smiles a little, despite himself.

"You'll still get Imbued after you swear your oath, right? Like you planned?" Isre says. "That way we can talk, even when we're far apart."

"Yes," Theren says firmly.

They make eye contact in the mirror.

"I'm sorry this is happening to you," Isre says.

Theren waits for the "but," for the reassurance he's sure is coming. But it doesn't. Isre just grips Theren's arms and lets that simple statement hang between them.

4

An hour later, Theren is buckling himself into a seat on one of the Sword's Sparrows. Fenn and Kesia are across from him.

Theren has only been in run-down public shuttles before this, where all the walls were fingerprinted and scratched with the names of past passengers. But this ship is polished. The interior is covered in sleek metal panels, with lights outlining the jump seats and the central walkway.

His mother's hands are deft with the safety straps. The Talusar take elixir from all the places they've conquered, and they give it to their child soldiers at age eleven, so they can fly ships until they get infected at sixteen. Kesia was one of them. Conscripted. Forced to swallow elixir, despite her religious objections. Taught everything about ships: how they worked, how they broke, how to fix them, and how to fly them.

Then, like all Talusar, she was infected. She died. And two days later, she came back to life.

After that, all the flight skills she'd learned were no longer useful.

"Hang in there," the pilot says. "Some people find this trip unsettling."

Kesia snorts. The ship lifts away from the shuttle bay floor so smoothly Theren hardly feels it. The pilot eases them forward, through the open gate and into the black. As they turn, Cedre Station, barrel-shaped and bright, takes up the entire view, big as the moon. Tethered to it is the *Sundial*, a large ship—but still tiny by comparison to the space station beside it—from generations past that will one day carry a crew in pursuit of another planet that supports life. A planet they know for a fact is out there, because before the spread of the Fever . . . it contacted them.

Theren's body lightens as they move away from the station's gravity. He focuses on keeping his meager dinner down.

They turn to face the planet. It looks farther away than Theren expected. He doesn't recognize anything in the patches of clouds, white and wispy, or the dark oceans beneath them. He's surprised by how bright it is; he has to squint to see it. It's supposed to be his home, but he feels no real attachment to it. He was born on the spaceship *Hoatzin*, while the exiles waited for the Sword to either grant them refugee status or blast them out of orbit. So "home" is Cedre Station. "Home" is creaking metal and stale air.

Their speed increases gradually, but it's still obvious when they leave Cedre Station's gravity completely. His clothes lift away from his body, and his shoulders press up into the safety straps.

"Why did you want to leave?" he says to Kesia. She'll know what he means. She usually does.

"I told you," she says idly. "I was pregnant with you, and suddenly the fifty percent chance of you dying from Fever was unbearable to me."

Her hand comes up to her stomach, as if in remembrance.

"I guess I just wondered if there was another reason," he says.

She gives him an odd look, but doesn't answer.

"Our ancestors were cold-weather people," she says, and she points ahead of them. "From the northern continent, there under that grouping of clouds. I didn't know this myself, but I met an epocha once, and she told me. She saw snow. Red cheeks."

Apart from the augurs, most Talusar had the gift of retrocognition—they could see a past they had not experienced themselves. It was most common to see someone else's recent past at a touch. But there were rarer gifts. The ones they called "epocha" saw much further back. Decades. Sometimes more. They were considered holy, and lived sequestered in monasteries . . . except for Rava Vidar, who supposedly embodied the spirits of long-dead warriors. Her mother had argued that such a special gift should not be wasted in a monastery, and the emperor had agreed.

"Do you like it?" Theren asks Fenn. "Being a Knight?"

Fenn snorts, and tips his head back against the wall. "Does it matter? It's this or I get deported."

Theren watches Earth grow larger in front of them by fractions.

✦ ✦ ✦

In the early days of Cedre's existence, the megacity of Losan was the reason Cedre Station survived. It was the first quarantine zone, protected by the miles of desolate land that surrounded it. It provided food and resources when the space station had none. A fortified city of laborers, some wealthy—those who had inherited successful farms, or livestock, or factories—and some less so—those who were in the employ of Cedre's elite.

He and Kesia spent the night at a hotel near the water, a clean but cramped establishment with fresh fruit at breakfast that he savored like it was the nectar of forgotten gods. He spent most of the morning listening to the waves hitting the sea wall. He was too nervous to wander the city with Kesia, who reappeared in the afternoon looking windswept and frantic. Nervous for him, he thinks, though she would never admit it.

Then he took a bath—an impossibility on Cedre Station—and dressed in his blue jacket, and just like that, his freedom ran dry, like the last sip from a glass.

Now they're on their way to the ceremony. The Sparrow coasts over the cluster of tall buildings in the city's downtown, where most of the population lives—buildings in other parts of the city were razed over a century ago to make room for other, more useful structures. The downtown area, though small, looks like a whole world to Theren, lit up neon, the streets packed with people. Before he can get a good look at it, it's behind them, and all that's left ahead of them is a sea of greenhouses and solar farms and low, flat buildings that house livestock. Except, of course, for the Getty.

The Getty is a white sprawl on a hill. It was built in a time before the Fever, all white tile and glass, manicured gardens littered with sculptures. It was a museum. It still is, but it's used more often as a place of ceremony.

"Will the other Knights be there?" Theren says.

"Yes," Fenn says. "But it's a high-security event. Very limited guest list."

Theren doesn't see the other Knights often, but he attended their oath ceremonies. Fenn and Lisia were the first, eight years ago, when Theren was twelve years old and gawky with his collar itching his throat. Furik and Maeve were next, four years ago, a small affair that included the exiles and a handful of government officials.

But this . . . he has no idea what to expect from this.

Kesia looks uneasy, like the motion sickness has finally hit her.

He feels the shift in air pressure as the ship's elevation drops, and he chances a look out the window. Red and orange lights glow in the nav panel, in front of the pilot. And beyond it, the Getty, white, curved in places, like it's following the shape of the land. The Sparrow slows, and shudders as it descends to a landing pad just south of the building. Theren watches the pilot's hands move. Finally he hears the hiss of decompression, and the hatch door opens.

The landing pad is painted with the seal of Cedre, which is an abstraction of the planet below and Cedre Station above, connected by the line of the shuttle's path. *Everything for the Cedrae is about Earth*, Kesia said to him once, *and everything for the Talusar is about the Fever*. It seems to be true.

Waiting for them on the landing pad is a young woman with messy hair and an uneven smile. Maeve Martin, one of the other Knights.

Maeve bobs her head to Kesia. "Mrs. Forint." But when she turns to Theren, she relaxes. "Hey, kid."

"I'm taller than you," Theren says. "You can't tousle my hair anymore."

"That rule sounds made-up." Maeve reaches up in an attempt at a tousle that Theren smacks away.

He and Maeve didn't really know each other until Theren's stepfather died. She came to the funeral, and every few months she took the shuttle to their apartment and insisted that Theren and Isre come with her to a movie, or the arcade. She helped them put up twinkling lights in their living room on Kesia's birthday; she tutored Isre in Hànyǔ; she brought Theren to his first party. And she made the prospect of his oath seem easier, because at least when he was a Knight, he would spend more time around her.

But now he's not swearing his oath to the Sword of Cedre, as she did. Instead, he'll be the only one swearing it to the Sword's secondborn, Elegy. So he won't get to see much of Maeve. Or anyone.

"Fenn!" Maeve says, as Fenn descends the hatch steps. "You look like someone peed in your cereal, as usual." She grins, and Theren is surprised to see that instead of snapping back at her, Fenn just rolls his eyes. "Lisia's waiting for you in the Room of Ceremonies."

"Noted." Fenn gives Theren a look. "Don't mess it up, Forint."

He walks past them and disappears around the side of the Getty. Maeve addresses Kesia: "They prepared a room for both of you to rest a moment before the ceremony and meet everyone. I volunteered to escort you."

Kesia nods. Her jaw is tight.

They follow Maeve through a side entrance. Most of the building's exterior is covered in white tiles or pale stone; the interior, too, is stark. There are paintings on the walls in gilded frames; sculptures of glass and bronze arranged in the spaces between, the ancient and the less-ancient keeping company.

Maeve says, "When I took my oath, I got here an hour early. Pretty sure I used the bathroom every five minutes. Furik thought I was sick or something."

"Nervous bladder," Kesia says.

"Most people wouldn't share that so openly," Theren points out.

"I'm not most people." Maeve grins. Her smile is her best feature, wide and infectious.

They pass a room that's empty except for a huge feminine figure, a story high, chiseled from stone. Theren slows to look at it.

"Ah. Cassandra," Maeve says. "In the myth, she's a prophet who's cursed never to be believed."

Kesia taps the plaque on the wall. "The artist reimagined her as Zhu Hualing."

Zhu Hualing was the first scientist to write about the Fever after the Empty Time, which was a blank space of about a century in their planet's historical records. No one knows much about her, just that she was the first person to describe the Fever as a virus instead of a miracle.

The statue stands with open hands extended, a seer begging to be heeded. Theren looks up at her face for a few seconds, then rushes to catch up.

Maeve leads them to a small, clean room. "I'll go let them know you're here," she says, and she disappears into the hallway.

A table in the corner holds a jug of water and glasses—Kesia makes a beeline for it. There's a table, chairs. Windows that overlook the lawn. On one of the walls is a line of old photographs. Theren draws closer to them automatically. They're pictures of Losan from a long time ago. The colors are faded, but he still gets a sense of them, the peach-red of clay roof tiles and the parched green of desert trees.

"It seems like another world, doesn't it?" a wry voice says from behind him.

An older woman stands in the doorway. She wears gray robes stained salt-white at the bottom. An augur.

Kesia makes the sign of the Fever over her mouth, and bows. Theren just stares. The augur's hair is close-cropped and gray, and she looks at him in an unfocused way, as if she's also looking through him to the room beyond. She speaks English, but in a halting way, like she's not sure of her words.

"Theren Forint," she says. "I am the primary augur of the Cenobium. Primary is just a polite way of saying 'oldest.'" She smiles a little.

"Augur," he says. He realizes a beat later that he said the word in Talusar. The augur's eyes glint. She looks at Kesia.

"The other Knights didn't speak it so automatically," she says. "You are to be commended, Ms. Forint, for teaching your son properly."

"Thank you, augur." Theren has never seen his mother so hesitant. "May I ask why you're here?"

"I asked to conduct this particular ceremony," the augur replies. "Elegy Rosyk is the subject of a very important prophecy, and my presence may help to usher her along the path I hope she'll walk. The Sword was kind enough to agree."

And no wonder, Theren thinks. If the prophecy is, as Fenn said, a prediction of Cedre's triumph over the Talusar, the Sword would probably hand her secondborn daughter over to the Cenobium if she thought it would improve Elegy's odds of fulfilling it.

"The others will be here momentarily," the augur says. "But I wanted to see you in the present before we begin."

Her eyes are gentle and solemn. She stands in front of him for a moment and as she looks at him, her expression changes. She looks . . . sad.

"I'd almost forgotten what you looked like before," she whispers.

"Before what?" he says.

But the augur only shakes her head.

"I sometimes forget the sequence," she says. "Seeing you has helped me to put things in order. Thank you." She looks to Kesia. "It's time for us to go. He must meet the Hope of Cedre alone."

A look of conflict contorts Kesia's face, briefly, and she rushes toward Theren, throwing her arms around him. Theren stiffens, at first, unused to his mother displaying affection so publicly. Then he hugs her back.

"I'm sorry," she whispers into his ear, and he's not sure what she's apologizing for.

5

Elegy stands in her underwear, staring down at the dress. It's black, a simple sheath that falls straight down from the shoulder. She thought putting it on would help her to put the whole persona on, like an actor donning a costume, but suddenly she doesn't want to.

This happens every few minutes now, this feeling of disconnect between who she is and who she's been told she is. The Hope of Cedre. It sounds like a joke, only no one's laughing.

She bites down on her thumbnail. There's still salt under all of her fingernails, even though she's scrubbed her hands more than once since yesterday. With a sigh, she shakes out the dress and steps into it, leaving the back unzipped as she searches for her shoes in the small closet she shares with Shir. She wanted to wear her formal military uniform for this, but the Sword refused. *You have to look more human than that.* Elegy didn't quite understand—soldiers were human, weren't they? But the Sword's intention was to announce Elegy's place in the prophecy tomorrow, along with pictures of this ceremony, and when they circulated, she couldn't look like a piece of military propaganda. Even if that's exactly what the Sword wanted her to be.

Elegy can't think about that right now—how this will be used. She has to focus on salvaging her marriage.

She finds her shoes and straightens, the straps dangling from her fingers. Shir is in the doorway.

"Hi," she says to him.

"I think the last time I saw you in a dress was our wedding," he says.

He hasn't said much since last night, when she woke him to tell him about the prophecy. He didn't get upset—at least, not visibly so. He just sat by the window with her and watched the sun rise over the buildings of Losan. Then he went for a run, and when she asked to go with him, he said no. *I need to think.*

"Yeah, well," she says, "it wouldn't really be practical on a search and rescue operation, would it?"

Shir smiles. She's so relieved to see it she almost bursts into tears.

"I'm so sorry," she says softly.

"Shit, El," he says, and he crosses the room to take her hands. "This is not your fault. I didn't mean to make you feel like it was." He squeezes her fingers. She put her wedding ring on properly today, so it shines on her left hand, warm gold.

"What the augurs told you is a miracle," he says, like he's decided something. "If saving Cedre means you'll love two men at once . . . well, it'll be worth it. And maybe you won't. Maybe they misinterpreted something. It *doesn't matter.*" He touches his forehead to hers. "I love you, and I believe in you."

She nods, even though his words make her feel uneasy, unbalanced. Yesterday feels like a dream already, standing on that mirror, the sky reflected back at her, the sun burning through the oculus overhead. Shoulder to shoulder with Rava Vidar, the Butcher of Calgara, supposed container for the souls of dead warriors. *Tumult and rupture.* It felt so huge in the moment, big fate, big responsibility. But now, it's . . . less. Now she has rough tile under her feet and Shir's warm hands in hers, and *this* is reality. The man she loves, and the promise she made to him.

He might believe in this prophecy. But that doesn't mean she has to.

"We'll carry this together," he says.

"I love you," she says.

He kisses her like they just survived something—and maybe they did. His hands are tight on her waist; his teeth scrape her lower lip. She presses closer, and his hands slip around to her bare back, the dress still unzipped. His fingers trail up her spine, and she shivers.

"We're going to be late," he says, against her mouth.

"I don't give a shit," she answers, and she drops her shoes on the floor. He tugs the dress down from her shoulders, and they spill into bed together like they've been poured from a pitcher.

✦　✦　✦

The Getty is up ahead. White and lonely on its hill, a relic of the city that was.

It's odd to think of a Losan that wasn't packed with high-efficiency farms and greenhouses, small factories and water purification plants. The nation of Cedre has never been just one land mass—it's a constellation of them spread across the globe. The Talusar have been putting out each star in that constellation by force, one by one, for hundreds of years. Now there are just three left on the planet's surface: the megacity of Losan, in the western hemisphere; the continent of Austra, in the east; and north of it, the island chain of Nusanta.

In the very beginning, Cedre Station struggled to survive. All of Cedre tried to help, but Austra was a haven for those fleeing the Fever, and a base of operations for the military, and Nusanta was embroiled in conflict with the Talusar, and all the other territories—conquered now, of course—were too small to offer much to Cedre Station. Only Losan had plenty to give, and that's the reason Cedre Station exists now.

Shir eases their ship down to the landing pad. The Sword waits at the edge of it, her hair pulled back so tightly the wind doesn't budge it. She's wearing her formal military uniform, deepest red with all kinds of patches on the sleeve to indicate her status, her service, her honors.

"You're late," she says, and she says it to Shir, like it's his fault.

"Couldn't find my shoes," Elegy says. "It's only ten minutes, anyway."

The Sword's eyes narrow by a fraction. Ten minutes is significant to her, no doubt.

"Everyone else is here, and the Getty has been secured," the Sword says. "Just a precaution. This ceremony is highly classified. No one knows who you are yet."

"Aside from 'the spare,' you mean."

"I wish you wouldn't call yourself that." The Sword sniffs in a way that seems disapproving to Elegy. "Your Knight has already arrived. You should go meet him."

"Meet him," Elegy says. "What am I supposed to say, exactly? 'Sorry you got traded away to the state before you were even born, hope it's not too lame for you'?"

"We are not guaranteed infinite choices in this life," the Sword says. "You and I know that as well as he does. If you wouldn't want to receive his pity, perhaps you should not offer yours."

She turns on her heel and walks into the building. Stung, Elegy follows. She hadn't thought of it that way—that from the moment the augurs summoned her, they winnowed down her choices. Her path is so narrow now there's only room for one person to walk it. The same is true for her Knight.

To be honest, she pities them both.

"You're ready to go to Cedre Station with me after the ceremony?" the Sword says, over her shoulder, as they walk past the endless galleries of the Getty. "You can meet with my army there, after the announcement, to determine your rotation of guards."

"Not sure why I'll need a guard—isn't that what the Knight is for?"

The Sword raises an eyebrow at her. "A little redundancy never hurt anyone."

"I'm also not sure why I have to announce myself as the Hope of Cedre like some debutante."

"If you ever intend to lead anyone, you need them to know what you are." She looks over her shoulder, and her eyes soften a little. "Larke wants to spend some time with you, anyway."

Larke is the Sword's other daughter. Technically Elegy's sister, though Elegy rarely thinks of her that way. She already has a sister: Hela, who promised her a bottle of whiskey when all of this is over, even though she wasn't important enough to be invited to the ceremony.

Elegy stops in the doorway of one of the galleries, and stares up at the statue of Cassandra inside it. It's the statue's expression that catches Elegy's attention. The furrow of her eyebrows—she's frustrated. No one listens to her.

"She looks a little like you," Shir says, in her ear.

She does, Elegy thinks. Something in the set of her mouth, maybe. Turned down at the corners.

"Let's hope that's just a coincidence," she replies.

6

Theren is alone. The sun is setting, and the land around the Getty is turning orange, like it's on fire. He hears footsteps approaching, and he buzzes with fear.

A woman enters the room. She wears a black dress, simple, and her brown hair is pinned back. He barely looks at her face before his posture is straightening, his head bending. He knows this is Elegy Rosyk, Hope of Cedre, daughter of the Sword.

A man follows her in. He wears a formal military uniform—crimson, with sharp shoulders.

"Oh! You must be Forint," the man says. He's handsome, his hair dark and curly, his skin tan and freckled across the nose. He smiles, and his teeth are white. He extends a hand. "I'm Shir Alexios. This is Elegy Ahn."

Theren's never heard the name "Ahn" before. It must be her father's name.

Theren shakes Alexios's hand. He has a good grip. Not too hard.

"Guess we're all going to be spending a lot of time together," Alexios says. He must be Elegy's husband, then. Theren wonders what this will be like—standing in the background while Elegy and her husband build a life together. Silent and watchful.

"Yes," Theren says. "We will."

"Interesting choice of *ensemble*," Alexios says. "Just something you had lying around?"

All Theren can do is stare at him. He isn't sure how to answer—how to explain that it's not like he's swimming in formal clothing at home, that his mother gave this to him, that she brought nothing with her to Cedre but her memories and the child in her womb, that he wants everyone to remember why he's swearing this oath—

"Shir." Elegy's voice is low and clear. "Can you give us a moment?"

Alexios gives Theren a strange look. "Yeah, all right." He kisses Elegy's cheek, nods to Theren, and steps out of the room, closing the door behind him.

Theren's eyes drop. He doesn't know how to be around her, this woman he's about to swear an oath to. This woman who's supposed to save Cedre, whatever that means.

"Sorry about that. When he's nervous, he *talks*," she says.

She's fidgeting with her hands. Twisting her fingers together and pulling them apart. She must be nervous, too.

"Hey, eyes up," she says, and he obeys without thinking. He isn't expecting the bare terror he sees in her face. It eases some of the tension in his jaw.

"I just thought we should meet before the ceremony," she says. "I'm not—I'm not someone people swear oaths to. I don't know how to do this."

She's young. Older than him, but still—young, just beginning. And pretty, too. High cheekbones, warm eyes.

"Why is *he* nervous?" Theren says, just to have something to say.

Elegy's hands still. "Well, yesterday a bunch of augurs blew up my entire life, so I think he's afraid of what it will mean. Even though he's pretending not to be."

She laughs. An awkward silence falls as her smile fades.

They're more alike than they are different, he realizes. Yesterday they were both living the lives they chose. Today . . . not so much.

"I'm a soldier. I work in search and rescue," she says. "I travel a lot. All over, actually. And I don't really need protection. So this . . . this Knight thing, it can be what we make it."

He wishes he could think of something to say. She thinks she's offering him some reassurance that his life won't be boring, but he doesn't want her life. He's not interested in exploring this planet; he never has been. He grew up on Cedre Station, looking toward the *Sundial* for the future. Hearing about the people from another world who once beckoned them out. And he always wanted to meet them. To go out of the solar system. Away from their destroyed planet.

He wants the life he had.

"I know you didn't choose this oath," she says. "But—you're willing to swear it, right? Nobody's threatening you with death if you don't?"

It's a harder question to answer than he expected. He went through the day without thinking about an alternative—put on the clothes, got on the ship, and walked into the Getty, and nobody held a blade to his back. But of course, they can't force him to take an oath. All he has to do is refuse to speak.

But he's lived his life with an unfinished sentence dangling over him.

His citizenship. His belonging. His mother risked everything to get him here. This was the cost. And he can hardly fault the cost for being costly.

"Yes," he says. "I'm willing."

"Okay," she says. "I think we have to go now. Are you ready?"

No, he thinks.

"Yes," he says.

✦ ✦ ✦

The room where the ceremony takes place was once the main entrance of the museum. It's round and three stories high, the walls mostly glass. Skylights in the ceiling let in the orange glow of the harvest moon, now rising.

He's outside now, alone and waiting to be summoned in. From here he can see that the exiles and their eldest children—the Knights of Cedre—stand around the circumference of the room, in shadow. Among them are Cedre soldiers, there to protect the handful of government officials therein who are witnesses to the proceedings. And of course, there's the Sword of Cedre herself. It's a small group, compared to the last ceremony, but the thought of all those eyes on him still makes him itch.

The Knight oath is over a century old. There has always been a Sword of Cedre, and that Sword has always had at least one Knight. Usually the Knight was prepared from childhood, raised alongside the Sword. He wonders what happened to whoever was originally supposed to serve this Sword, then supplanted by the children of exiles. Maybe she absorbed them into her private army.

The wind is cool, now that the sun is gone, but heat still emanates from the concrete beneath him. It occurs to him that he can still run. He's alone now. He can sprint across the courtyard and tumble down the hill and into the streets of Losan.

But then his mother would be cast out of Cedre. And if the Talusar ever found her . . . well. She wouldn't survive it.

The door to the building opens, and the augur beckons him in. He doesn't hesitate.

It's dark in the cylindrical room, but he can feel the pressure of a dozen sets of eyes staring at him. Standing in the center of the floor is the augur, and just behind her, Elegy Rosyk. No—Elegy Ahn.

He stops in front of the augur, as he was instructed, and waits. Silence falls over the hall. The augur lifts her hands, and speaks loud enough to fill the space:

"People of Cedre. People of the stars, unchanged by Fever and spared of its caprice. For over a century you have stood in opposition to an enemy far more populous and advantaged than yourselves. So often we are defined by what we oppose, and Cedre is no exception—when it took shape, it embraced a pluralistic system of governance, rather than the empire of the Talusar. Leaders would be chosen, not shaped from birth."

She tucks her hands into her sleeves, and turns to nod at the Sword of Cedre, standing off to her right.

"But Cedre's need to defend itself against the Talusar became too great," she says. "Cedre is, above all else, talented at survival. So they designated one woman as Cedre's defender. Her sole purpose would be to guard it against the Talusar, and that duty would be embedded in her blood, such that her children, and her children's children, would inherit it. Her name . . . was Rosyk."

Someone calls out a phrase in a language Theren doesn't speak. Though he can't translate it, he knows its meaning: *May the Rosyka endure.*

"She was called Cedre's Sword," the augur continues, "and her twin sister swore that as the Sword kept her eyes on the Talusar, her twin would keep her eyes on the Sword. She became the first Knight of Cedre. And since then, the role of Knight has not been inherited, but compelled by devotion, arising in each generation like a seed breaking through the earth."

Theren's hands are starting to tremble. He searches the crowd for his mother's face. He can't find her.

"In this generation, the Knight has come from the soil of an impossible choice. His mother chose to forsake home, and country; language, and culture; history, and name . . . for the good of her child and her future." The augur's eyes fix on Theren's. "She and her company turned their backs on the Fever, but the Fever has answered, nonetheless, providing a prophecy, and a new path for Cedre to reclaim more of what it has lost. So it isn't to the Sword that this Knight will swear himself, but to Hope—the hope that Cedre will endure, and prosper, embodied in a single person with the Sword's purpose in her blood."

He can't see Elegy's face. Her head is bowed, casting her eyes in shadow.

"Who takes this oath?" the augur says, and just like that, it's Theren's turn.

"Theren Forint," he says, his voice a little too rough, a little too quiet. He swallows hard.

"Kneel, Theren Forint."

He sinks to his knees on the polished stone, and sits back on his heels. He hopes no one can see the scuffing on the soles of his shoes, which his mother unearthed like buried treasure from a bin in a resale shop a few years ago.

The augur steps back, and Elegy steps forward. She clasps her hands in front of her, and though she doesn't fidget, he can see how tightly she's holding herself.

"Theren Forint, are you here of your own free will, taking this oath in full knowledge of the commitment it requires?" the augur asks.

"Yes."

"Do you swear your loyalty to Elegy Rosyk, daughter of the Sword of Cedre, to hold her interests above those of your friends, your kin, and yourself?"

Hey, eyes up, he hears Elegy say in his memory, and he forces his eyes to hers. She's staring at him with peculiar intensity.

"Yes," he says.

"Do you swear your blade to her, to make every effort to protect her, even if the cost is your life?"

"Yes."

"Do you swear to keep this oath for as long as you draw breath?"

Elegy closes her eyes, her throat working as if she's trying to swallow, and Theren waits for her to open them again before replying, "Yes."

"Then you are a Knight of Cedre. May you be a shield for the daughter of the Sword."

Theren releases a heavy breath. The augur steps to the side and accepts a tray with a knife and a pebble on it. He'd almost forgotten this part—every Knight got a tracker embedded, like the Sword herself and, he assumes, Elegy. He looks at the knife, small and deadly sharp, and his mouth goes dry.

Its purpose is symbolic as much as practical: it will seal his oath with pain. Even the Cedrae, with their pretensions of advancement, understand that pain can be powerful. In this case, a demonstration of commitment—though small—where simple words don't quite manage it.

He unbuttons the first few buttons of his jacket, and then the shirt beneath it, and pulls the fabric away from his right shoulder. Elegy picks up the knife, and stands in front of him again. She touches the tip of the blade to his chest, just beneath the juncture of collarbone and shoulder. Her eyes flick up to his as if asking a question. He nods.

The pain of the first cut is manageable. But when she uses the knife to press the tracker pebble into the wound, the pain is intense. White-hot, it spreads from the point of the blade and reaches down into muscle and bone and nerve as she presses deeper. He clenches his jaw and breathes through his nose, forcing himself to count to five. Elegy withdraws the knife on "four," and she holds a square of gauze to the puncture wound she left behind.

It's done.

He's on his feet again, accepting a strip of medical tape from the augur, when he sees something outside. A dark shape moves fast across the concrete where Theren was standing a few minutes ago. Then in the distance, a low wail, the sound of the Losani emergency alert system.

The wall that surrounds the city has been breached.

The room erupts into hurried conversations, in a handful of languages. Then the glass doors shatter. Talusar soldiers wearing copper-bright febra armor surge into the room—right toward Elegy.

He's been afraid before, in his life: when he got lost in the market as a child, when he thought he had failed an exam, when he prepared for this very ceremony . . . but all that fear is meaningless now in the face of this wordless terror.

He's a Knight. He swore. He swore his heart, his sword, his life. It's his duty to throw himself in front of Elegy, as the closest one to her, as the only one who can help her now.

Their eyes meet, hers so wide he can see the whites around them.

He turns—

And runs.

7

Elegy lurches back as glass sprays across the floor. An arm wraps around her back, and she knows without looking at him that it's Shir—knows by the way he feels, warm and strong, his fingers around her rib cage, half dragging her, half carrying her away from the dark figures now filling the room. She hears her mother's voice shouting commands: "Take her up!" "Summon the shuttle now!"

She's been on the other end of this so many times. Swooping in at the tail end of an attack to get Cedrae soldiers out. She's been the one who sees it from above, the one who has a plan, the one who the Talusar didn't see coming. But none of those skills are translating now. She doesn't know how to be the focal point, how to be the life that needs saving.

She smells smoke and eucalyptus oil. Shir dabs the oil under his jaw because he knows she likes the smell of it. He shoves open a door and the light of an exit sign reveals they're in a stairwell. His eyes find hers, reflecting red.

"We need to run," he says, and finally Elegy is in the present again.

She grabs his hand, and starts up the stairs, hiking up her skirt with her other hand. At the first landing, she kicks her shoes off and looks down to see the Sword not far behind them. The Sword shoves a broom—where did she get that?—through the door handle to slow down anyone who might follow them, and she runs to catch up to them.

"Where's your fucking Knight?" the Sword demands.

"Don't know," Elegy says. She forgot to look for him in the chaos. Maybe he's dead. "Who are they?"

"Some of Rava's soldiers, if I had to guess. Seems we were betrayed by one of our own."

"Shit," Shir says. "An exile?"

"Seems likely." The Sword leads them up, past the top floor of the building, to a door with roof access. She throws it open. The roof is hot from the day's sun. The Sword points to the far edge. "There. The shuttle will arrive soon. Get her on it."

"What about you?" Elegy says.

"I'll be right behind you. I need to get some of the others out."

"But—"

"I," the Sword interrupts her, her eyes locked on Elegy's, "am not as important as you are. Go."

Elegy is about to argue when something hits the rooftop a few feet away and sticks there. An arrow. There's a figure on the roof of one of the other buildings, illuminated just enough by moonlight that she can see their shape against the night sky. They wear their hair in a crown of braids.

Rava Vidar wore her hair in a crown of braids.

Shir cries out in alarm and moves in front of Elegy, his hand forcing her head down, his chest pressed to her back. She hears an arrow hit him—the impact of it, and then the wet gurgle of pain from his mouth.

She cries out, and his hand presses her head down even harder. Her knees start to buckle under the weight of him, now falling against her.

"Use me as a shield," he chokes into her ear.

She screams, and falls to her knees, her husband still wrapped around her. Another arrow whistles toward them, and his muscles jerk as it hits him. He makes a strangled sound, and Elegy screams again. Lights flood the rooftop, the shuttle hovering next to it. The ting of metal striking metal—an arrow hitting the side of the shuttle.

"Time to go!" the Sword says, from behind her.

Shir's body is just a weight, now. She no longer feels his breath crackling against her back.

The Sword grabs her arm and drags her out from under him. Elegy strains against her mother's hold, strains toward Shir. She makes desperate, wordless sounds, unable to voice her refusal to leave him.

"We'll come back for him!" the Sword shouts at her, and she's too strong for Elegy to resist; she drags Elegy toward the edge of the roof. The tile scrapes Elegy's bare feet.

Shir—

"Grab her!"

Someone wraps their arms around her middle and heaves her into the shuttle. She falls to the floor, and hits her head on the metal grate. The ship is moving, flying away from the Getty. Elegy turns back—

It's too dark to see anything but the Sword's silhouette against the rooftop. An arrow hits her mother in the gut, and her body arches around it, and she looks like a dancer, contracting and releasing, limbs long and oddly relaxed, as if this is all a part of the plan.

Then she falls.

A scream freezes in Elegy's throat.

Rava Vidar, with her crown of braids, just killed the Sword of Cedre.

8

Theren didn't touch dirt until he was six years old. His first-year class went on a day trip to the garden district of Cedre Station, and it seemed like a long journey, to a child. They had to take the high-speed tram and everything.

In the plant nursery, a horticulturist explained the basics of how plants grew and what being in orbit did to them. Then she laid out trays of seedlings for them to plant themselves. They were vegetables. Tomatoes and cucumbers and bell peppers—it was hard to believe they started their lives as little sprays of green.

Theren chose one of the bell peppers, but he couldn't get a good grip on his trowel, so he dug a hole with his fingers instead, and nestled the plant in its place, and squeezed the moist earth between his knuckles before piling it around the roots of the pepper plant to keep it stable.

On the way home, he looked at his hands and saw that despite washing them, there was still black earth under his fingernails.

He didn't think he would ever become more acquainted with dirt than that, his mother standing with him at the kitchen sink and scraping it out from under his nails with a little brush. But then a Talusar soldier is chasing him into the woods, knocking him down, and pinning him face down in the dirt, so he tastes dirt on his tongue. It fills his nose with the smell of growing and rotting.

It's only then that he realizes: he ran. Instead of fulfilling his oath, instead of performing his duty, he ran. And the Hope of Cedre might be dead because of it.

+　+　+

The soldier brings him, still bleeding from the nose, to a small unit of Talusar soldiers who are holding the other Knights captive. Fenn and Lisia, Furik and Maeve, each of them scraped and battered to varying degrees. None of them managed to escape. *This*, he thinks, *is the cost of not training us properly.*

Maeve and Furik embrace him, relieved to find him alive, but Fenn stares right through him, like he's made of glass, made of water.

One of the soldiers takes out a knife and sterilizes it with fire. Then two of the others force Furik to kneel. Maeve starts screaming, and Lisia sobs, and Fenn throws himself at the nearest soldier, only to be put in a chokehold. But Theren stands still. He doesn't think the Talusar dragged them away from the Getty just to execute them. Why would they bother?

"Your tracking devices need to be removed!" one of the soldiers finally shouts—in English—over the chaos.

After that, there's calm. One by one, each of the Knights kneels as the soldiers peel their clothes away from their shoulders and dig the knife into flesh to root out the devices buried there. Each of them screams and thrashes and bleeds. It's only when Theren sees one of the soldiers put all the tracking devices in a bag and mount her horse to ride away that it really hits him: now there's no way for anyone in Cedre to find them. And he doubts they'll put too much effort into saving the people they only gave citizenship to begrudgingly.

The Knights are on their own.

Then the Talusar take them to a clearing where horses wait for them. When Theren first gets on the animal's back, at the insistence of one of the soldiers, he's terrified. It's bigger than he expected, a snorting, powerful creature of solid muscle. He isn't ready for how forcefully it bounces when it moves, how he has to clench his legs and shift his weight to stay on. They put Maeve on the same horse, so the two of them are pressed together more intimately than either of them wants, smelling each other's sweat.

They ride along trails that only the Talusar seemed to be able to discern. By the end of the first day, there's dirt everywhere—in his ears, in the corners of his eyes, in the rims of his nostrils, in the cracks of his lips. Dirt chafes skin already raw and red from the sun, though they only travel for a few hours in the day. His skin is unused to unfiltered sunlight. In all of the Cedrae's romantic talk of home, they never mention how many ways this planet can hurt you.

But even the most abnormal things, the most terrifying things, become normal after some time. By the second day, it doesn't matter how bad either of them smells, it doesn't trouble him when the horse breaks into a gallop, and he doesn't notice the constant burn of thirst in the back of his throat. He doesn't struggle to sleep when the sun is high. They rotate through the horses, to give them breaks, and he gets used to the gentle ones and the touchy ones alike. He gets used to the guilt burning in his chest, a reminder of how he failed. He gets used to everything.

He stops looking for Cedrae rescue ships on the third day.

The soldiers offer no explanation for where they're going or why they're going there—or why none of the Knights are dead yet. They don't know if any of their parents survived the Getty attack or not. Theren keeps listening to the low conversations the soldiers have in Talusar, but they don't speak much, not even to each other. Instead, they follow the orders of the woman at the front of the pack, their obvious leader.

He knows what the emperor looks like, and even his niece, Ileth Vidar, thanks to the news, but all other Talusar leaders he only knows by name and by rumor. This woman is young for the position of authority she holds, which means there has to be something about her, some skill or heritage he doesn't understand. She's taller than him, and the plates in her febra armor are made to look like feathers. Her hair is the color of flax, a rare shade, and she never looks at any of them. Her eyes are always on the horizon.

+   +   +

Some Cedrae want to search for another planet to call home, one free from Fever. That's what the *Sundial*—the ship that hovers beside Cedre Station like a tiny moon—is for: an exploratory mission in pursuit of the extrasolar visitors that once invited Earth to participate in a greater interstellar order. That was before life on Earth almost ended.

Theren had always understood the desire to seek refuge on another planet. He was never interested in reclaiming Earth from the Talusar, as some Cedrae insist on attempting instead of sending the *Sundial* on its mission. But he understands the longing for Earth better now. Now that he's walking on the planet's surface.

Earth is different than he imagined. In moments when he can set his terror and remorse aside, he marvels at it. The mountains surround them from all sides, and in the dark, there are no glimpses of the horizon, no beautiful vistas, just the impression of dark, massive shapes against a dark sky. But then they reach a valley, and the sky opens up in every direction, and the moon can't crowd out the light of the stars. Cedre Station, too, glows above them, the shape of a barrel or a cork, reflecting the light of the sun. The *Sundial*—so small it's almost nonexistent next to Cedre Station—hovers beside it like a promise that Theren will never get to keep.

He saw so clearly the size of Earth on his descent, but the only way to understand how large the planet is is to trip tiredly across it. To ache from head to toe from the sheer force of its gravity.

Every so often, when they stop to give the horses water, and everything is still, he can hear the silence of the desert. The wind, the call of a bird, and nothing else. There were no silent places on Cedre Station, always humming with electricity and air flowing through the vents and the distant clanging of one thing or another.

They ride through stretches of strange trees, oddly human in shape, with sharp protrusions and scaly trunks. Furik cuts his hand trying to touch one when they stop for water, and the Talusar soldiers sneer at him when he asks for a bandage. Lisia ties a handkerchief around his palm to stanch the bleeding.

Only one of them tries to escape: Fenn, at the end of the second day. That's the day a Cedrae ship passes close enough for them to hear its hum. When he sees it, Fenn digs in his heels as hard as he can, sending the horse into a canter with him clinging to its back. One of the soldiers swears and gets on her own horse, which is faster than Fenn's, even with the head start. She brings him back within five minutes, forces him to his knees on the hard ground, and whips him with the reins until he screams for mercy. Maeve begs in four languages for her to stop, none of them Talusar. Theren can't move, can't look away.

The leader looks on, her expression unchanging. She's the one who gives the order to stop, eventually, just holding up a hand and then turning back toward the horizon.

Theren knows there's no point in escaping. The Cedrae won't find them, have probably stopped looking. They can't outrun the Talusar, either. And even if they somehow manage to, they'll be alone in the desert with no water and no food and no survival skills. This place is as good as a prison for people like them.

On the fourth day, Maeve props her chin on Theren's shoulder and speaks against his ear.

"See that?"

At first, he thinks she's talking about a rock formation up ahead. The rolling hills around Losan, with their dry brush and occasional tree, have turned sharp and bare, and the shapes they make look inorganic and strange to him. But then the dark mass in the distance catches moonlight, and he sees that it's metal.

It's two Sparrows, parked side by side in the desert.

Maeve swears against the top of Theren's spine. "Where the hell are they taking us? Why aren't we dead?"

"I don't know."

"Quiet," one of the soldiers—the woman with her hair in a knot on top of her head—says to them, in English.

As they near the two Sparrows, he sees that they're parked beside the ruins of an old building. It's so old, in fact, that he can't even guess at what it used to be.

The leader swings her leg over her horse and lands heavily in the dust. The other soldiers follow suit.

Theren's legs are so sore it's difficult to get off the horse. He lets Maeve go first, holding her hand as she jumps down, and then he slides off, graceless, almost falling to his knees. Both of them go to help Fenn, Maeve taking one of his hands and Theren taking the other. As he dismounts, Fenn bites his lip to keep from crying out, and sags against Theren, gasping. The back of his shirt is stained with blood.

"Line them up," the leader says, without looking up from her horse. She's undoing the buckles that hold the saddle to the beast's back, her long fingers stained black with dirt.

Theren tries not to react to what she says. Lining them up feels like a prelude to killing them, but there's no way the Talusar spent all that effort getting them here just to execute them. So he doesn't resist when one of the soldiers grabs him by the elbow and jerks him around so he stands next to Maeve.

The leader finishes taking the saddle and bridle off her horse, and leads it to a bucket of water where the soldiers are setting up their own animals. Finally, she walks along the row of Knights, pausing next to each of them to look them over.

"What a fine collection we have here."

She stops in front of Lisia. "The Useless Knight, who still can't ride a fucking horse . . ."

She moves on to Fenn. "The Stupid Knight, who tried and failed to escape . . ."

She moves past Furik and Maeve, and stops in front of Theren. "And the Coward Knight, who ran rather than defend the so-called Hope of Cedre."

He feels the others' eyes on him, and grits his teeth. He didn't tell them why he was caught in the woods instead of captured in the ceremony hall with the others.

"Oh, they didn't know that, did they?" the woman says, leaning closer to Theren. Her eyes almost glow in the moonlight. "They didn't know someone so *weak* walks among them?"

His face burns with shame. She turns on her heel, about to continue her pacing, and he makes himself speak.

"I may be a coward," he says, in Talusar, "but at least I'm not a murderer."

She freezes, mid-step, and turns to stand in front of him again. In his periphery, he sees the other Knights' heads turning, feels their eyes on him. Kesia always told him to be discreet about the fact that he speaks Talusar, and now he understands why. Apparently the other exiles were too focused on assimilating to teach their children their native language. He seems to be the only one who knows it.

"You speak Talusar," the woman says. "What's your name?"

"Forint." He trembles—with anger, with fear, with shame, he's not sure. She gets a strange, eager look in her eye.

"Right," she says softly. "I see the resemblance now."

He doesn't know how she could. She was a child when his mother fled Valla.

"How many are dead?" he says, before he can stop himself. "Who?"

"I don't keep a record of the traitorous pigs I slaughter. I just make them into meat."

The rage that surges through him is so intense it locks up his muscles. He couldn't have moved if he wanted to. She smiles a little, and steps close again, looking down her nose at him.

"You have a choice to make, Theren Forint," she says, in English this time, and he *knows* he didn't tell her his first name.

"Nyx!" she says, calling out to one of the others. "Bring her."

Dread turns his stomach like a bad meal as one of the soldiers standing with the horses moves toward the doorway of the abandoned building and disappears inside. The woman—the leader—studies his face like she's seen something fascinating.

Then his mother emerges from the nearby ruins.

The last time he saw her, she was in a starched white shirt and black slacks, blue stones glittering in her ears, her hair loose. Now she's dressed like a soldier, black canvas pants tucked into boots, a rough-woven shirt. She looks as tired as he feels, like she too has spent the last few days wandering the desert—and of course, she must have, to meet them here.

Her eyes find his with trepidation.

She's not bound. She's not bruised or scratched. She's here of her own free will.

"I knew it," Fenn says, from down the row of Knights. "You fucking *snake*!"

He surges toward Kesia, making it only a step before the leader catches him by the throat and forces him to his knees. Theren hears him choke, and gurgle. He doesn't turn to look. He can't move. He's just staring at his mother.

"Behave," the leader says to Fenn, and she releases him. He coughs, and heaves into the dirt.

"What have you done?" Theren says to Kesia, roughly.

"I wanted you to be free," she says. "I wanted us *both* to be free."

It's a strange thing to hear when he's spent the last few days as a captive.

"Your mother made a bargain," the leader says. "A clever one. In exchange for her help, I have promised to test you all instead of executing you immediately."

"What does that mean, 'test us'?" Lisia says, her eyes darting to Fenn's.

"It means they'll infect us with Fever and see if we live," Furik says. "But what if we survive?"

"The Fever makes a person new. Makes a person Talusar," the leader says. "If you survive it, you will be a citizen of Valla. I will find a place for you to adjust to Talusar society."

"And who the hell are you?" Fenn says.

"She's Rava Vidar," Maeve replies softly. "Obviously."

The moment she says it, it does seem obvious. Who else could this woman be but Rava Vidar, daughter of Ileth Vidar, rumored to be the living vessel of ancient warriors?

Rava's mouth quirks into a smile, as if she knows the effect her name has, and she's pleased by it. Reality sinks into Theren piece by piece. His mother made a deal with Rava Vidar. Traded away her Cedrae citizenship, her loyalty, her *decency* . . . why? Because she didn't like Cedre? Because she regretted letting the Sword make him a Knight?

For his freedom, as if that was something the Talusar would ever actually give him?

"As I said, Forint," Rava says, "you have a choice to make. You can't avoid the Fever, either way. But if you renounce Cedre, you and your mother can go together to Valla, where you will occupy positions of honor in the monastery there. Or, if you refuse . . . you can count yourself as a Knight of Cedre, and face what they face."

There's good strategy in lying to her—in renouncing Cedre, knowing it's just words, and lying just long enough to escape and return home. But his reaction is so visceral, so automatic, that he can't control it.

"I'm not renouncing my people," he says.

Kesia's eyes are fixed on his. "Theren. Don't be a fool."

He ignores her.

"I'm a Knight of Cedre," he says. "I took an oath."

"I suppose I can't fault you for trying to salvage your backbone," Rava says. "I will ask you again in your second life. Perhaps you'll change your mind after you die."

She turns away, and makes a gesture of dismissal at Theren's mother, who obeys. For just a moment, the Knights stand alone in a line in the desert, as the sun begins to peek over the horizon.

✦   ✦   ✦

They bind the Knights' hands behind their backs, and march them into one of the Sparrows. They sit three on one side of the ship, two on the other—Fenn and Lisia, inseparable as always. One of the soldiers comes through to strap them all in, crushing their bound wrists against their backs.

Sitting in the pilot's chair is a girl. She's lanky, awkward, like she just shot up and doesn't know where her body ends yet. She wears her hair in one tight braid, beginning at her widow's peak and ending at her spine. She's not wearing armor made of febra—a metal that reacts protectively to the energy field produced by Fevered blood—since she's not infected. She's in a flight suit, instead. But she looks at them with the same disdain the other soldiers do.

"You're a fucking idiot," Fenn says to Theren, as the engines spin up.

"Fenn . . ." Maeve says.

"You should have just done what she said," Fenn says roughly. "Then you could have at least found a way to save all of us."

"And if he had, you would have called him a traitor no matter what he did to help us." Lisia tips her head back and closes her eyes. "Why do you have such a hard-on for hating him?"

Fenn eyes Theren, but he doesn't speak again.

Theren tries not to think, but he can't stop memories from flashing in his mind. Kesia at the dinner table when he was a child, admonishing him for not speaking in Talusar. Kesia pressing a practice sword into his hands that was almost too heavy for him to lift. She was careful to present herself as fully integrated, but when the two of them were alone, she spoke of her home wistfully, she performed the sign of the Fever over her mouth, she read Talusar poetry out loud—

And then, just days ago. The blue-and-copper jacket in its garment bag. Kesia disappearing all day when they got to Losan. Kesia looking uneasy as they landed at the Getty; he thought it was motion sickness. The way she sounded when she said, *I'm sorry.*

How long has she been planning this? A week, a month, a year? Or was this always the plan, twenty years in the making?

Did she only go to Cedre with the exiles to wait for the right moment to strike?

Two of the Talusar soldiers who dragged them here step into the Sparrow and strap themselves in. One of them is right next to Theren—the woman with her hair in a high knot.

"How many of them do you think will survive the Fever?" the bearded soldier across from her says. "Two? One? We've got a pool going."

"This one can understand you, Ranos," Hair Knot says, jerking her head toward Theren.

"So?" Ranos says, and he looks at Theren. "You want in? Not sure what you can bet, but I'm sure you're good for it."

"Fuck you," Theren says.

Ranos looks at Theren for a moment, then says, "I mean, skinny and scared isn't usually my type, but you're not half bad."

Hair Knot throws a glove at him, and hits him in the face. He throws it back, hitting her in the knee. The ship buzzes in anticipation of takeoff. A low voice comes through on the ship's radio, and they lift away from the ground. Theren expects something bumpier than what he gets—the child pilot's hands are quick on the controls, all the awkwardness of their movements gone as they do the choreography of takeoff.

"He's too skinny to survive it, I think," Ranos says, once they're in the air. The desert spreads out in front of them, orange in the new morning light. It's flat where they are, but in the distance, there are mountains.

"It has nothing to do with what you look like," Hair Knot replies. "The Fever sees strength better than we do." She performs the sign of the Fever—three circles traced with the tip of her thumb—over her mouth as she speaks.

"Ever the zealot, Nyx."

Maeve nudges Theren with her elbow.

"You understand them?" she says.

Theren nods.

"How do you know it so well?"

"We speak it at home," Theren says, and with a twinge in his chest, he amends: "We spoke it at home."

Fenn snorts. "So she raised you like one of them, this whole time."

Theren wants to argue, but he isn't sure he can.

"Did you have any idea?" Maeve says, her voice gentle.

"No."

Theren looks out the window. The desert land is turning green, the mountains rising, rocky and lush, from the plain.

9

The monastery sits at the edge of a green lake, high enough in the mountains that there's still snow on the ground. It looks like a wooden layered cake, the tiers widening as they descend. The posts around the entrance are carved with flowers and with the sign of the Fever, three interlinked circles, one for the life before infection, one for the life after, and one for the Fever itself.

Ranos and the woman—Nyx—escort the Knights, their hands still bound behind them, into the monastery and down creaking hallways to a wide, bright room. A stove sits in its center, a chimney funneling smoke outside, and arranged around it are colorful cushions. It's the first comfortable place any of them have been in since the Getty.

Kesia is already standing inside it.

"This is a sacred place," she says to them. "It houses our most honored citizens: those who see deep into the past, who we call 'epocha'; and those who can pass the Fever by breath, who we call 'priests.'" Hearing her say "we" with such ease makes Theren feel sick. "The people here are all peaceful. They are also protected by our highest laws. If you attack them, if you so much as move threateningly toward them, you will be burned alive. Understand?"

As she speaks, Ranos moves from one of them to the other, cutting the ropes that bind their wrists.

"They'll bring food and water," Kesia says. "This will be the last meal you have before exposure to Fever. This is to give you strength. But there's no evidence that strength helps you survive the Fever. It just prolongs your death. So if you want a quicker end, don't eat."

Ranos and Nyx leave. Lisia chokes on a sob and sinks to the floor, her hand clamped over her mouth. Maeve sits next to her, an arm around her back. Kesia is lingering by the door.

"Theren," she says to him.

"There's nothing you can say to me that I want to hear," he says. "Not anymore."

He can see that it wounds her, and he feels regret, but only for a moment. He's here in this place, staring down death, because of her.

"You can't be angry with me forever," Kesia says.

"I can be angry with you until I die," Theren says. "And thanks to you, that'll be in a few days' time."

She stares at him. He doesn't think she knows what to say. Neither does he. When she walks out of the room and closes the door behind her, it's a relief.

"These people are insane," Fenn says. "They bring their own here to get sick and die, and they call it a holy place."

Theren sits, rubbing his wrists where the skin is raw. He feels strange. Detached, almost. Like he can't bear to be in his own body, knowing it will soon betray him.

The notion of "surviving" the Fever is a flawed one, a kind of translation error. The Fever is fatal, and the death it brings about is total. No heartbeat, no brain waves, nothing. And then, as if time is running backward, the body puts itself back together again. The heart starts. The lungs fill.

The eyes open.

It's no wonder they call this place holy. What else do you call a place where people routinely come back to life?

Lisia's sobs subside. She and Maeve sit clutched together, quiet, as the others stare into the coals of the stove and wait.

✦   ✦   ✦

A woman comes that evening to get them. Older, her face lined, wearing a deep blue robe with a heavy hood. The sleeves are stitched with copper thread in a repeating pattern: the three interlinked circles, over and over again, so tiny he doesn't recognize them at first. She wears a necklace of black stones that creeps all the way up to her jaw.

Nyx follows her in, her hand poised over the knife at her side. But none of the Knights even stand up, let alone move against the—priest. Monk. Whatever she is.

"I am an attendant to priests of the Fever. I will take you one by one to be prepared for the ceremony." Her English is slow and deliberate, each syllable pronounced. "Which of you would like to go first?"

No one moves.

When he was a child, Theren feared the monster under the bed, the monster in the closet, the monster in the dark. So his stepfather gave him a mechanical flashlight. *Better to know what's there than fear what isn't,* he said, and this sounded like a profound insight to Theren. After a few weeks of shining the flashlight under the bed, into the closet, into the dark apartment . . . he stopped feeling so afraid.

The Fever has been waiting in the dark all his life. It's time to meet it.

"Let's get it over with," he says, and he comes to his feet. He didn't eat with the others; he doesn't want a slow decline. The dread of death is probably worse than death itself.

Maeve gets up, too. Hugs him. Furik wraps his arms around them both. Lisia touches Theren's hand where it rests on Maeve's arm. Theren lifts his eyes to Fenn.

Fenn nods. It's more than Theren expected.

The woman ushers him into the hallway, and then falls into step beside him, her hands clasped before her.

"He's the one who speaks Talusar," Nyx says to the attendant.

"And he's the one ready to meet our God," the attendant says. "How fitting."

Despite the dark wood that hems them in on all sides, the hallways feel open, their ceilings vaulted. They pass through a narrow, two-story-high space with stained-glass windows on either side. The images are of a fragmented Earth, thrice-encircled; of a woman in a blue robe performing the sign of the Fever over her mouth.

"I thought anyone could pass on the Fever with their blood," Theren says, as he pauses to look at the windows. "What makes priests different?"

"Their breath is the breath of a god," the attendant says. "There is no wrong way to meet the Fever, but the ideal is through the air. 'What a clever-strange thing it is, that life's deepest mystery is gently adrift, like a seed carried by the wind,' like the poem from—"

"Volyn," Theren says quietly. "I know."

Kesia read him that poem once. She told him that some people shed enough of the Fever virus to transmit it through breath, but she didn't tell him those people were considered holy, marked and robed and sequestered here in a monastery.

"Then you already know that it's good to receive the Fever from one who is Fever-blessed to speak it into your body."

Theren knows no such thing. But he follows the woman down stone steps and into a basement. The air feels moist. Nyx opens the door, and gestures them in.

The room below is long and narrow, with a deep pool in the center, full of dark water. All along the edge of the pool are arches and columns, with lanterns positioned at intervals to fill the space with dim, flickering light. It reminds him of the temple where Isre was Imbued. And maybe the infection is a kind of Imbuing.

Shuffling through the space on light feet, all around the pool, are people in blue robes—deep blue, like the sky after sunset.

"No one here will harm you," Nyx says to him. "But you must do as they say, or I'll hurt you."

The attendant reaches for Theren's hand. When she touches him, she freezes, and stares up into his eyes. Her own are shadowed and dark. Her hair is the color of ashes.

"I see a man," she says, and she sounds like she's far away. Her hood falls away from her head, and he sees a tattoo on the side of her throat, but he doesn't know what it means. She squeezes him tightly. "A man descending into darkness. Your father, I think. He is not what you think he is, your father."

His father was a Talusar soldier. His body is buried under a tree outside of Valla.

"You must be mistaken," he says to her. He stares at the mark on her throat. Does it mark her as an epocha?

Is she looking into his past? Kesia lied about being loyal to Cedre, lied about betraying everything he'd ever known—did she lie to him about his father, too?

"Unmistakable," the attendant says, and she releases him. "Come."

He follows her to the edge of the pool, and he stares as she kneels and starts to untie his shoes. He crouches, stilling her hands, and their eyes meet again in the half-light.

"What is this?" he says.

"A ritual of cleansing," she says. "You can't stand before a priest without it. Don't be bashful. You aren't the first I've seen, and you won't be the last."

He hears Nyx moving toward him, and he releases the woman's hands. She keeps at his laces like there was no interruption. The room is hushed, the others busy in the shadows, where he can't see them.

It helps that she's quick and businesslike, tugging off his shoes, peeling off his socks—spotted with blood at the heels and toes. She doesn't object when he unbuttons his own trousers and steps out of them. His face is hot. He tries to ignore it.

"Get in," she says, leaving him to take off his underwear and undershirt. She walks away, and Theren hurries to undress and get in the water.

It's warm, and clearer than it looks, only dark because of the deep color of the tiles that line the pool. He stands with water lapping at his rib cage, and waits. One of the other attendants wades in, and then another, and another. They surround him.

He smells smoke. One of them holds a copper bowl with something burning in it. They wave it under Theren's nose, and by instinct he breathes it in. It burns his lungs. He coughs, and his head swims, his muscles relax. He's still awake, still aware, but he feels even more distant than before.

It's easier to submit to their attentions after that. To the hands pressing him down into the water, and guiding him back up again, then working soap into his hair, his shoulders. The sight of them, and the lanterns, is dizzying. He closes his eyes and he's not sure whether he feels fingers in his hair, along his knuckles, over his legs—or if they're just phantoms.

They guide him out of the pool, and dry him off. Someone dabs oil on his sternum, on his forehead. Someone else walks around him with a thurible in hand, sending smoke into the air, floral and green, thick enough to choke him. They clothe him in a blue robe and leave his feet bare. They give him a cup of water to drink, and it tastes like mint.

His head is heavy. He expects Nyx to mock him when he has trouble walking, but she doesn't. She just takes his elbow and guides him toward the door.

"You're all right," she says. "One step after another."

He feels a pulse of fear, but it's far away, somehow. They walk toward the stairs together, and down a hallway, and another hallway. The lanterns catch his eye, smear together, glitter at the corners. Nyx ushers him through a set of double doors, and then he's in a church.

It's not really a church, but it feels like one. Holy. The floor is stone; the walls are wood. A light source glows between the gaps in the wood; he can't identify it.

In the center of the room are two chairs facing each other. He knows one of them is for him.

He moves toward it, and he's aware there are other people at the edges of the space, that one of them is Kesia, that another one is Ranos, but that doesn't seem important anymore. He sits. The fear that was just a prickle a moment before seizes him like a fist.

A man steps forward, into the moonlight, and sits down across from Theren. He wears blue and copper. He takes down his hood, and Theren sees that he's young, his cheeks rough with a beard, and there's a tattoo on his throat that looks familiar. His skin is light brown.

"Nisov is my name," he says to Theren. "And I'm a priest of the Fever."

There's movement in the room—people making the sign of the Fever over their mouths. Ranos. Maybe Kesia. Theren clamps his mouth shut, an instinct.

"I know you're not foolish enough to think you can stop breathing the same air as me," Nisov says gently. "Your path is set. You can either move along it, or be dragged down it. But time doesn't run backward, and neither can you."

Theren fights the haze in his mind, fights to think this through. Surrounded by Talusar. Surrounded by wilderness.

"The Fever is your birthright," Nisov says. "You are Talusar, and until this day you were a child, untested by the world. After it, you will be an adult, or you will cease to be. It's not for us to predict."

Nisov leans forward, so close that his face is just inches away from Theren's. Theren is too dull-minded to pull away, though he knows Nisov's closeness is a strategy: get as much of the Fever airborne as possible.

"The Fever always kills," Nisov says. "To be infected with it is to face death. Some surrender, and some withdraw. But to face death is to change."

There's something about this that settles inside Theren like an anchor. He wants to change. He wants to become a person who wouldn't run away from an oath seconds after swearing it. He wants to be someone who wouldn't have fled the Talusar.

He wants to be anything other than Rava Vidar's "Coward Knight."

"You must welcome this change," Nisov says, and he puts a hand on Theren's knee. "There's no other way."

All of Theren's life has been about avoiding this. Cedre Station is a quarantine zone because the Cedrae don't believe in acceptable losses. They believe all they can do in the face of the Fever is fight to save as many people as possible. Yet here he is, unnecessarily breathing the same air as someone who can pass on this virus, who may already have done so. Nisov is right—he can't go back. It's too late now.

"Some people choose a holy kiss," Nisov says. "Though it's not a requirement."

Theren wants to laugh; he wants to scream. But he also wants this to be done, and done thoroughly. So he nods.

He nods, and Nisov angles his mouth over Theren's and kisses him, gently. A simple press of his lips, but Theren's fate is now sealed, for better or for worse.

"I believe you can survive this," Nisov says as he pulls away.

✦　✦　✦

The descent into fever goes in stages.

First is the warmth. It hits him in the late morning, when the sun is high. The others are back from their own rituals, dressed in blue like him, smelling of anointing oil and smoke like him. They're all sleeping on their own thin mattresses, which are arranged in a row on the floor in the bare room where they'll all die.

At first, Theren thinks the room is getting warmer from the heat of the sun. He sweats through his shirt, through his socks. Then he looks at the bowl of water in the corner of the room, with the cloths folded next to it, and realizes: this is how it starts. The Talusar know.

He wets one of the cloths and lays it across the back of his neck.

By the time the others wake up, sweaty and confused, he's already moved on to chills. His body shakes, and he ignores it, fetching water for the others.

"Gee, thanks," Fenn says, as Theren passes him a wet washcloth. "Coward."

"Leave him alone," Lisia says. She's leaning against the wall, her eyes closed, the wet cloth on her forehead.

Fenn asks him, "Do you know what happens next? Did they tell you?"

"What happens next," Theren says, "is we die."

+   +   +

Next come the aches. For him, the pain is just enough to make him restless.

For the others, it's agony. They whimper and moan, sweat and pace. Contorting. It's a few hours before he realizes it's the elixir in their blood causing all the pain. His mother told him it was agonizing when the Fever devoured elixir.

When he turned sixteen, his mother made him promise he wouldn't get Imbued until after he took his oath. Was she already planning to betray Cedre then?

The blue-robed attendants from the baths come in to check on them after a while. They watch the other Knights pace and weep, mutter to each other about how far along they are. When they reach Theren, the old woman looks down at him and clicks her tongue.

"He'll be dead soon," she says. "You can see it in his eyes."

It's almost a comfort.

That night, he starts to hallucinate.

He wakes to his mother sitting at the end of his bed, looking up at the stars, at the glow of Cedre Station. Moonlight glints on her teeth. He only knows it's not really her because of what she's wearing—her Cedrae clothes, a crisp white shirt and blue stone earrings.

"I thought I had prepared you to act," Kesia says. "I thought my instruction would foster bravery in you. But I suppose you can never know what someone is made of until they're tested."

Kesia's eyes flash with anger, and she lunges at Theren, seizing her son's shoulder and pinning him to the mattress. She digs her thumb into the wound there, and says, "You have been tested. You have been revealed."

Theren bites down on his fist to keep from screaming.

+   +   +

Kesia soon morphs into Zuza, who skips from Knight to Knight, as if she's checking on them, laying a hand on Maeve's damp chest as she thrashes on the ground, peering into Lisia's ear as she chews on her own fist. Fenn tosses and turns, moaning.

Zuza says, "Serves him right. Hope he dies." She pauses, and laughs. "I guess you're all going to die. But I hope it takes, for him."

"Don't say that," Theren replies.

"Why not?" She grins. "I mean it."

On the bed next to him, Maeve turns over. She's shaking so hard her teeth keep chattering.

Maeve says, "Theren. You're hallucinating."

"I know," Theren says. "But she shouldn't say that."

+   +   +

"I tried to make it work. I tried for so long. But I was lonely," Kesia says. She's not wearing Cedrae clothes this time. She's in the clothes Theren saw earlier, black pants tucked into boots. Hair pulled back. She has her head on the mattress next to Theren's, her body mirroring his. Their hands are right next to each other.

"I thought it would be different there, on Cedre Station," Kesia says. "I thought I would be freer there. But I was lonely, instead. And then, when the other Knights came of age . . . I saw how they lived. How the Sword just used them as props in a political game—like someone who teaches a wild animal a trick and wants you to be impressed, not with the wolf, but with the man. I didn't want you to be her wolf. So I started to pursue other options."

"I'll never understand," he says, "no matter how many times you explain."

"Listen." She lays a hand on his cheek, and he wonders, not for the first time, if she's actually here. "Rava won't just release you, any of you. She can't execute you once you survive the Fever—it's against Talusar law. But she can find an excuse to lock you in the Crucible. That's a prison—and a fighting arena. You'll never survive it. None of you. So when you wake up, you have to pretend something has changed. Pretend you've forgiven me, so you can go with me. You can hate me all you like after that, as long as you do it. Understand?"

She seems so real.

"I'm about to die," he says. Her hand feels cold, and then warm.

"It's all right. I was dead once," Kesia says. "I came back. So will you."

"Maybe."

"Theren," Fenn says. "Shut up."

"You'll talk to them, too," Theren says. "You'll see."

+ + +

He never finds out whether she's real or not. Because soon after that, his heart stops, and that's all.

The perfect Talusar is not a man,
    he is a mountain
altered by the fiercest weather.
No one bears pain like he does,
for he has had to.

—VOLYN,
"THE PERFECT TALUSAR"

BEFORE

It takes the man days to find the right place.

The plant is not like other plants. It doesn't thrive in the sun. So he avoids open stretches of land: the sprawl of deserts, sunlit meadows, and even the dappled light of a forest floor.

The man regrets not being able to linger. The Cloistered Planet is more beautiful than he imagined it would be. He'd thought of it as a barren place, a place where people had chosen familiarity and ignorance over knowledge and growth. But even from afar, it was beautiful—the deep blue of its oceans, the swell of its continents. He's seen planets overtaken by cities, planets where civilization can only survive in remote corners, planets that can't grow anything at all. This one is a jewel by comparison.

He wishes he could wander its surface forever. But he came with a job to do, and so he does it, finding dark, shaded places and testing the soil for compatibility. When the right spot appears, it's anticlimactic—just a small cave in a rocky stretch of land, not too far from the coast of whatever continent he landed on.

He finds a patch of soft earth and digs a deep hole there, in the dark, and unwraps the plant so that he can nestle it in the ground. Then he reaches into his pocket for a knife and digs it into his fingertip. Blood wells up from the wound and he holds his finger over the base of the plant, where the foreign soil intermingles with its native soil.

A few drops fall before he sits back on his heels and sighs.

"I'm sorry to leave you here," he says. "But I did my best to make sure you would be safe."

The plant remains still, its leaves drawn up into the teardrop shape that seems to be a protective response to the environment. It almost feels like a judgment.

The man stands, picks up his shovel and the cloth he wrapped around the sun-shy leaves, and walks toward the cave entrance. Just before emerging into the brilliance of day, he turns back to see that the plant has unfurled just a little, so it glows soft green.

The man smiles, and leaves the cave.

What he sees when he emerges isn't what he expected: his little hop-per ship, perched on a lonely patch of grass in the middle of nowhere-in-particular. The ship is still there, yes, but pacing in a circle around his craft . . . is a woman.

He goes still. He's not supposed to interact with the local population. Hundreds of years ago, the people of this planet didn't respond to the invitation to join the rest of the evolved worlds, which means they're sup-posed to be left alone. But they share a common—and relatively recent—ancestor, so they look the same as him, work the same way he works. And his research survey suggested that people on this planet speak quite a few languages. So there's no way for her to know that he's from *elsewhere* un-less he does something obvious to give it away.

"Hello," he says to her, knowing she won't be able to understand.

She wears sturdy, dusty boots and clothes the same light brown as the land that surrounds them. Her hair is pulled back, revealing a strong, square jaw. And she's carrying a sword—he really should have noticed that first.

He puts up his hands to show her he's not holding any weapons.

"What are you doing here?" she says, and his blood runs cold.

She's speaking a language he knows. Her accent is off, of course—some words are barely intelligible, and the form of "you" she uses is archaic. But he pieces the sentence together anyway.

"You speak Aczeran?" he says.

How is it possible that this woman speaks Aczeran? A language can't develop the same way on different worlds by happenstance. If she speaks Aczeran . . . it has to be because someone *brought it here.*

She frowns at him.

"Is that a dialect of Talusar?" she says. "Where are you from? The east-ern continent?"

The man doesn't know how to answer. Even stranger than the woman knowing Aczeran is her not *knowing* that she knows it. What did she call her language—Talusar?

The woman taps the side of his ship with her sword to get his attention.

"Ileth Vidar won't like hearing that a spy sent by the emperor's son is flying so close to her territory," she says. "And you know what she'll like even less? Knowing he's been developing an advanced ship like this one."

He says, "I'm afraid I don't know what you mean. I'm not a spy. Cer-tainly not for the son of your emperor."

The woman narrows her eyes at him.

There's something appealing about her face, he thinks. Something strong and polished as glass.

"I swear it," he says quietly.

"Oaths mean nothing to me," she replies. "Show me proof, or lose your head."

He looks at his ship, parked right behind her. He can show her the navigation records, but he's not sure she'll believe what she sees.

"If you think I'm not serious about you losing your head, you're making a severe miscalculation," the woman says.

"Oh, I have no doubt," he replies.

10

Elegy leans back in the chair, her spear across her knees. The house smells like mildew and cigarettes, and there's a pile of knitting on the side table.

The back door opens. Elegy feels like a wire that's gone live, but she forces herself to stay still. She hears the man—Robbie, and any man who chooses the name "Robbie" for himself is suspect, in her opinion—pouring himself a glass of water in the kitchen. She hears the gurgle of his swallow. When he steps into the study to find Elegy sitting there, spear at the ready, he freezes.

"Hello, Robert," she says, and she picks up the ball of yarn with her free hand. "I didn't think a man like you would have an interest in the fiber arts."

"It's very soothing," Robbie says. "Who are you?"

"I'm a Scout. People hire me to find things. Someone hired me to find you."

Robbie's eyes dart toward the door and back again. He obviously doesn't have a talent for subterfuge. Elegy picks up her spear and points it at him.

"Whatever you're thinking about doing is dumb," she says. "So don't do it. It'll just be exhausting for both of us."

"I haven't committed any crimes."

"And I'm not a Peacekeeper, so I don't really care whether you've committed a crime or not." Elegy sits forward. "Though in your case, you absolutely have."

That Robbie Meacham is a criminal makes this job easier, but even if he wasn't, she would have had trouble turning it down. The person who hired her has information she needs. Information about the Talusar. Robbie Meacham's freedom is a small price to pay for that.

She can tell he's about to run. In fact, she's counting on it.

Within seconds she's proven correct, as Robbie hurls his water glass at her and takes off. The glass hits the wall next to Elegy's head and shatters, spraying water everywhere. Robbie doesn't move toward the front door, since that would mean running toward her—he goes for the back, which is perfect, just as planned.

Elegy gets up, spear in hand, and walks toward the exit. By the time she makes it outside, her sister Hela has Robbie pinned to the pavement.

"You—fucking—!" Robbie says, his mouth full of pavement. Hela, still holding him down, punches her own leg in a move that would have struck Elegy as odd if she didn't know what it was for. Hela wears a bulbous ring on her middle finger, and the blow triggers a puff of sopora from it, which she points at Robbie Meacham's face. He inhales it and slumps.

"We've got five minutes until he starts wriggling again," Hela says, checking her watch. "Again, I have to question the fairness of this team dynamic. All you do is talk to him, and I'm the one who has to tackle him? I thought I was the senior partner."

"We can trade places if you'd like. But we both know I'm no good at tackling."

"I could use a drink," Hela says. "You?"

"Yes."

Together they haul a heavily sedated Robbie to his feet and walk toward Hela's Finch, which is parked at the end of the alley.

✦   ✦   ✦

They take a bound and gagged Robbie Meacham to a tavern called the Dustbowl in the middle of nowhere. Really—nothing around it for miles in every direction. It's in the Barrens, which is the stretch of land between Talusar country and Cedrae country, where citizens of both—and neither—intermingle.

They don't love Scouts there. They don't love Scouts anywhere, really.

Elegy's father was a Scout. He was an improbable choice for the father of the Sword's second child, and a downright scandalous one, at the time. Scouts didn't exactly have a stellar reputation. In the past, they partnered with the Cedre military to bring in criminals who fled Losan, but then Scouts started taking bribes from said criminals, and Cedre soldiers started coming up with any excuse not to pay Scouts for their work, and now, most Scouts want nothing to do with the military, including its Peacekeeping division.

Instead, Scouts now pursue justice—or vengeance—for other people, like bringing in Robbie Meacham; or they find salvage that's too deep in Talusar country for anyone else to dare seek it out; or, on some rare occasions, they help Talusar refugees find safety.

That was her father's specialty. And it's her father who got her this Talusar contact, from beyond the grave.

Hela stays in the car with Robbie while the exchange takes place. She tries not to talk to Talusar, as a rule. So Elegy is alone when she sits down across from the man, a glass of whiskey in hand.

"I held up my end," she says, as a greeting. "Now it's your turn."

His name is Deji—short for something, probably, but he never said—and he's maybe forty years old, his face carved up with scars. She thinks he might have been Talusar military in another life, but she's not sure. He responds well to directness.

"What do you want to know?" he says.

"You said you saw some movement," she says. "Close associates of Rava Vidar."

"I did," Deji confirms. "They passed through a little outpost called Duchess. Months ago."

"And this is notable . . . why?"

"Well, Rava wasn't with them, for one thing. And she's always with them." He sips from his glass, which has some clear liquor in it, no ice. There's never any ice at the Dustbowl. "And for another thing, there's only one place they could possibly have been going."

Elegy knows the area around Valla, the nearest Talusar city, pretty well, but it still takes her a second to picture it. Duchess is three hundred miles away from the city, and it barely even has a tavern. But it serves an important function: it's where people stop when they're on their way to the Cenobium.

"Rava's lessers were going to visit the augurs," she says.

"Now I gotta wonder why Rava Vidar sent her nearest and dearest to the Cenobium without her," he says, leaning closer to her. "I asked around—discreetly, of course—and I keep hearing the same damn thing."

"Which is?"

"That she's planning something. Something catastrophically big." He sits back, and drains the rest of his glass. "The last time Rava Vidar was cooking up something big, the Sword of Cedre died. So that's the caliber of shitstorm we're talking about."

That's what most people remember about that day, the day of the Getty attack: the Sword of Cedre died. Not many people know that a little-known primary by the name of Shir Alexios died, too. But his face is all Elegy sees when she thinks of Rava's big plans.

Shir thought Elegy was the Hope of Cedre, and he died to save her. After that day, she pretty much decided never to be the Hope of Cedre again. Fuck prophecy. All she cares about now is stopping whatever Rava Vidar is doing.

"I'm sorry I don't have more specifics," Deji says.

"That's all right," she replies distantly. "You'll owe me one."

+   +   +

After putting a still-woozy Robbie Meacham on the back of Deji's horse, Hela and Elegy get back in the Finch and fly out to their house in the desert.

"House" still doesn't seem like the right word for it. It's a chrome-plated structure, long and narrow, with a ramshackle addition hanging on one side, and a showerhead fixed to the back. There's no reason to worry about privacy out here—other than a few cacti and a small grove of Joshua trees, it's rocks, rocks, rocks for miles.

She likes the emptiness of it, and even the heat. But more than either, she likes that it doesn't resemble anything about her old life.

Four years ago, after the ceremony at the Getty, she was supposed to fly to Cedre Station with her mother and announce herself as the Hope of Cedre, the focal point of prophecy, the future savior of their people. But when Shir died, and the Sword with him, Elegy fled, instead. Now there are rumors about a prophecy, rumors about the Hope of Cedre, but no confirmation.

Come back when you've got your head on straight is what the new Sword of Cedre, her half sister, said to her then. *And we'll pick up where you left off.*

Never gonna happen was Elegy's reply. She had no interest in being the subject of prophecy, and she doesn't believe in a single "savior of Cedre," no matter what the augurs said. So now she's here. Working as a Scout, living with Hela in the desert. She may not be happy, exactly, but she can get out of bed again, which feels like an achievement.

"Do I want to know what your meeting was about?" Hela asks her as she parks the Finch.

"Big storm coming," Elegy says. "Courtesy of Rava Vidar."

"Fantastic," Hela says, and they get out of the Finch.

Elegy climbs the rickety front steps, then props up the screen door with her toe as she unlocks the front door.

"You think it has to do with that fulcrum thing?" Hela asks her. "Like she's trying to figure out who the fulcrum people are?"

Hela is the only person alive—aside from the Sword—who knows all the details of what the augurs told Elegy. And they only talk about it when they have to.

"Probably," Elegy says. "I can't think of another reason Rava would send someone to the Cenobium on her behalf. But I don't know what they told her—she asked different questions than I did, so who knows if they even talked to her about a 'fulcrum'?"

She who moves the fulcrum controls the outcome. The augur's voice haunts her still.

"You haven't seen any of the signs?" Hela asks. "The storm. Someone who can see the past. The—"

"No." Elegy cuts her off before she can continue. *Fuck prophecy*, she reminds herself. "And I'm not looking. I'm focusing on Rava, not the cryptic shit the augurs said to me four years ago."

The augurs may have declared themselves to be politically neutral, but they're still people—and they're *Talusar* people. The Sword may trust them, but that doesn't mean Elegy has to.

"You want dinner?" Hela asks her. "I'm heating up yesterday's."

Elegy sets her bag down by the door, and says, "Sure."

She steps through the kitchen—it only takes one stride—to give Hela enough room to work, then passes the little table to reach the desk against the back wall. It's piled high with their father's old things: weapons that are too dull or rusted to be useful, yellowing notebooks with his scribbles fading into their pages, and . . . the box.

"Don't start," Hela warns her. She's standing at the stove—which consists of a burner and a hot plate—poking a pot of savory porridge with a wooden spoon.

"I don't want to argue about it," Elegy says, as she takes the lid off the box. "I just want to know *why* you don't want to get rid of it."

The box contains "artifacts"—that's what Keen called them, anyway. Elegy's word for them is "junk." They're scraps from an old ship—knobs and handles and even a chunk of metal from the vessel's side. They're odd, there's no denying that. Unfamiliar shapes and designs. The metal is warm in color, like copper, but dull as lead and as strong as tungsten. Her father insisted it was unlike anything found on Earth.

"He loved collecting them," Hela says. "And I loved looking for them, for him."

"So you don't believe him. That an alien walks among us." Elegy gives Hela a sly smile.

Hela returns it.

"I think you know intelligent life exists out there and has in fact *contacted us*, so you shouldn't be so scornful of the idea that it's also secretly landed here," Hela says.

"They made contact at a *distance*," Elegy points out. "From somewhere between Mars and a sea of asteroids, in fact. Pretty sure we threatened to blast them out of orbit if they came any closer than that."

In the time before Cedre, before the Talusar, before the *Fever*, Earth received an invitation. It spoke of a greater interstellar order beyond their solar system. The governments of Earth were just trying to decide whether to respond to the message or not when a string of catastrophes struck—the exact nature of them is lost to history, as is the data associated with the invitation. The intended purpose of the little ship next to Cedre Station, the *Sundial*, is to try to trace the invitation's origins back to its source. Those who oppose the *Sundial*'s launch call it a pointless search—the universe is so vast that finding the people who sent that message would be like finding a single grain of sand on a beach, a disastrous waste of precious resources. Those who support the *Sundial*'s launch call it Cedre's only path forward—it's either succumb to the Talusar, or find another world.

Regardless, Elegy has grown up with the knowledge that there are others out there, others who are intelligent and capable of interstellar travel. But that knowledge is abstract. The idea of encountering one of them here on Earth still sounds ludicrous. Even now that Earth doesn't have the weaponry to stop an unidentified ship from landing, who would come here? This is a planet of ruins.

Hela turns off the stove. "It's not so silly to think that whoever and whatever invited us to meet with them also sent a scout to quietly investigate us. And with the Talusar controlling everything, it's also not silly to think that Cedre wouldn't have heard if they uncovered evidence of it."

Elegy nods a little, conceding.

"I guess not," she says. "I just . . . when I remember Dad, I try not to think about how obsessive he was. And he was most obsessive about this."

"He was *most* obsessive about collecting cat figurines," Hela says, gesturing to the shelf above the stove, where cat figurines of all sizes and styles are arranged in no particular order.

She pours the savory porridge into two bowls. It has protein powder in it, but also greens from the market in Twentynine, and onions that Elegy stole from a garden in Losan the last time she was there.

"You know you're a Cedrae citizen, right?" Elegy says, as she takes the bowl from Hela. "You still talk about it like you don't belong to it."

"Well, *you* spend eleven years in Silvis and then call yourself a Cedrae," Hela says.

Hela was born Talusar. When she was eleven, her parents arranged for a Scout—Keen Ahn, Elegy's father—to take their daughter somewhere safe rather than risk her dying by Fever. Keen had flown deep into Talusar country to get her and tried to find a family in Losan that would take her in . . . but she'd fit in so well with Elegy that she stayed with them, instead.

Her accent is gone, for the most part—trained out of her so she wouldn't draw attention to herself. But she still doesn't think of herself as Cedrae, which is her prerogative.

Together they sit in the pair of chairs behind the house, bowls balanced on their laps, and watch the sun set.

"It's been four years exactly since Shir died," Elegy says, at one point, watching the rocks turn a brilliant red.

"Yeah. You want to talk about it?"

Elegy takes Hela's bowl and her own, and walks toward the house. Just before she passes through the door, she says, "No. That's all right."

That night, Hela sleeps in the bed that's wedged into the house's addition, and as she always does when the weather accommodates it, Elegy sets up a cot outside, under the stars.

For a long time before she falls asleep, she stares up at Cedre Station, glowing like a second moon, and its constant companion, the *Sundial*—duller, and tiny as a distant star, but still visible in the night sky if you know where to look.

✦　✦　✦

The next morning finds Elegy in the Octopus, the one café-restaurant-bar in the collapsing desert town of Twentynine. She's drinking coffee. Aki—the bartender, and a former Scout himself—warned her that it would be sour, but she wasn't prepared for *how* sour. She puts three sugar lumps in it to cover up the taste.

She's on edge, her knee bouncing so hard it's making her chair squeak. Maybe it's the coffee.

Or maybe it's the fact that Isre Din, brother of former Knight Theren Forint, will be here any minute now.

Two weeks after the Getty attack, the office of the Sword sent her a message: they'd received a box full of bloody tracking devices from Rava Vidar, along with a note declaring that all five Knights were dead. So Elegy flew to Cedre Station for the funeral. She stood in the back, out of sight. And she only spoke to Isre Din.

If you need anything, she said to him, on impulse more than anything, *reach out to a Scout named Inexplicable.*

Four years passed with no communication, so she assumed Isre Din was out of her life forever. But last week, he requested a meeting.

The door to the Octopus opens. It's too bright to see Isre clearly until he's right in front of her, looking nervy, like he might bolt any second.

He's different now than the boy she spoke to at that funeral. The playful quality is gone from his face. His hair is cut too short to show a curl. He stands very straight.

"Your—" he starts, and she thinks he's about to call her "Your Grace," the honorific typically used for the Sword's family—which she can't allow. So she interrupts him.

"Inexplicable is the name I told you to use," she says. "Sit."

He blinks at her for a moment, then sits. He looks around the Octopus, his eyes landing on the bartender, who's picking at his cuticles.

"Aki," she calls out. "If you're not busy . . . mind strumming a little?"

Aki startles at the sound of her voice, but nods. He reaches under the bar for his lute, then sits down to tune it. He's not a skilled musician, but the sound will offer them some privacy.

"Better?" she says to Isre.

"Yes. Thank you."

He's still so upright.

"Are you a soldier, Isre?" she asks.

He looks surprised. "Yes. Enlisted after the Getty attack. I'm a technician, though."

She nods. She was too hazy with grief to notice, at the time, but there was a surge in enlistment numbers after the Sword died, and a surge in bloodshed, too, as Cedre sought revenge against the Talusar . . . unsuccessfully. She wonders what Isre Din was planning on doing before his brother was killed and his mother betrayed Cedre. She's willing to bet it wasn't joining the army.

"Are you really a *Scout*?" Isre says, with just a hint of the scorn she expects from a soldier.

It was a huge scandal when the Sword chose a Scout to raise her second child. Keen liked to say the late Sword—Annika was her name—was more interesting than people gave her credit for. All she ever said to Elegy about it was that there was strategic advantage in having one child raised by an "outsider."

"Scouting is the family business," Elegy replies tartly.

"And you'd rather be doing that than fighting Talusar in the army, like you were before?"

"There are a lot of ways to fight the Talusar," she snaps. "And dealing with bullshit military hierarchy is a waste of my time. What can I do for you?"

He hesitates a little. Behind him, Aki starts plucking the lute strings, sending gentle music toward them.

"I need to go to Valla," Isre says. "I thought . . . if you knew a Scout named Inexplicable, then you might know someone who can take me there. I didn't realize that Scout would be *you*, but . . ."

"You need to go to Valla," she repeats. "Why?"

He hesitates again. His perfect posture collapses a little.

"Isre, I'm not going to help you until you tell me what's going on. So you may as well just spill it."

"A month ago, I got a message," he says. "Asked for a meeting, and referred to something only someone close to me would know. I couldn't help myself—I went." He lifts his gaze to hers. "It was Kesia."

She feels like someone just tightened the strings on a corset, forcing her to straighten, to stiffen. Making it hard for her to breathe.

"You went to a meeting with a traitor," she says.

"I didn't know it would be her."

"Who else could it have been?" she demands, her voice low.

"I thought . . ." He sighs. "I thought it would be *him*."

Him. He means Theren.

"He's dead," Elegy says.

"No, that's the thing." Isre laughs a little, and it's tinged with desperation. "He's not. That's what Kesia wanted to tell me. We've been misled. He's not dead. He's alive, and he's a prisoner in Rava Vidar's house, and I have to—"

He chokes a little. She can hear the end of the sentence anyway. *I have to get him out.*

"She must have been lying to you," Elegy says. "Manipulating you."

"I asked her for proof. She had this." Isre reaches into his pocket and takes out a photograph.

It's been a long time since Elegy touched a photograph. Not many people in Losan bother with them. Paper—especially this kind of paper—is a precious resource, and film is even scarcer. Among the Talusar, it's more common, since there are only so many ways to document things without elixir.

Elegy holds it like it's hammered gold, cupping it in her palm. The image is grainy and grayscale, but she recognizes in it the young man who knelt before her in the Getty. Only . . . he's not quite that young man anymore. His face is rough with a beard. He's not looking at the camera; he's touching his mouth, an idle movement. There are two straight lines tattooed between his first two knuckles—tattoos he didn't have before.

Theren Forint. Alive.

Her ears are ringing. She can still see him in that antechamber before the ceremony, his eyes lowered. *Hey, eyes up*, she said to him, then, to make him look at her. She almost wants to say it again now, to the still image of him.

Her Knight is alive.

This can't be a coincidence, Deji telling her Rava's planning something big, and Kesia telling Isre—after *four years*—that his brother is still alive. But she doesn't know what the connection is, or what Kesia's motivation could possibly be.

There's only one way to find out.

"So," Isre says. "Can you get me to Valla?"

"You want to try to infiltrate Rava Vidar's house?" she says distantly.

"I know it sounds insane. I know I'll have to stay in the city for a while. Get to know it. Make a plan." He scratches behind his ear. "But I have to try. Okay? I have to try."

She nods.

She doesn't think Isre should try. He doesn't know how to deal with the Talusar. Doesn't know how to sneak into Valla and watch Rava Vidar's house and figure out how to slip in and out unnoticed.

But she does. And maybe a part of her has been waiting for a reason to try.

"I'll make arrangements," she says.

They talk logistics. What time to leave, what day. What supplies he should bring. They agree to meet in a week's time, and she watches him go.

But she's not going to meet him in a week's time.

She's going to set out for Valla in the morning. Alone.

11

Hela slept with the quill under her pillow again, so the feeling of an incoming message draws her out of sleep. She sits up in bed, that annoying pulling sensation in her fingertips.

She sits down at her desk, quill in hand. It looks like a feather made of metal—modeled after an eagle feather, she thinks, though she isn't sure. It's designed for elixir messages, so it won't actually stain whatever she writes on; it'll just make the text of the message visible to her. When she holds it, she feels the elixir in her blood waking up. Spider veins of white light wrap around her hands, and she writes.

> *Dear Dreadful,*
>   *You come highly recommended by a friend of mine as a trust-worthy and capable Scout, and I am hoping you'll agree to a find-and-retrieve of low to moderate risk. The package in question is small and not in Talusar country, but in the Barrens—however, I am not in a position to make the journey myself. If you are amenable to this request, I will forward you the details as soon as I am able.*
>   *Sincerely,*
>   *Dr. Canterbury*

As a rule, Hela doesn't like to do retrievals. They usually involve going into Talusar country, and she has no interest in going anywhere near the people she left behind as a child. But she makes exceptions for the Barrens, and she could use the money.

She sweeps the quill across the desk to erase the message, and then scribbles her agreement.

Scouts use aliases, and so do those who hire them, given how legally questionable their requests usually are. Scouts tend to choose adjectives, but she doesn't know what "Dr. Canterbury" is supposed to tell her about the person requesting this job. Still, her reply is tied to the original message. It'll get where it needs to go.

She sets the quill down. The trailer is empty—Elegy must have left for the Octopus already. But a pot of coffee waits for Hela on the stove. She was a little nervous to live with her sister again as an adult—what if they fought like they did when they were teenagers?—but it seems like the time in the military did Elegy good. She's neat, wakes up at dawn, and never forgets to make enough coffee.

Hela's joints creak as she crosses the trailer in pursuit of a mug.

✦ ✦ ✦

Hela's Finch is old and beat-up, but it still flies in a straight line, so she hasn't bothered to replace it. Of the two of them, Elegy is the one who loves a shiny new gadget; Hela will use something until it breaks, and often even after that point.

She ignores the puttering sound it makes as she dips down to fly low over the empty land. No land is truly empty, of course; even a desert has bunchgrass and brome and creosote. But from above, this land is yellow brown and smudgy as an oil painting. She's searching for a cave opening, as Dr. Canterbury instructed. This is her fifth pass over the coordinates he gave her; he warned her the location of the plant wouldn't be exact, but this is getting ridiculous.

As she turns the Finch to take her sixth loop around the area, she sees it: a dark patch in the land beneath her, like a sunspot in the corner of her eye. It's worth a try. She guides the Finch toward a rocky area that seems sturdy enough to hold it.

She pops open the driver's side door and climbs out. It's like climbing into an oven, the air hot and close. She drops to the sandy soil and presses one hand over her left eye. She learned that trick from Keen Ahn—get one eye used to the dark before you walk into it.

She grabs her all-purpose bag and locks up the Finch, even though there's nobody out here for miles. Dr. Canterbury didn't tell her anything about this plant other than the fact that it glows in the dark, and she probably doesn't need to know anything else. Before she left, she looked up bioluminescent plants, and as far as she can tell, they don't exist. Bugs, sure. Plankton, yes. But plants? Not without the intervention of science.

She's not sure what Dr. Canterbury is into, and at this point in her Scout career, she knows better than to ask. Maybe this is a secret Cedrae or Talusar government experiment; maybe he discovered a brand-new species; maybe he's just lost his mind. It's not her job to guess.

She steps into the cave, and uncovers her eye. It's disorienting at first, seeing muted cave interior with one eye and total darkness with the other, but she steps farther, letting the cold, damp air envelop her.

She's six steps into the cave when she sees a soft green glow up ahead.

She keeps her steps slow, careful. There could be a sharp drop or a pit in the rock up ahead. But the good doctor told her light would only scare off the plant's bioluminescence, so she can't exactly take out a flashlight and start waving it around.

She reaches it, and drops into a crouch. The plant is about the size of a fern, its leaves large and flat near the root and tapering at the ends. A vein of color runs down each one like a trickle of water.

"Well, damn," she says.

Good thing she packed a trowel.

+ + +

She didn't bring a pot, so she wraps up a big ball of dirt—and the plant itself—in an old T-shirt she finds in the footwell of the Finch, and buckles it all in like it's a baby. As soon as she steps into the light of day, the plant's leaves pull into a teardrop shape, showing her their dull purple undersides. But there's not much she can do about the sunlight.

She flies back to Twentynine, which takes about an hour. The trailer was never supposed to be a permanent home—it was Keen's Scout base, where he kept all of his weird "artifacts" and the salvage he wasn't able to get good money for. But when he died, Hela and Elegy agreed that El would get Keen's Losan apartment and Hela would get Twentynine. And El's sure as hell not going back *there* now, to the apartment she shared with Shir.

Hela is the one who packed it up for her after he died. Actually, for those first few weeks, Hela did damn near everything for her sister, because Elegy could hardly tie her shoes.

Not that she minded. When Hela was eleven, she came to Losan in mourning, having been sent away from her home and cut off from her parents in one fell swoop, and it was Elegy who took care of her, Elegy who taught her English, Elegy who first called Hela her sister. All Hela has done the past few years is return the favor.

She's careful with the plant bundle, hugging it close as she unlocks the door to the trailer and then nestling it in the empty sink. There's an old pot behind the house where she used to have a cactus; it'll do, for now.

She's got dirt in all the creases of her hands and under each fingernail when she notices the note, written on the window over the sink in erasing marker. It's from Elegy.

> *Hela—*
> *I'm doing something stupid. I won't be back for a few days, but don't forget—that military tracker is still embedded in my shoulder.*

So if you need to find me, call Primary Ciro Arias and tell him I said it's another King's Canyon.

I'm sorry in advance. It couldn't be avoided.

Love you,
El

Hela stares at that "love you" like it's a curse. They never say "I love you" to each other. But Elegy used to say it every time she was about to go on a particularly dangerous search and rescue mission.

"Fuck," Hela says to the kitchen counter. She braces her dirt-streaked hands on the edge of the sink, and then kicks the cabinet beneath it so hard she leaves a dent.

12

Elegy knows two strategies for getting into Valla.

In the military, it's all about speed. Child soldiers—still pre-infection, and thus capable of using elixir—give the Talusar access to the same radar technology as the Cedrae, but they're slow to deploy. So if a Cedrae ship is fast and precise, it can get into Valla without being intercepted.

Speed won't work for this mission. She needs to be patient in Valla—to wait and to watch. So she has to rely on another approach: her father's. Keen Ahn taught her that sometimes you can't avoid getting caught, so the trick is to get caught by the right people at the right time.

She sets her flight path to take her southeast of Valla, where there's a Talusar outpost on the very edge of nothing. No towns, only one settlement, for miles in every direction. It's a shit assignment for shit soldiers, and they're bound to be bored and disaffected. Easy to bribe.

Losan and Valla are a thousand miles apart, but it only takes an hour to fly there, even in her little Hummingbird. She flies overnight while it's still dark, all her lights off and the night-vision projection over the windshield so she can see. She has a filtration mask with her as a precaution, but she doesn't put it on—only priests of the Fever can spread it by air, and she's unlikely to encounter any, sequestered from society as they are.

In the back of the Hummingbird is a stack of skin mags and a crate of medical supplies, always useful in Valla, with less of a penalty for smuggling. She coasts low, weaving between the mountains. The clouds provide cover from the ground, but nothing can fool the radar. She'll make it as far as she can.

An arrow bounces off her windshield when she's twenty miles away from Valla. It doesn't penetrate the glass, but it leaves a star-shaped dent right in Elegy's line of vision. She can't see the archer, but she knows a warning shot when she sees one, so she dips down in a clear sign of surrender.

She touches the Hummingbird down in a clearing beside a river. The sun is coming up now, so everything is awash in blue. She takes a deep, slow breath. *Don't panic*, Keen would say. *No soldier wants to haul your ass all the way to Valla. They're looking for a way to get out of it, so give them one.*

She gets out of the Hummingbird just as the soldiers break through the tree line. She puts her hands up.

"Hey there," she says to them, when they're still a ways off. She speaks her clearest Talusar.

There are three soldiers, one holding a bow, the other two more casual, their weapons not even drawn. None of them are wearing febra armor—a good sign, because it means they aren't used to facing any action.

"Identify yourself," the one on the left says. He's tall, but rangy. Light brown hair, the color of honey.

"I'm Ella Locke," she says. "Didn't mean to get so close to the city, I got turned around."

They're close now.

"Hands on the ship," the soldier on the right says, and Elegy obeys. The soldier does a quick, lazy pat-down as her golden-haired counterpart peeks into the back of Elegy's Hummingbird. He produces one of the skin mags, and raises his eyebrows at Elegy.

She smiles a little. Shrugs.

"Just giving the people what they want," she says. "I was headed for Twin Cliffs."

Twin Cliffs is a small village nearby, just a few miles outside of Valla. Relaxed and quiet.

"Then you have to head out on foot from here," the soldier says.

The soldier in the middle—the one with the bow—eyes Elegy suspiciously. He starts to walk around the ship. She's made sure her Hummingbird is nothing special: unmarked, with parts only from Losan, and never the best ones. Never military.

"Yeah, that's the plan. Two trips and I'm gone," she says. "Listen, I'm happy to compensate you for your trouble. And your discretion."

She glances at the skin mag, now open in the soldier's hand as he looks over one of the spreads.

"And you're welcome to keep that," she says.

The soldier who searched Elegy snorts. "She's got you figured out, perv."

The archer is still moving in his slow circle around the Hummingbird. He pauses, crouches next to the bumper.

"How much are we talking?" the golden-haired one says. "For your compensation?"

"I don't have a lot of Talusar coin. A hundred, maybe."

"Make it two. And you gotta be out before dusk."

"Hey," the archer says. His voice is rough. "Come look at this."

Elegy looks behind her as the golden-haired one kneels next to the bumper, shoulder to shoulder with the archer. She doesn't know what they're looking at. The soldier grabs something and pulls, hard, detaching it from the underside of the Hummingbird. He stands, and holds it up to examine it more carefully.

It's a metal disc, half an inch thick, with a short antenna attached to it. One side is polished metal. But when the soldier turns it over, Elegy sees the seal of the Sword etched into the side.

The archer raises his bow, arrow notched and ready, and points it at her.

"This is a tracking device," the archer says to her. "From the Sword of Cedre. Want to tell us again who you are?"

Elegy's mouth goes dry.

"I don't know how that got there," she says, and it's not a lie.

"Sure you don't."

"You don't understand," she says. "I really don't. I've never seen it before, there's no reason the Sword of Cedre would be—"

The archer steps forward. Touches the point of the arrow to her forehead. It digs into her skin. She feels her heartbeat everywhere—throat, cheeks, fingertips.

Larke Rosyk, current Sword of Cedre, had someone put a tracker on Elegy's ship.

And now she's going to die because of it.

"Hands behind your back," he says. "I'm sure someone in Valla will be very interested to know who you really are."

+ + +

"Let's practice," Shir said to her, once, after they kissed but long before they got married. She remembers it so clearly: he was sitting across from her in a white T-shirt that was just a little too tight through the shoulders. His hair was damp at the back of his neck from a shower.

"Shir," she said, rolling her eyes. "We both know if I ever get captured by the Talusar, I'm pretty much toast."

"Don't say that." He folded his hands in front of him on the desk. "Never say that. There's always a chance of survival, and your job—your *duty* is to find it. Understand?"

It was still strange to switch gears the way they were—that morning he pulled her into a broom closet, pressed her up against the wall, and slid his hands under her shirt; this afternoon he was Primary Alexios again, teaching her how to endure a Talusar interrogation if she was ever captured.

She sat up straight, and folded her hands in front of her, just like he had.

"Only low-level Talusar interrogators resort to torture," he said. "The high-level ones are truthsayers—memory readers. It's hard to lie to a memory reader. Even if you keep your mouth shut, they'll see what they need to see. The good news is, most memory readers read the very recent past. Which means that if you plan ahead, you can create false memories that feel as vivid to them as the real ones. To create chaos in your memory."

"I do remember this from basic, you know."

"Chaos," he said, as if she hadn't interrupted. His eyes were bright as sunlight through honey. "Through the introduction of not one, but several false memories that you begin cycling through in your mind from the second you set out for your mission. So what do you do when you get captured?"

"Don't panic," she said. "Cycle through your false memories. Pick one or two sensory details every time."

"Good," he said. "Now I'm going to give you a scenario, and you're going to talk me through false memories, one by one."

"For future reference, you may want to refrain from putting your tongue in my mouth on days when you want me to focus," she said.

He grinned. "Call it a test of your mental strength."

✦   ✦   ✦

She crafted the false memories as she went, as any good Cedrae soldier would. Most memory readers can't tell the difference between an event that actually happened or a remembered dream—or a remembered fantasy, if you concoct one that's vivid enough. But as they bind her hands behind her back, she pictures the invented scene again, just in case. She's already presented the story that she's a smuggler, but any smart memory reader will see, even in her recent memories, that she's actually a Scout. The trick will be keeping the memory reader's attention there, instead of letting them dig any deeper—to Isre, to the conversation they had in the Octopus.

She laid the groundwork for herself, too. Before she left, she went to the Octopus and claimed a—very real—job from its bulletin board. The job is to retrieve a message from someone in Twin Cliffs.

In the invented scene, she's meeting with her contact, who has the face of Robbie Meacham. He shows her an image of the person she's supposed to meet in Twin Cliffs: a grizzled, graying man with a port-wine stain on his forehead.

Then she loads the skin mags and medical equipment into the Hummingbird.

The false memories she created on her way here just have swapped details in each scene. The sequence of events stays the same, but the faces revolve—Robbie Meacham becomes Isre Din, the man with the birthmark becomes Hela—and in each one there's the smell of cooked meat, the feeling of a cold glass in her hand, the heat of the sun on her face as she loads up the Hummingbird. The layers of contradictory memories will confuse the memory reader, who won't be able to tell what's real and what's imagined, if Elegy's done a good job.

They're not careful with her. When the archer hauls her up on the horse in front of him, he almost wrenches her arm out of its socket. He's pressed too close, too warm, but he doesn't try anything. The horse, though, terrifies her. It tosses its head and whinnies. Its body bounces her painfully. It's cold here, in the mountains; her fingers are stiff and numb.

She can't help but notice, as they ride the narrow road to Valla, that it's beautiful. She's been to a lot of places on Earth, but she hasn't lingered in any of them. Here, she has the time to feel surrounded, swallowed by the mountains on every side. The sunrise is an eruption of color, and the higher the sun rises, the more color spills into the valley in which Valla finds its home, like a can of paint tipping over.

They bring her through the streets of Valla on horseback, and all the way to the foot of the cliffs that border it on the west, where House Vidar stands waiting.

It's a strange kind of luck, that the seal of the Sword of Cedre was alarming enough to the archer that he decided to bring her here—here, where Theren Forint is allegedly still alive somewhere. This is exactly where she intended to go, just not how she intended to get there.

Her head is clear. She's faced death hundreds of times. Dodged bullets aimed by child soldiers firing out of an open Sparrow hatch. Fought Talusar soldiers with only her spear in hand. Once, she fled soldiers on horseback by hiding in a tree until they passed, confused, beneath her. She's a Scout and a former soldier of Cedre; she's not easily rattled, not anymore.

But she still knows, with an eager kind of detachment, that the odds of survival are not in her favor.

House Vidar is a feat of engineering, a compound built into the side of a cliff. The archer marches her through a door at the bottom of the mountain and to the foot of an interminable staircase that hugs its face. Through narrow slits in the walls, she sees the city that fills the valley. A lively place, full of open-air markets and people strumming old instruments and even, in a park they passed, clusters of people playing a board game in the cold, their hands in gloves and their cheeks bright.

A woman greets them at the foot of the stairs. She's Elegy's height and wears her dark hair in a long braid. Elegy wonders if she has status in Rava's house, if that means she was present during the Getty attack. But she remembers nothing from that night except Shir's weight against her body, and the metal grate of the shuttle between her hands just before she turned back to see . . .

Rava Vidar on the rooftop, with her hair braided into a crown.

"I received your message," the woman says to the archer who captured Elegy. "Where's the tracking device?"

He reaches into the pack at his side and offers it to the woman. She holds it up to her eye like it's a diamond and she needs to determine its clarity. She weighs it in her palm.

"The Sword of Cedre," she says.

Elegy comes back to herself abruptly. She's supposed to be playing a part.

"There's been a mistake," she says, in English.

"Speak again, and I will pull out one of your fingernails," the woman says to her—no heat, just fact, her English clear enough despite a thick accent. She turns to the archer again. "Anything else on her ship?"

"Blank. All the parts seem to be Losani."

"Okay." She takes a bag of coin from her back pocket and hands it to the archer. "You did well. The commander is pleased."

"Pleased enough to reassign me?" the archer says. "I shot the ship down, Nyx, did you tell her that?"

Nyx. She tries to remember the name.

"I gave her your message, and you were quite clear about your many achievements," Nyx says. "As to what she'll do with you, I don't presume to know the mind of our commander, so you'll have to wait and see."

The archer sighs. He pockets the coin, turns around, and goes back the way he came. Nyx grabs Elegy by the elbow and pulls her up the stairs. All the rooms in the house are on the right, since the staircase is built into the side of the mountain. After so many steps Elegy loses count, Nyx takes her through the only door on the left. Hanging above the doorframe is a portrait of an older man with a pale, craggy face, a pair of antlers fixed to the wall behind him so it looks like he's growing them from his shoulders. The emperor, Icar Talus.

Nyx drags her into the stone room and leaves her there, in the cold, for a long time.

13

They take her shoes and her jacket.

In theory, Elegy knows how to do this—how to be cold, and how to be alone, and how to be afraid.

She knows the rhythm of it, how it jerks her mind in different directions, if she's not careful; how it tells her to do whatever she can to escape, even if it means giving information to the Talusar. She won't—she knows that, too. She'll shiver and she'll sweat and she'll lose time. Her throat will burn from thirst and her muscles will ache. She'll remember the real and the fake memories alike. Maybe she'll suffer, and maybe she'll die, but she'll never give them anything useful.

For the crime of helping a child flee Valla, they killed her father. Then they killed Shir. And the Sword.

They won't take anything else.

After a length of time she can't measure, her interrogator comes in. She's short and pale with greasy hair. There's dirt under her fingernails.

"My name is Satka," she says, in English. Her voice is higher than Elegy expected, and raspy. She lisps a little on the *S* in her name. "Do you know why you were brought here, instead of interrogated by police?"

Elegy doesn't answer. The first lesson of being interrogated is not to say anything, if you can help it.

"Because we have seen quite a few tracking devices in our time, applied by Losani police," Satka says. "But the *Sword* . . . well, the Sword only keeps track of people who work for the Sword. Which means you are interesting to Rava Vidar."

She puts her hands on her knees and leans forward, closer to Elegy's face.

"Bad things happen to those who are interesting to Rava Vidar. Now I've been polite, I've introduced myself, but you haven't reciprocated. So tell me . . . who are you?"

Elegy tastes bile.

"My name is Ella Locke," she says. "I'm a smuggler. I don't know how that tracking device got on my ship."

Satka smiles a little.

"I sincerely doubt that. But fine. It's a place to start." She cracks one of her knuckles. "You know, people like to debate the place of pain in memory reading. For me, it's essential. Pain lays a person bare. It shakes up the order in a well-ordered mind, so I can sort through its contents at my leisure. So let's get started, shall we?"

Elegy's training taught her this, too—to endure pain.

Satka was clearly trained in the opposite. She inflicts exactly as much pain as she intends to, without causing too much damage to continue. Every so often she stops, bends down to look Elegy in the eye. Searching her memories, Elegy reasons. That's what Talusar truthsayers—high-level interrogators—do. It's strange to her that someone can dig into her brain without her even feeling it.

She cycles through the false memories like a mantra, even though it's too late for that to be helpful. Satka isn't a mind reader.

Chaos, Shir says.

Chaos, Elegy answers.

As time wears on—just how much, Elegy doesn't know—and Elegy says nothing other than her fake name, her fake identity, her fake story, and her mind apparently yields nothing of use . . . Satka gets frustrated. She grabs Elegy's arm and twists it out of the socket.

Elegy screams like she hasn't screamed since she was a child. With wild abandon.

She lets her rage stay shapeless. She thinks about what the Cedrae soldiers say—that it's still better to be captured here, in Rava's territory, than in her mother's along the eastern coast. It could be worse. It can always be worse.

Satka stalks out of the room. A servant comes in a moment later to set a glass of water down in front of Elegy. Elegy scrambles to pick it up with her still-functioning hand, pouring water into her mouth. Water drips onto her shirt in her eagerness. The burning in her throat subsides. She sets the glass down and looks around.

The room is beautiful and old. Round, two stories tall, with stone walls carved with grasses and pine needles, flowers and leaves. The ceiling is unfinished rock, showing veins of color, a record of minerals past. The chandelier itself is a tight cluster of tiny lanterns, each lit with a single flame. She wonders how long it takes to light them all.

She's kneeling. Her knees ache from the gritty floor. The chandelier is right above her, its flames flickering every now and then from the draft. She hears footsteps outside, but that's nothing new—there's no insulation in this grand house, and she hears every servant passing by, every change of the guard.

This time, the footsteps stop at her door.

Satka walks in first, followed by a man with a C-shaped scar on his cheek, and after them both: Rava Vidar.

Rage and revulsion scorch Elegy at the sight of her. It's been four years since this woman killed Elegy's mother and husband. Until this moment, she believed she was too weighed down by grief to feel anything more than cold fury. She's pursued information about Rava, piecing together her revenge, but she hasn't turned bloodthirsty. Shir wouldn't have liked it.

But right now, she wants nothing more than to wrap her hands around Rava's throat and squeeze until the light leaves her eyes.

Focus, she tells herself. One of her arms isn't in its socket. She's weak and bruised and surrounded by enemies. Now isn't the time. Now is the time to *pay attention*. Every moment she spends here is an opportunity to figure out what Rava is planning, to observe her, to find out something about her that Elegy didn't know before.

Rava looks the same as the last time Elegy saw her. She wears her hair tied in a hasty knot, instead of her distinctive braid, and her clothes— simple, but fine—are rumpled. There's mud caked on her boots. She has the look of someone who doesn't have to care about how she looks. Someone who is *someone*.

Rava squints at Elegy. "Her story?"

Satka picks at her cuticles without looking down. A nervous tic, Elegy observes. She must have failed to find anything useful in Elegy's mind.

"She won't say a thing other than what I told you, Commander. Not a single word."

"I didn't realize you needed her to *say* anything. That's the advantage of a memory reader, isn't it?"

Elegy remembers the silhouette on the rooftop, and Shir's weight against her—

And she forces herself back to the present.

"I saw the same things over and over," Satka says. "Several iterations of what seems to be the same memory, only—the details are switched around, inconsistent. Incompatible with each other."

"So you're saying she's trained to resist a memory reader," Rava says, looking down at Elegy. "Can't imagine why a smuggler would require such skills, can you?"

She closes her eyes, and sways a little. It hurts to breathe. She tries not to react to what Rava is saying—it's useful to pretend not to know Talusar, and she doubts the guards who captured her told Nyx what language she spoke to them.

"No matter," Rava says. "Fortunately for me, I have a different sort of truthsayer at my disposal."

"I'll go get him, Commander," the man with the scar says.

Him. Like it's a name.

"Thank you, Ranos."

The man—Ranos—leaves the room, closing the door behind him. Satka is still picking her cuticles. She watches Rava, and Rava watches Elegy. For just a moment, Elegy is worried Rava will recognize her—but she wore a mask in the Cenobium, at her mother's insistence.

"My name is Rava Vidar," she says to Elegy, in English this time. "Do you know how the Cedrae military instructs its soldiers to resist Talusar interrogation?"

She crouches in front of Elegy, balancing her elbows on her knees. There's ease in her posture, like she does this kind of thing every day.

"They tell them to begin each mission with a tangle of false memories that bewilders the average Talusar memory reader. Even an above-average one, it seems. So the manner in which you have resisted us so far has all but confirmed that you are who we suspect you to be. At this point, whatever story you have cooked up for later on is completely useless to you. So I will offer you a deal."

She has a knife at her hip—within reach, if Elegy were more physically capable. It's long enough to scrape the floor. There's a vine etched into the handle.

"If you tell me who you really are before my other truthsayer gets here, I will let you live out the rest of your days in Talusar prison," she says. "I'm going to get the information I need either way. My truthsayer is never wrong. So there's no need for you to die. Surely you want to survive this?"

Her voice is low and urgent.

"Let me tell you something your leaders may not have bothered to share with you. Four years ago, I went to the augurs at the Cenobium, and they told me that my fate is to attain victory for the Talusar over our Cedrae enemies."

She has such confidence, Elegy thinks. *Of course she does.* Rava has been a warrior her entire life, and a legendary one for a third of that time. Of course she believes the prophecy. Of course she believes her triumph is inevitable.

"I've already begun to fulfill it," she says. "I'm the one who killed your Sword. And with what's coming . . . well, you'd be better off in a prison in Valla than in Cedre."

Elegy's breath catches.

Something's brewing. Something big.

And from the recesses of Elegy's memory, the voice of an augur: *She who moves the fulcrum controls the outcome.*

"So no matter whose secrets you keep, and how bravely you face what's ahead of you," Rava says, her voice low and poisonous, "you will still lose. Unless you accept this deal."

Elegy stares up at her, helpless with rage. With grief. She isn't sure she'll be able to talk without screaming.

"No thanks," she says, as casually as she can manage.

Rava smiles. "You'd be more convincing as a smuggler if you weren't quite so brave."

She comes to her feet just as the door opens again. This time, a man follows Ranos into the interrogation room.

At first, when he's still in the shadows by the door, all she can see is that he's tall and imposing. And then he steps into the light cast by the chandelier, and the flames flicker over stern eyebrows and messy dark hair and the two bars tattooed on his right hand, and she recognizes him.

Theren Forint.

He stops at Rava's shoulder and waits, his hands clasped behind him. For the first time, it occurs to Elegy that he may be here of his own free will. When she imagined him in House Vidar, she thought of him locked in some basement cell subsisting on bread and water—not serving as Rava's special truthsayer, the one she uses when her other one fails. Maybe Kesia kept Theren's true loyalties to herself when she talked to Isre. Maybe this was all a trap, and Elegy just fell into it.

Rava turns toward Theren, and he inclines his head to her, respectful. She puts a bent knuckle under his chin and tips his head up so he's looking at her.

For a moment she just stares at him, and it's strange, the way her face goes slack, like she's not looking at anything at all.

Then she blinks, like she's surfacing from sleep, and says, "Your time belongs to me. Why, then, are you late?"

"It won't happen again, my lady."

"No, it won't."

She removes her hand. Theren's next swallow is labored.

"You won't be able to fool this one with your training, *smuggler*," Rava says—to Elegy, even though her eyes are still locked on Theren. "He reads hearts."

The only Fever gifts Elegy knows about—apart from the augurs', of

course—have to do with memories. Seeing them. Sharing them. Even erasing them. She's never heard of a "heart reader," whatever that is. Her best
guess is that he can feel the emotions that memories provoke while he
reads them, which is bad news for her—her feelings are bound to give her
away.

Which means that if Theren Forint *has* turned traitor, and he realizes
who she is . . . she's dead.

"Get to work," Rava says to him, in Talusar this time.

He turns to face Elegy as Rava recedes into the darkness near the door.
She braces herself for his recognition, not sure if it will benefit her or be
her downfall . . . but it doesn't come. It's as if he's never seen her before.
Is she that forgettable?

"I hear you're a smuggler." His voice is quiet.

"She doesn't speak Talusar," Satka says, still plucking at her cuticles.

"Yes she does." He crouches in front of Elegy, putting them on the
same level. "Don't you."

It's not a question. Light shifts across his face, and she realizes that he's
beautiful now. Time has carved out his jawline and cheekbones, and stolen
the boyishness from his face. His eyes are dark and focused.

"You're not a smuggler. I think you're a soldier."

She doesn't know what to do now. She tries to let her mind go blank.
Tries not to react, even emotionally, to anything he says. But her heart
betrays her. She is a soldier. A part of her always will be.

Theren nods. "A spy, probably. Easy enough to figure out, since you're
certainly not here to fight. I wonder what it is you want to know."

"She works for the Sword," Rava says. "What concerns the Sword most
in Valla?"

"You do," Theren says simply.

Elegy has no idea what he's seeing, what she's projecting, but she's had
enough of it.

"I've never heard of an interrogation without any questions," she says,
in English. She's not going to confirm that she speaks Talusar, no matter
how obvious it now seems.

"A spy for the Sword in Valla. Here to observe Rava Vidar. Alone," he
says, as if she didn't speak at all, and then he frowns. Shakes his head. "No.
Not alone. How many others?"

She feels a thrill in her chest, despite her efforts to remain neutral. She
didn't come with any others. If he believes she did, then he can't possibly
be as good as Rava Vidar thinks he is.

"A partner? No, more than that."

He shifts closer to her. From here, she can see how spare he is—muscled, but no softness anywhere, the bones in his shoulders showing through his too-large shirt.

"Two?" he asks, and then he nods.

Rava turns to Satka and barks an order: "Lock down the city. Offer a reward for information."

"Yes, Commander." Satka leaves the room.

Elegy doesn't dare move.

"Enough for now," Rava says. "It'll be easier once we find her cocon-spirators. Let them all decide how much they trust each other." She smiles a little. "Let her wonder what's become of them."

Theren looks at Elegy for just a moment longer, his expression unread-able. *He's exhausted*, she thinks, and she's not sure why she thinks it, be-cause he's Rava Vidar's truthsayer, and why does she care if a traitor looks worn all the way through, like a scrap of old fabric?

Then he stands. Rava moves into the light again.

"I'll expect you to be ready once we find them," she says to him. "Don't be inattentive again."

Theren is taller than her, and since he wasn't that tall the last time El-egy saw him, she supposes the rumors are true—the Fever can regenerate a person larger than they were before. That explains Rava's extraordinary height. He bows his head to her, and she puts a hand on the back of his neck, briefly. It's not affectionate—instead, it seems almost threatening. She watches the halting rise and fall of his breath.

Then Rava releases him, and he walks out of the room, leaving Elegy with Rava and Ranos.

"No one surprises him," Rava says, in a murmur, like she's talking to herself.

"Your orders, Commander?" Ranos asks.

"Tie her to a chair. I don't want her to sleep."

She raises an eyebrow at Elegy, then sweeps out of the room.

14

Elegy doesn't sleep.

Outside these walls, Rava's soldiers are searching the streets of Valla for her imaginary coconspirators, and the idea of them on an impossible errand would amuse her, if she wasn't in so much pain. Her shoulder. Her jaw. Her entire body, really.

She doesn't understand how she did it. How she fooled him, this man that *no one surprises*, according to Rava. Theren Forint, who apparently reads hearts, didn't recognize her, and didn't even come close to the truth about her. It seems impossible.

She listens to the footsteps in the hallway. The changing of the guard comes at regular intervals. In between, there are quick, purposeful feet—servants working into the night, if it's even night at all. She tips her head back to look at the chandelier. A few of the lantern wicks have run out of fuel now, and the flames are sputtering out one by one. She counts the disappearing ones like shooting stars. Four, then seven, then nine. Soon she'll be in total darkness.

She waits for the next changing of the guard, and it doesn't come.

Instead, there's a long silence and then running footsteps. Another flame flickers out above her as the lock to the interrogation chamber shifts. The door opens, and Theren Forint lopes in.

At first, all she sees is red. Red, wet palms. Red streaks on his arms. Red dots on his face. A knife dripping red on the floor.

He's covered in blood.

"Your Grace," he says. He drops a bag at her feet.

She stares up at him, her mind blank. She tries to remember if she saw any hint of recognition, any suggestion of her true identity during that interrogation. But there was no sign.

Whatever else he's become, Theren Forint is now an excellent liar.

"You know who I am?" she demands.

He nods, and limps around her. She hears him fall to his knees, and he heaves a breath against her back as he eases the wet blade under the ropes that bind her to the chair. He saws at them until they break, and then moves on to the ones across her chest.

"My shoulder is dislocated," she says.

"Okay. Stay there."

He moves around the chair so he's crouched in front of her. His eyes are full of tears, but he doesn't seem to be aware of it. He takes her wrist in hand, and carefully brings her arm in front of her, then rotates it so her elbow is out. His other hand falls heavily on her shoulder. Their eyes meet. He breathes in, and so does she.

As she exhales, he presses so hard it makes her scream. She feels her shoulder shift back into its socket. The relief is instant, the feeling of wrongness resolved.

"Better?" he asks.

"Yes."

He opens the bag he dropped earlier and takes out a pair of boots with socks stuffed inside them. She stalls his hands as he starts to unroll the socks. He's shaking.

"I've got it," she says. "Gather yourself."

He sets the boots down, but stays crouched there as she puts the socks on, and then picks up the left boot. There's something etched into the leather—a design. It's a circle of vines, continuous, like an ouroboros. The same vine is tattooed between his thumb and forefinger, not circular but following the curve of his hand.

His eyes are closed, his head bowed.

There's no time to wonder. She shoves her feet into the boots and pulls the laces tight. They're big for her, but the socks are thick. She stands, and so does he.

"Let's go," he says. He seems steadier now.

He leads the way out of the interrogation room, knife in hand. As she passes the open door, she looks back to see the key in the lock, metal, the size of her fist. She wonders how he got his hands on it.

She trips after him, shocked by how painful it is to walk. At the end of the corridor is the body of a guard, his arms sprawled out in front of him, his legs tangled. He must have been mostly dead before he hit the ground. The floor is wet with his blood.

Theren moves on quiet feet up the stairs, sidestepping the guard's lax fingers. He's more graceful than he has any right to be, at his size. She moves in his wake, holding her ribs with one hand to steady them as she breathes, and skimming the wall with the other, to keep her balance.

Theren moves faster than she can, so she trails behind him. Sometimes darkness swallows him, and sometimes moonlight stretches through the tall, narrow windows on the other side of the hallway, and lights up the bloodstains on his arms.

They pass another body, this one leaning against the wall, like the guard was only sleeping on the job. She looks away from it as they pass.

This is why they haven't run into anyone yet: Theren cleared a path for them in blood.

She thinks of the man—boy, really—that stared up at her during the Knight ceremony, pale with fear.

They pass half a dozen rooms, built with wide windows that show the mountains and the city of Valla below. Then, without warning, Theren doubles back and pushes her into an alcove she didn't even see. He stands so close to her she can feel heat coming from his skin, but he doesn't touch her. He puts a finger against his lips.

Then she hears them. Footsteps, coming their way. She clenches her jaw. Theren steps out of the alcove.

She sees only impressions of what he does then. His tall, rangy body grappling with another. Grunts and moans. Theren turns, fast, throwing his opponent against the stone and then—a sickening gurgle as the knife goes in.

Theren steps back into the alcove and flicks his fingers. *Come.*

She stumbles after him, stepping over the body—no, not a body yet. The man is still alive, dark blood spilling from a tear in his throat.

She keeps moving. Up, past three more rooms before Theren takes a sharp left. He shoves his way through a door, and cool air washes over her, smelling of cedar. They're outside. The moon shines above them—a half-moon—crowding out the light of the stars.

Rava's house follows the ridge of a mountain, and built into the small valley behind it is a long, low building. She knows by the smell that it's a stable.

And in front of that stable is the man with the C-shaped scar on his cheek. Ranos.

Ranos tosses a knife from his left hand to his right. Despite this showy display, he looks troubled, his mouth pinched.

"She thought you would go down, to the road," Ranos says. "You kept everyone busy searching the city."

"I'd rather not kill you, Ranos."

Ranos snorts. He tosses his knife again, so it's in his left hand instead of his right. Theren's knife is in his left hand, too.

"You know I can't let you leave." Ranos's voice echoes. Everything else is silent, even the wind. "Not with everything you know."

"You can. You just don't want to."

Ranos shrugs. "Whoever *that* is . . ." He points at Elegy with his knife. ". . . I hope she's worth it."

Theren laughs, a little hysterical, and then lunges.

It's a quick, artful move, but a half-hearted one—no sooner does he move toward Ranos than he's moving away, light on his feet. Ranos thrusts anyway with his knife; Theren dodges, and they face each other, weapons held ready. For a moment they're at a standstill, shifting forward and back by inches, each movement aborted before it can take shape.

"You think I don't know your tricks?" Ranos says.

"I know you know them. But that doesn't mean they won't work."

Ranos grits his teeth and pounces, slicing down. Theren is already moving, somehow; he holds up his forearm, and the blade cuts through his shirt, carving a red line on his skin. Ranos strikes again, and Theren's other arm goes up, this time closer, to block Ranos at the wrist. Ranos strikes again, and is blocked again. Elegy doesn't know how Theren is doing it, how he isn't so much reacting to Ranos's movement as moving *with* him, like the choreography was long set and he already knows the steps.

Ranos screams into his teeth, frustrated; he takes a swipe at Theren, and the other man lurches away from the knife, his back arched. But he isn't fast enough this time—the knife plunges into his side.

Ranos grins with brutal pleasure, and Theren dances back, hunched but undeterred. Elegy watches as his eyes sharpen and he stumbles around Ranos, turning his opponent in an uneven circle. He reminds her of a mountain lion—patient, muscles bunching in anticipation of movement, and then—uncoiling, sudden.

Ranos stabs again, and this time, Theren catches him by the arm. With his other hand, he stabs toward Ranos's neck. Ranos pins Theren's wrist against his shoulder, the blade inches from his throat, and they struggle against each other. Theren is taller, but Ranos is thicker, stronger. Sweat shines on his forehead.

Then Theren drops the knife that's in his left hand, and catches it with his right, waiting below. He stabs Ranos in the gut.

Ranos screams as Theren yanks the blade out, and he crumples, coughing blood on the ground. Theren drops to his knees, clutching his own side, where blood is already soaking the top of his pants.

The two men look at each other.

"You know what she'll do to me," Ranos says. "It would be more merciful to kill me."

Theren lifts the knife between them, and holds it over Ranos's throat. His body shudders. Heaves.

The knife clatters to the ground.

"I'm sorry," Theren says. "I can't."

They have to move. Elegy limps toward him, and touches his shoulder, making him flinch.

"Let's go," she says. "Now."

Theren presses a hand to his wounded side and staggers toward the stable.

Inside it, the air smells like hay and manure. It's not as unpleasant as she expected. She hears snorting and shuffling. It's too dark to see the animals they pass, but she gets impressions of them, the toss of a mane, the stomp of a hoof. He stops at the third stall from the end and steps into it, murmuring to the animal, too low for her to hear.

He leads it out of the stall and she lurches away, still not used to how big horses are up close. It's black, but not jet black—there's a patch of white on its nose, like a beacon in the dark. Theren points to something a few feet away. Her eyes aren't trained for dark stables with no electricity, but she fumbles for whatever it is. A stool.

She drags it to the animal's side. Theren leans into the horse's neck for just a moment. Then he steps up and, with a grimace, throws his leg over the saddle. He holds out a hand to help her up.

Her turn. She moves closer, startling when the horse tosses its head and snorts.

"Foot in the stirrup," he says. "Then—swing your leg. Don't think too much."

She puts her hand in his. It's tacky with blood. She guides her foot into the stirrup—and then throws her leg over the animal's back. Pain burns through her. She bites back a groan, and slumps against Theren. He's sturdy as a wall.

"Hang on," he says, and she can't wrap an arm around his middle, given that it's gushing blood, so she hooks an arm under his and rests her palm on his chest. She holds on tight as he urges the horse forward, out of the stable and into the night.

✦   ✦   ✦

They ride as fast as the mountain trail allows. The journey takes them down into the seam between the two mountains that House Vidar straddles.

About twenty minutes after their hasty departure, when the path narrows and they have to slow, he calls over his shoulder, "Do you have a way out?"

She can feel his heartbeat against her palm, much too fast. He needs a doctor, now.

"I still have a tracker in my shoulder," she says. "We just need to get far enough away that it's safe for them to pick us up."

He urges the horse on. She can feel every shift of his body like this, pressed against him. Every stutter of air into his lungs. It's too much to know about a stranger, even if he is a stranger who once bound his life to hers with an oath.

They go up and around a rock garden where boulders the size of houses lie cracked and moss-covered, and then down, into dense trees with thick underbrush. There's no trail here. Elegy watches little creatures in the trees flitting from branch to branch, weaving in and out of the leaves with the buzz of insect wings.

They're quiet except for the sound of hooves on rock. A cloud drifts away from Cedre Station, rendering it a stark white spool above them, and in the moonlight, she looks at the tattoos on Theren's hands—black bars between the knuckles of his right, and on his left, the vine she noticed before, between his thumb and index finger. She wonders what they mean. She knows priests of the Fever have tattoos, but on their throats, not their hands.

She hears splashing. They're at a low point between two peaks, and the horse is walking in a stream. She feels the strength go out of Theren's body, and she stiffens with alarm.

"Hey!" She jostles him. "Hey, wake up!"

He straightens, rouses.

"This is far enough," she says. "Let's get down before you fall off."

She's hurt, but not as hurt as he is. Gritting her teeth, she swings her leg over the horse and drops to her knees in the stream. The water is cold, but shallow, only going up to her calves. She offers Theren a hand, and he takes it, and all but topples into the water. She helps him to the bank of the stream, where the earth is wet and smells clean.

The horse turns and trots away, going back the way it came.

"Stay awake," she says. "I'll activate my tracker."

Theren sits, and braces himself against his bent knees. She steps away and positions her thumb over the hard spot in her shoulder muscle where the bead was inserted. She pushes down until red light flashes deep inside her body, lighting up her bones for just a second before receding. Relief makes her fingers numb.

When she looks back at him, she can already see blood seeping into the ground beneath him.

"Let me see," she says.

He shakes his head.

"Fine." She pulls her sweater over her head, so she's just in the T-shirt beneath it. The air is so cold she's already shivering by the time she's folded it and reached for his side.

Theren jerks back, but he lets her press the sweater to his wound.

"We thought you were dead." She's been speaking Talusar to him this whole time, and he's never corrected her.

It's just one of a thousand things she needs to say, to explain, and probably not the right one to start with, but it's too late now.

She adds, "They sent us your trackers in a box. All bloody."

"Only Lisia and Furik died from Fever," he says. "The others died—after. But—"

With his free hand, he tugs his shirt to the side to show her a silvery scar right above his collarbone.

She knows he's the same person who swore the oath. But the scar more firmly connects the two men in her mind: this is him, her Knight, whose death has been hanging over her for four years. He's alive.

"We had to cut them out," he says. "Or the Fever would have forced them out."

She hears something. A hum—an engine. Undulating, as if the craft is slowing. The humming gets louder, and louder, and she comes to her feet. Now she can see it—a dark shape moving through the sky, fast. A Sparrow.

They got here quickly. They must have already been looking for her, thanks to the device Larke planted on her ship. The one that almost got her killed.

Before it gets too loud for him to hear, she says, "I would have come for you sooner, if I'd known you were alive."

Theren is staring at her, *staring*, like he's confused by something she said, only she doesn't know what.

Then he says, "What do you mean? You came here just for *me*?"

The ship descends. She crouches next to Theren and lifts his arm over her shoulders so she can help him stand. For a moment, as the wind picks up, and the gears of the hatch grind together as it opens—as all these mechanical, distinctly Cedrae noises churn around them—their faces are close enough that she doesn't have to shout.

"I came to get you out," she says. "Obviously."

15

Theren's memories of waking up after the Fever killed him are dreamlike. Coming back to life felt like . . . surfacing.

His mouth tasted like rot. His feet twitched, and he blinked, but he couldn't see anything but light. He heard conversation somewhere nearby, but it was garbled.

He moved his fingers, his toes. Something came to mind—his mother, digging her thumb into his shoulder. Fenn moaning in pain. The priest of the Fever touching his chin.

Rava Vidar saying, *You have a choice to make.*

The memories felt far from him.

He sat upright. He was in a dim room with a blue tile floor. The windows were covered, giving the place a close feeling.

"Easy," someone said.

He startled. He'd forgotten he wasn't alone.

A second voice said, "Fifty-three hours from death to rebirth."

Hands touched his shoulders. In front of him was a blue blur. He heard someone pouring liquid into a cup, and then the cup was against his lips, and he drank. It was water, flavored with mint and orange peel. The cup disappeared, and someone dabbed at his face and throat with a cloth.

His vision sharpened a little, and he could see it was a woman tending him. The same older woman who took off his shoes in the baths.

"Welcome to the next life," she said to him.

He felt odd. A moment ago he had been confused and exhausted. But at her touch, the haze lifted, and he was . . . sharper. Brisk. Like he was about to finish a task.

"You've been dead for about two days," the woman said to him. "You're the first of your people to wake—or not wake. Here. Drink it slowly. You'll feel weak for some time."

She put a cup in his hands, and he clutched it to his chest. When her hands left his, the haze returned.

He drank from the cup. Time was slippery. It felt like only minutes later that she checked on him again, but the water in his cup was gone.

"I'm bigger," he said, and he wasn't sure where that observation came from. But it was true. He felt bigger. Broader. His legs were longer.

"That can happen," she said. "The Fever regenerates your body after days of deterioration, and sometimes it does so enthusiastically. Your joints may ache for a while, but you'll adjust."

She handed him a bowl of dried fruit to eat. His hands shook as he picked up a fig.

He'd been dead for two days.

When the fruit was gone, the old woman returned, and held out her hands to help him stand. When he touched her, he felt it again, that sharpness. Wakeful. His muscles shook when he got to his feet, but after a moment of leaning on her—she was stronger than she looked—he stabilized.

"You've been summoned by Commander Rava Vidar," she said.

She draped a blanket over his shoulders, which he clasped over his chest, already shivering. Then she led him down the hallway. They were in another part of the monastery now, moving in a different direction—deeper into the maze of rooms. They turned a corner and she knocked on a heavy wooden door.

"Come in," a voice called from the next room.

He entered a sitting room. In it, Rava Vidar sat beside a lively fire. Behind her, on a sofa, were two others—fierce-looking people with incongruously turned-up noses. One of them was the soldier who had bet on the Knights dying. Ranos. The other looked like his sister.

And of course, standing off to the side was Theren's mother.

Kesia rushed toward him, and a feeling of relief suffused every part of him—but that wasn't right, was it? He didn't feel relieved to see her. He felt sick. If he focused on it, he could feel that, too, the two contradictory emotions taking up equal space inside him.

It was as if there was a new layer to him that hadn't been there before. Skin, then muscle, then *this*.

It occurred to him, as he noted her expression, that he might be feeling *her* relief.

But that was nonsense. People who woke from the Fever saw the past, saw the future. Not . . . this.

Kesia reached for him, and he backed away, almost losing his balance before his back hit the wall.

"It seems the new version of him doesn't forgive you, either, Kesia," Rava said, drawing his attention back to her. She wore a green sweater. He'd only ever seen her in armor, before; it was unsettling to see her as a person instead of a soldier.

"You lived," she said to him, and she picked up a glass from the table in front of her, and sipped from it.

"I did." His voice came out rough. He'd barely spoken since resurrecting. *I resurrected*, he thought, deliriously.

"The others died a day after you," Rava said. "We'll know tomorrow whether they'll return or not."

He remembered Kesia—a hallucination, or maybe not—lying beside him on the pallet where he died, telling him that Rava had no intention of freeing any of them. Instead, she had just come up with a more creative way of killing them: the Talusar prison. The Crucible.

"And then, when they do wake, you'll put them in your Crucible," he said. "Where they'll probably die anyway."

Rava raised an eyebrow at Kesia, then set her glass down and stood. She wore a ring on her left hand, febra shaped into a single continuous vine. "Your mother negotiated for you all to be infected, and it's against our most sacred laws to hold a person accountable post-resurrection for crimes they committed before it. So I had to come up with a way to contain you all without killing you."

The Talusar faith insisted that a person resurrected by Fever was a new person. And the ruling family—Rava's family—was supposedly devout. But Rava looked like she wanted to roll her eyes when she said the words "sacred laws."

"It's not against your 'sacred laws' to imprison someone for no reason?" he asked.

"Oh, I'll give plenty of reasons," Rava said solemnly. "Regardless, my point is—you are alone, for now, unobserved by your fellow Knights, and free to make your own choice. So will you go with them to the Crucible, to fight and suffer and probably die? Or will you renounce Cedre and go with your mother to become a free citizen of Valla?"

He felt something strange. A flickering. Like there was a candle lit behind his breastbone, and its flame was fluttering in the wind.

"You won't let me be a free citizen of Valla," he said distantly.

She laughed. "Are you doubting my word?"

"Yes," he said. "You're offering me a choice to fulfill your end of the bargain you made with her." He gestured to his mother. "But you're only willing to do it because you think you know my choice already."

Rava Vidar was never going to let a Knight of Cedre move freely in Valla. Only a fool would believe otherwise.

"Let's see if I'm right," he said. "I choose freedom. I forsake Cedre, I forsake the Knights. I choose Valla, instead."

He felt the candle flame sputter out. The faint smile she wore as she played with him disappeared. He was right. Of course he was right.

She was never going to free him.

He looked at Kesia. "This is why you don't make deals with devils."

Kesia looked stricken. She hadn't seen this coming; that much was clear. But Theren only nodded and started toward the door.

"I look forward to seeing you fight," Rava said to his retreating back.

✦   ✦   ✦

Now, in the forest outside of Valla, Theren shudders at the sound of the Cedrae rescue ship descending: the gears shifting, the pulse of the engine. Warm blood gushes over his hand, even through the sweater Elegy gave him to stanch the bleeding.

The word "why" waits on his tongue. Why—why would the Hope of Cedre, the sister of the Sword, the person he abandoned in her hour of greatest need, ever risk her life to get someone like *him* out of Valla? He's desperate to know. But Elegy's already turning away, waving her uninjured arm to get the pilot's attention.

Wind rages around them both as the ship dips down to hover over the water. The hatch opens, and standing just inside it is a soldier in bright crimson, his black hair tied back. He jumps down before the craft has come to rest, and runs up to Elegy—now halfway across the river—to throw his arms around her.

"Fuck you for scaring me that bad, Ahn," he says, into her hair. Her answering laugh is muffled by his jacket.

Theren feels the forest at his back, quiet and dark. He considers disappearing into it. He could stumble into the trees and find some still place to take his last breaths. It would be a more peaceful end than he's dared to imagine for himself in a long time.

As if she heard his thoughts, Elegy breaks away from the soldier and turns back. Her eyes lock on his.

"I'll chase you," she says, in Talusar. Talusar's pronouns all carry some indication of status, and she addresses him like a perfect equal. That form of address is archaic. Unfamiliar. Perfect equality is nearly impossible— and even if it wasn't, it certainly wouldn't apply to him and her.

When he replies, he selects pronouns that acknowledge the gulf of status between them. Her, the fated savior of the whole goddamn planet. Him, the disgraced son of a traitor, practically a traitor himself.

"If you knew what I'd done," he says, "you might let me die instead."

"You aren't dying here." She feels heavy—with exhaustion, with sadness, with *decision*. The combined weight almost brings him to his knees.

He looks at her, her bruised jaw set. At the blue-white lights coming from the ship's hatch. At the soldier's bright uniform. At the dark smudge of trees all around them.

He already knows he'll do as she says.

The soldier who greeted her prickles with alarm. Theren feels it crackling in his temples.

"I'm assuming he can't infect me," the soldier says to Elegy, in English.

"Of course not, Arias; I'm not stupid," she says. "And I should be clear of any other exposures. Not that it really works that way."

"I know, I know. But we still have to take precautions. It's protocol."

"I remember."

She waits as Theren limps through the cold water toward her, his arm pressed so hard to his side that he can't feel his fingers anymore. The soldier's—Arias's—eyes burn into him for a moment, and then he turns and climbs back into the ship.

By the time Theren makes it up the hatch steps, a wall of sturdy plastic is extending from the ceiling of the ship to the floor. A barrier to protect against the Fever. There are three soldiers on board: the pilot, Arias, and a third, a small, solid young woman with unnaturally red hair that matches her jacket. All of them wear filtration masks, the emergency kind made of stretchy, sticky material that adheres to the skin—like a gum bubble that burst over a child's mouth.

The lights in the ship are so bright he has to squint. He's not used to bright lights anymore, after four years in Valla with only fire and moon-light to see by. The chemical smell of the ship makes him feel woozy; the last time he smelled something like that, he was on his way to meet Ileth Vidar, and—

He forces the memory out. The hatch door is closing, and the ship is already pulling away from the ground. It gives a lurch, and he stumbles into the wall to brace himself. *Let pain be the whetstone that sharpens the blade of you*, Satka says in his memory, but he's run out of sharpness. Instead, he lets himself go to his knees, bracing himself with one hand on the grate floor.

He hears something about a first aid kit. Everything sounds like it's underwater. A hand touches his shoulder, and he jerks away from it before realizing it's only Elegy's; she's the only one on this side of the barrier with him. He looks up at her, blinking slowly.

"Sorry." She holds up a bottle of wound sealant. "This won't do much for you, but it'll be better than nothing."

"You keep using the wrong 'you,'" he says to her.

"I know exactly which 'you' I'm using. Lift up your shirt."

If he bleeds much more, he'll pass out, and he'll be at everyone's mercy. So he sits back on his heels and, with trembling fingers, lifts the hem of his shirt up over his hip, exposing the deep, wet gash in his side. He pins the fabric under his elbow to hold it away from the wound.

Beyond the plastic barrier, he hears Arias hiss at the sight, sympathetic.

"Who is he?" Arias asks Elegy.

"He's Cedrae. Feel free to ask him yourself."

He's Cedrae, he repeats to himself, but he's not, is he? The only thing guaranteeing his Cedrae citizenship was the Knight oath. And he broke that oath almost as soon as he swore it.

Elegy tears open a packet of gauze with her teeth. He recognized her right away in the interrogation room. No one looks quite like her—that particular combination of heart-shaped face, wide-set eyes, and freckle-dusted skin.

She reaches for him like she's reaching for a wild animal, afraid it will lash out. He's still as she presses the gauze to the wound with one hand and pops the cap off the wound sealant with the other. She holds the gauze down for long enough to make him stifle a moan of pain, then takes it away and sprays the sealant over the split skin. It won't pull the edges together, but it creates a seal more effective than her balled-up sweater or his forearm.

The sealant stings, fierce, and he sways into the wall. Circulation is returning to his fingertips.

"You shouldn't have come," he says. It's all he can think to say. She must not know, must not remember, that at the first opportunity he abandoned her.

Coward, Fenn says, in his memory.

"You're welcome," she replies, a little sour. She caps the wound sealant and drops it into the first aid kit, then moves away, sitting with her back against the same wall he's leaning against, her boots propped up on the metal floor.

"I'll alert Losan Stronghold's hospital so they can prepare the tests," Arias says. He clears his throat a little. "Should they send extra security?"

Elegy glances at Theren.

"No. Primary Arias, this is Theren Forint." He feels a sharp pain, and he's not sure if it's his or hers. "He used to be my Knight."

✦   ✦   ✦

An hour later, they reach Losan.

He's just clinging to consciousness, but the sight of the city brings him back to himself. The sun is just cresting over the mountains behind them. It glints on the glass buildings packed into the valley. The sight makes his breath catch in his throat. He didn't grow up here, but for his entire life Losan was a symbol of Cedre, one of its jewels.

Unbidden, a line from a Volyn poem surfaces in his mind. *I crave a place I've never tasted.*

Elegy crawls to her feet as they approach Losan Stronghold, which is a cluster of concrete structures on the edge of the city. She opens a compartment in the wall and takes out two filtration masks. One, she attaches to her face, covering her downturned mouth with smoky iridescence. The other, she offers to him. His fingers are trembling so badly it takes him a few tries to hook the mask over his left ear. He chokes as the material adheres to his face. He tastes plastic, and he strains for air, even though the material is permeable.

"What happens now?" he says to her, as the ship touches down on the roof of the Losan Stronghold hospital.

"They'll fix you up," she says. "They'll have questions for you. As will I."

His lips feel numb, like they do when he has too much to drink. "And what will they do to get the answers?"

He can't read her anymore. He's too depleted. But a crease appears between her eyebrows. "They won't hurt you."

He snorts.

"They won't," she repeats, more firmly this time.

"Don't," he says. "Don't pretend that you're not going to rip me open. It's insulting to us both."

The hatch door opens, and the stairs extend to the ground. Her eyes are still on his when the paramedics charge into the ship in their orange hazmat suits. One of them holds a thermometer up to Elegy's forehead; another asks to prick her finger so they can test her blood for Fever.

At the sight of him, though, they hesitate. He's glad that he can't feel them. He already knows how he looks, drenched in blood, dressed as a Talusar.

They set a gurney down next to him, the black canvas stretched taut between two polished poles—shiny, everything here is so shiny—and he complies, tipping his body sideways so he can ease himself down onto it. They lift him, and the jolt makes blood gush around the edges of the wound sealant.

The sweet, fresh air of dawn turns into the chemical clean of the hospital. His nose burns. Everything is plastic, the walls and floor draped in it. Fever containment protocol, which is justified, in this case—his blood can pass the Fever to anyone with an open wound.

The ceiling is all lights and white panels. No place in Valla was ever this stark. They transfer him to a metal table, sliding the canvas gurney out from under him in one practiced motion. A light above his head turns on, making him wince. It's hot, and too bright—

He feels the cold line of scissors against his stomach, against his arms and legs. They peel the fabric away from his body, and he shudders at the cold, and he wishes he could cover up, or run, anything to feel less exposed—beside him, he hears a frantic beeping that he distantly realizes is his heart, now hooked up to the monitor—

"Gotta take him down to the basement," someone says. "That's where all the old surgical equipment is."

"Knock him out first. It'll be easier."

The man leans over him, a hard plastic anesthetic mask in hand, and peels the filtration mask away from his face. When he gasps, the man covers his nose and mouth with the anesthetic mask, and then everything disappears.

✦   ✦   ✦

An hour after his surgery, he wakes.

They fixed him. He may not have elixir in his blood to repair his body, but even the most rudimentary equipment the Cedrae have is better than Valla's. His wound is now sealed shut, a neat red line. It's smeared with some Cedrae healing potion that will speed his mending tenfold. And the whole thing is protected by sealant, to keep it clean. He's fuzzy-headed and confused, but no longer in pain.

He's in a bright room, in only shorts—a new pair, the fabric synthetic and skintight. An Eye hovers over him.

"Your test results are not yet ready," a level voice says through the Eye.

"Let me save you some time. I'm Fevered."

"Until we receive them," the Eye continues, as if he hadn't spoken, "you are under strict quarantine. Per our guidelines for soldiers returning from captivity, we are required to document the scarring on your body. Please stand."

"I'm not a soldier," he says, and he feels foolish, talking to a floating eyeball.

"Nonetheless, the Sword of Cedre has ordered that we follow the same protocol," the voice says. "We are authorized to use restraint if you do not comply, either physical or chemical. Do you have a preference?"

He puts one leg over the side of the bed, then the other, and stands, his head swimming so badly he has to brace himself against a nearby table. The Eye buzzes over and hovers at chest height. Its aperture expands and contracts as it documents the old scar on his chest. Then it shifts to one on his side. As it moves, the voice speaks.

"Please confirm your name for the official record."

"Theren Forint," he says, resisting the urge to swat the Eye away as it moves in too close to his rib cage.

"The length of your captivity?"

The Eye flies behind him to document the scars on his back. His shoulders tighten, and he brings a hand up to his head, which is still swimming.

"I don't—" He shakes his head. "I don't know. Four years and change. Are you finished yet?"

The voice doesn't answer. The Eye darts from scar to scar, making Theren twitch. Then it zips around his head and hovers at eye level.

"Thank you for your compliance," the Eye says. "We have changed your status in the system from 'deceased' to 'living.' You will be escorted to the showers shortly."

He sits on the edge of the bed, and takes slow breaths.

Primary Arias arrives a few minutes later to escort him to the showers. When Theren asks for something to wear on his way across the hospital, he receives an apologetic look.

"The more you wear, the more they have to incinerate later," Arias says. "It's a short walk, I promise."

So he follows Arias down the hallway almost naked. He tries not to stumble or weave, though he still feels muddled by anesthetic and painkillers. The floor is freezing on his bare feet. Everyone they pass—doctors, nurses, soldiers—stares at him. And no wonder. He's so tall now, and the smears of dried blood and antiseptic stand out against his pale skin, made even paler by the bright, cold lights. He tries to stand straight, to look right through them.

By the time he makes it to the showers, he's shaking. He draws the curtain between him and Arias, strips off the shorts, and turns on the water. The spray drums against his chest. He braces himself against the wall and leans forward, so it hits the back of his neck.

The length of your captivity? he hears again.

And his reply: *Four years and change.*

He feels hysteria rising in his throat like vomit. He stuffs a fist in his mouth. Ranos, and the tart, sharp feeling of him distinct even in memory, on the ground asking for mercy Theren couldn't give him; Theren's hand covering a guard's mouth as he slit the man's throat; Rava's boots stuffed into a shoulder bag. The knife, sticky with blood. Elegy Rosyk telling him she would chase him if he ran from her.

He chokes on a sob, and sags into the wall, face-first.

"You all right?" Arias asks him through the shower curtain.

He wants to disappear. More than that, he wants—not to die, exactly, but to be unmade. To have never been.

He takes his fist out of his mouth, sucks in a breath, and says, "Yes."

16

When they come for him, he's at least wearing clothes, this time. Standard-issue Cedrae military casual dress: a white T-shirt tucked into black canvas pants, which are themselves tucked into black boots. The door opens, and he jolts awake. He didn't intend to sleep, but the anesthesia is still coursing through him, and he can't seem to stay awake for more than an hour at a time.

Three soldiers in black uniforms stride into the hospital room. They have silver seals stitched on their sleeves, which means Cedre special forces, Army of the Sword. They're more clean-cut than the soldiers he's seen so far, all three with the same brutally short hair. None of them are afraid of him, which is a relief.

"The Sword wishes to speak with you," one of them says. Tall, with deep brown skin and a shaved head that shines in the light, and the name GREEN stitched on his chest. "On your feet."

Theren has been waiting for them. He doesn't know this Sword, but if she's anything like her mother, she doesn't want to waste time letting someone like him recover from his injuries before interrogating him. Better to do it now, while he's weak.

Maybe he should expect better of the Cedrae, but he doesn't. He feels nothing. Detached, like a kite with no flying line to tether it to the ground.

He gets up, and follows Green out of the room. The other two fall into step behind him. They pass Arias at the coffee machine on their way out, and he looks like he wants to object—but there's no objecting to the Army of the Sword. Even Theren, four years removed from Cedre culture, knows that.

A sleek Sparrow waits for them on the landing pad, its engines on. He follows Green on board, and buckles himself into one of the seats.

"It's a short flight," Green says. "To Losan City Hall."

It's more explanation than Theren was expecting. He didn't realize to what extent four years in Valla had conditioned him not to ask questions until now. He's used to going where he's told, when he's told, regardless of how he feels about it.

The ship takes off, smooth and easy. It's nearing dark, and the city lights are dazzling even from a distance, bright signs for businesses he doesn't understand, technology he can't use, locations he doesn't remember. The streets, too, are lit up, lines of light that make up the grid of downtown. Their ship coasts for a while, and finally touches down on the landing pad of city hall.

It's a new building, by Losan standards, a pillar of black glass that comes to a sharp point at the top, like an arrow aimed at Cedre Station. The dock is off to the side, a few stories elevated for ease of use. They touch down, and as Theren unbuckles himself, he thinks that he once would have found Green intimidating, but now, all he can think is that at least he isn't Satka.

Or Rava.

Green asks for his wrists, and Theren complies, seeing no other option than to let the man bind his hands with hard plastic. He follows Green into city hall, where walls and floor are black tile, a glasslike material that seems to show neither footprints nor fingerprints. Theren hasn't seen anything like it before. Four years is time enough for change.

They stop at an opaque glass door. Green touches a sensor, the elixir in his hand lighting up for a moment, and the door opens.

The room beyond is dim, so Theren can't tell how large it is. He can see a handful of people sitting along the edges. Standing in the center of the room is a huge table, and it's illuminated from above and below, so it looks like an aquarium. Seated at the far end is the new Sword of Cedre, Larke Rosyk, flanked on one side by General Thompson of Losan Stronghold, and on the other by a man Theren recognizes but can't place.

He's never met this Sword, Larke Rosyk. He's only ever known her as the heir. Before Elegy heard her prophecy, he was supposed to serve her with the rest of the Knights, and he heard she was as exacting and stern as her mother. By the look of her, that assessment seems right—her darkest-red military jacket is buttoned up to her throat, and her hair is smoothed back into a tight knot. She has even lighter skin than him, and a high, narrow nose. The only feature she seems to share with Elegy is her freckles.

He doesn't like the feeling of her. There's something claustrophobic about her. She's as focused as the point of a needle, and he's certain she'll be just as precise when she interrogates him. Why she feels the need to conduct this interrogation herself is unclear to him, but he thinks it must have something to do with his mother. The woman responsible for Larke's own mother's death.

"Mr. Forint," the Sword says, and she gestures to the chair at the other end of the table. "Sit."

Green pulls out the chair for him, and he sits gingerly, resting his hands on the table in front of them. Larke's eyes catch on the tattoos on his hands with interest.

"Your Highness," he says to her.

"Welcome to Losan. Have you been here before?"

"Once," he says, stiffening a little.

"Ah, right. On the day of the Getty attack." She gives him a cold smile.

On the day your mother betrayed my mother, she may as well say. But she doesn't need to. He can tell by the ripple of feeling that goes through the room that anyone who didn't recognize his name before does now.

The Sword tilts her head to the side, like a bird.

"Earlier I received a brief description of the events that brought you back here, courtesy of my sister," she says. "I understand we all owe you our gratitude for bringing her safely back to us."

Theren doesn't reply. He knows she's building toward something, and he knows he won't like whatever it is.

"What I'm not sure I understand is why you were even in a position to accomplish this feat. Why you were permitted to move freely enough through House Vidar to acquire a key, a weapon, even a horse."

He thinks of the forest where he almost died. Quiet and cool, the pine needles rustling in the wind.

He doesn't want to be here. He would have chosen death, instead, if Elegy hadn't stopped him.

"My sister says you were summoned to interrogate her when other methods had failed," the Sword says. "So it sounds very much as if you were acting as one of Rava Vidar's lessers. Is that the case?"

"No," Theren says. A beat too late, he adds, "Your Highness."

He hears murmurs all around him. Feels the press of everyone against him. But his focus is on the Sword.

"We have also uncovered intelligence that Rava Vidar is planning something significant. Do you know what it is?"

Memories drift into his mind. Rava coming back from a long journey, looking frustrated. A whispered conversation with Ranos that stopped when Theren walked in. Satka disappearing for days at a time without explanation. But none of them add up to anything.

"If I did," Theren replies, "it would have been the first thing I said upon my arrival."

The Sword opens her mouth to speak, but she's interrupted by the door opening. Every head in the room lifts. He doesn't need to turn to know who it is; he can feel that it's Elegy. She's like cold, clear water.

He isn't sure—and he can't explain it, if he's correct—but he thinks a frisson of fear goes through the Sword at the sight of her.

"Your Grace," the Sword says. "What are you doing?"

"Attending the debriefing, Your Highness," Elegy says, with a casual tone. "I assume my invitation got lost, because it wouldn't make sense to exclude me, would it? After all, I can corroborate Theren's account of our escape."

There's a chair on the right side of the long table, tucked under the tabletop. She drops a duffel bag she's carrying, pulls the chair out, and sits, looking clear-eyed and cheerful. Despite this, her hair is mussed, and she's missed a button on her shirt—her arrival was clearly rushed. Her arm is in a sling. She doesn't look at him.

"You are, of course, welcome to join us," the Sword says.

"Lovely." Elegy smiles a broad, warm smile at General Thompson. "Good to see you again, sir."

"Your Grace," he says to her, nodding. "I see you still have a flair for the dramatic."

Elegy winks. "Don't let me interrupt. Oh, except for this." She reaches into the duffel bag and takes out an Eye. Thin lines of light spread down her fingers and the tendons in her hands. The Eye hovers, and then zips around the perimeter of the room like a beetle.

"What," the Sword says flatly, "is the meaning of this?"

"Oh," Elegy says. "I rented it from the library. It just seemed like you'd forgotten that debriefings of Cedrae citizens are required to be recorded for the official record. So I thought I would lend a hand." She smiles. With her downturned mouth, even a smile looks skeptical. "And this must be a debriefing, not an interrogation, because Theren is twelve hours post-surgery and still doped up on painkillers, which, if it *was* an interrogation, would be a violation of Cedrae's ethics laws."

The forced cheer of Elegy's tone grates on the Sword. He can feel it. The only outward sign she gives, though, is a brief clench of her jaw.

"Well, as you say," the Sword says, "this is not an interrogation. It is also not a debriefing. It's a hearing, intended to assess the measures that will be necessary and appropriate in the handling of Mr. Forint's situation."

Something about the word "measures" makes his heart stutter. Cedrae doesn't allow the administration of pain or deprivation in interrogating enemies of the state, so it's not torture he's concerned about, it's truth serum. A perfectly calibrated concoction that suppresses deception, encourages speech, and lowers inhibitions.

It was given to each of the exiles when they first arrived on Cedre Station and cleared quarantine. And all his mother would say about it was that it was a profound violation.

"I apologize for my interruption," Elegy says, her voice suddenly cold. "Please. Go on."

"I was just about to ask Mr. Forint to explain why, if he is not one of Rava Vidar's lessers, he found himself in a position to interrogate you in House Vidar."

"There's no 'if,' Your Highness." He's relieved that his voice comes out steady, despite his racing heart. "I wasn't afforded any status in House Vidar."

"Oh?" Larke leans forward, ever so slightly. Her focus is back, as needle-sharp as it was before. "Then how would you describe your role there?"

"Rava . . ." He's aware of how the name sounds in his mouth, familiar, like he's spoken it a thousand times. And he has, he has. "Rava Vidar made use of me as she would a blade. I had all the status of a valuable weapon, and no more."

Larke laughs a little. "Surely she has more skilled warriors in her house than a Cedre-born captive."

"That's not the kind of weapon I mean," he says. "I read people. Preternaturally."

"You would hardly be the first among the Talusar to read memories," Larke says. "Isn't that what their truthsayers are typically known for?"

"I don't read memories." He shifts in his chair. He doesn't like discussing what he can do. It makes him feel like he's stripping down in front of everyone. "I read their—feelings. Which includes deception."

If this surprises her, she doesn't let on.

"As someone who also occupies a powerful position, surely you can understand how I might be uniquely useful as a truthsayer."

"I can see how such a weapon would be difficult to wield, if the truthsayer in question comes from among your enemies," she says. "It's difficult to trust the word of someone like that, whatever his special talents, if he isn't loyal to you."

"How is it that you think Rava Vidar won my loyalty? By dragging me across the desert and infecting me with Fever? Or was it by killing all my friends?"

"Watch your tone."

He squeezes his hands into fists in an attempt to get feeling to return to his fingers.

She's not listening to him. Not really. Her mind is made up, and he won't be able to dissuade her. But maybe he can force her to admit it.

"What is it you've decided, Your Highness?" he says to her.

This seems to catch her off guard. "I beg your pardon?"

"You've already decided something about me. I think it would save everyone a lot of time if you would just tell me what the hell it is."

Her eyes search his. All around the room, people shift in their seats, uncomfortable with her silence, with his daring, with both.

"Fine." She folds her hands on the table in front of her, and leans into them. "I will indulge you, Mr. Forint."

The plastic bites into his wrists. He tries to calm down.

"You are the son of an exile, conscripted to serve the office of the Sword when you were a child. Judging by the intelligence I have collected from the other exiles in the wake of the Getty attack, you are the only one of their children who was raised as a Talusar—taught to fight, to speak their language, to follow their customs. Your mother, Kesia Forint, then proved her true loyalties by betraying my mother and sister to our enemies, resulting in my mother's death. An occasion on which you were . . . less than helpful, I think you might agree."

He winces.

Coward Knight, Rava called him.

He blocks everything out as hard as he can. He doesn't want to feel Elegy's shock as she remembers that the man she just risked her life to save betrayed his oath at the first opportunity. That if he hadn't, maybe her mother, her *husband*, would have survived.

The Sword goes on: "And now you turn up four years later in House Vidar, apparently the sole survivor of the Knights, serving as Rava's trusted truthsayer. So what I have decided is that, like your mother before you, you are not loyal to Cedre."

His feet are numb now, but he doesn't think it's from the cold.

"Did you ever interrogate a Cedrae captive for Rava Vidar?"

"No, Your Highness," he says, quiet now.

"Not many Cedrae captives make it all the way to Valla, I suppose. So would you say you primarily assisted Rava Vidar with the political machinations and maneuverings of her own kingdom?"

"Yes."

"And, perhaps, with Cedrae traitors who were eager to do business with our enemies?"

"From time to time."

"You admit, then, to strengthening the position of one of our deadliest enemies? To aiding in the treasonous activities of our very own disloyal citizens?"

He can feel, now, the focus of the Sword's certainty. The needle of her, digging into the heart of him. There's no answer to her questions but "yes," and no defense possible. He tries to steady himself, to breathe. To find an answer that doesn't land him directly under the truth serum needle.

"Wow. Well, that got intense fast," Elegy says. He doesn't look at her, but she's using that same brisk, casual voice she affected before. "Already moved straight to the accusation stage, and I didn't even get to ask my own questions."

"Your own questions," the Sword says.

"Yeah, you know me, I just *cannot* turn off this pesky curiosity," Elegy says. "And besides, it seems like you might need some help, Your Highness. There are a few things you're leaving out."

"Oh, by all means," the Sword says, gesturing to Theren. "Have at it. You're the one he almost got killed, after all. More than once, for that matter."

"Debatable," Elegy says, with a forced laugh. "But all right."

She stands, and takes a pocketknife out of her back pocket. She flicks it open and reaches across the table toward Theren's wrists.

The Sword straightens—somehow—even more. But she doesn't object.

For just a moment, Elegy's eyes meet his, steady. Then she cuts through the plastic around his wrists.

"Palms flat on the table," she says to him.

He does it without understanding why. But as the Sword, General Thompson, and the unidentified man on the Sword's left all lean forward to see his hands, he remembers the tattoos. On his right hand: two simple black bars, stretching vertically between his knuckles. On his left, a fragment of vine that twists between his first two fingers and follows the curve of his hand to the base of his thumb.

"What does that one mean?" Elegy says, pointing at the black bars.

He stares at her. She just waits for his response.

"The bars are markers of time served in the Crucible," he says.

"The Crucible." She sits in her chair again, the knife stowed in her pocket. "I don't think I remember what that is."

It's a lie. If Elegy lying had a sound, it would be a sudden discordant note on a pipe organ.

It's the Sword who answers.

"It's a Talusar prison." Her anger is building, just a simmer now in the pit of his stomach that doesn't belong to him. "Distinguished by its particularly brutal practice of pitting prisoners against each other in hand-to-hand combat, for the entertainment of Valla citizens."

"Right, right." Elegy looks at Theren again. "So how long did you spend in the Crucible, then?"

"Two years," he says.

"So you weren't in House Vidar for four years," she says. "Only two."

"What is the point of this, Your Grace?" the Sword demands. "I hardly see how the length of time matters—"

Elegy smiles, again with that forced cheer.

"Sorry, Your Highness. I'll get to that," she says. "First, though, I want to talk about the other tattoo, Theren. Looks like a vine. Did you choose it?"

He tenses. "No."

Elegy isn't even listening for his response. Instead, she's digging around in the bag she brought in. She produces a pair of familiar-looking boots.

Theren's mouth goes dry.

Elegy carries them to the other end of the table and deposits them right in front of General Thompson. The soles are clean, but the leather is still wet from the river she waded in during their escape.

"Can you look at the tongue of the right one and tell me what you see, sir?" Elegy says.

Thompson gives her a wry smile. He picks up the right boot and peeks at the tongue.

"There's a vine etched into the leather," Thompson says.

"Interesting," Elegy says, and she leaves the boots there when she returns to her seat. "Whose boots are those, Theren?"

How did she figure it out? He doesn't remember mentioning to her that he took the boots from Rava. He wouldn't have.

"They're Rava's," he says.

"Thought so. I noticed that vine in quite a few places when I was in House Vidar. The handle of Rava's knife. These boots." She nods to his tattoo. "Your hand. What does it mean?"

He understands, he *knows* why she's doing this, but that doesn't stop him from hating it.

"The boots belonged to her father," he says, spitting the words out like they're poison. "The vine is the symbol of the Vidar family."

Elegy's voice loses its energetic quality as she says, "It seems to me that it's used to mark valuable possessions. Am I wrong?"

He remembers, now, that she saw him bow to Rava. Heard him call her *my lady*. Watched him receive that reprimand. *Your time belongs to me.*

He can't look at her.

He switches to Talusar, and asks Elegy, in a low voice, "Is this how you see me? As some tortured innocent in need of saving?"

"Answer my question," she replies.

"As you've already said," he says. "It's used to mark weapons or possessions."

"Which one are you?"

"Take your pick," he snaps.

He remembers it so clearly. Rava's hand on his wrist like a manacle, holding him down as the tattooist worked. Her fingers were cold and strong. The needle was painful, but the worst part of it was that she had invited her lessers to bear witness, so there could be no mistaking what he was from that day forward. Not a man, but a tool.

"I think I've been patient with your theatrics thus far, Your Grace," the Sword says. "Get to the point."

"All right," Elegy says. "There are a few Cedrae laws about acting under duress. I won't bore everyone with the precise legal definitions for 'duress.' But imprisoning a person for two years in a place where they must endure constant violence certainly creates the conditions for it. Forcing them to serve in a state of constant debasement also qualifies. And when someone acts under duress, our legal system is inclined toward leniency."

The Sword's simmering rage reaches a boil.

"I don't need to be reminded of what my own legal system values," the Sword says. "I am more aware of it than you are."

"Are you sure? Because I know you want to use truth serum, which is only legal if its use saves lives that are in *imminent danger*—"

"We are at war, and exceptions must be made for extreme cases that put Cedre at risk!" the Sword snaps. "He has information we need, and we can't trust him well enough to allow him to provide it without the use of truth serum—"

His ears ring.

He thinks of waking in the hospital, stripped bare, sluggish and stupid, unsure of who had touched him, and when. It was bad enough when it was his body they stripped his control from. But his mind—

"This man saved my life. I won't allow you to violate him."

"You won't *allow* me," the Sword says, and the silence that greets her words is so sudden and so tense it almost rings. "Who are you to give me orders?"

"I would never presume to give you orders, Larke," Elegy says. "But four years ago, the augurs told me that I was fated to bring Cedre victory over the Talusar, so I hope you'll trust my instincts and heed my advice."

The collective shock in the room is so intense Theren flinches at the feeling of it, like electricity in his skull.

"This is probably not how you wanted me to confirm the rumors to the people in this room," Elegy says. "But I am the Hope of Cedre, and they were going to find out eventually."

Elegy and Larke lock eyes for a long, tense moment.

"Then I will ask you for your advice, *Elegy*," Larke says. "But only if you confront exactly what it is that he did to you."

Elegy frowns at her. Theren squeezes the edge of the table, hard, as Larke's palms glow, the elixir that runs through her veins activating. She gestures, and an image appears in the space between them—the table is an obsidian. Hovering over it is an image of Elegy Rosyk with the augur at her side. Kneeling in front of her is Theren.

"I don't need to see this," Elegy says quietly. "I was there."

"You were there, but I don't think you remember," Larke says. "Let me ensure that you do. Watch Mr. Forint, please."

Theren watches the hologram shift and move as Elegy plunges the tracker into Past Theren's shoulder. Then the windows shatter, and as dark figures stream into the room, Past Theren is already moving, hurling his body away from Elegy, away from the windows—

Running. Like a coward.

He watches as a dark-haired man, recognizable as Shir Alexios only by the familiar way that he puts a hand on Elegy's waist, dives at his wife to protect her from the onslaught of Talusar soldiers. Theren feels pain so sharp and so fierce it couldn't possibly belong to him. It's emanating from Elegy, so intense he can't block it. A grief that runs deeper than any he's felt himself.

"Turn it off," Elegy says, her voice dark and flat.

"Do you know how long Mr. Forint hesitated before running from you? Because I've watched this dozens of times, and I've timed it."

"Turn it *off*!"

Larke does. The obsidian goes dark again.

"A fraction of a second," Larke says. "No hesitation, in other words."

Elegy's eyes close.

"Tell me," Larke says. "What do you think I should do with this man who left you to die? Celebrate his return? Reinstate him as your Knight?"

Theren thinks again of the dark, still forest.

Elegy sits still for a long time. He can feel her pulling herself together—nipping and tucking the pain until it fits inside her again. She clears her throat, and answers.

"I suggest you offer him a trade: freedom, in exchange for his contin-ued cooperation in providing valuable intelligence that aids us in our fight against Rava Vidar. Intelligence that will be independently verified, as with any other asset or informant, no truth serum required."

Larke surveys Elegy for a long moment.

"And you?" the Sword says. "I assume, since you were so comfortable using your role to persuade me to show mercy to this man, that you're now ready for your four-year pity party to come to an end? To make a public statement confirming your status, and then work to serve Cedre, as our mother intended four years ago?"

Elegy looks away. At her fingertips, resting on the table.

"Yes," Elegy says, and she's heavy with dread, so he's heavy with it, too. "Of course."

"Fine, then," Larke says, her eyes shifting back to Theren. "*If* your initial intel proves useful, Mr. Forint, you can begin easing back into Cedre society. If it doesn't, we will revisit the idea of truth serum. Understand?"

The tension in Theren's shoulders eases somewhat. He unclenches his jaw.

"Yes, Your Highness," he says.

"Green, please escort Mr. Forint back to Losan Stronghold," the Sword says, raising her voice a little. "And Mr. Forint . . ." She switches to Talusar. "Give me a single reason to revoke this offer, and I will dig around in your mind at my leisure."

Her speech is clumsy, but unlike Elegy, she uses the right "you."

He leaves the room without looking at either of them.

+   +   +

The hallway beyond is dim and empty. Green leads him a hundred meters at a clip, then glances at Theren and idles.

"Take a moment," he says.

He must look bad for Green to notice. Grateful for the reprieve, Theren leans against the wall and presses a firm hand to his side. The wound aches, and so does the rest of him.

He expects to feel relief, but all he feels is confusion. Exhaustion. Elegy agreed to enter the public eye as the Hope of Cedre with all the dread of a woman going to her own death. She did it for him, and she did it knowing he failed to protect her at the Getty. He wonders if she really considered what that meant—what she could have salvaged of her life, if he had stood in her path like he was supposed to. Like he *pledged* to.

He tips his head back against the tile, and hears his name.

"Theren."

He opens his eyes to the primly pursed mouth and pale gray eyes of Julia Martin. Maeve's mother.

He searches her face automatically for signs of Maeve, but it's been too long since he looked at either of them. Instead, he remembers Maeve talking about formal dinners at her mother's house, with starched white tablecloths and more forks than a person could ever need, and her mother running a finger up her spine to remind her to sit up *straight* for once—

"I take it by the way you're looking at me," Julia says, "or rather, by the way you *aren't* looking at me . . . that my daughter is not alive in Valla."

"No, ma'am," Theren says quietly. His stomach twists. It might be her reaction, not his. Sometimes it's hard to tell.

"I assumed as much." Her voice is tight. "Did she die from Fever?"
He shakes his head.

"Lisia and Furik did," he says. "The others—after."

"I will tell the other parents so," she says. "Did you see it happen? Maeve?"

It's strange to hear such a question in English. In Talusar, the question would be one of identity. *Were you a witness?* He finds himself unable to lie to her, and unable to tell the truth, at the same time.

"Yes," he says, unsteady.

Julia nods, slowly. Her eyes skip from his bruised jaw to the hand he's still holding against his wounded side.

"You're not well," she says. "But when you are, I will speak with you again."

He's not sure if it's a promise or a threat. She turns, and walks back toward the debriefing room.

17

Hela sits at the rickety table in the trailer in Twentynine and watches a drop of water clinging to the faucet. It'll fall any second.

Elegy has been off "doing something stupid" for twenty-four hours now, and even though she warned Hela she'd be gone for a few days, Hela has been a wreck since she read that note over the sink. She can't focus on anything, and her teeth are gritted so hard they keep squeaking.

After the water drop falls to the sink, she gets up and fumbles in the desk drawer for one of the headache tinctures she keeps stashed everywhere she goes. She finds one rolling around in the back of the drawer, uncorks it, and looks at the plant she retrieved for Dr. Canterbury. She hasn't told him, yet, that she found it in that cave. She keeps *almost* doing it . . . and then forgetting.

The sun is setting, so the plant's leaves are starting to unfurl. She's only had it for a day, but she'll miss its gentle glow when it's gone. It feels almost like company.

Hela downs the vial.

"I hate it when she does this," Hela says to the plant. People say it's good to talk things out—does it still help if the thing you're talking to doesn't have ears? It's worth a try.

"She leaves a note when she wants to avoid a conversation," Hela says. "And she avoids a conversation when she knows it would be easy to talk her out of whatever she's planning on doing."

Hela pulls the chair out from under the desk and sits. She pokes the tip of her finger into the earth at the base of the plant, to see if it's dry.

"Do I water you?" she says. "You don't like light, so maybe you don't like water, either." She frowns. "But that's not how plants work, is it?"

It's been a while since her secondary school biology class—the one she nearly failed—but she thinks all plants need sunlight to live. It's part of that whole photosynthesis thing. So why does this one shudder away from the sun?

She frowns. One of the plant's leaves seems to be moving. She sits up, sure that her eyes are playing tricks on her, but no—the leaf is slowly shifting to the side, toward Hela. Her mind goes blank as she watches it turning toward her. Just one leaf, with its vein of green light, questing like an outstretched hand.

Maybe it's just instinct. Maybe she's losing her mind. But she reaches back, pinching the leaf delicately between her thumb and forefinger.

And then everything gets weird.

+ + +

It's almost like falling asleep, the way the new surroundings unfurl around her. Wherever this is, it's dense with plants, and strange ones. Purple vines spill across a stone walkway; blue-tinted leaves the size of her head dangle from the ceiling. Under faint lights in the corner is a cluster of orange flowers that pinch closed and burst open seemingly at random, like winking eyes. Hela reaches out to brush her hand over the lightly furred branches of a nearby sapling. She can't feel anything.

She's in some kind of greenhouse, that much is clear. Above her, between the vines that cling to the glass, she can see the night sky, dotted with stars. But there's a strange white band across it, like a rainbow without color, like a bridge over the planet itself.

She's so focused on it that she doesn't see the woman until she's right in front of her. She startles, stepping back into the dirt behind her.

The woman is beautiful in a harsh way, her brow dark and straight, her mouth spare. Her eyes are what strike Hela most, big and haunted, as if she sees more than she wants to. They fix on Hela, wide with alarm.

Then the woman says, in Talusar, "Fuck."

The woman, the night sky, the greenhouse—they all disappear at once, and Hela finds herself back in the trailer in Twentynine with her hand hovering over the plant.

She laughs a little. She must be stressed if she's hallucinating beautiful women in otherworldly greenhouses. She sits back and contemplates the empty vial of headache tincture she just opened—maybe it was contaminated, or maybe Keen indulged in more illicit drugs than she was aware of.

She gets up and goes into the tiny bathroom to wash her face. She needs to go to sleep—she'll sleep, and she'll wake up to a new day, and Elegy will come home and she'll forget all about the strange, cursing woman standing among the leaves.

+ + +

It's the following evening when she hears the Hummingbird arrive. It's an unmistakable sound out here in the silence of the desert. It pulls Hela's focus from the book she's reading, and she crosses the trailer to nudge the front door open with her knee.

The Hummingbird isn't Elegy's, and Hela considers ducking back into the house to get a weapon before she sees the driver through the windshield—definitely Elegy.

Relief makes her body weak. She slumps against the doorframe, arms crossed, feeling wobbly. The Hummingbird touches down on the dirt behind Hela's old Finch, and Hela can tell it's military-issue just by the shape of it, though the emblem of the Cedre army stamped on its side is a dead giveaway.

Elegy climbs out of the ship with difficulty. For the first time, Hela notices the sling her arm is in, and the bruising around her face—already faded thanks to one potion or another. Her hair is limp and greasy, like she hasn't washed it since she left.

Hela's throat feels tight. Without saying anything, she steps back into the trailer to put the kettle on. She's busying herself in the kitchen: two mugs, two tea bags stuffed with dried chamomile and lavender—courtesy of Agatha, the older woman who delivers their water tanks every week—and two spoons with honey still clinging to them. Elegy steps into the trailer and Hela wants nothing more than to punch her, like she would have done when they were a lot younger.

Instead she says, "Well if it isn't the *Hope of Cedre*, come to bless me with her presence."

She pours the now-boiling water over one of the tea bags and sets it down on the table behind her, trying not to slam it. It would be a shame to waste tea just because she wants to murder her sister.

"You're pissed," Elegy says.

"Yeah, I'm pissed." Hela slams the other spoon down on the counter and gives Elegy an incredulous look. "You left a *note*? And you come back two days later looking like someone beat you with a shovel—"

"It's not *that* bad—"

"—and I didn't even know where you were going, but I'm guessing, based on context clues, that it was fucking Valla—and you were *alone*—"

"Dad told me Talusar territory is best navigated solo," Elegy says. "No smuggler would travel with a buddy. And it would have gone just fine, but Larke put a tracker on my ship and they found it—"

"Don't blame the Sword for this." Hela points the spoon at Elegy. Honey drips from the end of it onto the floor. "If she put a tracker on your ship, it's because it's her job to keep the Hope of Cedre from dying, and you're not making it any easier."

"Please don't call me that."

"Why not? 'Lies serve neither the speaker nor the listener,'" Hela says, quoting an old Talusar saying that her mother used to love. And if that's not a measure of how upset she is, nothing is. She tries not to think about her mother.

Elegy sits at the table behind the mug that Hela prepared for her. Her grimace of pain makes Hela soften a little.

"It's not what I am," Elegy says. "That's why not."

Hela sits down across from her. She's had this argument with Elegy a thousand times, and she's not going to have it again. As far as she knows, she's the only one who knows all the details of what the augurs told Elegy—the only one apart from the Sword, that is. Elegy insists the augurs must be wrong, or lying, or manipulating her. She's determined to approach Rava Vidar like a soldier, not like the subject of prophecy— probably because she thinks being the subject of prophecy is what got Shir killed.

Hela, meanwhile, waits and watches for the signs the augurs told Elegy to look for. A storm and the trio of the fulcrum: a Vidar, an augur, a man.

"Where did you go?" she asks. "And why?"

Elegy clears her throat, and tells the story: Isre Din telling her that her Knight is alive, the journey to Valla, the tracker that gave her away, the interrogation that somehow didn't, and the escape that she recounts in so little detail that Hela assumes it was a lot more traumatic than she's letting on.

When she finishes, Hela sits for a while, stirring her spoon. She never met the Knight. She found the whole "compulsory oath swearing" thing to be about as backward as infecting your child with Fever to give them magical powers. But she knows that Elegy has felt the weight of that oath for the last four years, unreasonable as that is.

"It's not your fault he was kidnapped by Talusar," Hela says. "Do you know that?"

Elegy sighs a little, and stares into her teacup.

"It's not that I felt responsible for him being taken," she says. "It's that . . . they took a lot of my people that day. And then Isre told me I could get one of them back, and . . ." Her voice falters a little, and she stops, letting the unfinished sentence hang between them.

"I get it," Hela says, even though she's not sure she does, or can. "How is he?"

"Stable. Well-adjusted. A real peach."

Hela snorts. The light above the sink buzzes. In the corner, the plant is starting to unfurl again, its leaves creaking a little as they pull away from each other.

Elegy says, "He bolted during the Getty attack, did you know that? I didn't remember—it was too chaotic. But Larke reminded me."

"I didn't know that, no."

Elegy nods. "He was twenty. He was scared, and it was never his choice to be my Knight to begin with."

"Right," Hela says.

"So I don't blame him."

"All right."

Elegy glances at her. Hela keeps her face as neutral as possible.

"Should I?" Elegy asks. "Blame him?"

"El . . . that's not something I can have an opinion about."

Hela never watched the footage of the attack, though it played in news pavilions for months after. Every time she saw it, she looked away, not wanting to see Shir's last moments play in front of her—not wanting to see Elegy's greatest horror, either.

She'd liked Shir. Sure, he was a soldier, and soldiers and Scouts didn't get along well. But Shir seemed different from other soldiers, less concerned with hierarchy and law and protocol and more interested in getting things done. In getting people saved. When he found out Hela was Talusar, he just grinned and started speaking that language instead, his accent atrocious and his vocabulary full of holes. *What?* he said to Elegy, when she sighed with embarrassment. *I gotta practice or I'll never get better.*

It was hard not to like Shir, really.

So she understands why Elegy might blame anyone and everyone who contributed to his death. Blame isn't a precious resource, to be stored up and given to the one person who really deserves it. It's a thrashing many-headed monster, big and mean and sprawling.

"What's that?" Elegy says, pointing at the plant in the back of the trailer.

"Some weird goddamn salvage I can't bear to turn in," Hela says.

Elegy raises an eyebrow, and she's about to ask more when she stops and frowns down at her hands.

"Sorry," she says. "Urgent message."

Hela sips her tea as Elegy goes to the desk to pick up the quill. Delicate lines of light, like seams, trace their way down Elegy's fingers and arms, ending at her elbows. Her eyes go unfocused. She starts writing in hand-writing that isn't her own, prompted by the elixir in her veins.

Only she can see the message she's writing. When she finishes writing, she looks irritated. "Footage of a little stunt I just pulled leaked to the news pavilions, and Larke is probably going to kill me."

"Well," Hela says, and she drains the last of her tea from its cup. "She'll have to get in line."

18

Elegy spends the next day shrouded in desert heat and silence, ignoring everything. She feels the tug of messages in her fingers, messages she's refusing to read, and she knows there are half a dozen tasks she's neglecting, including simple things like laundry and clipping her fingernails. But she gives herself time to sit in the evening shade and watch the sun set behind the rocky hills.

But the day after that, she dares to go to Twentynine to watch the news holograms in the central pavilion. News pavilions are Cedre institutions, usually located in the center of a well-populated neighborhood or district. They used to be community spaces, but Twentynine's is just a glitchy hologram in the middle of town playing national news on a loop.

The news about the "Hope of Cedre" has leaked, and now everyone has an opinion about who she is, where she's been, and whether this means the Cedrae government should abandon the *Sundial* program altogether. After all, they reason, if there's a prophecy that says Elegy can *save Cedre*, maybe there's no need to find a home on another world.

When she steps back into the trailer afterward, she sees Hela at the table with a cup of coffee. Her expression is troubled.

"You saw the news," Elegy says.

"Parin wrote to me about it," Hela says. Parin is a friend of theirs, a fellow Scout. If he wrote to Hela about Elegy declaring herself to be the Hope of Cedre, it must be widespread.

"Larke's been asking me to 'come out' for years now. Guess this isn't quite what she had in mind."

"She's not going to be happy about them blaming her for your long absence," Hela says. "The attendees of Forint's debriefing apparently observed some tension between you two, and now people are speculating that she kept you away from the public to prevent you from seizing power."

"That's absurd." Elegy pours herself another cup of coffee and sits down across from Hela. "She's the firstborn. She's the rightful Sword. Everybody knows it, especially me."

"Yeah, but you're chosen by *destiny*. And they might respect Larke, but no one likes her."

"What's to like?"

"Exactly."

The heat from the coffee warms Elegy's cheeks. "She'll hate me more than usual."

"You did storm in there and make her look like a goddamn idiot. Does this really surprise you?"

Elegy shakes her head. As a child, she spent a month of every summer with Larke on Cedre Station, learning from their mother and her various underlings. And even then, Larke was cold to Elegy. The reason why isn't a mystery. Larke's entire life was about duty; Elegy's entire life was about choice. Their mother had neglected her, but she had controlled every aspect of Larke's life, and even Elegy could agree that was probably worse.

Then, when the augurs gave someone a huge, important destiny . . . it was Elegy, not Larke. And she didn't even *want* it. Didn't even *believe it.* The greatest insult.

"Why does she even want me back in the public eye?" Elegy says. "She hasn't pushed that hard for me to come back before now. In fact, she lied her entire ass off to keep the army from charging me with desertion four years ago. I owe her for that."

"It's not like you went on a four-year vacation. You basically turned General Thompson into your pen pal. You're the only reason she knows Rava's now cooking up something extra-special for us all."

It was true: Elegy had spent the last four years earning money as a Scout, but also pursuing leads about Rava Vidar and the movements of the Talusar, which she had then forwarded to General Thompson when they turned out to be valuable. So it wasn't like she'd been doing nothing.

"I hate politicians."

"Yeah, they're gross." Hela yawns. "Anyway, Losan Stronghold even reached out to *me* this morning to make sure you know you're going to be debriefed whether you like it or not. So you'd better head over there before they show up and arrest us both."

Elegy has no interest in returning to Losan Stronghold, but she knew this was coming. They let her rest for a day, but they need to debrief her while the memories of Valla are still fresh in her mind. She downs the rest of her coffee in one gulp and gets up to find her nicest boots.

As she passes the glowing plant, she reaches out to run a finger down one of the leaves. It's too bright in the trailer for it to unfurl.

"You still haven't told that guy you found it?" she says to Hela.

"I put him off for a while, told him I had to delay my trip," Hela says. "I just want to find out what it is first."

Elegy raises an eyebrow at her. "You know, it isn't a pet. It's a plant. It doesn't have a brain."

"Neither do you, but I still keep *you* around," Hela replies, and she gets up for another cup of coffee.

+ + +

Lydia Parekh greets Elegy at the entrance to Losan Stronghold, a proud smile on her face as she introduces herself as "Tertiary." Lydia and Elegy went through basic training together. Parekh was fast, but had trouble climbing in the obstacle course, and never did figure out how to make her bed correctly.

Parekh's entire left leg is in a brace. "I'll be back on active duty in a month or so. Gotta let elixir rebuild the bones in my leg first."

Elegy gives a low whistle. "What happened?"

"Got shot out of the sky by a twelve-year-old Talusar pilot," Parekh says, wrinkling her nose a little. "Everybody survived, but I cushioned my Primary's fall with my femur."

"Good of you."

Losan Stronghold is painfully familiar, a place she walked with Shir at her side. It's a cluster of stark concrete buildings, each of them artfully geometric but intimidating. All around them are plants—tall cypresses and sprawling bougainvillea in pink, orange, and red; groves of lemon trees and pomegranates and guava; agave plants and prickly-pear cacti.

Parekh leads her to the administration building, which has a polished wood floor and ornate, delicate light fixtures that contrast the relentless concrete, and drops her off at General Thompson's office for her debriefing with a lazy salute.

"Good seeing you," she says. "Primary."

"Not anymore," Elegy points out.

"Sure, sure."

Elegy is nervous when she steps into the general's office. He seemed happy enough to see her at the "debriefing," and he was the one who had granted her an early discharge four years ago, but that didn't mean he forgave her for abandoning her post.

The general comes to his feet when she walks in, and offers her his hand to shake. His smile seems warm enough. He's an older man, his brown skin lined, but only at the corners of his eyes and mouth, the kind of age that comes from too much laughter. His face is the same as the last time she looked at it—across Shir's urn as it was lowered into the ground.

"Miss Ahn," he says. "You look better."

"That healing elixir does good work. Barely a twinge in this shoulder anymore."

"I meant you look better than four years ago, but I'm glad to hear our medical treatments are still effective." He sits down, and gestures to the chair across from him.

She swallows hard. She doesn't remember what she looked like four years ago, after the attack. Just that things like brushing her hair or washing her face had felt impossible.

"I thought I would conduct your debrief, since the information you'll provide about Rava Vidar is highly sensitive," he says. "But first I wanted to ask you why you've tasked one of my Primaries—Arias, obviously—with babysitting your Knight." He folds his hands on the desk in front of him. "Something that you don't actually have the authority to do. The Hope of Cedre is a political role, not a military one, isn't it?"

"Right." Elegy winces a little. "I was concerned about how Larke would handle Forint's . . . reintegration. He's a valuable asset."

"Is he."

Elegy leans forward. "He was Rava Vidar's *truthsayer*, sir. Think about what he must know about this big attack she's planning, even if he's not aware of it yet. We need to be securing his loyalty, not potentially compromising it with harsh methods."

General Thompson looks thoughtful. He taps his desk with his fingertips.

"As it happens, I share your concerns, which is why I also told Arias to keep an eye on him," General Thompson says. "Forint was pulled into questioning the morning after that 'hearing,' the second the anesthesia was out of his system, and he's already back again this morning. It's not how we usually do things, particularly when someone is healing the old-fashioned way from a significant injury."

Elegy shakes her head. "Putting too much pressure on him could backfire."

"I'm aware." General Thompson clears his throat. "But Miss Ahn, you are no longer an officer in this army. You can't continue to order around my soldiers."

Elegy's cheeks burn. "Yes, sir. I'm sorry about that, sir."

"*Unless*." And here he raises an eyebrow at her. "Unless you negotiate with your sister to give the role of Hope of Cedre some authority that it doesn't presently carry."

"I beg your pardon, sir?"

"You have a choice, Miss Ahn." His voice is gentle. She's always liked that about him—he never needed to shout to get his point across, not even in basic training. "You've agreed to enter the public eye, but you can do so as a political pawn of the Sword, or you can use your status to bargain for more authority. It's up to you."

She meets his eyes. They're warm brown, and more calculating than one would expect, based on how calm and kind the general is otherwise.

"I'm not sure I believe in the prophecy," she says.

If he's troubled by that confession, he doesn't let on.

"You don't need to believe in something in order to make use of it," he replies. "Prophecy or not, you do good work, Elegy."

He clears his throat.

"Now why don't you tell me how you found yourself arrested in Valla with a stack of pornographic magazines in your backseat?" he says. "Or is that just a wild rumor?"

✦   ✦   ✦

Dread weighs in her stomach like a bad meal as she finishes recounting her time in Valla. She knows where she has to go next: to see Theren Forint. And it's the last place she wants to go.

She crosses the courtyard, packed with cacti, to the barracks. Few soldiers live in Losan Stronghold, usually the ones recovering from an injury, like Parekh, or the ones whose work takes them all over the planet, like Arias. And there's a short hallway of empty rooms reserved for "special guests"—those who require more security.

That's where she finds Arias, leaning against a doorframe at the end of that hallway. He turns at the sound of her footsteps, always alert, and smiles, his eyes crinkling at the corners.

It's hard to remember, now, how he looked the first time she met him. Covered in blood, his face ashen, his eyes blank. He was the sole survivor of a mission gone awry, and when she and Shir responded to his distress call, he was barely able to give his name. But after months of healing, he'd asked to join search and rescue, and it was where he still served.

Over his shoulder, Elegy can see Theren Forint facing one of the walls of his new room, staring up at a grid of paper—little squares tacked in place with pins. Talusar characters all over them.

"Never thought I'd see you at the Stronghold again," Arias says.

"Never thought I'd be here again."

Arias glances over his shoulder at Theren, then touches Elegy's elbow to steer her away from the door.

"This isn't good, El," he says to her, his voice quiet. "He needs to un-clench, and they're just putting him under more and more pressure."

"I know. I'm working on it."

"He asked to talk to you yesterday, but apparently the office of the Sword wasn't keen to pass along that message."

"Of course they weren't. What does he want to talk about, do you know?"

Arias shakes his head.

"Well, I can take it from here," she says. "Thanks."

She takes Arias's place in Theren's doorway as Arias walks away. She looks at Theren's broad shoulders, squared off with the wall.

The room around him is sparse and small. The bed—made with sharp corners—looks too short for him, but that's probably unavoidable, given his height. There's a neat stack of clothes on top of the dresser, all military-issued casual, like the white-on-black ensemble he's currently wearing. A door on the opposite wall leads to a tiny bathroom. His wall of paper is right next to a small desk.

She thinks of him in his blue-and-copper suit, kneeling in front of her in the Getty, and then Shir's weight against her back—

He turns, fast, like he heard a sharp sound. When he sees her, he freezes, and she wonders if he even knew Arias was gone, or that she was there.

"Your Grace." His voice is rough. She assumed, when she first met him, that he was coming down with something, but it's just the way he speaks, like each word has to fight its way out.

"I sent your brother a message yesterday." It was the one task she completed yesterday, in fact. "He knows you're here. I'll try to set up a visit."

He looks surprised. "That's— Thank you."

"You should know, he's the one who told me you were still alive. Your mother contacted him to tell him." She watches his reaction carefully. "Did she know you were alive all those years?"

But there's no need to measure his reaction. He admits it readily. "Yes."

"So why did she contact Isre only recently?"

"I don't know."

"You have no ideas?" She's aware that she's interrogating him now, and it's probably the last thing he needs, but she can't stop herself.

"I assume it's not a good sign, whatever her reasons," Theren says. *Something's coming. Something big*, a voice in Elegy's head whispers. "But I have no greater insight into Kesia Forint's mind than you do, Your Grace. We saw each other only rarely in Valla, and our interactions weren't friendly."

"Really." She frowns a little. "Your own mother? The only person you knew in Valla?"

"Everything I endured in Valla was a result of her betrayal." Bitterness creeps into his voice. "So no. We were not—are not—friendly."

She wants to press harder. To make sure. She even wants to see what happens when she makes him angry—if pushing him too hard makes him reveal something new.

Instead, she gestures to the wall of paper. "What's that?"

"A timeline. Of my years in House Vidar. I thought it might help me remember things more clearly."

"You're having trouble?"

"According to Specialist Gylle, my intelligence has been useless."

Elegy knows Gylle, Theren's interrogator. The late Sword talked about her with a sour twist to her mouth. Larke, however, seems to have no qualms with her. It's that, maybe, that prompts Elegy to ask, "She's been all right to you?"

"Yes."

The answer is too quick. The silence that follows is tense as drawn wire. The sun emerges from behind a cloud, and casts a shadow of leaves across the floor. She watches as they turn over in the wind. The branches of the lemon trees outside are heavy with fruit.

"A reliable source told me Rava Vidar is planning something," she says. "Do you know anything about that?"

"Yes and no," he says. "For the past few months she's been . . . under strain. More volatile. More secretive. But there was never anything concrete, except maybe . . ." He turns back to the grid of paper and taps one of the squares. It's almost blank, just a scrawl at the top and the bottom. *Summer—Kesia visit*, and *Hallway—Rava. Hurt?*

"I have a gap," he says. "In my memory."

Kesia visit, she reads again. He doesn't call her "Mom" even in his own notes.

"A gap. I assume you mean more than just forgetting something."

Theren nods. He plucks the paper off the wall, crumples it into a ball, and tosses it on the desk. His sleeves are pulled up to his elbows, showing thin scars that crisscross his forearms. She doesn't think they're self-inflicted—too haphazard for that—but she can't think of where else he could have gotten them.

"Are you familiar with the categories of Fever gifts among the Talusar?" he says.

She steps back to lean against the wall, arms folded. Some of the pages on his wall are dense with writing. She can't read all of it from where she stands, but what she does read veers into the abstract. *Night meeting* is certain enough, but *dry, porous rock* is nonsensical. So is *swarm of insects.*

She runs a hand through her hair, and considers his question.

"I know most of the Talusar can see recent memories. That they particularly honor the epocha, who see distant ones. And there are some who can project other people's memories. Rumors of some other variants, too. What am I missing?"

He sits on the edge of the bed, and his hand reaches for his side, automatically, as if it's still tender and he feels the need to protect it. His skin is still dark along his jaw and at the corner of his eye, lingering bruises.

"A few. Among them—those who erase memory, and those who alter it."

She looks at the paper crumpled on his desk. The gap, the space he can't remember. "You think someone erased your memory?"

"No, that work is—indelicate. I would show other signs of brain damage." He speaks of it so casually, this cruelty, and maybe cruelty *is* casual to him, after the life he's led for the past four years. "I think someone buried my memory. And no one would have dared to do that unless it was at Rava Vidar's behest."

"No one would have *dared*," Elegy says, dubious. "Are you that scary?"

He rubs his thumb along the vine tattoo on his left hand, as if he's trying to erase it. His eyes skirt hers. "No one touches Rava's things."

His next swallow is labored enough to be noticeable.

"What you're implying is that if Rava thought a memory was important enough to bury, it's probably something we want to know about," Elegy says.

"What Ranos said. About . . . how he couldn't let me leave, with 'everything I know.'" He frowns. "I must have found out something significant. Something she knows is still accessible to me. So it's important that I retrieve it."

"Is there a way to do that?"

He nods. "One of the exiles. Julia Martin."

Elegy remembers the woman from the interrogation, giving an elegant bow to Larke after Theren was escorted from the room. All buttoned up. She reminded Elegy that most of the exiles had been high-status in Valla, and they had brought as much of their wealth with them as possible.

She says, "Larke is the one who actually knows Julia Martin. You should have told her about this, not me."

He meets her eyes with peculiar focus, unblinking. In this light, his eyes look black as space. She feels disassembled by them.

"While I'm aware that you and your sister both hate me," he says, "I thought that of the two of you, you were more likely to listen to me."

If he'd asked her, she wouldn't have used the word "hate." But he didn't ask. He didn't think he needed to. "I don't *hate* you."

He comes to his feet, and she steps back, automatically, her shoulders hitting the wall. It's as if she keeps forgetting how tall he is, over and over again.

"You do, though," he says.

The bright greens and yellows of the orchard, showing through the window, frame his face.

"Is this what you do?" she snaps, suddenly annoyed. "You just . . . tell people what they're feeling, like you know them better than they know themselves? Bet you're a real hoot at parties."

"What I am is someone who left you exposed to Talusar violence without a second thought. Someone who *betrayed you*."

He says it like it's a blow. As if she could possibly forget that he'd turned on her in a fraction of a second.

She says, unsteady: "You were—"

"Young?" he says. "Does my age change how much the Talusar took from you?"

She doesn't understand why he's doing this. Why he seems to want to make whatever anger she feels toward him worse.

"Does my youthful inexperience bring your husband back to life?" he asks, and her reaction is sudden, a step toward him, a hand raised to point a finger in his face—

He flinches, but doesn't move, and she thinks of the way Rava Vidar put a hand on his neck right after the interrogation, how it made his breath stutter, but he still didn't pull away; she thinks of how he snorted when she assured him no one at Losan Stronghold would hurt him. Suddenly, him reminding her of Shir seems like he's feeling for the edges of her anger, just so he knows where they are.

"You're trying to provoke me." She steps closer to him, and tips her head up to look him in the eye. "Congratulations. You succeeded."

She grabs his chin, lifts his head a little. He freezes. She's well aware that he could hurt her if he wanted to. She thinks he could probably leave the Stronghold, and Losan itself, if he wanted to. He could clear a path for himself in blood, as he did in Valla.

But here he stands. Perfectly still, and letting her grab him, even though his chest is rising and falling faster by the second.

"What do you expect me to do now?" she says, quiet, her hand squeezing tighter. "What was Rava Vidar's approach—would she hit you? Or just insult and degrade you? Maybe both at once?" She can feel the scratch of his stubble under her fingers. "What would you do if I did—just let me?"

His breaths are uneven. He still doesn't move.

"Yes," he admits.

She looks up into his eyes, which are dark and full of trouble. "Do you think letting me hurt you would absolve you of what you've done?"

He doesn't answer.

She releases him. Her fingertips, her cheeks, her eyes—they all burn. She turns away, but doesn't leave—not yet.

"I'll speak to Julia Martin about your missing memory," she says. "You're right—it seems important that we know what Rava was so desperate to hide."

She walks out of the room, and she's just past the threshold when his voice stops her, rough as always.

"Thank you."

19

It's obvious when Cedre Station's gravity catches her—Elegy's hair falls across her cheek, and the weight of her dress settles against her shoulders again.

Evacuation Day is the celebration of Cedre's founding, three hundred years earlier. The earliest records to emerge from the Empty Time—the black hole in the planet's historical record—described a Talusar decree requiring that every person receive their god, the Fever. All across the world, so-called heretics rebelled against the decree, refusing the Fever. After a great deal of bloodshed, the Talusar, then not as mighty as they are now, permitted the heretics three quarantine zones where they could live separate from the Fever: Losan, Austra, and Nusanta. Evacuation Day marks the day that deal was made. No one knew then that the Talusar would go back on it mere decades later.

Everything else that made Cedre what it was—the restoration of Cedre Station; the repurposing of city land for food, water, and production; the colonies all over the world who chose to fight the Talusar from where they were instead of evacuating—came later.

Evacuation Day, Larke insisted, was the best day for Elegy to make her public debut as the Hope of Cedre. Elegy, thinking of General Thompson's insistence that she didn't need to believe in the prophecy in order to make use of it, agreed. It was as good a time as any to finally confirm the rumors—and going public will give her some political leverage over Larke, in case she needs it.

Her mother's intention had been for the Hope of Cedre to become a political advisor to the Sword. She gets the feeling that Larke would rather hurl herself into the sun than listen to Elegy's advice on anything.

Hela chose her dress. It's a black sheath, its only adornment the overlapping metal plates that make up the strong shoulders, like the scales of a fish. It looks like armor. *You should look like a warrior, not a politician*, Hela said, her head over Elegy's shoulder in the mirror. Elegy had only nodded.

The loading dock doors in Cedre Station open, and the ship drifts toward the space. Elegy's palms are sweaty. She wipes them on her skirt.

All she can think is, *Shir is supposed to be here for this.*

That was their plan: go to the Getty for the Knight ceremony, then fly together back to Cedre Station for the formal announcement.

I'll be right next to you, Shir said. *Bursting with pride.*

And now here she is, wincing as the ship touches down, listening for the closing of the loading dock doors, unbuckling herself. Standing, straightening, checking her reflection in the hand mirror Hela shoved into her tiny, ineffectual purse. She tucks a strand of hair into the tight knot at the back of her head, and leaves the purse behind. She's not carrying a bag the size of a waffle into Cedre Station.

At the top of the hatch steps, she breathes deep. She's jumped out of hatches like these dozens of times, spear at her back, only jungle or desert or mountains in front of her, Talusar soldiers waiting just out of sight. She was never this afraid.

She goes down the steps.

A crowd stands at the bottom, held back by barriers made of delicate rope. Flanked by guards in black uniforms just in front of the barriers is Larke. She wears her formal military uniform—such a dark red it's almost black, and more gilded than her casual uniform, the buttons shiny and the braiding over her shoulders glittering. Her face is powdered enough that her freckles don't show, the only thing that makes them look like sisters buried under makeup.

As Elegy descends, Larke gives her a warm smile, which almost makes Elegy stumble. Larke has never looked at her like that in her life. When she reaches both hands for Elegy, she gives a warning look, and Elegy reaches back. Larke pulls her close, and kisses her cheek. With her mouth still close to Elegy's ear, she says, "Play along."

Elegy isn't good at playing along, but she tries to smile. She has her father's perpetual pout, so she's not sure it's effective. Larke loops an arm through hers and turns toward the crowd, her teeth white and her eyes crinkled at the corners. Elegy can't help but stare. She's never seen Larke look so . . . *normal*. Like a sister Elegy might have grown up with, instead of the one she inherited after their mother's murder.

"We'll go through the maintenance tunnels to the banquet hall, and then stop at the monument for a picture," Larke says. "Just smile for the crowd."

Larke knows how to smile for a crowd. How to wave, and wink at children to make them squeal with excitement, and how to move at just the right pace toward the door at the back of the dock, the one that leads to the maintenance hallways. Elegy just follows along, her face frozen in an almost-grin and her hand clenched around Larke's arm.

Once the door closes behind them and no one is watching, Larke lets go of Elegy and brings a hand to her forehead.

"Well, that was almost a disaster," Larke says. "Could you have looked more like I was leading you to your execution?"

"You didn't warn me the entire population of Cedre Station would be waiting for me in the dock," Elegy says.

"I didn't think it would be such a problem."

"I'm a *soldier*, Larke. Not exactly used to being on display. If I'd had to fight them off with a spear, maybe—"

"You're a *Scout*," Larke says icily. "I'm given to understand you're all talented at subterfuge."

Elegy stiffens, but she knows better than to respond in kind. She understands why Larke is angry, after what happened at Theren's "hearing," and she's afraid of making it worse.

"Let's just go to the banquet," Elegy says.

They walk through the maintenance tunnels in silence, flanked by Larke's guards. Elegy listens to the churn of machinery and the hiss of steam and the clinking of her dress's scales, and tries not to think about what awaits her at this banquet. Questions about where she's been. Sympathy for what she's lost. Expectations as heavy as dread.

When they emerge from the tunnels, it's crowded, since everyone has to move through a small antechamber on their way to the banquet hall. At first, no one notices them—not until they reach the antechamber itself. Inside it is a stone plinth, and on top of the plinth is a decryption device.

No, she reminds herself. *Not a decryption device*—the *decryption device.*

When the visitors from outside the solar system first contacted Earth, it was through a crash landing. An object—the records aren't clear about what it was, exactly—fell through the atmosphere, and all that survived the impact with the ground was the decryption device, a heavy metal cylinder with tiny characters inscribed all around it. No one knows how long it took Earth to make sense of the message the cylinder carried, but when they did, they read an invitation to meet at a set of coordinates just beyond Mars.

It was there that Earth's ship linked up with an extraterrestrial craft. There are no transcripts of the conversation, no explanations of how a conversation successfully took place between people who didn't speak each other's language. All that's left is a fragment of a report from an Earth representative upon her return. *We have been invited to join a greater order,* she said. *We do not know exactly where they were from, as they refused to tell us for their own security—they're as wary of us as we are of them. But if we agree to their terms, they'll lead some of us there, to another world.*

Of course, they never managed to come to terms before Earth nearly destroyed itself.

Elegy stares down at the decryption device, trying to read the characters inscribed on its otherwise smooth surface. The only language she recognizes are bits of Old Hànyǔ, but she can't read them.

"No one knows how they knew one of our languages," Elegy says. "To this day."

"There are theories." Larke is standing at her shoulder, looking impatient. "Come on, smile for the picture."

There's a man with an old-fashioned camera standing across the plinth from them. While Elegy was staring at the decryption device, he seems to have cleared the room of everyone but her and Larke. Larke links arms with her and smiles; Elegy does her best to smile, too. The man with the camera steps aside, leaving their path to the banquet clear.

Elegy reluctantly continues on.

The banquet hall is huge and lofty. In its center is a large, sprawling tree with delicate orange-yellow leaves. Above it is a light fixture, as big as the tree is wide, that fixes a beam of white light on the branches.

All around it is the shimmer of water. At first she thinks it's a pool—but then she sees someone walk across it, and she realizes it's glass. Beneath the glass are the tree's roots, stretching out in every direction and tangling with the structure of the ship itself, all its struts and ducts and pipes.

"There's one just like it in the *Sundial*'s arboretum," she hears a man say as she passes, in conversation with someone else. "Grown from seeds from the same mother tree. So that when the *Sundial* launches, it will carry a piece of Cedre with it forever. Poetic, don't you think?"

The man in question is wearing a pin shaped like the *Sundial*, the symbol of the Pilgrimage Party, the one that advocates for sending the *Sundial* in search of the visitors' planet in the hope that the Cedrae will be welcomed there. It's optimistic of him to speak of the *Sundial*'s launch with such certainty. The Restorationists—those who are determined to reclaim Earth from the Talusar instead of seeking another home—have the majority, now.

Where we come from is where we belong. That's their motto.

There are people everywhere, gathered in clusters with plates in hand or seated on the chairs that are arranged here and there around low tables. The food comes from buffets in the back corner, and it's a decadent array of dishes, some of which she doesn't even recognize, some of which she does. She thinks her father would have liked to see so many different kinds of dumplings all in one place like this. He used to philosophize about dumplings—almost every culture had one, even if they called them by different names or prepared them in different ways. They were like a symbol of Cedre.

Elegy rushes toward the first person she recognizes: General Thompson. He sits in a group of chairs with a drink in hand, wedged between two people in uniform, one older and one younger.

His eyes light up when he sees her. "Miss Ahn. Lovely to see you again so soon."

She smiles. Something tight and hard in her chest releases. "General."

"Let me introduce you to General Ngozi Okoro of Temasek Stronghold in Nusanta—"

The woman stiffens, and Elegy knows immediately that she'll never be referring to General Okoro as "Ngozi." She's the younger of the two soldiers, her hair dyed indigo and her nails painted an incongruously muted pink. She looks skeptical as she bows her head and says, "Your Grace."

Elegy returns the short bow, feeling uneasy. Even though "Your Grace" is the appropriate honorific for any close family of the Sword, it still feels like an ill-fitting shoe to her.

"—and General Jeda Saetang, leader of Naarm Stronghold in Austra—"

He gestures to the soldier on his left, who's older than Okoro. They wear a ring in their septum that's a gesture of nonbinary identity. Their hair is worn in a high knot. They offer Elegy a smile.

"You're welcome to join us, Your Grace," Saetang says to her, gesturing to the chair behind Elegy. Elegy is aware of eyes on her from all directions. She perches on the edge of the seat with her skirt arranged around her.

"We were just talking about that dustup last year about our name," Thompson says. "The anti-Cedre people."

"What is it they actually called themselves?" Saetang asks.

"There was an acronym," Okoro says, her voice clipped. "As a general rule, I don't memorize acronyms."

Thompson asks, "What was the issue again? Something involving the root word of Cedre—"

"*Ceder*," Okoro says. "An old word for yielding. Since we yielded Earth. Their position was that we shouldn't wear our surrender as a badge of honor."

Saetang looks thoughtful, but Elegy snorts.

"You don't agree?" Saetang says.

"What a person is willing to give up in order to save a life says a lot about them." She thinks of Theren, running from her in the Getty. Unwilling to risk his safety for her life. She clears her throat. "The same goes for a nation. We gave up our land for our people. I'll wear that as a badge of honor."

"Your sister told me you're a bit of a . . . *Pilgrimage* supporter," Okoro says, as if the word "Pilgrimage" tastes bitter. "I'm not surprised to discover you don't long to return to our planet."

Pushing off the *Sundial*'s scheduled launch by a decade was easily the most controversial decision Elegy's mother had made as the Sword of Cedre. All the Swords before her were in favor of the Pilgrimage. They had advocated for the *Sundial*'s refurbishment, citing Cedre's small population size—just over three million—as an argument for seeking a new planet, one free from Fever.

The decryption device that carried the visitors' first message is the key to the Pilgrimage's plan. It emits a signal that some Cedre scientists insist they can trace, if they're given enough time and resources. Once they succeed, a crew that includes a group of Cedre's representatives will set sail to make contact. It's a distant hope, but then, so is the hope of reclaiming Earth from the Talusar.

Elegy's mother, on the other hand, was a Restorationist. She dreamed only of returning to Earth. These days, the majority of people on Cedre Station agree with her. They see their planet not as a real place—a place with as many problems as Cedre Station, if not more—but as a distant paradise. And who willingly surrenders a paradise?

The movement had picked up steam in the last ten years, thanks in no small part to Larke.

"I'm Losan-born, General," Elegy says to Okoro. "Of course I long for Earth. I just long for something else more."

"Like no more war?" Saetang supplies.

"We must always fight for the things we want," Okoro argues.

"I wouldn't get the wrong idea about Miss Ahn here," Thompson says. "More than most, she joined the army to fight the Talusar."

Okoro looks unimpressed. Elegy gets the feeling, based on the familiarity with which Okoro called Larke "your sister" a moment ago, that she's close to the Sword—which means she'll never be a fan of Elegy.

"Yeah, we remember your team pretty well," Saetang says to Elegy. "You served with Primary Shir Alexios, right? May he rest in peace."

They raise their glass, and drink.

Elegy touches her heart with two fingers, since she doesn't have a drink of her own to raise.

"Search and rescue, yes, I remember," Okoro says. "Though I was lower-ranked then. And you were just behind Talusar borders the other week, weren't you, Miss Ahn? What was that for?"

Elegy shrugs, and says, "Private rescue mission."

"A hell of a way to put yourself at risk," Okoro says.

Yes, Okoro has definitely been talking to Larke.

"I don't consider my life more valuable than other people's," Elegy says.

"Noble of you."

"You caught me. I love to sound noble."

Their eyes lock for a few seconds longer than is comfortable. Saetang clears their throat.

"You need a drink, and I need a refill," they say. "Come on, Your Grace, let's hit the bar."

Elegy stands, and lets the general lead her over to the bar, nestled on one side of the room near the food tables. When they're a few steps away, the general leans a little closer.

"Sorry about that, Okoro's just a pill."

Elegy shrugs. "I've met worse."

"Bet you have." Saetang's eyes glint a little. "Friend of mine told me there's a rumor going around that you're a Scout."

Elegy tries not to react. "Wild rumor."

It's not illegal to be a Scout, but it's not the kind of thing you broadcast when you're trying to maneuver in *respectable* society. Especially when you're ex-military.

"That's what I said." They reach the bar, and Saetang orders a glass of red wine. Elegy gets gin.

"If you were a Scout, I know that would scandalize quite a few people," Saetang says. "But it wouldn't scandalize me. We're a rougher sort in Austra. We work with Scouts all the time."

"If I see any Scouts, I'll let them know."

Saetang laughs, and touches their glass to Elegy's.

A clinking sound catches Elegy's attention, and she looks around to find its source. Larke is standing at the base of the tree, glass of wine in hand, beneficent smile on her face. Elegy doesn't trust that smile.

"Good evening, everyone," she says, and though her voice isn't amplified, it still carries through the space. It's a talent she must have learned from their mother.

"Elegy, would you come up here, please?" Larke's voice is warm. Everywhere, heads turn and eyes find Elegy. Her face heats, but a path clears in front of her, so she walks it, not knowing what else to do. She squeezes the stem of her glass so hard she worries it will crack, and stands beside Larke under the tree.

"I'm so pleased that my sister is finally recovered enough to join us," Larke says, with that same warm smile. Elegy stares at her, her mind going blank. *Recovered?*

"Especially on this day, Evacuation Day, which is so meaningful for our people." Larke looks out at the crowd. "Perhaps you all heard rumors, years ago, that the augurs had given us a great gift: a prophecy that declared Elegy Rosyk the Hope of Cedre, destined to lead us in triumph over the Talusar."

In the air above them, Eyes swarm like bees, recording this moment to be broadcast in news pavilions all over Cedre.

"I am pleased to confirm those rumors for you today," Larke says, and she takes Elegy's hand, which is hanging limp at her side as she tries to root herself in the present. Larke's fingers squeeze her tightly. "And it is with that prophecy bolstering our confidence in Cedre's triumph that I am announcing a renewed effort to reclaim Earth from our enemies."

Elegy stiffens. She feels like she's waded into water that's deeper than she expected, and she's lost touch with the bottom. No—she feels like Larke has *dragged* her there.

Their plan had been to announce Elegy as the so-called Hope of Cedre—not for Larke to use her as Restorationist propaganda.

"There has always been considerable risk in sending the *Sundial* out to contact outsiders we have no real knowledge of," Larke says. "Assuming we could even find them, there's no guarantee they will be sympathetic to our cause or peaceful in their approach." Elegy hears harsh whispers from the crowd, presumably coming from their Pilgrimage-supporting attendees. "With these risks in mind, I think it's wise to redirect resources from the *Sundial*. There's no reason to launch if we already have a planet to call our home. Instead, I intend to convert the *Sundial* to a museum, to commemorate the great work that our people have done over the centuries to prepare for any outcome, no matter how difficult it is to achieve."

Elegy tries to pull her hand away from Larke's, but Larke is holding her too tightly. She feels trapped in her own anger like a fly caught in honey. Cedre has been preparing the *Sundial* for its mission since its founding, aware of how impossible it will be to fight an enemy that outnumbers them ten to one, as the Talusar do. Though sentiment has been shifting in the last decade, she never thought the *Sundial* would turn into a *museum*.

And she never thought Larke would use her to justify it.

Larke raises her voice as the crowd starts to mutter.

"Our orbit has encircled Earth for all my life," she says. "This planet, which gave us all life, which still sustains us, has felt like an unreachable, impossible dream. But now it is within our grasp, and we must close our fist around it."

She raises her glass with her free hand. Her knuckles are white where they grasp Elegy's fingers.

"'Where we come from is where we belong,'" she says.

Elegy remembers what General Thompson told her—that she could either be a pawn of the Sword or a tool.

Larke raises her glass even higher. Elegy wrenches her hand out of Larke's, but it's too late—most of the crowd is already joining the toast, a sea of glasses held aloft.

"'Where we come from is where we belong,'" they murmur.

20

Theren's head throbs. He probes at the corner of his eye to relieve some of the pressure, and looks up at the image of a man projected above the obsidian glass between him and Specialist Gylle.

Again.

The man in the projection is familiar in the way that some faces are always familiar, whether you'd encountered them before or not. Theren has been searching the recesses of his memory for the man's face for the past hour. The problem isn't that he's coming up empty—it's that he's come up with too many possibilities, too many meetings that Rava called him to, too many bland faces.

Specialist Gylle taps her neat fingernails on the table in front of her. She's a woman of precise lines, whether it's the angle of her hair along her jawline or the shoulders of her jacket. She feels, to him, like touching the pad of his thumb to the edge of a razor. If he makes one wrong move, she'll cut him.

Every day for the past week, he's sat in this room for hours, going over every face she wanted him to recognize, every name she thought he might have heard, every detail he could summon from the miasma of memory that was the last four years. There are no windows here, no adornments. Just a table with an obsidian in its center and two chairs. Just Specialist Gylle's gray eyes narrowing every time he fails to answer a question to her satisfaction, and the ringing of her voice when she makes a demand.

"I don't know," he says to her, and she's already shaking her head.

"You aren't even trying, Mr. Forint."

"Not *trying*?" he says. "A mind isn't a mine; you can't just chisel into it and expect to find a diamond."

"At this point I would be thrilled to discover anything of value at all," she replies. "So far you have brought me nothing of clarity, nothing of substance. Did you have your eyes closed for four years, Mr. Forint?"

He clenches his teeth so hard they squeak. "If you would just—let me get some rest."

She sweeps her fingers across the obsidian, and the image of the man between them disappears.

The first day he sat across from her, she told him his cooperation would be rewarded with restored privileges. The first of those privileges would be seeing his brother. At the end of every day, though, she informed him that he hadn't been cooperative enough yet.

When will you give me something of value, Mr. Forint? she asked him at one point.

When I unearth this goddamn buried memory, he thought, but couldn't say. Elegy said she would work on it, and he believes her. But he knows how crucial it is that he remember whatever it is Rava wants him to forget.

"I was told that your brother was dear to you," Gylle says. "I see that's not really the case, or you would feel more urgency about reuniting with him."

He feels nothing from her. She may as well be a machine.

He doesn't know if he'll ever see Isre again, an idea he'd gotten used to when he was in Valla, but now that he's home—he feels like he's going to be sick.

"You can of course rest, if you feel no such urgency," Gylle says. "Or we can continue. The choice is yours."

Theren takes a deep breath.

"Show me again."

+   +   +

That night he dreams of a hand in his hair.

It begins tenderly, fingers scratching along his hairline, tweaking a curl above his ear. Teasing. *You need a haircut.* He can feel the whisper in his ear, Fenn's whisper, and his warm hands.

The hands change, then, the fingers stricter, wrenching his head to the side. *Look at me when I speak to you*, an order spoken in a low voice. Satka, maybe, demanding his focus. *Fucking get it together, Forint.*

And then gentle again, but sickening this time—his insides squirming, his skin crawling—

He wakes with a start in his too-short bed in Losan Stronghold. He chewed his knuckles as he slept, and now the pillow is spotted bright red.

He knows where he is, but he also doesn't. He lurches into the bathroom, his shoulder hitting the doorframe hard. He fumbles under the sink for the shaving kit and the scissors. The scissors come first; he leans over the sink and grabs chunks of his hair and saws at them. His hand is red with blood, but the wounds are shallow.

He just wants to look like a person no one ever touched in violence. Brand-new and unhurt.

He takes out the shaver next, fastens the right guard, and turns it on. The buzzing steadies him. His hands stop trembling. His breaths slow. Short, prickly hairs cover the sink. He changes the guard once, twice more. Cleans up the edges. Trims his beard.

When he's finished, he looks older and harder. He looks more like himself. He wipes the stray hair from the sink basin and throws it in the trash, cleans the shaver and puts it away. He washes his hand and sits at the desk to dab at the cuts with wound sealant from the first aid kit he found in the bathroom cabinet.

By the time he's finished, showered, and changed, Gylle has come for him. As usual, she looks him over, unimpressed, and leads the way down the hall in silence.

Theren still feels strange, like he's not inside his own body. He taps his fingers together, one by one, to ground himself. His hands feel like they're the wrong size, or on the wrong body.

"Forint?"

A hand falls on his shoulder. It takes Theren a moment to recognize Arias standing in front of him in the hallway. He pulls away, and Arias lets him, but leans in to meet his eyes again.

"Okay," Arias says. "Gylle, I'm taking him to med bay."

Theren finds the words out of nowhere, thinking of Isre. He wants to see Isre, and in order to do that, he has to give Gylle what she wants. "I'm fine."

"Sure you are," Arias says. "Gylle? Med bay."

"This is in direct violation of the Sword's orders."

"File a complaint with General Thompson if you like," Arias says. "But he won't want to hear that you pushed a *voluntary informant* living in his stronghold into a dissociative episode."

Gylle eyes him, then continues down the hallway, her shoes snapping on the tile. Arias's hand settles on the side of Theren's neck; he jerks back again.

"Sorry," Arias says. "If I take you to med bay, they'll give you a sedative. Is that what you want?"

Theren shakes his head. "My brother. She won't let me see him."

"I'll handle it. Just tell me what would help you right now."

"I need . . ." He feels an itch under his skin, deeper than he can scratch. "I need to move."

"Okay. Let's go, then."

Arias leads him out of the barracks. He greets almost everyone that he passes with some degree of familiarity. They stare at Theren. He wears his last four years in some obvious way that he can't control. But none of them say anything to him.

They walk through the orchard to the next building over, the training facility. The air smells sweet and sharp, guava and lemons. The branches scratch Theren's cheeks.

The training facility, like all the other buildings in Losan Stronghold, is all concrete. Straight lines. It smells like sweat and shoes, like the training room on Cedre Station where his mother taught him sword forms and made him watch the Talusar fight again and again. The familiarity doesn't help with the feeling of unreality. Where is he, and when?

Then he's wrapping his hands, like he's done a thousand times, and choosing a pair of gloves. He stands in front of a heavy bag and it's all automatic, it's all easy.

There, somewhere in the middle of a drop of sweat rolling down the back of his neck and the slap of his fist against the canvas, he finds himself back in his body again. Heat builds in his muscles and it's a relief to move, to do what he's best at. He can't remember the details of every meeting with Rava, but he can do this.

✦   ✦   ✦

The next day, when his door opens, it's not Gylle waiting on the other side, it's Arias.

They go to the bigger training room, this time. It's a wide elliptical space that reminds him of a church sanctuary. Huge oval windows in the far wall let in the sun. All around the edge of the room is a track.

They run. Arias is faster, or maybe Theren is just recovering, but Arias also surrenders after just a few miles. Theren keeps going, his body remembering. He's used to running at higher altitudes, where the air is thinner and the ground is uneven. This smooth, flat plain feels like nothing beneath his feet.

When he finishes, Arias is sitting in the corner, a bottle of water against his lips. Theren didn't ask why Arias was at his door earlier; it didn't even occur to him to try.

"What happened to Gylle?" Theren asks.

"It takes you a really long time to ask questions," Arias says.

"I'm not used to receiving answers."

Arias swallows more water, then offers the bottle to Theren. Theren is shocked by the offer, at first. Not many Cedrae will even share bottles with each other, let alone with someone who's Fevered. Theren can't pass the Fever through his saliva, and Arias knows that, but still—the fear runs deep.

He takes the bottle and drinks.

"General Thompson intervened on your behalf," Arias says.

Theren frowns. "Why?"

"Because Ahn—sorry, *Her Grace*—asked him to, and he trusts her." Arias gets up and straightens his shirt. "Gylle's tactics aren't working. We all know that. Elegy wanted to try a different approach."

"So you're my new interrogator."

"I was under the impression you agreed to be cooperative, and you don't need an *interrogator*. Was I wrong?"

"No. No, you're not wrong."

"Then I'm just here to help you make sense of things. That's all."

The doors to the training room open, and a few soldiers stumble in, sleepy-eyed and barefoot. They freeze at the sight of Theren, falling into each other. Arias jerks his head to the side, an invitation to follow him, and Theren does, slipping past the soldiers and into the hallway beyond.

Arias says, "Do you know how Elegy and I met?"

Theren shakes his head.

"When she was in the army, she was in charge of search and rescue with Shir Alexios. We met because my squad was ambushed just outside of Nu-santa and I was the only one who survived. I sent out a distress call, and search and rescue answered. Saved my life and took me back to the base to recover."

They walk side by side. Theren clasps his hands behind him, at the small of his back, like he's in parade rest even now. Arias pushes through the front door with his hip, a wry smile on his face.

"Recover." Arias snorts. "Really they wanted a debriefing, only I couldn't give it to them. Everything that happened . . . it was all weird and jumbled. Like somebody jostled a puzzle and the pieces all separated. So they gave me three months of leave, and I spent it gardening on Cedre Station."

"Gardening?"

"Badass, I know."

They walk across the hard-packed dirt and into the orchard. Theren still has scrapes on his cheeks from walking through here the day before. Today, he ducks under the branches, following Arias to a wooden bench that stands between two lemon trees.

"And gardening . . . fixed it?"

"I have no idea what 'fixing' it would even mean." Arias sits on the bench, and Theren stands across from him. "But it helped a little. The more I could unclench, the more things made sense. It wasn't like I suddenly remembered better—more that I could see how the pieces were supposed to fit together. I put them in some kind of order, as best I could, and that's what the army needed me to do."

"So, what," Theren says. "You think if we go running together, I'll be able to give coherent intelligence?"

"Mostly I think if we go running together, I'll be in much better shape. But yeah, I think that if you sleep well, eat well, and get some exercise, you might finally be able to relax."

Theren runs a hand over the bark of the lemon tree. It's smooth, almost like skin.

Arias asks, "So that man Gylle was showing you the other day—what was the problem there, exactly?"

"I think . . . I think I know his face from the time when Maeve Martin had just died. I couldn't—" Theren pauses, not sure how to explain. "At that point, I wasn't really . . . there."

"I understand." Most of the time when people say that, Theren thinks they don't. But Arias really might. "Let's skip that whole stretch of time. When did the haze start to lift?"

He thinks of the paper covering one wall of his new quarters. He divided it, not by month, or by season, but by *event*. Maeve's death, to start. And then—

"I met Rava's mother, Ileth Vidar." Theren's hand, when he brings it up to cup the back of his neck, is trembling. "And she decided to help Rava bring me to heel."

Arias lifts his eyes to Theren's. "How?"

Theren runs his thumb along the vine tattooed on his left hand.

"Ileth is . . . we call them 'sutora.'" He drags his fingernail over one of the leaves inked on his hand. "She creates memories. Or alters them. She made me remember things I'd never done. Horrible things. She . . . *broke* my reality, she . . ."

He can't tell if it's Arias's gut that's churning, or his own. He feels separate again, distant from himself.

He doesn't think about those memories, the ones Ileth created, if he can help it. He buried them as deep as they could go.

"Rava got me away from her eventually." Theren looks down at his hands. "She taught me to recognize the false memories."

It wasn't that difficult, once he knew what to look for. Ileth was good at her work, but she didn't understand Theren's gift, so the memories from her never felt like he was actually in them.

"Rava promised to keep me away from Ileth, if I was . . . cooperative. So."

"So you were," Arias says softly.

The wind blows hot against Theren's cheek. He nods.

"Let's talk about what you did for her, then," Arias says. "Rava called you a truthsayer, but obviously you weren't a typical Talusar truthsayer."

"Deception is easy for me to read. Having me around meant people couldn't lie to her," he says. "Allies. Potential allies. But more than that— Rava was raised to be her mother's muscle, not a politician. She's awkward and charmless. I helped her to navigate people."

"What kind of people? Ileth?"

Theren hears something ringing in the distance. An alarm, maybe, or a siren—

"Sometimes. Her underlings, sometimes. And mostly—the family. The Talus family."

"She needs help navigating her own family?"

Theren nods. The ringing is getting louder. "They're all devout worshipers of the Fever, and she's . . . not. And they see her as a brute. Even those absurd legends about her among the Talusar, about her containing the souls of ancient warriors, they're designed to make her feared. Set apart, but not equal."

"Absurd legends," Arias repeats. "How absurd? I mean, I know she's not housing a bunch of souls—"

Theren shakes his head.

"I only have suspicions, based on what I saw," he says. "But I think . . . I think Rava is just an epocha, and Ileth invented the lie about her daughter channeling ancient warriors so she could justify keeping Rava out of the monastery."

His hands are shaking. Arias gets up, reaches for him. This time, Theren lets him. Arias squeezes his fingers and releases them, squeezes them and releases them. It's more soothing than Theren expected.

"I got too close to the truth once," Theren says, and his mouth feels clumsy, hard to move. "She didn't take it well."

Arias opens his mouth to ask another question, then squints at Theren. "I can see we've reached our stopping point for the day."

"I don't know why this keeps happening."

"I do," Arias says sadly. "It's all right. You did well. Let me walk you back to your room."

21

Theren waits for Isre in the shade of a piñon pine, in the green space behind one of the Losan Stronghold buildings. A line of cypress blocks the view of the city's sprawling greenhouses and high-efficiency farms. It's hot, but he likes the heat, and the smell of the earth, and the sound of his feet scraping the ground.

Since the day before he's felt raw, like everything is too loud, too bright, too rough. He doesn't know why he's here—why he's now allowed to see Isre when he hasn't given Arias anything of substance. Just a suspicion; just speculation.

The back door of the nearest building opens, and Arias steps out, followed by a young man with light brown skin and black hair. Lean and narrow, with an eager stride. Isre.

Theren comes to his feet just as Isre breaks into a run. He collides with Theren and laughs, the sound muffled by Theren's shoulder. His short hair tickles Theren's jaw. It takes him a moment to bring his arms around Isre; he's too bewildered by how different this feels, now that Theren is bigger and Isre is older.

Isre pulls away, wiping his eyes with the heel of his hand. "How are you so much *taller*?"

Theren smiles a little. "Fever."

"Fever." Isre touches the back of his hand to Theren's forehead. "Holy shit."

They move back into the shade of the pine tree, where there's an old wooden table coated with dust and pine needles. Theren sits across from Isre, and Arias stands apart from them, his back against the trunk of a tree. He has to listen in—Theren still isn't trusted enough to be left alone.

Theren is struck by the memory of his last day with Isre, Isre standing behind him, almost his height, asking him to get Imbued after he swore his oath, so he and Theren could stay in touch. Only that Isre was gangly and hunched against his own new height, and this one sits straight and has stubble on his chin.

"You're a soldier," Theren says to Isre.

It's an old habit, from years of reading people for Rava. It's easier to just tell people what he suspects about them and read how they react than to ask them questions, which are as likely to prompt lies as truths. He realizes, too late, that he doesn't want to read Isre, doesn't want to know the tangled mess that his brother is feeling. Isre's concern is already itching at the back of his neck, too persistent for him to block. He must not look well.

"They told you?" Isre says.

Theren shakes his head. "Your posture."

"Impressive. Yeah, I'm a technician," Isre says. "Used to be a pilot, but I went where the need was."

Isre was always good with technology. He liked to play with old machines, the kind no one in Cedre used anymore. He could open something up and tease it apart and make it work again. To Theren, all of that was so far out of reach that Isre seemed like a miracle worker. So he's not surprised to hear his brother is a technician.

It's the pilot that Theren can't see in him—that's the part of Isre that Theren doesn't know. Not yet, anyway.

Isre touches Theren's hand, and it takes all of Theren's self-control not to pull away. Warmth sinks into him, and he relaxes a little. This is his brother in all ways but blood. As Arias has been saying for the past few mornings, *You don't need to be ready to fight right now.* It's almost helping.

"I heard you were hurt," Isre says. "Enough to need surgery."

"I'm all right." Theren lays a palm over his ribs. The wound is still sealed, just in case, but it's closed now, thanks to Cedre healing. "Arias said you flew in from Cedre Station. Do you still live there?"

Isre shakes his head. "I have a friend who does, asked me to volunteer my time to look over their escape shuttles. I live in Losan, though. Needed a change, after . . ." The pain in him is like the deep ache a person feels in an old injury, right before a storm. "After."

They're only skimming the surface, talking about *work*, as if that matters to either of them now. But it's easier than talking about what else is between them: Kesia's betrayal. The Knights' funeral. Isre's secret dealings with a Scout who turned out to be the Hope of Cedre. The four years Theren spent in Valla. Theren knows they can't stay here, apart from it, for much longer—but he can't bring himself to take the plunge.

"I live between a bakery and a little dairy," Isre says. "Wind blows one way, it smells like fresh cookies. Wind blows the other way, it smells like manure. It's kind of like reading your fortune every day."

Theren smiles. "And today?"

"Chocolate chip."

Isre's laugh fades too quickly, and Theren knows the respite is already over. He braces himself.

"How long have you been here?" Isre says to him, softly.

"Almost two weeks."

"Why wouldn't they let me see you?"

"The Sword is suspicious of me." Theren glances at Arias, who's making a show of not listening in, gazing through the cypress branches at the city beyond them. When Arias doesn't stop him, he goes on: "Mostly because of Kesia, though that's not all. I've been—cooperative. To earn back their trust. But it will take time."

Isre raises his eyebrows. His curiosity itches in Theren's head.

"You call her 'Kesia' now," he says, as if that's anywhere near the most important thing Theren just said.

"After what she did, she's lucky I'll even say her name."

"She helped you, you know. She came to me—"

"Yes. I heard."

"Then you know she's not all bad."

"I know no such thing." He says it a little too harshly. Theren is squeezing his hands together so tightly his fingers are starting to go numb. He pries them apart and rests them on the table in front of him.

Isre's eyes drop to the tattoos on his hands.

"She's known exactly where I was for the last four years," Theren says. "Don't you think it's strange that she suddenly came to you after four years of letting you believe I was dead? She was perfectly content to let me endure—" He cuts himself off.

"Endure what?" Isre says.

"Don't."

"I just want to know why—"

"Isre."

"—why you were gone for so long and then suddenly you were able to escape, like it was easy—"

"I said, *don't*!" Theren says, his voice lifting, almost a yell.

Isre and Theren sit in the quiet. There are distant voices, the chattering of birds, sirens from the city, but around them everything is still.

"It wasn't easy. It wasn't," Theren says, his voice tight.

Isre's eyes are glassy.

"I'm sorry," he finally manages to say.

Theren wants to tell him not to apologize. He doesn't want this—this tension between them, the uncertainty in Isre's eyes, in his hands, even in his posture. Like he's facing down a wild animal, and he's not sure what it will do next.

"I'm just so glad you're alive," Isre says, and Theren remembers, all at once, that Isre has a gift for this, for saying the one simple thing that Theren needs to hear.

He reaches for Isre's hand and closes his eyes. His brother feels warm and steady, like the low crackle of a fire at the end of an evening, exactly as Theren might have predicted, if he'd been asked.

"It's been terrible, not seeing you," Theren says, and just like that, the tension evaporates.

Isre squeezes his hand.

"So I got married at eighteen," he blurts out, like it's a confession. "That's probably the biggest thing you missed. Don't worry, it didn't take."

Theren lets out a startled laugh. "It didn't *take?*"

"Yeah. Only lasted a few weeks. Then I found out she was a criminal."

"I take it you mean that literally."

"Yeah. She was a con artist. She said her name was Harmony—"

"Never date someone whose name is also a concept."

"Now you tell me. Anyway, I'm not sure why I jumped into it so fast . . ."

And Theren lets Isre's warmth settle into him as he listens.

22

Theren is starting to remember certain things, though not the thing he most wants to—no, *needs* to—remember: the gap that Rava Vidar left him with.

Instead he can recall the day he moved from the Crucible to House Vidar. Nyx, Rava's right-hand woman, escorted him. She wore her hair in a long braid that brushed back and forth across her spine as she walked. All of his possessions—two changes of clothes, a clay bowl that belonged to Fenn, a silk scarf that belonged to Maeve—fit in one bag.

At the last second before he left his cell, he doubled back to retrieve a book of poetry from beneath his mattress. Orda—first his instructor, then his friend—gave it to him before he was released from the Crucible.

Then Theren followed Nyx in silence through the streets of Valla.

It was the most he had seen of Valla since his arrival, but he still couldn't be bothered to look at it. Maeve Martin had just died, and he was dizzy with grief. It didn't occur to him to run, or fight back, or ask questions.

When they arrived at House Vidar, she took him to the room he would share with three others, and according to Talusar custom, Nyx told him, he would get five days to grieve. Then he would be expected to work. Just what he would be doing, she didn't say, and he didn't ask. He hoisted himself into the top bunk and turned toward the wall.

He remembers that there was a portrait of the emperor, Icar Talus, hanging over the door, so he felt like the man's cold blue eyes were watching him as he slept. And he remembers that later, one of the others—a maid—took pity on him, and brought him food, and showed him where to bathe and wash his clothes, and told him who among the staff was lenient and who wasn't.

Then he remembers five days later, when Nyx came back.

"Put on your shoes and come with me," she said.

He did as he was told, almost out of habit. In the Crucible, he knew the consequences for disobeying orders, and they were painful. When you were a Crucible fighter, you couldn't afford to get hurt unless it was in a fight—if you got hurt in a fight, you were allowed to take time to heal, but if you got hurt outside of a fight, you had to face your opponent anyway, at a disadvantage. So there were no brawls in the Crucible, there was no defiance. It was too costly.

But when he stepped outside into daylight—dark clouds covered the sun, so it wasn't bright, but it was brighter than the windowless room where he had spent the past five days—he realized he was in House Vidar now, where he didn't know the rules, and he wouldn't be obeying some prison guard who just wanted him to stop lingering in the hallway. He would be obeying Rava Vidar.

Nyx brought him to a clearing of sorts, a circle of bare, packed earth that reminded him of the arena. Standing in the center of it was Rava, boots laced, hair tied back, arms folded. At the edge of the circle were Ranos and Satka, her other two closest subordinates. Each of them felt, to him, like biting into a lemon, only Ranos seemed a little less tart than his sister.

"Your friend Orda is at the monastery now," Rava said, without preamble. She wasn't lying; he would have known. "A position of honor, per our bargain."

He was the one who had guaranteed Orda's release from the Crucible, and he was relieved that Rava had done as she promised. She didn't always, as he well knew.

"Good," he said.

The feeling of her was like set teeth, the uneasy tension of two powerful things held just so.

"Ranos was confused as to why you didn't even try to ask for freedom for yourself," Rava said. She set a hand on Ranos's shoulder. "And I told him—"

Here she paused, and her eyes went blank, in the same way that Fenn's used to every time he saw a vision of the past. It lasted for just a few seconds, and then she snapped back to attention, removing her hand and continuing as if there was no gap at all.

"—that you don't ask for things you know you won't get. That the Fever gives you certainty where others can only guess. It's that certainty that brings you here."

She tilted her head. Her eyes looked paler in this gray light, almost unearthly. Just like the emperor's eyes in the portraits that hang all over House Vidar and all over Valla.

"Your capacity to know people makes you a potentially useful instrument. I frequently encounter the untrustworthy, the deceptive, and the cunning, and I don't have the time to put my trust where it doesn't belong," she said. "I say that you're 'potentially' useful because for as long as you persist in pointless defiance of me, I can't trust your assessments of others. And I must be able to trust your assessments of others."

Once she said it out loud, his purpose in House Vidar seemed obvious. Any leader, especially one who made so many deals with the scum of the earth, would relish the ability to know when people were lying. He offered her that. As long as she could figure out how to control him.

And her certainty—it meant she had a plan for that already.

"To that end." She tipped her chin up to look into his eyes. "We find ourselves here. You want to hurt me, and you need to see what will happen if you try." She spread her arms wide. "So go ahead, Forint. Hit me."

He didn't have to ask if she meant it. He was sure that she did. And judging by the total lack of surprise in any of the others, they were as sure of her as she was of herself. That rattled him. He was a good fighter, these days, but he wasn't an idiot. The Crucible had taught him to assess people right away, and he could tell by how Rava moved—quiet, graceful—that she was a good fighter, too. Too good.

"No," he said.

"No?" She grinned. "I offer you the opportunity to cause me physical harm without any repercussions, and you say 'no'?"

"I don't ask for things I know I won't get, and I don't get into fights I know I won't win."

"Admirable. But I think you're underestimating how badly you want to punch me even if you don't win."

She had a point there.

There was no tentative dance as he decided on a strategy. Instead, he charged at her with all the strength and speed he could muster.

She slipped from his grasp like water.

Usually, when people decided to move, there was a *change* in them just before—like a spark. In the arena, he had learned to pay attention to that spark, to move just a split second faster than everyone else. But Rava did things without even a moment of forethought, her reflexes and instincts so well-honed that he couldn't feel a goddamn thing. She fought without emotion, and without planning, and without a single trace of fear.

He doesn't remember much after that. He knows that he tried again and again to hit her, and only succeeded once, his fist connecting with her jaw so hard she spat blood on the dirt. The pain didn't seem to faze her; she just grabbed his arm, wrenched it until he saw stars, and knocked him down.

She hit him over and over. Until he could barely see, barely move. Until the others started to feel impatient, uneasy.

Eventually his legs were shaking too badly to support his weight. He knelt on the dirt, blood running down his chin, and she crouched in front of him. She had a swollen jaw, but she was otherwise untouched.

"You know, you take punishment like no one I've ever seen." Her pale eyes searched his. "I don't actually think that pain will be instructive to you. But there are other ways to break a man's resolve."

She touched his face. He couldn't move.

"And I assure you," she said, "I will find them."

✦　✦　✦

In the training room at Losan Stronghold, he squares off with Arias again, his hands up, palms bare. Arias bats at him with a glove, grinning, a teasing blow. Theren shifts back to avoid. It's always this way, with them. Arias rarely makes contact. But he's getting better.

Theren sees a hole in his guard. He reaches out, quick, and taps Arias's jaw, just to show him that he could have hit him, if he wanted to. "Hands up."

"Hands up, hands up," Arias repeats. "Will you ever say anything else?"

"When you remember to keep your hands up, maybe." Theren ducks under a punch, and slips past Arias, poking him hard in the rib cage.

When he looks up at the clock on the far wall, he sees Elegy beneath it, her arms crossed, leaning into the doorframe. He doesn't know how long she's been standing there, but he thinks it's more than a few minutes. He drops his hands.

Her hair is loose over her shoulders, and with her round face and full cheeks, it makes her look younger. Like a girl he would have gone to university with, in another life. But it's her eyes that betray her, so sharp they whittle him down every time she looks at him.

That could have something to do with how she *feels* when she looks at him, bitter and angry and curious, all tangled together.

"Ahn!" Arias says, grinning, easy—everything seems easy for Arias, though Theren knows that's not the case. Arias walks up to her and opens his arms like he's going to embrace her; she cringes, her nose wrinkling, and smacks his chest.

"Gross. No, thank you," she says.

"Ouch. Rejected. Just coming to say hey, or . . . ?"

"Sadly, no," she says. "Can we go somewhere to talk?" She looks over Arias's shoulder at Theren, and raises an eyebrow. "All of us?"

Theren walks in their wake down the hallway and out, through the orchard to the barracks. She's talking to Arias about the Evacuation Day banquet, and Theren isn't listening so much as he's watching her long fingers flutter through big gestures as she talks.

Arias takes them to his quarters, which are more comfortable than Theren's. There's a table in the middle of the room where he and Arias have sat, going over Gylle's list of suspects, trying to find something of value in Theren's memories. He's had more success recently than he did at first, but it's still just bits and pieces—an approximation of when a person met with Rava, a moment of the conversation he overheard, maybe.

And always, nagging at the back of his mind, is that gap—the memory he lost. Rava is up to something, and he needs to find out what it is, even if he has to rip it out of his own head.

Elegy sits at the table, and Arias takes a shirt out of his cabinet, sniffs it to make sure it's clean, then changes.

"Hey, whoa," Elegy says. "I didn't agree to nudity."

"You literally cut pants off my body with a knife once."

"You were bleeding."

"I was still naked."

Theren leans against the door. The room is in disarray, clothes piled on the unmade bed, a collection of water glasses on the nightstand, a dog-eared book resting on the pillow.

Arias sits across from Elegy, and props his feet up—still in boots—on the edge of his bed.

"So what's making you look so grim?" he says.

Theren cringes a little. He knows the answer—Elegy is in Theren's presence, which makes grief and anger well up inside her like blood from a fresh wound.

"Nothing," Elegy says. "Nothing new, anyway."

Arias looks from her to Theren and back again. "I'm missing something. Did you guys have a fight?"

"No," Theren says, and he shifts his focus to Elegy. "You have news, Your Grace?"

"I spoke to Julia Martin about helping you with your memory gap," she says to him. "She agreed to help you, but she had one condition. It was that you perform a Talusar ritual with her. Ring any bells?"

A weight settles in his stomach. He nods. "Erczet."

"So you've heard of it. She said it was a mourning ritual."

"It's a memory-sharing ritual," Theren says. "When there's no body to bury, but there's a witness to the death, the witness agrees to share memories with the family of the deceased, so they can . . . process."

"You can share memories?" Arias says.

"*I* can't. But one of the other exiles—Fenn's father—can project them from my mind."

Arias scratches behind his ear. "What if the person died in some horrific way? The family really wants to see that?"

"They think having closure, at last, is worth watching their loved ones die."

"Then they have no idea what it is to watch someone you love die," Elegy says tersely.

"Most of them *have* watched a loved one die," Theren says. "The Fever kills half of them before they reach adulthood."

"That's their choice."

"Is it?" he says. "Cedre would be so very welcoming to any Talusar who prefer their children remain uninfected, would it?"

Elegy doesn't answer.

"But what about you, during this ritual?" Arias says. "You'd have to watch these deaths, too."

"I've already seen them," Theren says. "That's the whole point."

"Yeah, but . . ." Arias frowns. "Seeing them again would be painful."

Theren looks at his feet. He's known since he spoke to Julia after the interrogation that she would ask for this. That's why she asked him if he was a witness to Maeve's death.

"This is the sole condition of Julia's cooperation," Elegy says, sharp. "If you want your buried memory, the one that could help us understand what Rava Vidar is planning . . . this is what you have to do to get it."

"Ahn, you can't ask him to do this," Arias says. "This sounds brutal, and he's already having enough trouble—"

"Arias, stop," Theren says quietly, keeping his eyes on Elegy's. "She's not asking. She's ordering."

Outside, the wind is blowing hard. Flecks of earth hit the window.

She looks away.

He says, "When?"

"They agreed to board a shuttle tomorrow morning." She clears her throat, and sounds more like herself again. "I wanted Arias here because I think someone who isn't an exile has to attend, to make sure you aren't exchanging sensitive information, and I assumed you'd be most comfortable with him."

She's correct about that, at least—he doesn't really want anyone in his memories, but if he has no choice in the matter, Arias's patient presence is the one he would prefer. It's a shame he can't agree to it.

Instead he says, "I think it should be you."

"You can't seriously be claiming to—"

"Be comfortable with you seeing into my mind?" He laughs a little. "No."

She's staring at him, and he wishes she wouldn't. He loses track of himself when she does. There's just always something new about her, every time he looks at her.

"But if you join me in this ritual," he goes on, "you'll be able to meet Rava as I meet her, with the Fever. You'll know her in a way that she'll never know you."

Before he recognized Elegy in Rava's interrogation room, he felt her. He was used to other people's anger feeling like heat, like burning deep in the belly. An agitated, unstable force. But hers . . . hers wasn't like that. It felt like an anchor settling cold and stable in his body, rooting him to the spot. A metal chain pulling taut, everything going still.

The chain pulls taut again now. Elegy nods.

"Fine," she says. "Tomorrow, then."

23

White is the Talusar color of mourning, so for the erczet ritual, Elegy wears white: white pants and a white jacket with a collar high enough to frame her face, and boning in the midsection that makes it look like old-fashioned corsetry. One of her only nice outfits.

Standing at the dock, watching the Sparrow that carries the exiles grow larger as it descends, she doubts the choice. The wind is blowing up dust. But beside her, Theren Forint is also in a white shirt—collared, tucked into his pants. It's not his shirt; the sleeves are too short for him, so he rolled them up as soon as they spotted the ship above them. He must have borrowed it from Arias. It fits him through the middle, but it's tight around his shoulders.

He doesn't have his own clothes, she realizes. He came here with nothing, and he still has nothing.

"How was your brother?" she asks him, just to fill the silence.

"Isre had to go to Cedre Station for a few days. He'll be back soon."

It's not really an answer.

He raises a hand to shield his eyes from the sun. The Sparrow is the size of an apple now, descending. It's cloudy, hazy, but it's always bright in Losan. She looks at the scars on his forearm. Faded, crisscrossing.

"What are those from?" she says.

"What?"

Without thinking, she touches his arm, and runs her thumb across one of the faded lines on the back of his wrist. He goes still, staring down at her fingers, tan against his light skin.

"Those," she says, and she releases him, quick, like he burned her.

"I trained with a vambrace." It's an old word, only vaguely familiar. He clamps his right hand around his left forearm, to show her. "It's a piece of armor. Sometimes in practice I forgot when I wasn't wearing one, so the blade . . ."

He drags a fingertip sharply along one of the scars, mimicking the cut of a sword.

"Oh," she says.

They both turn back to the landing pad, where the Sparrow is so close that a cloud of dust is lifting to meet it. She can feel the vibrations of its engine in her skull. She's relieved when it touches down and the hatch opens, so the engine can gentle.

The erczet ceremony has to be small, Julia told her, because a memory projection can reach only a few people at once. So each Knight has one representative. Julia Martin is the first off the ship. She wears a knee-length white dress, stiff and professional. Elegy researched the exile families that morning, and she thinks it's Ivy Amalka, Lisia's mother, who comes next. She looks wan, like she might have gotten sick on the plane. Tor Kovek, Fenn's father, comes next. He's tall, and his coloring is lighter than his son's, his hair as gold as Rava Vidar's and his skin only a little darker than Theren's. At his side is Jiro Heather, Furik's father. His white trousers are rumpled from the flight. Elegy sent him a bouquet of paper flowers when his wife died, two years ago.

Julia looks confused when she sees Elegy, but she recovers quickly, giving her a quick bow. "Your Grace. What an unexpected honor."

"Hello," Elegy says. "I'm here—"

"Her Grace is here as my guest," Theren says, and judging by the way Julia takes that in, it must be explanation enough.

She can't sense emotions, but if she had to guess, she would say the exiles all feel about Theren the same way she does: they would trade his life for the ones they lost in an instant. Here he is, among so many people for whom his survival is a wound unto itself . . . and thanks to the Fever, he's cursed with knowing it.

"I reserved a room for us in the library," Elegy says. "Follow me."

Losan Stronghold has a beautiful library. From the outside, it matches all the other buildings in the stronghold: concrete. Inside, though, the concrete is arranged in a series of hollow triangles with panes of glass nestled inside them to let in sunlight. All the bookshelves are warm orange wood, and there are rugs everywhere, salvaged from times when such beautiful things weren't seen as an unnecessary extravagance. They're colorful and worn in places from the foot traffic, unraveling at the ends—at odds with the neatness of the rest of the space.

She leads them through the hush of the now-empty library and into one of the meeting rooms. The wall opposite the door is all windows that look out into a lush green courtyard—evergreens grow there, their needle-laden branches pressing up against the glass. The courtyard is in an artificial winter now, so there's frost on the windowpane. A row of chairs is arranged in a semicircle in the middle of the space. Facing the semicircle is another chair, standing on its own, for Theren.

Once inside, Tor turns to Julia.

"Well, do you want me to do the whole song and dance?" he says, running his hand through his hair. It stands up where his fingers were.

"If you're going to do a thing, do it properly."

"All right." Tor looks like he would very much like to roll his eyes.

Ivy Amalka takes her seat, with Julia Martin at her side, and then Jiro Heather. Elegy sits in the chair on the end. She's so tense her shoulders already ache.

Theren settles across from them all, the heels of his hands balanced on his knees. His fingers are trembling.

Tor takes a vial of dark liquid from his pocket. It looks like the water left over from painting watercolor, murky and opaque.

"Do you know what this is?" Tor asks Theren. Elegy notices the pronouns he chose, which indicate a disparity of status between them. If he wanted to, it would be within Theren's rights to argue it now—those negotiations are common, she's given to understand. But he doesn't.

"It's sovallan," Theren says. "It will slow my perception of time, to make the projection less chaotic, and cause memories to surface."

"Good."

Elegy wonders where Tor got it. There's no way he smuggled vials of a Talusar memory drug into Cedre as a refugee. Maybe it's better she doesn't ask.

Tor takes a small copper bowl from the bag at his side. He passes the bowl to Theren, who cups it in both hands as Tor pours the vial's contents into it. Then Theren drinks it in a single swallow, and passes the bowl back to Tor.

As he takes it, Tor says, "Loss is a burden."

"It's my honor to share it," Theren replies flatly.

She wonders how he knows this ritual so well. Has he done it before? Sat on the other side of it? Studied it?

Tor sets the bowl aside. Theren stares into middle distance, looking dazed. The drug must be taking effect.

Tor stands behind him, and puts both hands on Theren's head, fingers spread wide to frame his ears. He raises Theren's head, slightly, so he has no choice but to stare directly at Julia Martin.

"Tell us, Theren Forint," Tor says, "what became of the Knights of Cedre."

24

Elegy stands in an airy room, next to a stove—cool now. There are cushions around it, their colorful array at odds with the tension in the air, the *weight* in her, like a rock in her stomach.

She sees a young woman on the ground, lying on her back with her hands folded over her stomach. She's Lisia Amalka, and she's dead. Her body is beginning to swell as her organs break down.

Beside her, arranged the same way, is Furik Heather. His eyes aren't closed all the way, and Elegy itches to tug his eyelids down, to make it look like he's only sleeping.

Kneeling between them is Fenn Kovek. He's still. And beside Elegy is Maeve Martin. She glances at Elegy—no, at Theren, who's standing on Elegy's left.

But this is not a Theren she's familiar with. He's not the shorter, leaner boy who swore to be her Knight, and he's not the hardened man who rescued her from House Vidar, either. He's so pale he looks sick, with dark circles under his eyes. His body looks stretched out, far too thin for its size. It takes her a moment to recognize that the ache she's feeling in her limbs is his. It's as if her body is mirroring his.

It's strange that in the memory projection, she's separate from him. She was expecting to experience his memories as if she *was* him, but apparently that's not how Tor's memory projection works.

"Theren," Maeve says. "What should we do?"

A door on the side of the room opens. Nyx, Rava's right hand, walks in, her hair knotted on top of her head, and she steps back to let four people in blue robes enter. Their purpose seems clear: two go to stand at Lisia's and Furik's feet, and the others, their heads. They're here to get the bodies.

"Don't fucking touch her," Fenn growls at one of them, in English.

Nyx responds in Talusar, not to him but to Theren: "Get him under control, or he's going to die."

Theren must be the only one who speaks Talusar.

Theren crouches at Fenn's shoulder, despite the throbbing in his knees. He puts a hand on Fenn's back, and Fenn lashes out, shoving Theren so hard he topples.

"Get the fuck away from me," Fenn says. His eyes are red, and full of tears. "She just hasn't woken up yet, she'll be alive again any minute—"

"They're not going to wake up," Theren says, dragging himself to his knees again. "Fenn, it's been too long. They're gone."

"She is not gone!"

Theren grabs Fenn's shoulders as the robed ones pick up Lisia's body, and then Furik's. As they lift Furik from the ground, Maeve reaches out and sets one hand on his swollen ankle in farewell.

Theren squeezes tightly to keep Fenn from lashing out. Fenn's body shudders in his hands.

Theren whispers, "You can't hurt them, or they'll kill you. Understand?"

"Fuck you," Fenn spits at Theren. "Coward."

✦   ✦   ✦

The shift between memories happens without interruption. She was in that room, and then she's in another one. A bathroom, it looks like, judging by the tile floor—green and worn, cracking in places—and the basin of water on the ground.

Fenn Kovek is kneeling behind it, stripped to the waist, splashing his face. She doesn't remember much about what Fenn looked like before the Fever, but in its aftermath he's just muscle wrapped around bone, and it's painful to look at him. Off to the side, Theren—still obviously fresh from his Fever resurrection—is brushing his teeth.

Fenn pushes himself to his feet with a grunt, but he doesn't seem used to his body's new weakness—he tips to the side, and Theren is there to catch him, his toothbrush still sticking out of his mouth.

Based on the way they related in the memory before, she expects Fenn to snap at him. But instead his eyes go glazed and unfocused as he stares up at Theren.

"Fenn," Theren says. He takes one hand off the other man's shoulders to tap his cheek. "Fenn!"

Fenn blinks at him, and straightens.

"It happened again?" Theren says to him, his voice low.

"Yeah." Fenn closes his eyes, briefly. "More and more often."

"You could just tell them you're an epocha," Theren says to him. "Epochas are well-treated, well-fed—"

"—and fucking property of the Talusar state," Fenn snaps, sounding more like himself. "I would never see you or Maeve again, and I'd be so well-guarded there's not even a shred of hope that I could escape. No thank you, I'll pass."

"Where we're going is brutal. If I were you—"

"You're not the one whose brain is sending them decades into the past at random, so it's not up to you to decide," Fenn says. "Just keep your mouth shut."

He grabs a towel from a stack by the door, and wipes his face. Elegy hears tapping against the window—rain.

"I think I saw your father," Fenn says, before he walks out the door. "Looked just like you."

+ + +

The tap of the rain disappears, and in its place: a roar.

She hears it as if from a distance. A sweaty, shirtless man just toppled to the floor in front of her. He spits blood on the wood. Wheezes. And stands.

There's an audience around her, above her—layers of them, like she's in an amphitheater, but it's dark in here, so she can barely see their faces. She stands in the spotlight, in the heat, and all around her is the tangy smell of sweat.

She watches as another man, just to her left, steps forward, hands raised to protect his face. She takes in the bloody fists, the muscled torso, the expressionless face of Theren Forint. There's a cut in his eyebrow, and blood runs down the side of his head.

She's never seen him like this. Bare from the waist up, and thicker—well-fed and fit, like an athlete. His shoulders back and his spine straight. Confident. A master of this fight, of this place.

He has one black bar tattooed on his hand. One year in the Crucible.

His posture is relaxed as he advances on the other man, his movements fast and predatory. His opponent tries to punch him, but Theren catches it, twisting his arm brutally to the side as he hits the man in the face with his left hand.

Southpaw, she thinks, and she watches as the other man tries to pull away, but Theren shifts with him, effortlessly, following him around the edge of the arena and twisting, still twisting, wrenching the man's arm to strain the limits of his shoulder joint. Elegy cringes. The man screams, and Theren drives a knee into his side, so he goes down hard.

The man slaps the ground with his uninjured arm, yielding.

Theren raises his head.

She follows his gaze to Maeve, standing somewhere above in the first few rows of spectators, her eyes wide. But Theren doesn't acknowledge her. He just walks to the edge of the arena as everyone cheers and chants something. Their voices are muffled. He goes through a doorway that stands open beneath the seats.

There, beneath the amphitheater, the hallway is dark and quiet. Only a few people are milling around, chatting. They look at Theren but don't speak to him as he leans into a wall, his forehead against the stone.

His next breath shudders on the way out. She feels burning in her throat, in her chest. Deep in the pit of her stomach. Everywhere, burning.

Then Maeve's voice:

"Hello."

Theren straightens and pulls away from the wall. Maeve and Fenn are coming toward him, from the arena floor.

"What are you doing here?" Theren says, his voice rough. He speaks English, and it comes to him a little unsteadily, as if he's gotten rusty.

"Nice to see you, too," Fenn says.

"We came to talk to you about something," Maeve says.

Theren sighs, and nods. He leads them down the hallway, past a few people who nod to him and call him by a name Elegy doesn't recognize. Or—perhaps she does. *Intere.* It's a word that means "sifted together." If she had to guess, she would say that in his case, it refers to Cedrae and Talusar.

He opens the door to a small, bare room with no windows. When they walk in, lights flicker on as if triggered by motion—febra glass. When a person survives the Fever, their body starts emitting some kind of energy. Febra armor channels that energy into a shield, and febra glass channels it into gentle light.

There are a few chairs in the room, scattered here and there. A basin of water stands in the corner, on a table, next to a stack of towels, a box of medical supplies. This is a place for fighters to recover in.

Theren goes to the basin and scoops water into his hands, then drinks, long and slow. Once. Twice. Three times.

"I've never seen you like that before," Maeve says to him.

"Like what?" Theren splashes water on his face, then probes gently at the cut above his eyebrow.

"I don't know." She sounds troubled.

"She means you're fucking brutal now and it scares her," Fenn says. "As it happens, though, that's why we're here."

Theren picks up one of the towels and presses it to his bleeding head. He still doesn't turn to look at either of them. Elegy can't stop staring at the muscles in his back, shifting with every movement.

"Is this an intervention?" Theren says. "You're fine with the fact that we all have to survive by beating the shit out of people here, but it's not okay for me to be good at it?"

"It's not okay for you to like it, maybe," Fenn says.

Theren only laughs. He leans against the table that supports the water basin.

Elegy thinks it's an odd thing to say. It's obvious to her that Theren doesn't like it.

"What do you want from me?" he says.

"Why are you acting like this?" Maeve says. "We're your friends, Theren."

"One of you is afraid of me, and the other one only ever refers to me as 'Coward,'" Theren points out.

Fenn sneers. "Would you prefer your tough little arena nickname?"

"If you think they're calling me 'Intere' as a compliment, you have no clue what the word means."

"Both of you, stop," Maeve snaps. "I'm not afraid of you, Theren."

He gives her a look. "Did you forget you can't lie to me?"

"How could I possibly?" Maeve says flatly. "Fenn, tell him the idea. We're obviously taking up too much of his precious time."

Fenn crosses his arms, and eyes Theren for a moment.

"We think you should enter the Tournament next year," he says.

"I can think of less painful ways to die," Theren says. "The Tournament is all swordplay. I'm mediocre with a sword at best."

Maeve says, "You won't die. We know you're not good enough to win it as you are now, but we'll help you *get* good enough."

"Leaving aside the obvious question of 'how the fuck could the two of *you* help me with that,'" Theren says, "why would I care about winning the Tournament? She's not going to free me. The only way any of us are getting out of Valla is in a pile of ash, like Furik and Lisia."

Elegy feels a stab of pain right in the middle of her sternum.

"Ah," Theren says, touching his chest. "Still that raw for you, Fenn?"

Elegy touches her chest, too. That must be what it feels like when he reads people. She isn't sure what she expected—maybe more sensing, and less *feeling*. It's like he's sharing a body with Fenn, the same way she's sharing a body with him now.

"Fuck you," Fenn snaps, and something in him sparks, and he moves as if to grab Theren by the shirt, only he isn't wearing one. Fenn seems to remember—Elegy assumes, anyway—that he just watched Theren beat a man bloody.

"Go on," Theren says quietly, and it's not clear to Elegy whether he's goading Fenn or inviting Maeve to continue speaking.

"It's not about freedom," Maeve says, ignoring them both. "It's about what else happens when you win the Tournament: you stand in front of Rava Vidar without her febra armor on."

"And then what?" Theren says. "You want me to kill her with my bare hands?"

"Obviously not. Let us worry about getting you a weapon at the right moment," Maeve says. "As for our qualifications, we may not be good fighters, but we can still help you train, research opponents, strategize . . . and you can ask Orda to help you with technique."

"Orda isn't going to agree to that. His responsibility to us ended after he stopped being our teacher."

"He'll agree if you promise him his freedom," Maeve says. "You already said it—Rava's not going to free any of us. That doesn't mean you don't still get to ask her for something when you win. So ask for Orda's freedom, instead."

Theren looks at Maeve like he's sorting through her. Elegy can feel it, too, how he feels first the weight of her sadness and then, pushing it aside, the hard edge of her determination. It's like listening for each instrument in a symphony, one by one.

"Even if I somehow succeed, this will kill us all," Theren says. "You realize that, right? None of us will walk out of that arena alive, if I kill Rava."

"Don't really care," Fenn says. "As long as Rava doesn't walk out, either." He raises an eyebrow at Theren. "But if you're starting to feel cozy here—"

"Shut up," Theren says. "I'll do it."

✦   ✦   ✦

The practice sword connects with Theren's rib cage, and he heaves so hard Elegy thinks he's going to vomit. He holds up a hand, yielding.

"I'm starting to think," he says, between breaths, "that the two of you only agreed to this so you could beat the shit out of me."

He sits on the wood floor, and looks up at Fenn and another man standing over him with practice weapons still in hand. The other man is taller than Fenn, but lankier, his gray-brown hair cropped close to his scalp. His skin is paler than Theren's, and his eyes are sleepy and thoughtful.

Orda, she assumes. Their former teacher. She wasn't expecting him to be older.

"You can't rely on your Fever ability to get you through the Tourna-ment," Orda says firmly. "What you can do is remarkable, but swords are faster than hand-to-hand, and—"

"Teacher," Theren says, "I know."

"He's not in charge of us anymore," Fenn says, wiping his forehead with the back of his wrist. His hair is long enough now to wear it in a knot. "You can call him by his name."

"I'm not surprised that one of the things you have failed to absorb about Talusar culture is the importance of addressing people with respect," Theren says, but he's smiling a little.

Fenn rolls his eyes, and steps away to drink water from a glass bottle in the corner. It's a gentler reaction than he would have had in the previous memory, Elegy thinks. Things must have softened between them in the interim.

Orda offers Theren his hand, and helps him to his feet. Before releasing him, Orda says, "Sometimes I think you've just forgotten my name and it's been too long for you to ask."

"You caught me," Theren says. "Orga, is it?"

Orda grins, and then his eyes shift to the clock over Theren's head. "Shit, I have to go. Don't forget to stretch and for God's sake, *sleep*. Big day tomorrow."

"For both of us," Theren says, and he looks at Fenn. There's an edge to his expression, something like fear. Orda nods, his mouth a grim line. He puts his sword away, claps Fenn on the shoulder, and leaves the small practice room.

It's a bare place, with worn wood floors and only febra glass burning copper here and there, powered by the Fever coursing through its inhabi-tants. The lights dim a little after Orda leaves. Theren puts his own weapon away, and steps backward into the middle of the room, beckoning to Fenn.

"Come on," he says.

"Fighting me alone isn't going to do you any good," Fenn says. "We both know you can beat me."

"It's not for me," Theren says. "Your opponent tomorrow is a tough one. I've fought him before, let me help you."

Fenn sighs, but he puts down his sword and follows Theren. His hands go up automatically to protect his face. Theren's hands are open, palms facing Fenn.

"All right," Theren says. "Hit me, if you can."

He's smirking. She's never seen him this way—confident, almost arro-gant, delighted by his own skill.

"Smug bastard," Fenn says, in English now that Orda is gone and it's just the two of them. But he steps and punches, hard. Not fast enough, because Theren's hand closes around his wrist, pushes down, and twists, so Fenn is doubled over beneath him before Elegy even registers the movement.

Fenn spits, "Let go of me."

"Power is not going to help you," Theren says, right next to Fenn's ear. "He's stronger than you. You have to be fast."

He releases Fenn and steps back.

"He's that much worse than any other opponent?" Fenn says.

"No. He's good, but not better than you are," Theren replies. "It's just . . ."

Fenn straightens a little. He has an odd look on his face. "You're worried about me."

"I'm always worried about you," Theren says hotly. "You and Maeve both."

"But . . . you hate me."

"Believe it or not, I've never actually hated you," Theren says. "Now try to hit me, and be quicker about it."

He puts up his hands. Fenn puts his up, too, but before he moves again, he says, "I've never *actually* hated you, either."

Theren smiles. Fenn punches.

+   +   +

"What are we doing here?" Fenn whispers, leaning close to Elegy's—no, Theren's—ear. They're in a crowded room with stone walls that she recognizes as belonging to the Crucible, only this isn't a fighting arena. The febra lights in the walls glitter like stars, and provide enough light to see a crowd of people dancing. In the corner, a group of musicians pluck and drum and sing.

"Maeve needs it," Theren whispers back, and he nods to her. She's picking three full glasses off a low table with both hands. She dodges someone's elbow on her way back to them.

When Maeve gets closer, Elegy can see that she's bruised and moving stiffly, like she's injured. A fight must not have gone her way. Or maybe it did, and this is just the aftermath.

"I have no idea what this stuff is, but we're drinking it," Maeve says, and she offers the glasses to each of them in turn.

As her fingers brush Theren's, Elegy can feel the frayed edges of her, as if she's on the verge of screaming.

"It's vado," Theren says. "It's made of sap and . . . something else, I don't remember. You've had it before."

He drinks it, and Elegy tastes it, sweet and green as a fresh-broken branch and so strong it burns her throat. Maeve makes a face as she swallows hers, but Fenn sips his, looking contemplative.

"You're like an encyclopedia of all things Talusar," Maeve says to Theren. "Do you know their dances, too?"

"No, but I know ours," he says, and he takes her glass and sets it down on a high table nearby. He offers his hand to Maeve, and they slip into the crowd.

It's a faster song now, and Theren moves capably through the steps of a dance Elegy only barely recognizes. Maeve stumbles along, laughing, though the expression looks painful, straining the cuts in her face.

"Thanks for this," she says. "I know you should be resting up for tomorrow."

"There are all kinds of ways to rest," Theren replies, but Elegy can feel how heavy he is—with fatigue, and maybe also with dread.

"Bet you can't get Fenn to dance."

Theren grins, and releases her hand. He walks up to Fenn, plucks the half-full glass of vado from his hand, and swallows it himself. Fenn glares at him, but Theren just slides the glass onto a nearby table and grabs Fenn's hand, tugging him toward Maeve.

"I am not dancing with you," Fenn says, but he follows anyway.

"Afraid I'll make you look bad?"

"Afraid I'll reveal my total lack of rhythm."

Theren just puts his hand on Fenn's side and steps closer. Fenn blinks up at him, like he's startled. Elegy doesn't need Theren's gift to tell her what that look means. It's all over Fenn's face.

"*Relax*," Theren says, laughing.

Fenn, still looking dazed, mirrors Theren's steps with his own, though he seems stiff and uncoordinated by comparison.

"See? Not a total embarrassment."

Fenn glares at him. Just as he's opening his mouth to give a sharp reply, his face goes blank. Distant.

"Fenn." Theren snaps his fingers in front of Fenn's face. "Fenn!"

"They're lasting longer than they used to," Maeve says, over his shoulder.

Theren doesn't look pleased. "Come on, let's get him out of here."

Maeve grabs Fenn's hand and pulls him toward the door. Theren follows, watching Fenn's tripping footsteps. They go down the hall, where the music is muted. At the end of it, Elegy can see two people moving against each other in a sensual rhythm, but they're otherwise alone.

Fenn blinks at Maeve, who's now tapping his cheek.

"Quit it," he says to her, after a moment. He sounds unfocused.

"What did you see?"

"Our parents," he says. "Crossing the desert."

Theren and Maeve exchange a troubled look.

"You're not going to be able to hide it forever," Maeve says to Fenn.

"Just another month, and then we'll probably be dead," Fenn says, with forced cheer.

"Or you could go live in a monastery, pampered and cared for—"

"No," Fenn says darkly. "If I do that, I'll be stamped with their seal, I'll go where they say, I'll do what they say—"

"Just like you do here!" Maeve brandishes her hand at him, showing him the single black bar tattooed between her fingers.

"There's more freedom in the Crucible than in the monastery," Fenn says. "At least here, I get to see you." He looks at Theren. "And you."

A warm, soft feeling—Elegy can't tell if it's Theren's, or Fenn's, or Maeve's, or if it's shared among them all.

✦   ✦   ✦

Another dark hallway—

Fenn stands with Theren beneath the dim glow of a febra light. Theren is teeming with nervous energy, bouncing on his toes. Fenn puts his hand on Theren's chest and presses him into the wall, gently, as if to steady him.

And then, a moment of hesitation—and Fenn steps even closer.

"Hey," Theren says softly. "Hey, what—"

"Just in case." Fenn touches his temple to Theren's cheekbone, and closes his eyes. "Just in case this doesn't go well—"

Elegy can hear the desperation in his voice, and she can feel it, too, in her own chest—the horrible itch of need. Theren stares at Fenn for a moment and then sets his hands on Fenn's shoulders—and slides them in, to the other man's neck, his thumbs touching just beneath Fenn's jaw to tip his head up.

He bends his head and kisses Fenn, softly. Fenn presses in, his hands on Theren's waist—

✦   ✦   ✦

Elegy walks alongside a horse in the desert at night. By the moonlight she looks to her left and sees Theren and Maeve atop the horse, Theren slumped

forward into Maeve, Maeve slumped back into Theren, like two cards balanced just so to keep the whole house of cards from tumbling down—

✦   ✦   ✦

In the hallway, she sees Fenn against the wall this time, Theren pinning
him to the stone and kissing his throat—the same occasion as before, or a
new one, Elegy can't be sure, and it doesn't really matter—

✦   ✦   ✦

"Focus," Tor says, back in the room in the Losan Stronghold library, his
hands tightening around Theren's skull. "Slow down, and focus."

✦   ✦   ✦

"Wake up." Orda's hand touches Theren's shoulder to wake him. He lifts
a lantern by its handle and sets it on a little table next to Theren's pillow.

Theren sits up, blinking sleepily at Orda. Elegy can't see anything about
the room except the two men's faces, a foot apart, the lantern light between them.

"What is it?" Theren says roughly. There's a bandage on his side, dark
circles under his eyes. Though he sounds confused, Elegy is getting better at reading his expressions, and he doesn't *look* confused. He looks re-
signed. Like he already knows what Orda is going to say.

"Fenn and Maeve were caught," Orda says. "This afternoon they snuck
out and tried to smuggle a knife into the Crucible, and they were discovered. I only just heard."

Theren sits up, swinging his legs over the side of his bed so he's facing
Orda. Orda stays crouched in front of him, his hands on either side of
Theren, braced against the mattress.

"What does this mean?" Theren says.

"Rava's guards suspected their intentions based on some of their other
behaviors. But Maeve confessed, and convinced them they were working
alone," Orda says. "We're in the clear. They'll be executed."

Theren covers his face with his hands.

✦   ✦   ✦

Then Theren's sitting on the edge of a bed, his fingers pressing into his eye
sockets. Elegy sits beside him. Her back aches, like she's been sitting there
too long without moving.

Where is she right now? And when? They're not in the Crucible, and
there are two bars tattooed on Theren's hand, so she knows this is later

than the last memory—yes, this has to be from when he was in House Vidar, only she can't imagine that a prisoner of House Vidar sleeps in this kind of room, simple but fine, the sheets silky and the bed frame carved—

Carved with vines.

She tries to place this Theren in the timeline. Both of his hands are tattooed, and she can see some of his ribs—he was healthier when he was in the Crucible, so this must be months after he moved to House Vidar, if not more. Old scars mark his bare torso. There are faded bruises on his side.

She hears the door open in the next room. Her entire body tenses in anticipation. He gets up, stiffly, and picks up his shirt, slung over the window seat. The fabric hangs around him like a tent. She follows him through the door.

The next room is bright, the huge windows on the far wall letting in the entire panorama of Valla below. Every other wall is covered with books. It smells like a library, with that same sweet mustiness, the scent of old paper.

Kesia Forint stands just a few feet from the doorway, as if she wasn't sure that she was allowed in. She's wearing casual clothes: trousers made of repurposed leather, a white woven shirt, old boots. Her hair is short, chin-length. She stares at him, and Elegy feels, through Theren, the interplay of her emotions—shame and relief and guilt and *God*, she suddenly doesn't care what else—for a few seconds before he shuts her out.

"What the fuck are you doing here?" he says to her.

"You've lost weight," she says.

Why are we here? Elegy thinks. *Why were you here?*

Theren looks toward the window, at the sunlight reflecting off the snowcapped peaks that surround Valla.

✦   ✦   ✦

Then Elegy is in a grand, bright hall.

Through the windows on either side of the room, Elegy sees the mountains with white peaks, the forests dusted with snow. Below, foot traffic in the streets of Valla has already packed it down and muddied it and turned it to slush.

Theren stands waiting in the middle of the room, looking worn and shabby compared to the polished blue tile. Orda is off to the side, his hands behind his back, also waiting. They exchange a look. Then the door behind Theren opens.

Elegy shudders to see Satka walking in first, looking exactly the same as she remembers, down to the chewed nail beds and the unwashed hair. Trailing behind her are Maeve and Fenn, bruised, hands bound, ushered along by Ranos.

Satka stops beside Theren and draws her sword. He tenses, but doesn't move as the blade touches his throat.

"Kneel," Satka says.

There are footsteps behind them, hard and steady.

"Now, now, Satka," Rava's low voice says. "There's no need for blades."

"I'm not going to kneel for you," Theren says—not to Satka, but to Rava, who walks past him. She's wearing the vest part of her febra armor, which is so polished Elegy can almost hear it humming. Her hair is tucked behind her ears.

Satka sheaves her sword. Theren and Rava stare at each other.

And then, Elegy is sorting through the layers of Rava Vidar.

She's not as chaotic as Elegy might have expected. There's stability in her, but she's rough, no polish, no ease. Elegy is surprised to discover a twinge of awkwardness, uncertainty. A flare of heat, deep within her, that she can't identify, and then, under all of it—

Fear. Not fear of Theren, Elegy thinks, or it wouldn't be buried so deep. But *fear*, nonetheless.

"You *will* kneel," Rava says to Theren, evenly. "One day, you'll do it because you're so used to it that it doesn't cost you anything anymore. But today, you'll do it because I have your friends in custody awaiting execution, and you wouldn't want to give me a reason to make their last hours more painful than they have to be."

She tips her head to the side, expectant. Theren glances at Maeve and Fenn. Maeve's cheeks are streaked with tears.

Jaw clenched, Theren sinks to his knees.

"Better," Rava says. "I'm surprised you're not begging for me to spare them."

"I don't ask for things I know I won't get," Theren says.

"Ah." Rava touches a fingertip to her mouth, considering him. "And you do *know*, don't you? That is what I hear about you, Forint. That the Fever shows you a person's heart. That you're never surprised. That no one is a mystery to you. A tremendous gift indeed."

Theren doesn't answer, but Elegy watches his labored swallow.

"For now, I appreciate it because it saves us time," Rava says. "I won't offer mercy to people who conspired to kill me. Your friends will die today. However, we do extend certain courtesies to those about to be executed. We allow them to choose how. And we allow them to choose *who*."

Theren sucks in a breath as it dawns on him, what this means, what she's not saying. Elegy brings a hand up to her mouth.

"No," he says. "I'm not going to *kill them*."

"Are you refusing?" Rava says. "It's your right to do so, of course. But I think your friends chose you because they would rather not die by an enemy's hand."

It almost sounds like kindness, Elegy thinks. She can tell it isn't cruelty, exactly. Rava looks curious—feels curious, like there's an itch she's desperate to scratch. Elegy thinks of Satka telling her that bad things happen to those who Rava Vidar finds interesting.

She clearly finds Theren interesting.

Theren slumps, bracing himself against the floor with one hand. "No. No, I'm not refusing."

Elegy marvels at it, then. How every time she thinks she's found the bottom of Theren's will to go on, he reveals there's another layer.

"Then you will prepare yourself," Rava says. "They die at sunset."

"No," Theren says, and he lifts his eyes to Fenn's. "Not him."

Rava looks amused. "Not him? And why not?"

Fenn shakes his head, but Theren is already speaking.

"Because he's an epocha," he says. "And it's forbidden to kill him."

Fenn looks stricken. Theren closes his eyes.

✦   ✦   ✦

The crackle of a fire. A plush, dark blue rug. Pale, bare feet walk across it to her, and she can't look up, because her head aches, her jaw *aches*—

"Look at me," Rava Vidar says, poisonous.

Despite the pain, Elegy's head lifts, as Theren's head lifts. He looks older, his cheeks sallow, his hair curling at the ears. They are years later, again. Both tattoos on his hands. Exhaustion in every part of his body.

Rava touches his chin, and her thumb comes to rest on his lower lip—

"Your friend Fenn is dead," she says.

✦   ✦   ✦

Theren, sitting in the chair in the library with Tor Kovek's hands on his head, lets out a soft moan, and brings his fist up to his mouth, biting down hard—

✦   ✦   ✦

Somewhere above them is the clamor of a crowd. Shuffling feet and the collective volume of hundreds of voices. Elegy leans against a stone wall, and Theren is beside her, his forehead against it. His hand bears two black bars, but the other one is blank. He's not thin and drawn, which means they must have gone backward again, back to the Crucible.

She looks intently at his face. How his breaths come in bursts. How, as the door opens to admit Orda, he opens his eyes to stare at the wall like he's trying to stare through it.

His eyes are beautiful, she thinks. A dark, rich color—chestnut. She's noticed it before, but not like this, standing so close to him.

"They tested Fenn," Orda says. "And they're taking him to the monastery now."

Theren nods, the rock scraping his forehead.

"He'll never forgive me," he says.

"You saved his life."

"He preferred death." Theren pulls away from the wall. "I don't want to feel your pity right now, Selio."

"I'm sorry about that," Orda says. "But I came to help."

Theren lets out a laugh that borders on the hysterical. "I'm about to execute a friend of mine in front of a fucking crowd. You want to *help?*"

"Yes." Orda stands by the door, his arms folded. He seems to be keeping his distance. "I assume you want to offer her a merciful end. Fast and as painless as possible. What you don't want is to make it worse than it has to be."

Orda takes a wooden dagger from his back pocket, and crosses the room to touch two fingertips to Theren's throat, right beside his esophagus, beneath his jaw.

"Bypass the esophagus," Orda says. "Push in at an angle." He replaces his fingertips with the point of the wooden knife, to show Theren the angle. "*Twist.* Commit to the movement, because it'll be much worse if you don't. Understand?"

Theren nods. Orda flips the knife in his hand, so he's holding the blunted blade, and offers it to Theren.

"Show me."

Theren takes the knife, and holds it to Orda's throat.

"You've done this?" Theren says softly.

Orda nods. "That's why I'm in here. A friend was very ill, and asked me for mercy. But she wasn't someone Rava was content to lose." He clears his throat. "It will feel worst tonight, when you try to sleep. It would be better if you weren't alone."

"I have no one left."

"You have me," Orda says, and he puts his hand on the back of Theren's neck. "I'm your friend. I always will be."

Theren bows his head.

Orda goes on: "Remember that this violence is a kindness. Maeve doesn't want to die alone. You bearing the horror of it for her—it's a profound gift."

Behind them, another door opens. Through this one, Elegy can see the arena floor—a larger, grander arena than she's seen in the Crucible before. The clamor of the crowd is louder now. A guard in febra armor stands waiting. Orda releases Theren's neck, and takes the wooden dagger from him.

Theren turns, and walks through the doorway. Elegy follows him past the guard and onto the polished wooden floor. She feels intense pressure from every side, the force of a thousand people bearing down on her through the Fever.

Standing in the center of it all is Maeve, dressed in a black shift, barefoot, her hair still wet from bathing. Whatever grand pronouncements of her guilt undoubtedly accompanied this occasion, Elegy thinks they've already been made, without Theren to hear them.

Guards flank Theren as he walks across the floor to Maeve. The crowd around them roars, but Elegy hears it as if through water. Theren reaches for Maeve, and she puts her hands in his. Terror fills Elegy, jagged and electric.

"I'm so sorry," Maeve says, in a rush of whispered English. "I needed to speak to you again and this was the only way, I'm so—"

"It's all right," he says, and maybe he would have said more, but Rava Vidar is walking toward them, surrounded by her own guards—Satka and Ranos among them. She's in full febra regalia, her yellow hair in a crown of braids, her eyes smudged dark.

"The condemned has requested a dagger," she says. The entire arena goes quiet at the sound of her voice. Elegy can't help but marvel a little. No one commands an audience quite like Rava Vidar.

One of the guards steps forward, and offers the dagger to Theren, handle first. It's a simple weapon, with a black handle, a short guard, and a straight blade. He takes it, and as he does, Elegy watches the guards behind him fan out in a semicircle, weapons drawn.

She wonders what he'll say—wonders what there is to say, in a moment like this.

"I changed my mind," Maeve says quietly, and she touches Theren's face. She leans in close to speak right against his ear. Elegy moves in close, too, so that she can hear.

"I want you to forget our plan. Survive instead," she whispers. "Please. Live, so you can go home."

She reaches for his hand, the one that holds the dagger. She lifts it up by the wrist, positions it over her throat. "Do it now. Before I lose my nerve and start begging."

"Maeve," he says, "you never lose your nerve."

He wraps his free arm around her waist, and presses the point of the knife to the side of her throat, just beneath her jaw. Their eyes lock together. He pushes the blade in and twists, in one strong motion, as committed as Orda commanded him to be.

He doesn't look away as she dies. Elegy wants to close her eyes, but that's not an option here, in this place—he saw it, so she has to see it, the blood gushing from Maeve's neck. Has to hear the cheering crowd that accompanies Maeve's end. Has to watch Theren sinking to the ground with Maeve still in his arms.

Has to *feel it*, in her own body, as the other woman dies.

25

Elegy opens her eyes to Tor's hands sliding out of Theren's hair. Theren collapses forward, catching himself with his elbows on his knees. He gasps. The room is silent except for the sound of his breaths. Behind him, Tor braces himself against the back of the chair, his head bowed.

Julia Martin—and Elegy can see the resemblance between her and Maeve, now, both gray-eyed and clever-looking—sits with her hands in fists on her thighs, breathing just as hard through a tight O. Silent, her eyes glittering with tears. Ivy has her arm across Julia's back, supporting her.

Julia stands, her body quaking—with anger, with grief, Elegy can't tell. Theren doesn't lift his head, but he slides out of his chair, coming to his knees in front of her.

He waits. Elegy waits.

Julia's tears spill over. She opens her mouth as if to speak, but no words come out. So she bends over him, takes his head in her hands, and presses a kiss to his crown.

Then she hurries out of the room, her hand covering her mouth.

✦   ✦   ✦

Elegy walks Theren back to his quarters, after—

After the others leave the room in a hush. After he seems steady enough to stand.

She leads him by the elbow, gentle fingertips pressed to gentle skin, until he yanks his arm away. The next time she looks at him, his eyes look clear, the sovallan worn off.

She's surprised by how badly the memories ache in her body, like they belong to her.

She leads them around the building to the orchard behind the barracks, the one just outside his window, and pushes through the back door. He follows her into his room.

"You can go," he says coldly.

She goes to the pitcher in the corner of the room, fills a glass of water, and offers it to him.

"Drink," she says.

He takes it, and sips.

"Are you going to pretend you didn't see it?" he says. "That you don't know?"

"I saw a lot. You referring to anything specific?"

He carries the water glass to his bedside table, then runs a finger along the headboard of the simple bed. She remembers, suddenly, the vines carved into the headboard of that bed he was sitting on, right before he saw Kesia. She wondered what a prisoner of House Vidar was doing in such a fine bed.

Why were you there? she wonders again, and then she thinks of Rava's thumb against Theren's lip, right before she told him Fenn was dead; she thinks of the vines etched on Rava's knife handle, on her boots, on Theren's hand—

"I'm referring to the memory of me in Rava's bed," he says, his back to her.

She feels cold. She can still feel him in that memory. His back ached from sitting there too long. His head hurt. He tensed *so hard* when the door in the next room opened . . .

"If you want me to pretend I didn't see it," she says slowly, "I will."

"What?" That gets his attention. He turns back to her and scowls. "After all you've seen—"

"What I saw is no more than I already suspected, based on what I saw in House Vidar."

"You already suspected." His hands are shaking. He nods, once, twice. "I see. You've already made some assumptions of your own." He moves toward her, slow, his voice lowering. "You think, what? Rava drugged me? Threatened me?"

"Is that what she did?"

"No." His voice stays low, his mouth curling into a smile. "I made the first move."

"I don't believe you."

"Believe me!" he snaps. "I knew that she wanted me, and I decided to take advantage of that. You don't have to care about someone to fuck them, you know."

She suspects he uses that word, harsh as it is, to shock her. It works. She presses her hands to her abdomen, an instinctive gesture to soothe herself, to steady herself.

"Okay," she says. "What did you get in exchange, then?"

He stares at her.

"Did you get . . . a position of respect? No, I guess you didn't. Even in the interrogation room, you spoke to her like a servant," she says. "Did you get untold riches?" She tilts her head. "Doubtful. I think it was much simpler than that—more food, maybe?"

She steps closer.

"More sleep?" she says, and then, carefully: "Less pain?"

His jaw tightens.

"If you tortured me, and I seduced you to make the pain stop," she says, "would you call me your lover?"

"Look at me!" he says, his voice loud, grating. He opens his arms. She does as he says, taking him in, all six feet and a handful of inches. And beyond that, broad and muscled and God, didn't she just see, firsthand, how deadly he could be?

He says, "How could anyone do something to me that I didn't want?"

The question makes her feel sick. She may not like him, may not forgive him for what he cost her, but she hates to hear him ask that question—as if his physical strength makes it so that no one can ever take his choices away.

"I'll call it—you in Rava's bed—whatever you'd like," she says. "It's not up to me to name the act for you. But you can't force me to condemn you for it, either."

It seems to deflate him. He was ready to fight her, maybe. Shock her some more. Or maybe he was just ready, so ready, to be guilty. He's probably been waiting for it since they got back. Holding this secret so close, and knowing that when people discovered it, they would hate him.

Hate him, for surviving Rava Vidar in every way possible.

"Is there anything else, or is that the worst you've got?" she says.

He sits on the edge of his bed.

"No," he says, after a few seconds. "There's nothing else."

She lingers in the doorway, unsure that she should leave him alone after an ordeal like that. His mind laid bare, his worst memories exposed to near-strangers. But she doesn't think her presence is much of a comfort, either.

She closes the door softly behind her, leaving him alone, in the dark.

26

All right, so . . ." Parin—Hela's friend, fellow Scout, and trustworthy confidant—scratches behind his ear. "Remind me again where the hell you found this thing?"

"In a cave north of here," Hela says.

They sit at the little table in the trailer, their knees touching. Between them is the plant Hela retrieved for Dr. Canterbury, who still has no idea that she was successful.

She's been friends with Parin since Keen died and she had to start making her own Scout friends instead of tagging along with him. Parin's Scout code name is "Incorrigible," which is at odds with his quiet, thoughtful personality—but it's not her job to criticize anyone else's Scout name, with hers being "Dreadful" and all.

Hela glances at the back of the trailer, where Elegy's old trunk still stands open, fabric spilling out of it. She had to dig deep to find white clothes for the erczet this morning. Hela wouldn't agree to an erczet if someone paid her—why invite pain that isn't yours into your mind? Life is painful enough already—but she's not Elegy.

Parin tosses his hair out of his eyes—a pointless exercise—and says: "And the windows are all blocked off because . . . ?"

Hela covered all the windows with heavy blankets and wood scraps that morning. "Because it doesn't like sunlight."

"It's a plant, though."

"Yeah. Tell me about it."

Parin nods, as if he's considering this. There's a tattoo on his neck—flowering branches that follow the contours of his throat.

"What happened the last time you touched it?" he says.

"I hallucinated." She frowns. "I think. I saw a woman, anyway."

"Was she hot?"

Hela smacks Parin's arm.

"What?" he says defensively. "If she was hot, isn't that evidence that you hallucinated her? *You* wouldn't hallucinate a woman who wasn't hot."

"Yeah, she was hot," Hela admits. "I just want you to observe me when

I touch the thing, and, I don't know. Be there to shake me if I go into a trance or something."

"Got it." Parin folds his hands in front of him. "Well—fire at will, Tausia."

Hela looks at the plant, stern. She's been handling it with gloves since the day she saw the woman, watering it sparingly and trying to keep it out of direct sunlight. She's still not ready to hand it over to Dr. Canterbury. For all she knows it's some kind of Talusar biological weapon, and it's dangerous in the wrong hands.

Maybe it's dangerous in *her* hands.

She shakes her head a little. It's just a plant. She props her elbow up on the table, and rests her fingertips lightly on one of the leaves, the one that's stretched out toward her like a reaching hand.

+   +   +

This time it's the woman she sees first, not the room she's in—lending some credence to Parin's theory that she's hallucinating. Hela hasn't been on a date in a really long time.

She's wearing gloves, the woman. Black ones, tight to her hands. Well-made—Hela knows quality when she sees it, though her own trailer is rickety and her pants are patched at the knees.

The woman is sitting at the edge of a stone path, in the same greenhouse she was in last time Hela saw her. Hela recognizes the lush vines dangling from the glass ceiling, and the white band that stretches across the sky beyond it—a day sky, this time, pale blue.

When the woman sees Hela, she jumps back, bracing herself on the stone path. She's dressed strangely, Hela notices—in layers that make no sense to Hela's eyes, leggings with long shorts over them, and a tunic over both, maybe a coat and a vest. All the fabrics are lightweight, their colors dark and rich and setting off her cream-colored skin nicely.

The woman comes to her feet. She's Elegy's height—above average, but not as tall as Hela. Her hair is such a dark brown it's almost black.

"Who are you?" Hela says.

"Be more specific," the woman says. Her accent isn't one Hela recognizes, but then, Hela has never spoken to any Talusar outside of Vidara territory.

"Okay," Hela says, drawing the word out. "Your name?"

"Akara," the woman says. "And you?"

"Tausia. But people call me 'Hela.'"

"Well met," Akara says, with a bob of her head. The response seems ingrained—good manners. If Hela had to guess, she would say the woman is high-status, but she's not addressing Hela like an inferior, and Talusar is always very specific about status. The terms she's chosen are the ones for uncertainty about social standing, and Hela knows she's being rude by using them right back—refusing to clarify—but she has no interest in telling this woman she's a poor Scout who is currently, at this very moment, sitting in a trailer.

"How are we here right now?" Hela says, gesturing to the greenhouse.

"The plant is facilitating it," Akara replies.

"Yeah, I figured that part out. But *how*?"

"I'm not sure about the exact biological mechanism that allows for it," Akara says, and Hela laughs.

"You're being intentionally obtuse."

"Yes," Akara agrees.

"Why?"

Akara brings a gloved hand up to her mouth, as if to bite her fingernails. Then she seems to remember the glove, and lowers her hand again.

"We have to be careful what we say," she says, "because there are those who see the future, and we don't want to reveal anything to them."

Hela puzzles over this for a moment. She doesn't want to sound like an idiot, but she has no idea what that means.

"Um," Hela says. "What? Are you talking about the augurs?"

"Augurs, yes." Akara looks relieved. "But they don't see all things at all times. Certain meetings, certain conversations, certain events—they prompt new visions. We must be careful not to provoke them. The less we say, the less risk there is of that happening."

Hela has a thousand questions to ask, and also none at all, her mind blank. This doesn't make sense. It feels like a dream.

"*Why* are we here?" she asks, eventually.

"I have a task for you, Hela," Akara says. "It's the only thing I'm permitted to reveal. The only safe thing to say, in a time when nothing is safe to say."

Hela stares at her.

"Find the one who makes it bloom," Akara says.

And the greenhouse disappears.

✦   ✦   ✦

When she opens her eyes again, Parin is sitting upright, his hands braced against the edge of the table. His eyes are wide.

"What?" she says. "What happened?"

"It got really bright and the leaves all reached for you at once," Parin says. "What happened on your end?"

"Hot girl," Hela says. "She spoke to me this time."

"In what language?"

Hela worries at her lower lip. "In Talusar."

Parin lets out a low whistle, and leans forward again, scrutinizing the plant.

"You've looked it up, obviously," he says.

"Obviously. The library had nothing."

"It seems to me you gotta find out more about this thing," Parin says. "Because if it's some kind of weird Talusar experiment, you have to tell someone."

She thinks of Elegy, who is right at this moment letting someone pour Theren Forint's memories into her mind. She doesn't want to add to Elegy's already considerable burdens.

"And if it's not a weird Talusar experiment?" Hela looks toward the back of the trailer, at the box of artifacts that Keen insisted were alien in origin. She thinks of the glowing band across Akara's sky, like the rings of Saturn.

"If it's not, then . . ." Parin shrugs. "You still have to know, don't you?"

Hela nods, looking down at the green-veined leaves of the mystery plant.

"I'll set up a meeting with the guy who gave me the job," she says. "Will you come with me?"

Parin doesn't hesitate. "You couldn't get rid of me if you tried."

27

Elegy considered flying into Losan to attend the meeting Larke invited her to—or summoned her to, hard to say. She misses the public square where she and Shir used to book a veil for just a few coins and then find a dank, sticky tavern afterward. Cedre doesn't allow much personal technology—quills, for messages, and a small selection of permits for private ships, but everything else is communal. The library, the news pavilion, the veils. It started as a way to conserve precious resources, but now it's a principle, as sacred as the Imbuing Pool. *We're in this together.*

She decides security is more important than nostalgia, in this case, since the summons is from Larke. So she goes to a veil in Losan Stronghold instead. She nods to the woman working the front desk in the administration building and walks the dim hallway, past a line of portraits depicting former Swords of Cedre, to reach the right room. She doesn't even pause next to the painting of her mother. No need to suffer unnecessarily.

The room is large enough to hold a group of ten, at least, and its walls, floor, and ceiling are all unadorned, but it's softly lit and warm. The veil stands in the center of the space, a simple metal arch with a shimmering curtain hanging from it. It reminds Elegy of a soap bubble.

She takes a deep breath, and steps through the veil. The veil fabric clings to her face, her hands. It wraps around her body like a blanket, a little stifling at first, and then the sensation recedes, and a line of ghostly, glowing figures appears in front of her.

She was expecting only Larke, so for a few seconds she stares at them, unblinking, as they resolve into familiar faces. There's Larke, of course. Her secretary. Generals Thompson, Saetang, and Okoro. *Their* secretaries. She seems to have walked into a very important meeting.

"—don't believe it's that simple," Saetang is saying. "The Talusar don't attack for no reason, even if we don't know what the reason is."

"They didn't take anything and they didn't kill anyone," Larke says. "We should offer our gratitude to whatever deities we do or do not believe in, and move on to more important matters."

She looks pointedly at Elegy. Larke seems to have abandoned their mother's affectation of dressing like she was in the army; she's wearing civilian clothes, pressed black pants and a starched white shirt. Pearl earrings. Her hair tucked behind her ears.

Elegy can't stop herself: "There was a Talusar attack where no one died?"

"There's a man with significant memory trauma, but otherwise nothing," Saetang replies.

"Then what was the point?"

"My question exactly," Saetang says.

"I did not summon you here to comment on military strategy, Your Grace," Larke interrupts.

There's a crease between Larke's eyebrows. Elegy is learning to dread that crease.

"I assume you summoned me for the same reason you invited me to the Evacuation Day banquet," Elegy says. "To be useful to you. Your Highness."

There's a bite to her words. She still hasn't forgotten how Larke dragged her up on stage to make her a symbol of the Restorationist cause. *Where we come from is where we belong*, indeed.

"'Useful.' Is that what you call it when one of my subordinates convenes a meeting of potential Talusar traitors without my knowledge or permission?"

It takes Elegy a moment to figure out what she's talking about: the erczet ritual. By "potential Talusar traitors," she means the parents of the former Knights of Cedre. And judging by the ever-deepening brow crease, Larke is *very* angry about it.

"The exiles—who, as far as I can tell, haven't done anything *potentially traitorous*—came here yesterday for a mourning ritual, Your Highness." Elegy keeps her voice level. "I didn't think I needed your permission for a mourning ritual."

"Describe this harmless 'mourning ritual' to me, then."

Elegy feels Okoro's eyes on her. Larke must have talked to her already. Larke must also already know what the erczet entails, or she wouldn't be asking.

"Erczet is performed when there's a witness to a loved one's death," Elegy says. "The memories of the witness are projected to the family of the deceased. In this case, Theren Forint was either a direct witness of all the Knights' deaths, or was informed of them, so I invited all the families to participate."

"Theren Forint is an asset of the Cedre government with significant knowledge of Rava Vidar and her associates," Okoro says, crisp. "You allowed his memories to be shared with civilians with no security clearance, without even vetting them first?"

Heat creeps into Elegy's face. "The Talusar exiles already have signifi-cant knowledge of Rava Vidar and her associates," she points out. "Julia Martin in particular served as House Vidar's memory healer before her defection—"

"All the more reason *not* to supply her with sensitive information now—"

"I participated in the ritual specifically to make sure that we had access to all the intelligence that could come from it," Elegy says. "I learned more from Theren Forint in one hour than your battering ram of a specialist did in days of constant interrogation."

"You wanted to make sure that 'we' had access. Right." Larke's hand tightens to a fist at her side. "Who do you think you're talking to, Elegy? I know there's no 'we' for you. There's only you, and what gets in your way, which in this case is the pesky responsibility of respecting the hierarchy of our government and military."

"I hid it from you because I was worried that if you knew it was possible to project Theren's memories, you would use it against him without even needing approval or oversight," Elegy snaps. "After all, we don't have any laws about using Talusar Fever abilities instead of truth serum."

"I see." Larke's voice has gone soft, almost soothing. "So you stepped outside of the law to keep me from stepping outside of the law. That makes perfect sense."

Elegy opens her mouth to respond, but she has nothing to say. She can feel her heartbeat behind her eyes. There's no real defense for what she did, she realizes that now. She was just so desperate to gain access to Theren's missing memory—to find out what it is he knows that Rava Vidar wants to keep hidden. She forgot that this wasn't a Scout mission, where the only important thing was getting the job done.

Larke must have made the same connection, because there's a look in her eye that Elegy doesn't like. It's the same look Hela gets when she sees a way to win at chess but doesn't want Elegy to know yet.

"I suppose I shouldn't be surprised that you think and act like a Scout," Larke says, and each word is so carefully weighed and measured that Elegy wonders if Larke has been planning to say this all along. If this is the whole point of summoning her to the meeting.

"Larke," Elegy says, warning.

"A Scout?" Okoro says. "Oh, right. Her father."

"Her father, yes." Larke's eyes meet Elegy's. "But she's been following in his footsteps for the past four years."

Cedre's military hates and scorns Scouts for operating outside of the law. If Larke wants to discredit Elegy in front of Cedre's military, to take away whatever social capital she has left after so many years in search and rescue, this is an efficient way to do it.

The silence that follows makes Elegy's chest tight with anxiety. Okoro looks like she found a bug in her food. Saetang avoids Elegy's eyes, their hands clasped in front of them.

Larke says, "You're not embarrassed, are you? I didn't realize it was a secret."

"If we could return to the issue at hand," Elegy says, fighting to steady herself. "The erczet ritual was part of a bargain I struck with Julia Martin in exchange for her help with Theren's memory. I believe what she can recover from Theren's mind will be of great importance to—"

"Julia Martin will soon be on her way to Austra to examine the witness to the Talusar attack that we were discussing when you came in," Larke replies. "Specialist Gylle will assess Theren Forint in the meantime, and if *she* approves of bringing in Julia Martin, we can revisit this discussion."

Elegy doesn't respond. She doesn't intend to wait for Gylle's approval in order to recover that memory—or Larke's. So there's no point in arguing.

Larke says, "I'll let you know when you can be 'useful' again, Your Grace. Until then, I suggest you make yourself scarce."

Elegy glances at Thompson, who gives his head an almost-imperceptible shake, and at Saetang, who still isn't meeting her eyes. Her face burns with humiliation. She wants to scream at Larke; she wants to tell her to go fuck herself. But she's not going to let Larke turn her into an impetuous toddler. She stands as straight as she can, her expression carefully neutral.

"Of course, Your Highness," Elegy says. "Though, as my *Scout* father used to say, sometimes when you leave a tool outside for too long, it gets too rusty to do its job."

Larke raises an eyebrow. Elegy gives her a respectful nod, and steps backward through the veil.

28

The sun is setting, and she leaves the Losan Stronghold cafeteria at a sedate pace, so it doesn't look like she's fleeing. Which is exactly what she's doing.

News of her Scout history has leaked from the meeting. One of the secretaries, maybe. If Elegy had to guess, she'd say Larke didn't count on this outcome—she wanted to compromise Elegy's authority with the other generals, but she didn't want the reputation of Cedre's prophesied beacon of hope to be widely tarnished. But there's no going back now. News is like a virus; once it starts spreading, it's almost impossible to contain.

Elegy just had a dinner meeting with Arias to discuss Specialist Gylle and the damage she'll inevitably do when she interrogates Theren next. All around them, soldiers stared at her and whispered. She felt like she was in primary school with the other kids spreading rumors about her father, all over again.

"You think the general would mind if I used the training room?" she asked Arias, as they returned their trays. She wasn't ready for the quiet trip back to Twentynine yet. She had energy to burn.

"El, he's the one insisting you step up, remember? I don't think he would mind if you started living in one of the rooms here."

He has a point. If anything, Thompson has seemed annoyed that Elegy wasn't demanding *more* power. But he might be angry with her now that he knows she conducted the erczet ritual on his base without telling him what it really was. He hasn't kicked her out yet, though.

They part ways at the archway of bougainvillea that separates the barracks from the training rooms. The sun is behind the mountains now, casting everything in moody blue light. A squirrel darts out of her path and disappears into a bird-of-paradise plant, which fills the air with the smell of pollen.

The training facility is empty during mealtimes, as usual. She goes to the end of the hallway to the biggest room—always her favorite, when she was a soldier—and a flash of movement catches her attention.

Theren is in the middle of the floor, alone. Instead of the oversized shirts he usually prefers, he's wearing a T-shirt with the sleeves bunched up around his shoulders, so his arms are bare. His feet are bare, too, his boots at the edge of the empty space with socks and laces tucked neatly into them. He holds a practice sword, a longsword made of synthetic material meant to imitate a real weapon's weight. She watches as he shifts from one defensive posture to another, bringing the sword up with both hands into high guard. He doesn't pause there, just turns and shifts into another, bringing the sword down and to the side.

His movements are fluid and controlled, the muscles in his arms standing at attention, his feet light and careful. It's almost like watching a dancer. Low guard turns to back right, which Theren turns into hanging right, fast, like he's flipping a knife in his palm. She has barely enough time to observe the angle of his elbow—perfect, of course—before he's moving again, just as quickly as before, abandoning fluidity for sharp, sudden movement. Inside left, the bottom of the sword tucked right under his armpit as if it's settled there a thousand times.

And it has, obviously.

She forgets about training—forgets about the whispers at dinner and the argument with Larke. All she can do is watch Theren Forint move.

But as he turns, he spots Elegy through the window, and drops the posture. Her stomach twists and she pushes the door open.

She hasn't seen him since the ritual. Since they argued about what his relationship with Rava really was. There's so much she wants to know about what she saw, about what happened to Fenn and Orda, about how Theren came to be a truthsayer in House Vidar, about what happened at the end of the Tournament.

Instead, she says, "Will you fight me?"

His eyes search hers. "If that's what you want."

She walks into the room, crouching next to his boots to untie her own. He puts the longsword away in the rack at the back wall, and stands facing it, considering his options.

She strips off her socks and pulls her hair back. By the time she's on her feet again, he's chosen two quarterstaffs. He offers one to her.

She takes it, and squares off with him. There's no reason to fear him. He's more likely to let her hurt him than the other way around. But standing across from him, she finds herself a little nervous. She's seen him fight. Not just in memory—in the flesh, blade in hand.

She pushes her trepidation aside and takes a swing at his arm. He's ready, blocking her blow just as soon as it lands, and then pressing her back with surprising force. She twists away with a grunt, and the fight is on.

She likes the quarterstaff. Always has. Her father taught her when she was a child, before moving on to the spear. He said a good Scout—and a good daughter of the Sword—is competent with at least one weapon, and she likes that a staff can become so many things. A shield and a sword. A lever and a trip wire. Another limb.

She lets it transform into all those things, sinking deep into instinct, so that she couldn't have formed a sentence if she tried. She's too busy watching Theren's feet, his hands, the shifting of his weight.

She's warm now, a trickle of sweat rolling down the back of her neck. She attacks with more force, testing him, teeth gritted. He sidesteps her, and she tries to catch him with his back turned away; he spins and blocks her, then swings hard at her staff so it goes flying across the room. She chases after it, bent, and picks it up in one motion; then she's on him again.

He swings at her legs, and she jumps, just barely clearing the staff. When she lands, she brings a blow down on his shoulder, but he's too quick, batting her aside. He seems to be getting better as they go, like a revving engine—driving her harder, faster, as he discovers how much she can handle.

Maybe that's *exactly* what he's doing.

"You're going easy on me," she says, breathless.

"Thought you wanted to let out some aggression."

"I did—" She swings; he blocks. She swings again; he blocks again. "I'm just wondering what would happen if you stopped going easy on me."

The next time she swings—fast—he blocks her and twists so she loses her grip on her staff. Then he brings his own staff behind her knee and flips her, hard, so she falls flat on her back.

She lays there for a few seconds, catching her breath.

"Well," she says. "I did ask."

He offers her his hand, and she lets him pull her to her feet. She drags an arm across her sweaty forehead.

She says, "Larke found out about the erczet, so she sent Julia Martin to Austra. She's insisting we get Specialist Gylle's approval before you can get your memory restored."

Theren stiffens, so Elegy adds, "I'll find a way out of it. I promise."

"You don't have to do that. I can find a way to—" His breath catches a little. "Make it work."

"No," she says.

She means to say something else. Maybe to explain why she won't put Theren in that situation again. Something about decency, about efficacy, about her experience with trauma recall—something reasonable. But she finds that the actual reason she won't let Specialist Gylle drill into Theren

Forint's mind again is because of Arias's description of the aftermath. Theren dissociating. Bloody knuckles, empty eyes. The little tremor in his hands. She didn't even see it herself, and she still hates the thought of it.

So she just leaves it at that. *No.* It's explanation enough.

"Something else happened to you," he says, and God, he always knows everything, doesn't he?

She shrugs. "Larke told everyone I was a Scout."

"Is that a problem?"

"The military looks down on Scouts. Thinks they're not trustworthy, not ethical, not . . . not people you give respect to."

He plants his staff on the ground and leans into it, one arm stretched high over his head. His shirt pulls up, too, showing a line of skin above his hip.

She tries to look away, but it's like a magnet, drawing her eyes to it no matter how hard she fights its pull.

"She did it because she's afraid of you," he says.

Elegy snorts. It's as much as Hela said the other day, as much as any news outlet has said—that Larke Rosyk fears the hold that Elegy could have, if she chose to. But Theren's dark eyes are steady on hers. That same brown that she looked so closely at in his memories.

"You forget who you're talking to," he says. "I'm neither guessing nor speculating."

Elegy replies, "Well, I'm not scary."

"To someone who enjoys their power, you are."

She scowls at him. "You think I'm making a play for Sword?"

"I think you don't have to." He nudges her staff, now rolling on the floor, away from them with his foot. "I think if you want it, it's yours. You're the Hope of Cedre, and your destiny gives you consequence."

She stares at him. She thinks of Shir telling her that what the augurs told her was a miracle. That he believed in her. There was awe in his eyes, and wonder, and it got him killed.

This isn't that. Theren isn't in awe. He's matter-of-fact and certain. She feels rattled, to be assessed so frankly by a man who sees too much.

"Don't call me that," she says.

"It's what you are, isn't it?"

Then he looks at her like he's peering into her, like he's staring into a microscope to see what she's made of.

"You don't believe it, do you?" he says.

"Stop doing that."

He demands, "You don't think you're the Hope of Cedre?"

"Just because you *can* invade my privacy doesn't mean you should."

He laughs, bitterly. "If you don't believe in the prophecy, what's the fucking point of anything?"

"It's my life, it's my *identity*, it's not your goddamn business—"

"It's everyone's business!" he says. "Because I've met the people who will be in charge if you fail, and I . . ." He laughs again, and it sounds more like a gasp, faintly hysterical. "I would rather die than live in that world, I would rather die."

"Then why didn't you?" she says, without thinking. She regrets it right away, her cheeks burning. But he only looks at her.

Stricken. He looks stricken.

"Forget it," she says. "Forget I asked, forget I came here—"

"No. No, I'll tell you."

He moves toward her, too quickly for her to pull away, and she's not sure she would have anyway. He touches her arms, just above her elbows. He's gentle, for a man so capable of violence, and then he's *right there*, warm and strong and bending to meet her eyes.

"When I met you, I was twenty and I had never been tested, I had never been afraid." His voice is rough, as usual, but quiet, like he's telling her a secret. "It tore through me like nothing I'd ever felt before, and I reacted to it like a child—no, even worse than that, like an animal."

She's transfixed by those dark eyes of his, which are fearful even now, the moment of his betrayal still as alive in him as Shir's death is in her.

"Since then, I have known much worse fear," he says. "I know that surviving as a coward is worse than dying."

He releases her arms, but doesn't back away, and neither does she, even though she knows she should.

"You hate me, and I'm glad you do, because I don't know what I would do with your forgiveness if you offered it," he says. "I'm not your Knight, because you won't have me, and I'm not bound by any oath, because the Fever swallows oaths, but neither of those things matters."

He touches his forehead to hers, the movement so sudden and so strangely intimate that she goes still.

"My life is still forfeit to you," he says. "My life is still yours."

The scent of him washes over her, sweat and lemon soap and mint, and then he pulls away, and picks up his boots, and walks out of the room without another word.

Elegy stands there, barefoot and silent, until the heat in her body subsides.

29

Hela doesn't like weapons. For one thing, she's not particularly good with them—she can throw a mean punch, but put a sword in her hand and it may as well be a kitchen knife, for all that she knows how to use it. But today she needs to get over it, because there's no way she's showing up at some guy's potentially creepy lair unarmed.

She felt the tug of a message earlier that morning, so early the sun was just clearing the horizon and Elegy hadn't even made the coffee yet. It took her three tries to get out of bed and pick up the quill. Elixir lit up orange spider veins along her arms, and she wrote:

> *Dreadful,*
> *I received your confirmation of retrieval with great joy, and will be delighted to host you at my home for the delivery of the plant. Please take precautions, as it is sensitive to sunlight. Attached are the coordinates.*
>
> *Sincerely,*
> *Dr. Canterbury*

There was no hurry to make the trek today, but she's between jobs and burning with curiosity. Parin volunteered to take her there, and he's a half hour late.

She's just shaking her sleeve down over her watch when the Hummingbird putters to a stop next to her parked Finch. She grabs one of Elegy's spears—spears are effective even if you haven't mastered the finer points—and the plant itself, covered in an old T-shirt to protect it from the sun, and leaves the trailer.

The passenger door of Parin's Hummingbird pops open. He's wearing a blue plastic visor for some reason.

"Hey there, sugar," he says. "Want to go for a ride?"

"Little old me?" Hela says. "Are you sure there's not some other girl you want to sweep off her feet?"

She sits in the passenger's seat and closes the door behind her. The plant is cradled in her lap.

"Who is this Dr. Canterbury guy, anyway?" Parin says, and he flicks one of the air vents so it's pointing at her.

The inside of his Hummingbird is covered in crumbs and wrappers. She tries not to think about what she might be crushing beneath her boots.

"Don't know, actually," she says. "He posted the job last week and it sounded weird and not too close to Talusar territory, so I took it."

"And then it started to connect you to a beautiful stranger. Are you going to leave it with him?"

"I don't know." Hela squeezes the plant tighter to her chest.

"You hear the rumor about the *Sundial*?" Parin says, his fingers tapping on the steering wheel. He could just set the autonav to take them to their destination, but she's never known Parin to sit that still for that long.

"What, that it was built by a society of aliens that have secretly infiltrated Cedre government?"

Parin laughs. "Nah—the Sword wants it converted to a museum, like she said on Evacuation Day. But the rumor is, the staff is just . . . not doing it, and hoping she doesn't notice."

"She's the Sword. She'll notice."

"Maybe, maybe not." Parin shrugs. "I'm not sure why the *Sundial* is in her purview anyway—she's not our only leader."

It's technically true—Cedre has a council of elected leaders called the Quorum who handle all the other aspects of government, resource distribution and the economy and transportation and criminal justice. But the Sword is in charge of the military, so for a nation at war, she's pretty much the queen of all the land.

"You ever think about trying to get on board the *Sundial* when it launches?" he says. "I hear they're still looking for people. You could be a janitor or something."

"The worst janitor they have," she says, with a laugh. "I don't know. I guess I'd go if Elegy went. But I'm kind of attached to this Earth."

"Yeah," Parin sighs.

It's where Hela and Elegy part ways. Elegy's always been interested in the *Sundial*, in finding out what else—and who else—is out there, in the end of struggling against the Talusar. She probably feels that way *because* of the prophecy. Wanting to stay on Earth, for Elegy, means believing what the augurs told her, means accepting that the weight of the world actually *is* on her shoulders. Hela doesn't blame her for refusing to believe that.

But Hela loves every inch of this planet. She can't imagine going to another one. And she thinks that whoever is out there beyond Earth's solar system is just as likely to mean Earth harm as they are to be friendly. Not worth the risk.

They fly for a while, Parin's fingers tapping like hard rain on the wheel, electronic music playing quietly over the speakers, the desert spilling endlessly beneath them. She's just starting to fall into a half sleep when she hears a chime.

"Getting close. You got an escape plan in case it goes sour?"

"Yeah. Fight my way out."

"Uh . . ." Parin raises an eyebrow at her. "How are you with that spear?"

"Good enough to stab a guy. You don't need to come in, if it sounds too exciting for you."

"Are you kidding? I am so goddamn bored."

He guides the Hummingbird lower to the ground, and then slows. Dr. Canterbury appears to live right smack in the middle of a junkyard, across a cracked road from a strip of ruins. She's hard-pressed to find an actual lodging amid all the rusting cars, piles of tires, and heaps of scrap as tall as a house, but eventually the collection of nonsense resolves into an actual concrete structure. She assumes that's where they're headed.

Parin parks next to the tower of old cars, and doesn't lock his doors, so they can make a quick getaway if necessary. Hela gets out, secures her spear across her back, bundles the plant under one arm, and leads the way to the good doctor's house.

The man himself pops up in the doorway before she gets to it. In some ways, he's exactly what she expected: rangy and worn, his skin browned by the sun, his unkempt hair tied back with a bandana. But he seems steadier than what she imagined—his eyes aren't wild, he's not twitchy. Good signs.

"You're Dreadful?" he says to her. She would be impressed that he guessed right, except she's obviously the one carrying the plant.

"Yeah," she says.

"Who's this?" he says, nodding to Parin.

"My friend," she says. "I'm not going into your house by myself, no offense."

"None taken, though we can just do the exchange here."

"That's the thing," Hela says. "I don't want money for this. I want information."

"Information."

She nods. "Before I hand anything over, I want to know what you know about it."

She expects resistance. But instead, Dr. Canterbury's eyes light up like a kid with a stack of birthday presents.

Well, shit, she thinks. She should have asked for money.

"I am always happy to supply information for seekers of the truth," he says. "Please, come in, both of you."

Hela glances at Parin, who mouths *seekers of the truth* at her, and together they follow Dr. Canterbury into his house.

The house is dark. All the windows are covered with black fabric. What little light there is comes from beneath: strips of light fixed to the edges of tables and desks, fish tanks, plant grow lights, a few glowing orbs on metal stands, lamps with hot wax bubbling up inside them, spotlights pointed directly at walls.

She's never been in a place with so much *stuff* in it. Most of it appears to be random: books stacked without any regard for subject or title, newspapers strewn across desks, plates and cups and mugs, computer keyboards, star charts, old photographs, busted clocks set to the wrong times, and in one corner, in one of the tanks, a rubber snake.

Dr. Canterbury leads them into the next room, which appears fractionally more organized than the rest of the house. In the center of the space is a table with junk arranged on it, mostly metal parts, but each one is labeled carefully.

The metal looks familiar to her.

Parin leans over the scrap, his hands clasped behind his back.

"Before I begin," the doctor says, "can I see the plant?"

"Sure." Hela carefully lifts the old T-shirt, exposing the plant to the dim room. The light from its leaves reflects in Dr. Canterbury's glasses. He lets out something like a gasp, and brings his hands together in front of his chest, almost like he's praying.

"My, my," he says. "How beautiful! I've only ever seen a cutting. May I?"

She doesn't want to give it to him, but she's not sure how she can avoid it. If she tries to abscond with it after he gives her the information she needs, things could get ugly. Surely there are weapons somewhere in this scrap heap of a house, and the man's reverence for the plant could easily turn to fervor.

Besides, it's *just a goddamn plant.*

She sighs, and offers it to him. He takes it in both hands, gingerly, and sets it on the table near the labeled scrap. He takes a small magnifier out of his pocket, and looks at the plant's leaves through it.

"What are you going to do with it?" she says.

"I'll run some tests," he says. "See if I can get it to propagate."

"Will you have to . . . remove its leaves?" She almost winces as she asks, thinking of all those leaves stretching toward her as if toward the sun, and the calming green glow of them.

"Several of them," the doctor confirms. "But the plant should rebound nicely. I was told they're very resilient."

Hela feels cold.

It's just a plant, she reminds herself. *It's just a* plant.

"You've seen one of these before?" she says.

"A mere piece of it," he says. "Over the years I've been gathering evidence, isolating its approximate location . . . but my resources are limited, you see."

Hela thinks of Akara telling her to *find the one who makes it bloom*. "The piece of it you saw . . . did it have any flowers?"

"No," Dr. Canterbury replies. "Why?"

"No reason. How long ago did you see it?"

"Over twenty years," the doctor says. He pulls away with the magnifier still in place over his eye, so one eyeball appears huge in his face.

"A little plant like this could live that long?"

"Yes," Dr. Canterbury says. "If it is, as I suspect, extraterrestrial in nature."

Hela raises her eyebrows.

"Extraterrestrial," she says. "You mean . . . an alien brought it here?"

Parin snorts, and tries to cover it by coughing.

"Are you skeptics?" Dr. Canterbury says. "A shame. I thought you were here for the truth."

"Well if I was looking for the truth, I wouldn't already know it, would I?" she says. "So why don't you tell me your theory? I promise my friend will be less . . . reactive."

She gives Parin a look. He shows her his palms in surrender.

"You have heard, of course, about the extraterrestrial theory of the Empty Time," Dr. Canterbury says.

"Um . . . no."

"Well, most scholars agree that the Empty Time resulted from a collection of global catastrophes—multiple epidemics and environmental disasters that dramatically reduced the human population on this planet, followed by a devastating attack on all digital records, which resulted in almost no information being stored from that time period," Dr. Canterbury says, and that's about what Hela learned in school, so she nods. "Good. Where scholars don't agree is in what exactly happened during the Empty Time that led to the dominance of the Talus family. Among the most puzzling mysteries: their language. The language bears no resemblance to any other language on this planet, so there's a theory that it's extraterrestrial in origin—carried here by an alien race."

"So you think the Talusar are descended from aliens?" Parin says. "Explains some of the fashion choices."

Hela can't bring herself to laugh at the joke. She's supposed to find this ridiculous, maybe. But given that she's just used a goddamn *plant* to communicate with a woman nowhere near her—*in Talusar*, no less—she can't find the humor in it.

"And then there's the launch," Dr. Canterbury adds. "I have footage of it."

"Launch?" she asks weakly. "Don't you mean landing?"

"I wasn't present for the landing, though evidence of it is scattered across this table," he says, gesturing to the scraps in the middle of the room. "They're not comprised of Earth materials. Your friend is welcome to examine them while I show you the footage, if you like."

Hela follows him through a narrow doorway framed with tinsel to a desk that takes up most of a little room. A grid of screens confronts her, lighting up all at once when he taps the keyboard. This kind of personal-use technology isn't legal in Cedre, so he must have pieced it together from old salvage on his own. She has no idea how all of it works, but after glancing back at her to make sure she's paying attention, he makes a video play on one of the screens.

"This is from deep in the desert, far outside of Losan," he says. "Between here and Valla. A little over twenty years ago."

The video was taken in broad daylight, so she can see the beige landscape surrounding it, the flat, dry ground that's so familiar in the Losani desert. Glinting in the middle of the screen is a gilded ship. The clarity isn't spectacular, but she can tell the shape of the ship is nothing like a Cedre craft—it's jagged and almost menacing-looking, not sleek like the Cedre military's Sparrows. She frowns. Is it a secret project of the Talusar? She wishes she brought an Eye to record this.

As she watches, a brilliant light surrounds the gilded ship, so bright it whites out the footage for a moment. And then in an instant, the ship is gone, the only sign of its presence the blackened ground it left behind. She stares at that scorched earth, baffled. She's never seen a Cedre ship leave that kind of mark when it launches, not even the large ones.

"You see?" Dr. Canterbury says.

"I see," Hela says. "My question is . . . how do you know it's not built by the Talusar, or a secret Cedre military project? Or even a development from one of the raiders—"

"Well, that was the first thing I considered," he says. "But that was before I found the scraps—they appear to be from some kind of launching apparatus, so they broke apart somewhere above Earth and scattered everywhere. And every analysis I attempted of their materials yielded strange results. Types of metal that don't exist, things like that."

"Incorrigible?" she calls out.

"This material looks weird as hell," he replies.

Hela chews on her lip. The launch footage is frozen on the bare, black ground where the ship used to be.

"Why were you out there?" she asks.

"Weeks earlier, I had met . . . a stranger in distress," he says. "A Talusar man, or so I assumed. He saw my tool belt and asked me to help him build something. I worked for the military, then, and decided it was better to play along than to communicate any suspicions to him. So I helped, and I managed to get a few recordings as proof. But when I took them to my commanding officer . . ." He scowls. "He mocked me. Close-minded boors, the lot of them . . ."

"You know, they really are," Hela says. "Do you mind if I replay part of it?"

The doctor opens his mouth to object, but Hela is already bent over the keyboard, moving the progress bar back so she can watch the launch again. It happens in only an instant, like it disappeared into thin air rather than pulling away from the ground.

She notices, then, that the progress bar has more time left on it than she thought. She advances the footage, and that's when she sees a woman standing near a rock formation, not far from where Dr. Canterbury is recording.

"Who's she?" Hela says, pointing.

Dr. Canterbury clears his throat. "I encountered her at the launch site. I assume that she, like me, was drawn by some kind of signal and went to investigate—"

Hela frowns. The woman is tall, like Hela herself, with dark hair.

"Did you speak to her?" she says.

"I may have."

Hela raises her eyebrows at the doctor.

"I don't mean her any harm," Hela says. "I'd just like to ask her a few questions."

"I don't think you'll be able to get in touch with her anyway."

"Because she's Talusar?"

Dr. Canterbury looks wary, guarded. "I didn't know she was Talusar at the time."

"I'm not . . . *accusing you*." Hela rolls her eyes. "Do I look like a Peace-keeper? I don't care if you get a beer with her every Wednesday."

Dr. Canterbury sighs. He adjusts the bandana holding his hair back.

"I don't see her anymore," he says, defensive. "I knew her before it all happened—"

"Before *what* happened?"

"Before the attack on the Getty!" Dr. Canterbury rubs the back of his neck. "I didn't know she would turn out to be—"

"Oh." Hela looks at the woman in the video, standing by the rocks with her head tilted up to the sky. "*Oh*. She's Kesia Forint, isn't she?"

She can't help it—she laughs. And then she stops . . . and laughs again.

✦   ✦   ✦

She's outside in the desert sun, dust clouds rising up around her boots, when she realizes:

She can't leave the plant there.

"Parin."

"Yep," he replies.

Together they turn around and walk right back into Dr. Canterbury's house, right through the first room with its grow lights and orbs and hot-wax lamps, and into the second room where the plant sits on the table amid all the metal scraps. Dr. Canterbury is at his wall of screens until he hears them come in.

"Did you forget something?" he says.

"I did, actually. Parin?"

Parin picks up the plant from the table as Hela tugs her spear free from its holster and points it at the doctor.

"I'm sorry," she says. "But I can't let you hurt it."

"I'm sorry, too," Dr. Canterbury says, and he reaches under his desk to take out . . . a gun.

For just a moment Hela stares at it, marveling. Guns haven't been in regular use for a long time, since they're ineffective against Talusar armor. In Cedre's more lawless years, they were popular among the criminal el-ement for use against fellow Cedrae, but Peacekeepers cracked down on that harder than anyone likes to admit, and now . . . she's never seen one in person.

But she's familiar with the concept.

She knows she should put her hands up and give him anything he wants. That's what you're supposed to do when someone points a gun at you; even Hela knows that. But instead she follows her instincts.

"Run!" she screams at Parin, and she throws her spear at Dr. Canterbury.

She doesn't have good aim. The spear flies only a foot before it stabs down into the doctor's boot. The gun goes off, so loud it sounds like the world is coming apart, and Hela is running, her arm over Parin's shoulders to push his head down.

Above her, a light bulb shatters and the bits of glass prickle in her hair, but she keeps running. She and Parin sprint across the junkyard, and the gun fires a second time as Hela wrenches open the driver's side door and heaves her body inside.

The windshield of the Hummingbird shatters, but she's already powering the ship on. In the passenger seat, Parin is hunched over the plant, protecting his head. Hela looks back for just long enough to see Dr. Canterbury with his gun in the air and a trail of bloody footprints behind him, and then she's launching, and flying as fast as she can in the direction of Twentynine.

"You all right?" she shouts at Parin, over the howl of the wind through the broken windshield.

"Just exciting enough!" he calls back.

30

"YOU did *what?*" Elegy demands, and across from her, Hela sighs into her whiskey.

Elegy has been in the trailer in Twentynine since last night, when she came home from Losan Stronghold too agitated to sleep. Hela was already passed out, so Elegy went outside to pace, rubbing at her face to get the sensation of Theren touching his forehead to hers out of her mind, out of her *skin*.

It didn't work.

Hela gave her a distraction this afternoon. She turned up with Parin in a Hummingbird with a shattered windshield, the plant she was supposed to be returning buckled into the passenger seat like an infant. She just confessed to the whole caper, including the part where she threw one of Elegy's spears at a man's foot and ran away without retrieving it.

"You," Hela says, and it sounds like she's struggling to stay calm, "do *not* get to lecture me about taking risks without informing you first."

Elegy bites down on her lip, and drinks the rest of her whiskey in one gulp. She can't stop fidgeting. It's gotten worse since yesterday—word of her dropping out of the army to become a Scout has hit the news pavilions, and even though the general public doesn't have the same distaste for Scouts that the military does, it's a move that doesn't exactly scream "emotional stability." The worst of the rumors speculates that the Getty attack sent Elegy into full mental collapse, whatever that means.

So it's almost a relief to find out Hela believes in an alien landing now.

"Fair enough," Elegy says, finally. "But . . . do you really think it was an alien ship?"

Hela runs her finger around the rim of her glass.

"If I tell you . . . are you going to accuse me of turning into Keen?" There's something vulnerable in her voice that startles Elegy into stillness.

"No," Elegy says, like it's an oath.

Hela leans back in her chair, still running her finger around the rim of the glass, until it sings a low, mournful note.

"The idea of an alien ship sort of . . . pieces things together for me," she says, after a long pause. "The way I saw that woman by touching a damn *leaf*, the way all those scraps Keen collected were made of nothing I can identify, the way that ship in the video launched . . ." She shrugs. "If there was an *otherworldly* person here, on Earth, that would make sense of all of it. Someone who planted the plant. Who launched the ship. Who knew Akara."

Elegy can't pretend she doesn't see the logic in it. And it's not like they don't already know there are people out there, people capable of communicating with them.

"What confuses me is Kesia Forint being at the launch," she says. "She was a soldier before she came to Cedre. So her being there says 'Talusar military' to me."

Kesia was a soldier before Cedre—and now after Cedre, according to Theren. What if she was a soldier *during* Cedre, too? Some kind of sleeper agent, placed in Cedre to activate at an advantageous moment—or a spy, sent to look into Cedrae technology? What if the ship was just a secret project they'd been developing all this time?

"I don't know," Hela admits. "Both theories seem plausible to me. But either way, I'd like to talk to Kesia Forint."

"Yeah." Elegy's voice comes out sounding hollow. "So would I."

Hela finishes her whiskey, and taps the empty glass against the edge of the table. "Well . . . what if we can?"

"What do you mean?"

"You said she sent a message to Isre," Hela says. "If we can trace that message back to its origins, we could send a response. Arrange a meeting."

"If this is some kind of long-term Talusar plan that's brewing," Elegy says slowly, "then we need to know what Kesia knows. But we have to be careful. She reached out to Isre after four years of silence for a reason, and we don't know what it is, or what she wants."

"So we find out . . . and then arrest her and try her for crimes against Cedre."

Elegy shakes her head.

"I want to say yes," she says. "But that's what a Peacekeeper would do, or what the Sword would do. Not what a Scout would do."

Hela sighs. "'Never burn a bridge—'" she begins, quoting their father.

"'That's still getting you somewhere,'" Elegy finishes. "Kesia's a link to Rava Vidar. She's not a predictable link, but she told Isre Theren was alive, so she seems to be willing to at least *pretend* to be a go-between. It would be bad strategy to take her out of play. Better to make use of her, if we can."

"I'd rather throw her directly into the sun. But okay. So?"

Elegy rubs a circle between her eyebrows. "So . . . find a way to contact her and set a meeting. Please."

Hela nods, and with a quirk of a smile that she almost means, says, "Is that my sister giving me an order, or the Hope of Cedre?"

Elegy glares at her. Hela winks.

"Just kidding. You're always both."

Hela gets up and takes Elegy's empty glass to the sink, along with her own. She's rinsing them both when she asks, over her shoulder, "Did you hurt yourself, or something?"

"What?"

"You keep touching that spot."

Elegy takes her hand away from her forehead, from the place between her eyebrows where Theren's skin burned into hers. *My life is yours.*

How dare you? she wants to demand. *How dare you say that, how dare you lay a hand on me, how dare you spit my emotions back at me, how dare—*

"The memory sharing, during the erczet," she says. "Is it supposed to . . . stay with you?"

Hela seemed surprised when Elegy told her she was going to do the erczet ritual. When Elegy asked her why, she only said that she wouldn't want to see four Knights die. But now Elegy is wondering if there's more to it than that.

Hela picks up one of the cat figurines on the shelf next to the sink. It's one of the realistic ones, painted to look like a tabby. She's turning it in her hands when she faces Elegy.

"It's intimate," she says. "Like you didn't just share a memory, you shared . . . a body." She runs a finger over the cat's ears. One of them is broken from the time Elegy knocked it off the shelf. Hela doesn't like to revisit the past, so Elegy doesn't move—if she moves, Hela might remember she doesn't talk about this sort of thing. What she learned among the Talusar. What her life was like there.

"They usually do erczet after battle, when one soldier survives and another doesn't. They say it heals what's broken between people," Hela says. "Some people praise the Fever for that, like it's an act of God. But my mother told me it was just what happened when you'd lived under someone's skin."

She turns, and sets the cat back down.

"That's not an easy phrase to translate into English," she says, "but you know what I mean."

"Yeah." Elegy is rubbing her forehead again. "Yeah, I do."

31

When Theren finally remembers something useful, it's not about that strange blankness in his mind that Julia Martin was supposed to help him fill before Larke sent her away. And it's not about Rava Vidar's big plan that casts a shadow over everything. Instead, it's about Ykev Talus, son of the emperor.

Theren dreams about it. Dreams about rain drumming on the windowsill of a dark sitting room in Rava's mother's house—and that explains why he struggled to remember this, because so much of what he experienced in Ileth Vidar's house was her layering false memories into his mind like icing into a cake.

In the dream, the air is close and hot and smells of petrichor. He runs a finger along the wood to catch some of the water. Behind him, a door opens, and he turns to see a man.

The man is older than Rava, but not by much. He's handsome, his face tan and his hair a light brown swoop over his forehead, threaded with gray. He has a strong jaw, and there's something familiar about him.

He reminds Theren of Rava's mother. Ileth.

Sitting on the sofa near the fireplace—full of lanterns, then, since it's too hot for a fire—is Rava, her hair loose around her shoulders. She wears a lightweight dress with wide sleeves.

"Ykev," she says. "It's so good of you to join me. I worried your feud with my mother would prevent you from so much as glancing in this house's direction."

Ykev Talus. Fear rises in Theren's throat like bile. Ykev Talus is the probable heir to the emperor's throne. Ileth Vidar's greatest rival.

"Your mother is at dinner with my father at the moment," Ykev says. "So I felt I was unlikely to run into her. Though she has more to fear from that altercation than I do, I assure you."

Theren isn't sure whether to believe that or not. Ykev doesn't have a reputation for showing mercy any more than Ileth does, but he's more straightforward. The kind of man who will stab you in the front instead of the back. If Theren had to choose an opponent, he would choose Ykev, but there's no relief in the thought.

Rava shrugs at the implied threat to her mother. Ykev's eyes shift to Theren—and to the vine tattooed on his hand.

"I see you've picked up your mother's affectation of marking her territory," Ykev says, and he crosses the room to Theren. He bends down, seizes Theren's hand, and twists until pain shrieks down Theren's arm. Theren bites back a scream.

"I thought we agreed no weapons," Ykev says, leaning closer to Theren's face.

"Come now, cousin," Rava says. "I bring you something nice to look at, and you try to break its wrist?"

Her voice is light and careless, but Theren feels the sharp twist of fear in her gut. It's different from his own low-level terror.

"Something nice to look at. Really." Ykev releases Theren and straightens.

Rava says, "Get up, Theren."

Theren's face is hot with humiliation, but he stands in front of the windowsill, the rain at his back. Ykev stares at him, his eyes like an unwelcome touch.

"Not bad." Ykev shrugs.

"He's a Knight."

Ykev's demeanor changes. Relaxes. He looks back at Rava, a smile playing over his lips.

"I heard rumors. I didn't know you'd actually succeeded in taking them from Cedre."

"They're dead, except for this one." Her answering smile is like the slash of a knife. "You asked me if I'd ever accomplished anything without my mother. Well, I invaded Losan. I murdered the Sword of Cedre. And I took her Knights. Here's the proof."

Ykev turns away from Theren, and sits across from Rava. "You have my attention. What is it you're proposing?"

"A temporary alliance intended to achieve a particular purpose."

"A particular purpose?"

Rava focuses on Theren. "Go. This discussion isn't for Cedrae ears, even if you're barely a Cedrae anymore."

Theren doesn't hesitate. He crosses the room and walks out the door. The hallway beyond is empty and airy, with polished wood floors and sturdy exposed beams in the ceiling. Everything smells like flowers.

He tells himself he doesn't want to hear what Rava is concealing from him, but he's already turning to press his ear to the door.

At that moment, a woman with bright red hair turns the corner up ahead. She wears Talusar military dress, with the symbol of Ykev's army stitched over her chest in copper. Theren lurches back from the door as soon as he sees her, but judging by her raised eyebrow, she knows what he was doing.

"You're Commander Vidar's," she says.

His face heats. He wants to say no, no he isn't, he's no one's, least of all Rava's. But the symbol tattooed on his hand says otherwise. And really, what's the point in pretending his life still belongs to him?

"Yes," he says.

"I'll walk you to her quarters, then," the woman says. "Come."

The hallway dissolves into nothingness. It's as if Theren is walking over a ravine. His stomach drops, like he's falling, and then he wakes.

There's a hand on him. His stomach lurches. He wants it gone; he wants to pull away from it. But he knows the cost of doing that too well. So he goes still, instead, and tries to keep his breaths quiet so she won't realize he's hyperventilating.

But then the hand withdraws, and he realizes that Rava Vidar never felt like this, like something warm and light. Ciro Arias crouches next to the head of the bed, his hands clasped in front of him where Theren can see them. His brow is furrowed with concern, but he keeps his distance.

"I'm sorry," he says. "I couldn't figure out the best way to wake you, but we've been summoned by General Thompson."

Theren turns on the lamp on his bedside table and sits up. The blankets are tangled around his legs, so it takes some effort to dislodge himself. He's wearing the loosest shirt he could find in the Losan Stronghold supply closet and a pair of drawstring pants; he has to change.

He grabs what's nearest and goes into the bathroom to get dressed and brush his teeth. The dream is still clinging to him—the feeling of rain on his fingertips, the pain in his wrist when Ykev twisted it. He shakes out his hand, like that will dispel it, and picks up his toothbrush.

By the time he leaves the bathroom, he feels more alert. Arias is standing by Theren's bed, leafing through a book of poetry Theren picked up from the Losan Stronghold library. It's a Cedrae poet from the Oneiromantic Period.

"This poem is pages long, and it's just about the petals of a lily," Arias says. "I've never thought that hard about anything in my life."

"Well, when the Oneiromantics were writing, Cedre had just restored the relics from before the Empty Time," Theren says. "They were afraid of what relying on technology would do to people, so they focused on the natural world, instead. Sometimes they focused a little too hard."

Arias gives him an odd look, and Theren feels, for a moment, like he's twenty years old again, a library custodian who was so desperate to be a university student that he followed along with the Talusar Poetry in Translation curriculum on his own time. It's a version of himself that he thought was long dead, killed by Fever and four years in Valla. Not as dead as he thought, it seems.

Arias asks, "Did they also romanticize dying of sepsis? Because before we got Imbued, a lot of people died of sepsis."

Arias sets the book down, and they walk down the hallway to the back door. The air is cool; it makes goose bumps prickle over Theren's arms. The sun is a long way from rising.

They walk to the administration building and down the empty, dark hallways to General Thompson's office, identifiable as such because the lights are on. The space is warm and busy, all the furniture the same polished orange wood, all the surfaces cluttered with keepsakes—sculptures shaped by child hands, notes in a child's scrawl, a line of mugs that declare him to be the world's greatest father. The man himself stands at an obsidian that's projecting a map; Theren doesn't recognize it, and his gaze doesn't linger on it. Because standing across the obsidian from General Thompson is Elegy.

He hasn't seen her since that day in the training room, the day he made a declaration she neither asked for nor wanted. *My life is yours.* Not a promise, and not an offering, but a fact, as sure as their planet's revolution around the sun.

He always tries not to read her. The sight of him tends to bring grief to the surface of her, like oil beading on water. And now, after she's seen his memories . . . if she pities him now, he doesn't want to know.

So he only skims the surface of her, now. Feels turmoil in her, and panic.

"Arias, Forint," General Thompson says. "Thank you for coming, I apologize for the hour."

Arias salutes the general, and touches Elegy's shoulder in greeting. She's staring at the map, her brow furrowed. She doesn't look at Arias, just covers his hand with her own, briefly, to acknowledge him.

"Show me where the ship went down, again?" she asks.

"What ship?" Arias folds his arms and looks up at the map.

Theren is suddenly aware that he's the odd one out. The only one who isn't in the military, and never has been. The only one who can't use most Cedrae technology. The one who's barely a Cedrae citizen, barely trusted, barely useful. He stands back, unsure of his welcome, and waits to be told why he's here.

"Julia Martin's ship went down on the way to Naarm," Elegy says, and a red light appears in the map projection, right off the coast of a land mass Theren now recognizes as Austra. "She was supposed to see if she could heal the memories of a witness who saw the recent Talusar attack on the base. The one where the Talusar didn't steal anything or kill anyone."

"Sounds like the Talusar didn't want Julia to fix that witness's memories," Arias says. "How long has it been since the ship crashed?"

"Two hours," Elegy says. "Our people have been keeping an eye out. So far no ships have launched, and there are no boats along the coast. So we don't know how the Talusar plan to get Julia off the continent."

General Thompson's gaze fixes on Theren. "That's why you're here, Forint."

"I—" Theren's voice comes out rougher than usual. "I'm not sure how I can help."

"You were kidnapped from Cedre territory and brought to Talusar territory in an operation planned by Rava Vidar," Thompson says. "We suspect this attack on Julia Martin was also planned by Rava Vidar, so it's possible she'll use some of the same strategies."

"And if she doesn't?" Theren asks.

"We can't guarantee we'll be right," Elegy says, with the tone of someone who's said this phrase before, or maybe heard it before, over and over again, until it became part of the fabric of her. "But we have to pick a path anyway."

She looks over her shoulder at him, and as grief spikes through her he realizes it must have been Shir who said that to her. Not Shir her husband, though—Shir her commanding officer.

"Okay," Theren says, and he steps closer to the obsidian, looking over Elegy's shoulder at the projected map, at the red dot that represents Julia Martin.

"After the Getty attack . . ." Theren begins, and Elegy stiffens.

Theren remembers the feeling of grit on his clothes, dirt and sand in every fold of skin; he remembers the bounce of the horse's steps and sitting so close to Maeve that his sweaty shirt stuck to her. He swallows down his shame at the memory of his own cowardice, the way it pricked at him and still pricks at him, and continues, "After the Getty attack, we traveled at least one hundred miles on horseback. Mostly at night."

"Where did you go?" Elegy asks. "Do you remember anything about the direction you traveled? The landscape?"

Theren tries to think about the angle of the sun, coming up over the distant hills—and then, when there were no hills left, just burning over the flat horizon as they stopped to sleep.

"Into the desert," he says. "Northeast, I think. And then—there were ships waiting for us, parked in the middle of nowhere. They flew us to Valla."

He feels Arias's eyes on his unsteady hands. Theren's hands always give him away. He crosses his arms.

"So if this kidnapping is orchestrated by Rava, as we suspect," Elegy says, "she's stashed a ship somewhere outside of Naarm, and they're headed there on foot."

"The question is *why*," General Thompson says. "Why not have the ships land somewhere close? Why travel such a long way to reach them?"

Theren says, "She's playing to her strengths."

"I'm sorry?"

But Elegy is nodding at him. "The Talusar fight better on the ground. Their ships are slower than ours. Let's say Rava has a Talusar ship pick Julia Martin up right next to Naarm. We would launch in minutes, and catch up to their ship before they can even reach top speed."

She's getting more animated, gesturing as she talks. Her hands are elegant, for a soldier, for a Scout. Thin fingers, almost delicate.

"But if the pickup point is far enough away from our base and close enough to the Talusar border, her ship has a better chance of crossing into Talusar territory before we can catch her in the air. And we can't pursue her across the border without asking for huge casualties."

It's true that Cedre soldiers are no match for the Talusar on foot. Everyone knows that. Important Talusar soldiers, like the ones Rava would assign to this mission, all wear febra armor. Febra armor, when worn by a Fevered soldier, channels the energy that a Fevered body produces into a shield. The shield renders projectile weapons like bullets or arrows useless. So a Cedre ship can't do much damage to a pack of Talusar foot soldiers. Instead, they have to land and engage the Talusar on the ground, where they're always outmatched.

"So," Arias says, picking up on Elegy's logic, "Rava stashes a ship as close to the nearest Talusar border as possible, and then . . . her soldiers travel there, knowing that if we do happen to find them—which is unlikely—we'll have to engage with them on foot, where we'll be at a disadvantage."

Elegy nods. "What's the closest Talusar border to Austra, and how long will it take Julia Martin's captors to walk there?"

"They won't be on horseback?" Arias asks.

"For a last-minute mission on Austra? What would they do, catch feral ones and tame them?" Elegy says. "Doubtful. I think they're on foot."

General Thompson touches the obsidian with his first two fingers, and the map changes. Suddenly they're looking at the southern hemisphere, and the general is pointing at a large island south of Austra.

"There's a Talusar settlement on that island. Small, but once they get to it, they would be out of our reach," he says. "It would be a short flight. I can ask Austra to fly along that border, but—"

"But we don't want Rava to know we've figured out their plan, or she'll change it," Elegy says. "How long do we have? How long a walk is it from the crash site to that pickup area?"

Arias holds one finger over the red dot that symbolizes Julia Martin's crashed ship, and another finger over the point on Austra that's closest to the nearest Talusar border. He squints.

"Half a day's walk, maybe," he says.

Theren thinks of the journey through the desert again. The heat rising up from the land, even though the air was cool after dark. He thinks of reaching that place in the desert where his mother revealed herself to be a traitor, the two Sparrows perched side by side nearby. He never had much hope for escape. But once he was in the ship, he knew he was lost.

"Prioritize finding the ship," Theren says, and he's aware, suddenly, that he's standing a little too close to Elegy, speaking over her shoulder. She's tense, her face angled just slightly toward him, so he can see the edge of her cheekbone. He steps back, and adds, "If you get to their stashed ship before they do, you can ambush them. Once they're in the air, though, they're gone."

"Find the ship," Elegy says, and she laughs. "Do you know how big Austra is? Finding that ship is like finding a single hair on a person's head."

"Not really, though. We know the area she'll launch from. That narrows things down," Arias points out. "And you and I are experienced at finding good launch spots."

"Let's go, then." She pauses, and gives General Thompson a hesitant look. "That is . . . if the general approves."

"You're not a soldier," General Thompson points out to her.

"But I am the right person to do this," she replies. "And you know that."

General Thompson sighs.

"As it happens, General Saetang invited you to Naarm Stronghold to review all the evidence they have of that Talusar attack. They said your . . . *Scout expertise* would be helpful," he says. "And they asked me if I would let someone fly you there. I doubt they'll monitor your flight path. So if you just *happen* to fly over a parked Talusar ship and then find yourself in the midst of a skirmish—"

Elegy grins.

"I'll have someone wake up Parekh," General Thompson says. "How many people do you need?"

"Well, Arias and Parekh, of course. And . . ."

Then Elegy turns toward Theren, and there's a little hesitation in the way she looks at him, like she's not sure she can stand it. He's not sure he can stand it, either, though maybe for a different reason.

In Talusar, he says to her, "Tell me what to do and I'll do it."

"I know you will," she replies, in the same language. "That's the whole problem."

He knows from the last time they spoke that she doesn't believe in her own destiny. Or maybe that she's afraid to believe in it, afraid of what it might mean. It can't be an accident that right after Shir's death, she gave up her rank, her authority, her power. And now she doesn't want to give Theren an order because she knows he'll obey it. She doesn't *want* that kind of authority over other people, the authority of the Hope of Cedre.

So he says, "Let me rephrase, then: I want to help you, if you'll allow me to."

She meets his eyes, then.

"All right." Her voice softens. "I'll allow you to."

32

Late that night, when the desert is dark and the only light in the trailer is the humming fluorescent one above the back door, Hela goes to the desk where the plant sits aglow. She doesn't touch it, because she's not sure if she wants to go to that dreamlike greenhouse place or not; she's not sure if she wants to speak to Akara again or not. Because she knows what she'll ask if she does, and she's afraid of the answer.

Are you on Earth?

Elegy is gone again, headed to Austra to do God knows what, so there's no one here to distract her. Instead of touching the plant's leaves, she sorts through Keen's box of artifacts, handling each scrap of metal like it's a delicate item of rare beauty. And though they aren't delicate, "rare beauty" might not be so much of a stretch. Hexagonal knobs with perfect corners. A curved fragment of an unknown ship. A handle so smooth it seems to be made from a single piece of metal. All made of that strange matte material, the one neither she nor Keen were ever able to identify.

I believe in the unknowable universe, Keen told her once. *Don't you?*

And she did, of course. But she's discovering there's a difference between "unknowable" and "unknown."

Sighing, she sets the handle down in the box and sits before the plant. She reaches for the leaf, and it reaches back, curling around her fingertip like an infant grabbing a finger.

She opens her eyes in the greenhouse, but it's dark now, and Akara is nowhere to be found. Hela steps onto the stone path and ducks under a low-hanging vine. The path leads to a central courtyard, and above it is a high ceiling made of diamond-shaped panes of glass. Through them she can't see many stars—the ring that stripes the sky is too bright.

She doesn't know much about planetary rings. That they're moons, maybe, broken apart and stretched—or that they're made of ice and rock. She searches for an exit, hoping to step outside the greenhouse, but Akara's voice interrupts her.

"You woke me," she says.

She's wearing what appears to be a silk robe, but it's not belted around her middle like the bathrobes Hela is familiar with. It buttons asymmetrically at her collarbone and hangs in liquid folds to her ankles, as pure white as the ring above them. Her hair, dark and thick, is piled on top of her head. Her face has the scrubbed-clean look of someone with no makeup on.

"I'm not sure how," Hela says. "Does the plant speak to you somehow?"

"In a sense." Akara crosses the courtyard, her feet bare, to stand closer to Hela. Hela wonders what would happen if she touched her—would either of them feel it?

"I've formed a connection with it, so it makes its needs known," Akara says. "Why have you come? I told you everything I can safely say. I've asked you to find—"

"—the one who makes it bloom. Yeah—do you have any idea how many people exist on this planet? You're asking me to find one stitch in a whole embroidery, here. Can you be any more specific?"

Akara hesitates. "It would be risky."

"So is me not getting it done at all, isn't it?" Hela looks up at the ring again. "Also, while I'm asking for stuff . . . if I'm going to do something for you, you need to do something for me."

"Oh?" Akara raises her eyebrows. "And what's that?"

"I want you to answer a question," Hela says. Her heart is racing. "Are we on the same planet right now?"

For a long time, Akara only looks at her. She seems capable of a preternatural level of focus; Hela would swear, in that moment, that she's the only thing Akara can see.

"No," Akara says. "I am very far away from you indeed."

"And this plant I'm touching right now," Hela says. "One of your people put it here? On my planet?"

Akara nods.

"We once invited Earth to join us on this side of the gate," Akara says. "We met with you in the stars, and made you an offer. You didn't accept it, so we left you alone. It's illegal to cross into a solar system that doesn't come to terms. But . . . someone broke the law. They planted that plant so that there would still be a way of speaking to you across the great distance that separates us."

Part of Hela wants to think it's a lie, or a trick. Another part thinks that it takes a real fool to deny the simplest explanation when it's right in front of you.

So she says, "Take a risk, Akara. Or there's a chance I'll never find the person you need me to find."

Akara takes a deep breath.

"To find the one who makes it bloom," she says, "seek the traitor's son."

33

When Theren approaches the landing pad ten minutes later, Elegy is there, standing across from a small, uniformed woman with her leg in a brace. Arias rushes forward to greet her. She does a lazy salute and then both of them start a complicated handshake that Theren can't quite follow. A technician light hovers near them, an opaque orb that almost seems to pulse like a heartbeat.

Elegy turns, and with the warm glow of the light catching her cheekbones, and an olive shirt bringing out the green in her eyes, the sight of her is like a gut punch.

"Secondary Parekh, this is Theren Forint," she says, gesturing to him. "Theren, this is Lydia Parekh. She'll be flying us to Naarm Stronghold."

"Hi. Wow," Parekh says. "Nobody mentioned you were this attractive."

Theren's face heats. Elegy cringes, her nose wrinkling, and sets her hands on Parekh's shoulders to steer her toward the Sparrow that's perched on the landing pad, its hatch open.

"What?" Parekh says. "I'm not flirting with him, I just don't see the point in pretending my eyes don't work, the way *you* seem to be."

Arias is a few paces behind them, laughing. Theren follows, his bag in hand. This time it's not full of borrowed military clothes. Yesterday Arias took him into Losan, armed with Theren's old bank account information—still active—and a list of necessities, to get him some clothes that weren't from the bottom of a Losan Stronghold closet, as he put it. Theren was shocked to discover that Arias had a lot of opinions about fashion. Theren managed to escape with a few plain collared shirts—the one he's wearing now is a deep navy, rolled up to his elbows.

They buckle themselves in, Parekh in the captain's chair and Arias and Elegy across from Theren in the back. The ship is too big for four people, but a smaller one wouldn't have enough fuel to get them to Austra. Parekh ties her hair back and readies the engine, her fingers dancing across the navigation panel as the elixir in her blood activates and she sinks into the ship.

He's not Imbued, so he can't quite imagine what Parekh is seeing right now, but his mother described piloting a Sparrow to him once. It wasn't like piloting a Hummingbird; she had to think about two things at once, see two things at once, *be* two things at once—herself, and the ship, coasting through the air. The training was rigorous, and not everyone who attempted it was successful—not every mind was built for that kind of flexibility.

"Secure?" Parekh asks.

"Hold on." Elegy, who hasn't buckled herself in yet, crosses the aisle to stand in front of Theren. She hooks her fingers over the safety strap that crosses his chest and tugs it, testing it. It's loose.

"You're not an experienced flyer, I guess," she says to him. Her knee brushes his. He doesn't respond—can't respond, because he's watching her fingers as she tugs the end of the strap to tighten it. She isn't touching him, but she may as well be, skimming the fabric that holds him fast to make sure it's secure.

Then, satisfied, she sits down and buckles herself in. "Parekh, can you at least *try* for a smooth takeoff—" she says.

They jerk away from the landing pad so sharply his teeth snap together.

"Never mind," Elegy finishes, sounding strained.

"I don't see you volunteering to drive!" Parekh looks over her shoulder at Theren. Her hands are faintly glowing. "She was like this in basic training, too, fussing over everything."

They fly west, toward the ocean. The flight from Losan to Austra is safer than most Cedrae journeys—the Talusar don't bother to patrol the empty expanse of ocean that borders Losan, and even if they did, they lack the ships to do it effectively.

Parekh flies them into the moon, which glints white on the water. Even in the dark, Earth is too beautiful to look at.

Arias is still examining the map, which is projected over the nav panel. He writes notes with a quill on the air beside it.

"Have you ever been to Austra?" Elegy asks Theren.

He shakes his head. Nonessential travel is for the wealthy, something he's never been. And Austra is across the planet, thousands of miles away from Losan. But he's heard stories of what it's like there, about its clear water, its bigger, fiercer animals. Like Losan, the city of Naarm has a sea wall, but theirs is older, concrete, with a mechanism in it to let a small amount of water in and out of the bay. A feat of engineering.

"The last time I went there I woke up to a spider on my face," Parekh reports from the captain's chair. "And it was not small."

She turns on music. A guitar, strumming, and a woman's voice layered over it in a language he can't identify.

"She was born on Cedre Station," Elegy says, as if that explains everything.

"Oh?" Theren says. "And you Losani are, what? Expert spider-handlers?"

Elegy's eyebrows pop up in surprise. She clearly forgot he's also from Cedre Station—not surprising, given that they reencountered each other in Valla. But she just says, "I'm only saying the station-born tend to be . . ." She pauses. "A bunch of wimps."

"Interesting." He folds his arms and sits back. "Then we'll have to put you in a spacesuit and see how you do adrift."

Parekh laughs. Everyone on Cedre Station has to experience a spacesuit drift when they're eleven years old, so they know how to handle themselves in an emergency. Theren loved it. It was like swimming without having to come up for air.

"It's part of basic army training," Elegy says. "I did fine."

Theren squints at her, like he's assessing her.

"Fine, I almost wet myself, is that what you want to hear?" But she's laughing. "You're very annoying, you know that?"

He thinks he should tease her more often—he's never seen her eyes light up like that before. He tips his head back against the wall of the ship as Parekh and Elegy reminisce about their army training days.

Parekh tells Theren that Elegy used to stay in the back of the group no matter how slow or hopeless they were, to make sure everyone finished as a team. "It didn't get us the best scores," Parekh says. "But we were all so closely ranked we got to sit together at graduation." He can imagine Elegy at the back of the group, the severe pout of her mouth, a line between her eyebrows.

Arias, meanwhile, is on his feet, staring at the projection of the map. He circles a few places on the hologram with his fingertip.

"Here, here, and here," he says. They all go quiet. "We should look for the Talusar ship in these places. They're closest to the Talusar border, and they're flat, relatively clear. Good spots for ships."

"We won't be able to see a parked ship from the air, thanks to all the tree cover," Theren says. "We'll have to search on foot."

"Parekh, how's your hip?" Elegy asks.

"Good enough," Parekh says, a little too quickly. She feels lively to him, like a beetle buzzing from one branch to another. A difficult person to read, especially compared to Elegy.

Parekh finds a place to land—a clearing at the bottom of a kind of bowl in the land, where she nestles the ship against the slope of a hill. It's not a hidden place, which leaves it vulnerable to the Talusar, but she activates the ship's security system as soon as she touches down. If anyone but her tries to connect to the ship's systems, the equipment will fry so badly it will be unusable. It's important that the Talusar don't get their hands on any more Cedrae ships than they already have, since ships are Cedre's only combat advantage.

Theren unbuckles himself, rubbing at his shoulder where the strap dug into his skin. Elegy is already outside, unloading the supplies she brought from Losan Stronghold with Arias. When Theren descends the steps, Arias tosses him a pack.

Theren holds it for a moment, drinking in the air, which is moist and temperate, unlike the dry heat of Losan. He listens to the trees shuddering in the wind, the insects chirping and buzzing. It's been months since he was in a forest, and he missed the sound of it, the smell of it. Even though it's still dark, he closes his eyes so he can focus on it.

When he opens them, Elegy is standing in front of him with a sword. Not a longsword, but a sturdy falchion, a little curved at the end. He takes it by the handle and tests its weight.

"Thought that would work for you," she says, a little stiffly. "Can't march through the woods with a one-handed longsword."

She has a spear already strapped to her back. Her weapon of choice. And apparently she knows his.

"It's good," he says. "Thanks."

When the ship has powered down and they're all outfitted with weapons and supplies, there's no debate about who's in charge. Elegy tells Arias to take point, since he's the best navigator, and ushers Parekh and Theren ahead of her—accustomed to leading from the back, he assumes, based on the stories Parekh told him.

Most Cedre soldiers aren't trained to be quiet. There's no need. So even though it's clear Parekh, Arias, and Elegy are trying to tread lightly, Theren can still hear the crush of greenery beneath their feet, and little bursts of breath as they forget to breathe through their noses. He also hears the cries of distant birds and the rustling of small mammals through the brush. They pass a shimmer of moonlight refracted over the threads of a spiderweb, and the earth yields to his boots in a way it rarely did in the dry mountains that border Valla.

They climb the hill that cradles the ship and move deeper into the trees. This area is lush. Ferns brush his legs as he walks, and when he sets a hand on a tree trunk to steady himself, it's mossy and soft. He was right to say they wouldn't see the parked Talusar ship from above—the trees are so dense here he can hardly see the moon.

"Look," Elegy says, and Theren searches the trees for some sign of the Talusar, but Elegy just laughs a little and comes to stand behind him. She's close, and she puts a hand on his shoulder to steady herself as she points at the trees above them. Under the bow of branches, there are spots of blue-white light. Like fallen stars clinging to the leaves.

"Glowworms," Elegy says softly. Though he can't really see her face in the dark, he can feel the pulse of wonder beneath the stress and determination. And—and he can feel her fingertips brushing his collarbone. He doesn't know if she remembers she's touching him.

For just a few seconds, they all stand and stare at the pinpricks of light, and Theren thinks that even though as a child, he only ever longed to go *out*—into space, into the stars—he keeps discovering little corners of this planet that surprise him with their beauty. Maybe the Restorationists have a point. Maybe there's something uniquely precious about Earth, something worth fighting to reclaim.

He glances at Elegy again, and wonders if she could be the one to do it, even if she doesn't believe it.

They keep walking.

✦   ✦   ✦

They walk the perimeter of the area Arias identified, a slow, arduous circle in the dark, like second hands ticking around a clock face. If their ship is at six o'clock, they walk forward in time, past nine and noon and all the way to three before they encounter anything except trees, ferns, rocks, and streams.

Then Theren hears it: a voice. He stops, and the others stop with him, all three of them going still. He hears the flutter of leaves, the rustle of animals, and the low, shapeless murmur of someone speaking quietly up ahead. Theren draws his sword and gestures for the others to stay where they are. He moves on soft, careful feet toward the sound.

The parked Talusar ship is just a shadow among shadows. It's perched in a clearing only large enough for it to launch, and no larger. Trees loom over it, their branches offering camouflage; it must have been here for a while, for the branches it broke on its descent to have filled out again. He sinks down, crouching among the ferns to see where the voice is coming from.

Whoever is guarding the ship—and there are probably at least two of them, if they're speaking to each other—hasn't lit a fire. The ship is shut down, its engine silent and its navigation panel dark. He could just charge in its direction and meet whatever comes, but he's not a fool—he may be good with a sword, but if there are three Talusar soldiers watching this ship, they'll kill him easily.

He's still considering his options when he gets a lucky break. He hears the scrape of a match against striking paper, and in the flare of light it produces, he sees two people hunched over the flame. Two Talusar soldiers, lighting the cigarettes they must have just rolled. One of them has the young, gaunt face of a teenager—the pilot, who can't be older than fourteen. The other is older than Theren, his head bald and his free hand balanced on the pommel of a sword.

Theren is more than capable of handling one soldier and one child, so he doesn't hesitate. He sprints toward the man and aims his blade low, beneath the protection of the febra armor. There's a flash of terror as the man sees him surging out of the dark. Theren's sword cuts easily through the soldier's clothes and through his skin; he groans, and lashes out with instinct instead of finesse, battering Theren's head with a fist. Theren drives his full weight into the man and they both fall to the ground.

This is what his body knows best: one person against another, strength against strength, the way it was in the Crucible. Some opponents were smart, devious, but in the end, it's difficult to beat someone who's bigger than you are, and Theren is counting on that now. He gets his hands around the soldier's throat, faltering only briefly when a knee drives into his rib cage. His hands slip down to the top of the armor, and he grabs it, lifts, and slams the man back down.

The soldier's head snaps back, and Theren puts his hands, and then his arm, at the man's throat again. He listens to the rattle of air as the soldier takes his last breath.

And then the buzz of insects, and the calling of distant birds, and the rustle of small animals in the brush.

He's fine. That's what he tells himself as he looks up to see the terrified eyes of the child soldier, the pilot taken from his family at the tender age of twelve and fed elixir like a drug. The boy is frozen, too scared to attack Theren even though that's what he was trained to do.

"Run," Theren says roughly.

The boy runs, stumbling over his feet as he sprints into the woods.

Theren's fine. He unfastens the dead soldier's febra armor and undoes the buckles holding his blade to his hip. Elegy and Arias come out of the trees to help him with the body, and Elegy's long, thin fingers cover his as she presses him gently away. His hands are shaking.

"Let us handle it," she says, and he sits, the undergrowth itching at his legs.

+   +   +

The sun hasn't risen yet, but there's a line of light over the horizon, like it's considering it.

Theren is wearing febra armor. He's worn it before only once, when Ranos agreed to indulge Theren's curiosity. Theren always wanted to know what febra felt like to the Fevered, or if he could hear it, its energy field a frequency that Cedrae ears couldn't detect. It didn't disappoint—when he put it on, he could feel it humming, like a gong that's just been struck.

It hums now, this other man's febra armor, even though it's not made for someone of Theren's size and build. It chafes in places, digs in others.

They're waiting for the kidnappers to arrive with Julia Martin. Parekh and Arias are in the trees. Parekh took a length of wire out of her pack and started walking through the woods with it, setting up a trip wire that will surround the camp. *When fighting Talusar soldiers*, she said, when he gave her a confused look, *even the second it takes them to recover from stumbling can be crucial for us.* The task Elegy assigned her was to identify Julia Martin and take her away from the fighting as quickly as possible.

Arias, meanwhile, pinpointed the direction the Talusar will be coming from, and then found a hiding place along that path. His job is to wait for the group to pass him, and then attack them from behind once they run into Parekh's wire.

Elegy is with Theren. Well, not *with* him—they stand six feet apart, each of them looking in a different direction. Not back-to-back, exactly, but close enough to it. Her spear is in her hands, and even though they've been standing there for the better part of an hour, she still looks ready. Not too stiff, not too relaxed.

He couldn't help but stare at her, once the haze of killing the soldier had passed. For someone who's been refusing to have authority of any kind, she took it up so effortlessly. Assessed the entire clearing in one glance, ordered the trip wire, assigned each of them a position. Her tone was authoritative but not commanding.

This was the person she was before she met Theren. Before she lost everything.

Theren sees movement in the trees, and forces himself to stay still. Elegy meets his eyes, and holds his gaze as she calls out, "Hey! Come and get us, assholes!"

For a second he gapes at her, uncomprehending. Why would she want to alert them to enemies in their campsite a second before she had to? But as the soldiers charge toward them, their febra armor glinting in the pale dawn light, he understands the logic: if they run toward Theren and Elegy, they'll all trip on the wire at the same time.

Sure enough, the wire sends them all sprawling. It would be funny if adrenaline wasn't stampeding through Theren's body. He sees Arias attack; he sees Parekh running into the trees to find Julia Martin; he counts fallen Talusar soldiers—six of them recovering their balance. He breaks into a run and stabs one of them right in the back. It reminds him of walking the dark hallways of House Vidar the night he escaped with Elegy, the way he had to kill the guards before they even became aware of him, just to ensure a clear path to the exit.

He hated it then, and he hates it now. But Elegy's presence has a way of bringing clarity to things. She needs him to kill these soldiers, so he will.

This time, he will.

Without hesitating, he turns to attack another one. This soldier's reflexes are better than he anticipated. He lurches away from Theren just in time to save his neck. But he's also lost his footing. Theren pursues him, feinting to misdirect him and then ducking low to stab beneath his armor. The blade slides right into the man's belly. Theren feels hot blood on his hand, and yanks the weapon free.

He feels Elegy next to him. Even in the chaos, she's obvious to him. Cold and clear as water. One of the others—the tallest and broadest of them all—has Elegy by the collar of her jacket, and she's fighting him off as hard as she can, clawing at his hand and screaming into gritted teeth. Theren picks up her fallen spear, rolling on the dirt, and swings it at the Talusar's head.

It hits the man hard in the shoulder, startling him enough that Elegy pulls away. Parekh screams for help deep in the woods, and Elegy shouts "Go!" at Arias, who takes off running. There are two Talusar left for Theren and Elegy to deal with, and both are advancing on Elegy herself.

Theren throws himself in front of her, and realizes he recognizes one of his attackers.

Her hair is bright red. He just dreamed about her. The guard who caught him eavesdropping on Ykev and Rava's conversation. The one who asked him if he was Rava's.

She's Primary Avka Becken, direct report to Ykev Talus.

Just what she's doing here, on a mission everyone assumed was planned by Rava, not Ykev, is unclear. But there's no time to wonder.

Becken rushes toward him and slices, clean and neat, across Theren's arm. He grits his teeth as he lunges to the right, to thrust his sword at her right side. As he does, he hears a grunt; Elegy, who's still behind him, moved left when he moved right, and is now slamming the spear into the other soldier's leg.

Something buzzes next to his head—not an insect, but an Eye, likely a Cedre military surveillance device drawn there by the fight. Theren ignores it.

Without hesitating, he and Elegy trade opponents. Theren moves left to counter the tall, broad soldier's longsword, the impact shuddering down his blade and rattling his bones. Elegy stabs right with the spear, keeping Becken at bay. Theren's focus narrows.

He keeps moving, his muscles burning as he shifts back and forth, countering one blade and then the other, and he can feel it as Elegy responds in kind, moving behind him, around him. Becken carves a line into his armor as he twists away from her, and he kicks back, missing her knee by inches.

Becken shoves him into the other soldier; he falls, and rolls, recovering fast to strike Becken from the side. She's too quick, too reactive; she blocks him, once, twice, as Elegy wards off the tall soldier with the point of her spear.

Then he hears a gurgling scream from the tall soldier as he collapses to his knees, revealing Arias behind him, sword in hand. Theren faces Becken, the last one remaining, and they fight in earnest, now.

Becken is at the center of a pinhole of focus, shifting in and out of the patches of sunlight on the clearing floor. She moves with ruthless efficiency, no flair to her technique but few weaknesses to it, either; she fights like someone to whom killing has become routine, and he is just another in a long line of bodies to put at her feet.

They trade attacks and parries, filling the air with the sound of metal on metal, Theren making good use of his height and reach, Becken outmaneuvering him. He buries himself in the feeling of her, attunes himself to the spark of decision in her that comes right before she attacks.

Then he swings hard, so hard he knocks the rapier out of her hands; it topples to the earth, and he touches his blade to her throat.

"I know you," Becken says, in a low, quiet voice. "Do *they?*"

He grits his teeth, and turns the blade, about to press in and end her—

"Stop!" Elegy orders, and he does, going still. "I have questions for her."

She's reaching into her bag for something. She takes out a vial of clear liquid.

"Swallow this," Elegy says to Becken. "Or die."

Becken eyes Elegy for a second, and then smiles a peculiar smile. She holds out her hand for the vial, and Elegy gives it to her. Theren is expecting Becken to do something—to grab Elegy, or to drop the vial and crush it beneath her boot. But instead she just unscrews the cap and pours its contents into her mouth.

It only takes a few seconds to work, whatever it is. Becken collapses like a puppet released of its strings.

Theren goes still, his ears ringing, his hand tight around the sword hilt. Elegy turns toward him, probes at one of the cuts on his arms, her eyes frantic with concern. He must look *wrong*, the way he did when Arias first rescued him from Specialist Gylle. *A dissociative episode*, that's what Arias called it.

When she sees that he's all right, she puts a hand on the back of his neck. He's startled by how good the contact feels, and how much he doesn't want it to end.

"You did well," she says. The rising sun is shining directly into her eyes, green as ivy. "It's done now. You're done."

He releases the sword, and covers her fingers with his, holding her against his neck for a moment. He nods. Her hand is cool and steady. *She* is cool and steady. And maybe that's the most startling thing of all: what a relief she is.

Over her shoulder, he sees Parekh limping out of the forest. Behind her, bruised and unsteady with her arm cradled to her chest, is Julia Martin.

"It's a long walk back to the ship," Elegy says, looking down at Becken's unconscious body.

Theren drags a hand across his forehead to wipe off sweat. "I can carry her."

34

"Oh boy," Hela says, looking over the rim of her mug at Isre Din, little brother of Theren Forint. "You're *adorable*."

Isre looks startled, reminding her of a deer in the woods who just caught sight of a predator. She rolls her eyes.

"Just sit," she says.

He does. He's not short, but he is trim and narrow through the shoulders, which makes him look smaller than he is. His hair is just long enough to curl at the ends.

This meeting came at a good time. She can think of exactly two people who qualify as a "traitor's son." One of them is on some kind of mission with Elegy in Austra. And the other one is right here, about to help her contact Kesia Forint—the traitor in question.

They're sitting under an awning in Losan's most central market, a few blocks away from where Hela spent her adolescence. It's late afternoon, but the sun is still hot, and Hela is wearing cutoffs and a tank top, like she would have at sixteen. Across from her is an old woman running a lemonade stand that's looking more appealing by the second. But she still has to finish her tea—hot, despite the temperature outside. She doesn't believe in icing it.

"Want something?" Hela says to Isre.

He shakes his head. "I'm fine, thanks. Just wondering what I'm doing here. Primary Arias wasn't forthcoming."

"I give you a state-mandated reprieve from work and you don't even want to take advantage of it?" She sips from her teacup, and sets it gently down on its saucer. "They really have you grunts brainwashed over there in Losan Stronghold, don't they?"

"Fine," Isre says. He disappears inside the café, and Hela drinks the rest of her tea in one swallow.

She has the plant waiting in her Finch around the corner, but she's not going to ask him about it yet. Contacting Kesia Forint for a meeting is more important.

When Isre returns, she's on her feet. She points across the street at a narrow alley. "That's where we're headed."

Isre looks at the mug in his hands, and then raises his eyebrows at her.

"Oh, you'll bring it back, don't worry about it," Hela says, flapping her hand at him.

Isre looks hesitant. "Why do you need to get in touch with Kesia, anyway?"

"I think she knows about an alien landing."

"You're messing with me."

"I would love to tell you I am," she says. "Truly. And sure, maybe it's not *aliens*, per se, maybe it's some kind of top-secret Talusar military tech pieced together by Imbued soldier children that will completely wreck Cedre if it comes to fruition. But your mom knows about it, and I intend to speak with her."

Isre stares at her for a few seconds, then takes a swig of his coffee. He wipes his mouth with the back of his hand.

"And if I don't want you looking at my messages?"

"Trust me, I have no interest in your diary or your assorted romantic liaisons. I need a single point of origin for the message your mother sent you to arrange a meeting. That's all."

Isre sighs.

"Screw it," he says. "Let's go."

They cross the street, sidestepping a group of children playing with marbles and a man trying to get the chain back on his bicycle. Over their heads, laundry hangs from a clothesline that stretches between the two buildings.

Up ahead is a door with peeling blue paint and a sign on the knob that reads OPEN. Before she reaches it, she turns back to him.

"Just so you know," she says, "this place isn't strictly . . . aboveboard. So this isn't something you should mention to your soldier friends."

Isre gives her a look. "You know, I kind of figured that from the 'walking down an alley that smells like piss' part."

Hela sniffs. She didn't notice the acrid smell in the air, which makes her worry about various other facets of her life. Shoes, for example.

She pushes the blue door open and walks into the shop. It smells musty, with a hint of stray dog. The stone walls are painted, but the paint is faded and flaking, as blue as the door. At one end of the cramped room is a wooden counter, also painted blue. A neon sign on the wall behind the counter advertises "elixir repair" with the elixir symbol—an old-fashioned bottle with a cork stopper—next to it.

A man emerges from the back room like he's materializing from nothing. He's far taller than she is, his face shrouded by a red hood. He wears a long red coat of the same material, heavy and thick around his shoulders.

She should have warned Isre about his flair for the dramatic.

"Dreadful," the man says, in a low, drawling voice.

"Recordkeeper," she replies, inclining her head. "I was hoping you might help me with something. For a fair price."

The Recordkeeper waits.

"My friend here received a message," she says, gesturing to Isre. "I'd like to find out its point of origin."

"This information is not yours."

"That's true." The first rule of dealing with the Recordkeeper: don't lie to him. "But I'd like to access it anyway, with his permission."

"You are prepared to pay?"

Because the Recordkeeper only deals in information, it's also the only thing he'll accept as payment. Hela already knows what to offer him.

"Of course," she says. "I came to offer you, not a discovery, but a mystery."

She reaches into the bag at her side and takes out a box small enough to fit in her palm. She unlatches it, and holds it out to the Recordkeeper.

Inside it is a leaf from the mystery plant. Hela didn't cut it off—it fell the other day, in the aftermath of the encounter with Dr. Canterbury. It's shriveled in death, but it still emits a soft green light, unlike any plant she's ever seen on Earth.

The Recordkeeper's fingers reach for it, and stop just shy of touching it.

"You say it's a mystery," he says.

"I can't identify the plant this leaf is from," she says. "And I don't know how it survives, since the sun seems to hurt it. I know almost nothing about it, in fact."

"And why should I accept a mystery as payment?"

"Mysteries are . . . perched at the very edge of knowledge," Hela says. She thought about this for a while, how to make it sound poetic, the way the Recordkeeper likes. "Where our knowledge fails, we have lingering questions. And those questions are the most interesting thing we have."

The Recordkeeper does love for things to be interesting.

He seems to consider this for a moment. Then he reaches under the counter and takes out a metal object, egg-shaped, about the size of his palm. It's striped with concentric circles, and one of them is a seam. When he opens the egg along that seam, there's a needle nestled inside it.

"Stab your finger on that needle," the Recordkeeper says to Isre.

"Um," Isre says. "What?"

Hela taps the edge of the egg. "Stabby stabby. Now."

Isre sighs, puts his index finger over the needle in the egg, and presses it down until it breaks the skin. Blood bubbles out of the wound, and he takes his hand away.

"What?" he says, when he sees her disgusted face.

"Needles gross me out."

"I'll cancel the acupuncture appointment I made for you, then."

That surprises her. She laughs as the Recordkeeper flips the reader closed around Isre's blood sample.

"The date of the message in question?" he asks Isre.

"February twenty-eighth."

The egg starts to quiver, almost like a chick is about to hatch from it, as it distills the elixir from Isre's blood sample. She listens for the hum as it feeds the elixir into a vial of base liquid also contained within the egg—that's what the Recordkeeper will inject. Whatever illegal modifications he made to his own elixir allow him to trace the origin of any message in his bloodstream, no matter how old.

The Recordkeeper produces a quill that was tucked into his sleeve. The metal feather is long and thin, curved at the end like a bowstring. The Recordkeeper bows his head, and starts to write.

Hela can't see the glow of the message he's writing, but she follows the nib of the quill across the counter just fine. It's a useful skill for a Scout, to know what other people are reading.

Luckily, this message is in all capital letters.

NEED TO MEET YOU. IT'S URGENT.
SLEEP TIGHT. I'LL SEE YOU IN THE PALE MORNING.

The Recordkeeper's head tilts. "In the pale morning?"

"It's . . . a reference to a private joke," Isre says. "It's what told me who the message was from."

"I see," the Recordkeeper says. He fumbles under the counter for a scrap of paper and a pen that's stained blue with spilled ink. Then he picks up the pen with his left hand and the quill with his right, and writes the same numbers with both, at the same time.

"Impressive," Isre says.

Hela almost curses out loud when she sees the sequence of numbers come together. They're coordinates, and she recognizes some of them . . . because she was *just there*. Or close to there, anyway.

Wherever Kesia Forint sent this message from, it's not far from Dr. Canterbury's dubious estate.

The Recordkeeper finishes and tucks his quill into his sleeve and his pen under the counter. He picks up the box with the shriveled leaf inside it and slides it into a hidden pocket in his robes. Then he bobs his head to her.

She bobs her head back, takes the paper, and says, "Thank you, Record-keeper."

He turns to disappear into the void again, but right before he does, he says, "You are welcome, Tausia Helasz."

She waits until she and Isre are in the alley again before she says anything.

"Well," Isre says. "That guy was weird."

"Yeah, but at least he's predictably weird." Most of the people she deals with as a Scout are odd in one way or another. Some are frightening, and some are harmless, but all of them have their quirks. She holds up the scrap of paper with the coordinates written on it and says, "I can't believe I gotta go back to that shithole."

"What is it?"

"Nothing, I was just way out in the middle of nowhere a few days ago and now I have to go ten minutes to the left of the middle of nowhere again," she says. "The message came from a neutral settlement—not Cedrae."

"Those exist?"

"Not technically, but practically, yes," she says. "I don't know how Kesia sent you the message, since she doesn't have elixir, but that's where it came from, so I have to go talk to the proprietor of that undoubtedly fine establishment."

"If Kesia gets back to you, can I come along?"

"If she gets back to me, I'll probably need you to." She takes the mug that Isre is still holding, now empty of coffee, and says, "I have one more favor to ask you."

"Need more of my blood?" he asks her. "Some spit, maybe?"

"Very funny." She crosses the street to return the mug, and Isre follows her. At least he's obedient—another good thing about soldiers.

They walk around the corner to the lonely alley where Hela's Finch is parked. She opens the passenger-side door, where the plant is buckled into the seat. She constructed a tent out of brown paper to shield it from the sun.

"Lift up that flap," she says to Isre, pointing at it. "And touch what's under it."

Isre looks at the paper structure, then at Hela. She winces a little. She probably could have made her request sound a little less like a prank.

"I think we've reached my limit on weird shit," Isre says to her.

"It's a plant," Hela says. "It's sensitive to light. And I just need to confirm something."

Isre sighs. "What'll happen if I touch it?"

"It'll give you eternal youth." Hela rolls her eyes. "I don't know what'll happen. Probably nothing."

Isre considers her for another long moment, then brushes past her and reaches for the brown paper. He lifts the corner of it up, and peers beneath it, at the softly glowing plant with its leaves drawn up into a teardrop.

He reaches out and brushes his finger against one of the leaves. Hela waits, staring at the plant, searching it for any sign of change.

It doesn't stir.

"Okay, then," Hela says. "Thanks. Be seeing you."

+   +   +

"Jodi pulled the pin from her hair and let her curls cascade over her bare shoulders. It was a hot day on the farm, and all the field hands were sitting in the apple grove with their lunches, so she was alone at the creek. Or so she thought—"

"What the retrograde hell are we listening to?" Parin says as he buckles his seatbelt.

"We have an hour drive ahead of us," Hela replies. "And I am invested in Jodi's future success."

"I can tell you exactly what happens—one of the farmhands is totally spying on her, she's furious at his audacity but also sort of turned on, they start a love affair but can't have a future because he's but a mere farmhand, they break it off, and then some contrivance makes it possible for them to be together, the end." He fiddles with the air vents.

"I bet you ten pieces that's not what happens," Hela says. "On account of I bought it in the 'ladies who love ladies' section."

They're driving over the most boring landscape imaginable. Hela flips a switch so the sun shade rolls down over the windshield, and leans her seat back.

She doesn't usually spend this much effort on something that's not an official job, but apart from her own curiosity . . . Elegy asked her to follow up on this. And even though she remembers Elegy as a grubby preteen girl with scraped knees and the inability to keep her mouth shut, she still can't pretend that Elegy isn't who she is. Daughter of the Sword. Hope of Cedre.

So if Kesia Forint, traitor to Cedre and accomplice to Elegy's husband's murder, is connected to this plant and its origins . . . Hela is going to find out what she can.

By the time they make it to the neutral settlement, where the bar—inelegantly named Bob's Bar and General Store—is nestled between two vacant buildings as flat and plain as they come, Parin is too invested in the story to get out of the car.

A farmhand didn't, in fact, happen upon Jodi bathing in the creek—that honor went to the mayor's daughter, who was cruel and cold and widely known to be a snob. A forbidden love affair followed, and Parin was currently begging Jodi to break it off for good, while Hela was arguing that such passion couldn't be denied.

"We've been sitting here for ten minutes," she says finally. "We can listen all the way back, come on."

Parin sighs, and they get out of the Finch.

Bob's Bar and General Store has dark windows and a glowing sign in the door shaped like a beer bottle. On either side are the bare buildings common to ruins in this area. They're built on top of old buildings, using the crumbled walls as a foundation. She thinks this place used to be a store, and she can't imagine a world with so many people in it that all these spaces were necessary. Even with all the Talusar and Cedrae put together, they couldn't fill all the ruins she's seen. The world was so much bigger before the Empty Time. Before whatever array of catastrophes destroyed it.

A bell rings as they walk into Bob's. On the left is a wood-veneer bar top, and a filthy tile floor with a few high tables clustered on it. On the right is a little store—a few shelves with cleaning products and wrinkled produce and stacks of towels and, of course, tobacco. There are a few people at one of the tables gathered around a small obsidian, watching something that looks like an old movie. And there's a woman behind the bar, older, a rag hanging over one shoulder.

She raises her eyebrows at Hela, like that's a greeting.

"Hey there," Parin says, sidling up to the bar.

"Save it, kid," the woman says. "Are you here to drink or are you here to cause trouble?"

"Do we look like trouble?" Hela says.

"Yes," the woman says, like it's obvious. "The only Cedrae who come out here are either Scouts or soldiers, and you don't look like soldiers."

"I feel like that might be a compliment." Hela thinks she might be half in love with this woman. "We're not here to give you any grief, we just want to know if someone's been by here recently."

"Lots of people have been by here, it's a bar," the woman says.

"All right." Hela sits on the bar stool. "Was one of them a Talusar soldier, a woman, kinda tall, middle-aged, asked for your help sending a message?"

"I think I would remember someone like that."

"That's not a no."

The woman braces herself against the bar top, her fingers tapping the wood. She squints at Hela for a few seconds.

"Listen," Hela says, lowering her voice. "Her son wants to get in touch with her. That's all."

"Her son? Why's he not here himself?"

"Because he's a Knight of Cedre, and he's got more important shit to do."

It's a risk, revealing Theren's identity to this woman. But if she's right about the woman's hesitation, Hela needs to back up her story with some concrete details to show she actually does know Kesia's son. Not that she actually does, but . . . no one needs to know that.

The woman looks her over for a few seconds, and then nods.

"If you leave a message for her here," she says, "I'll be sure that our mutual friend gets it."

35

It's pouring rain by the time Elegy and the others land at Naarm Stronghold. After the walk from the landing pad to the door, she's soaked to her skin.

Chaos greets their arrival, as Elegy figured it would. Theren radiates a kind of foreignness even when he *isn't* wearing febra armor and carrying the unconscious form of Primary Avka Becken over one shoulder like a bag of potatoes. Soldiers surround him, and he seems too tired to be bothered. He sets Becken down on the floor, and looks up at the blades pointing at him with a deeply unimpressed expression that almost makes her laugh out loud.

"He's with me," Elegy says to the soldiers, her voice weary even to her own ears. "But this woman"—she nudges Becken with her toe—"needs to be taken to a holding cell immediately."

"I'll go with them," Parekh says. She nods to Theren. "He's still bleeding."

"I can take care of it," Theren says, but Elegy shakes her head. She wants to get away from the wide-eyed stares of the soldiers in the entryway, and beyond that, she *needs* to see that he's patched up.

She just does.

They walk behind Arias and Julia Martin to the hospital. Arias has a steadying hand on Julia's elbow, and he has his head bent toward hers, listening. Elegy gives them space. Arias is good at taking care of people in aftermaths, maybe because the aftermath he himself endured—wounded, close to death, surrounded by the bodies of his entire team—was so horrific. He knows what not to say.

It's so early in the morning that no one intercepts them on their way to the hospital, and there's only one nurse working in the ward itself. Even with the storm raging, the room is so bright it's blinding, with tall, arching windows and every surface of the room white, white, white. The nurse takes Julia and Arias back right away, and Elegy beckons Theren toward the supply closet across the hall.

Theren tries to object again. She doesn't need to hear it. She knows he can patch himself up, even if the gash on his arm requires stitching—he can probably do it with a sewing needle and fishing line, knowing him, and he certainly wouldn't bother with any kind of painkiller. But the thought of leaving him alone in some stark hospital room to stitch his own arm after everything he just did because she told him to—and she *knows* he did it because she told him to—makes her chest ache.

"Just let me," she says to him, and he complies.

The supply closet has shelves and drawers on every wall, floor to ceiling, each one labeled and neat. It's large enough to accommodate both Elegy and Theren, but she didn't think about how it would feel to be in an enclosed space this small with him—tall, broad-shouldered, and still wearing febra armor. Her mouth goes dry, looking up at him, so she focuses on finding everything she'll need: antibiotic spray, wound sealant, healing ointment, a painkiller, bandages.

She saw him put on the febra armor in the forest with practiced hands, not realizing how complicated it is to fasten. She watches him with his fingers on the chest straps for a moment before she pushes his hands gently away. Tugging at the straps, she tries not to think about how immovable he is—tries not to think about sitting behind him when they fled Valla on horseback, how his muscles moved. She tries not to think about how they move now, shifting beneath her fingers with each breath he takes.

She manages to get the febra armor—a cuirass, she thinks it's called—off, and guide it over his head. There's a dark red mark at the side of his neck where it dug into his skin, too small for him; without thinking, she touches her thumb to it.

"What does it feel like? The armor?" she asks him, her thumb still touching his skin. He's too warm, the Fever heating his blood. She can feel his pulse. Or hers.

He says, "Like when you hold two magnets close together, and you can feel the energy between them."

The answer comes to him so easily, she thinks he must have given it before.

"Your arm," she says, after a moment.

Theren reaches over his head to grab the back of his shirt, but it's too wet; it sticks to his abdomen, and Elegy finds herself peeling the fabric away from his sides, her fingernails scraping at his damp skin. He tugs it over his head, and drapes it over one of the empty shelves, and she goes still at the sight of so much of him.

It's quiet. They're quiet. She stares at his defined shoulder muscle, at the fine dusting of rain that sits on his collarbone, at the white line of scar tissue that follows his hip. He's bare and warm and within reach of her, and when his eyes meet hers again, there's heat in them.

He's never looked at her like that before.

She forces herself to focus on the cut on his arm. It's still bleeding, but not so deep they need to find a doctor. With unsteady hands, she sprays it with antiseptic, then uses a square of gauze to wipe it clean.

"It's shallower than I thought," she says, because the silence has become strange, and she needs to fill it. "Might not even scar."

"I have so many, one more scar won't make much of a difference."

"Trust me. No one who looks at you is going to be thinking about them."

A moment too late, she realizes what she said, and her cheeks burn.

She sprays the gash with wound sealant, careful with the nozzle. It's only human to crave contact after so long without it, she reminds herself. For years, she couldn't stand a body near hers that wasn't Shir's. And then, once she could have tried again for some meaningless satisfaction, she was already in the habit of being alone.

Theren lifts his hand, and brushes the lock of wet hair that's stuck to her cheek back behind her ear. For a moment, his fingertips linger on her earlobe, and that heat is still in his eyes, and *God*—

She slides a hand behind his head and brings his mouth down to hers.

His response is fervent, almost frantic: his arm wraps around her back to pull her hard against him, and his lips part beneath hers. Desire lights up her body like elixir, and she lets out an embarrassingly eager sound, crowding him against one of the shelves. It creaks, and a bottle of antiseptic spray falls, but she doesn't care; she doesn't care; she doesn't care.

His hand gathers her shirt into a fist, and she does what she's wanted to do for days, without articulating it even to herself; she runs her fingers along the line of his jaw and down his throat to his collarbone. He kisses her harder, deeper, and she feels like every inch of her is prickling and sparking with desire; it's too much but she's not sure how it could ever, ever be enough. Her hand drops to his shoulder, firm with muscle, and her finger brushes the still-sticky wound spray.

Reality floods back in as she remembers the gash, and then how he got it, and then *who he is*, as in, Theren Forint, breaker of oaths and survivor of Valla and deadly sword-wielding almost-Talusar. Not some man she met at a bar, not some chance encounter on a mission—

Not Shir.

Breathless, she pulls away, her hand hovering over her mouth. She feels too warm. Too unsteady.

"We should find some dry clothes," she says.

Theren straightens. Runs a hand through his hair.

"Okay," he says.

✦   ✦   ✦

When she wakes, there's rain drumming on the windows, which is the first sign she's not at home. It doesn't rain much in Losan.

Last night, after—well, *after*, a helpful deputy of General Saetang showed them to the guest apartments, where Elegy and Parekh took one room and Arias and Theren took the one across from them. She thought it would be easy to fall asleep, but of course it wasn't, not with her body flushed and her thoughts racing. Memories of fighting for her life faded into the background. All she could think about was Shir, and the deep well of grief inside her, and then something new: fear. Fear that the well wasn't as deep as it should be.

She listens to the rain for a few minutes, now, as Parekh shifts in the bed next to hers. She's only been lying there for a few minutes when there's a gentle tap on the door. Then Theren steps into the room, a cup in each hand.

"Felt you wake up," he says, and she's too startled by the idea of that to do anything but nod. *No one surprises him* was Rava's assessment, and she seems to be right, most of the time.

But Elegy thinks she surprised him last night.

Theren moves on quiet feet to Parekh's bedside table, and sets a cup down there, then holds one out to Elegy. It's coffee. And not just the synthetic approximation concocted by a lab in Losan—actual coffee.

She takes the cup with a murmured thank-you, and sits up. Her body aches in odd places, muscles she forgot existed. She leans back against the wall, and cradles the cup against her chest. The blankets fall away from one of her legs, and Theren's eyes trace it from hip to ankle, once, before he looks away. She feels a line of heat all along that leg, like he ran a hand down it.

She tries to be casual, shifting the blankets back over her body. He leans against the wall.

"I found a coffee machine down the hall," he says.

"I'll recommend you for a medal," she replies. "What's going on out there?"

If he's surprised that she's determined to pretend nothing happened between them, he doesn't show it.

"Julia's wrist is sprained, not broken. She's resting," he says. "Everyone's talking about us. Mostly expressing doubt that we just happened upon that ship, given that you're the former Primary of search and rescue. And . . . there are some wild rumors about the Talusar soldier you made your ally."

He gestures to himself, and Elegy laughs.

"You did make an entrance," she points out. She runs a hand through her hair, and very carefully doesn't look at him as she asks, "Your arm?"

"Well-tended," he replies, and it doesn't matter if she looks at him or not—she blushes anyway.

She can't figure out how to ask him what she really wants to know. Not about his arm, but about whether yesterday damaged him in some other, deeper way. *Do you feel okay?* seems too intimate for them.

Parekh spares her from having to. She groans, and sits up. "Oh my God, is that coffee?"

"Special delivery," Elegy says.

"It's *real coffee*," Parekh says, marveling. She's upright now, sticking her entire nose in the paper cup. "Wonder of wonders."

"I'll let you wake up." He pulls away from the wall, glances at Elegy, and leaves the room.

Elegy swallows the last of her coffee, and sets the cup down next to her. She can feel Parekh staring at her, but she's not going to break the silence first—not going to give Parekh the satisfaction.

"It's all right, you know," Parekh says.

"What?"

Parekh rolls her eyes.

"Come on, I'm not stupid," she says. "He's gorgeous, and barely looks at anyone who isn't you, and you've been celibate for four years. It's biology. Shir would understand." She tilts her head. "For that matter, Shir would understand if it was more than biology."

"It's not," Elegy says firmly.

Parekh sips her coffee, her expression inscrutable. "I'm just saying, don't beat yourself up about it."

Elegy listens to the rain.

"Thanks," she says, after a while.

+   +   +

Shir always used to say that walking through Naarm Stronghold made him feel like he was inside a bubble. She understands the comparison—everything here is made of glass. In the sun, it's hot and bright, every surface reflective, too shiny to touch. In the rain, it's *loud*, the drumming echoing throughout the building. All the walls are sharp and angular, coming to points above them. From the air, it looks like someone swept up a pile of broken glass and left it there on the coastline.

At the center of the building is the old fort, an old-fashioned structure made of red brick that no one could bear to tear down, but it serves only as a museum, now. They pass it, roped off for repairs, on the way to meet Saetang.

They were invited here for a reason, and it wasn't to rescue Julia Martin. It was to review the evidence of the Talusar attack—the one in which the Talusar took nothing, hurt no one, and left a single memory-addled witness.

They meet Saetang on the landing pad, where the general is surveying their ship from a distance. It's parked right where Parekh left it, next to the entrance, bits of branches still stuck to its wings. Saetang stands under an awning, sheets of rain falling to the pavement right in front of them. Their boots are covered in its splatter.

"Your Grace," they say. "Interesting detour you took on your way here."

"Well, you know how it is," Elegy says. "You train yourself to search and rescue for long enough, and you end up searching and rescuing completely by accident."

Saetang's smile is knowing. "And the fact that your sister didn't approve a mission is, I'm sure, mere happenstance."

Elegy doesn't have anything to say to that. She just shrugs.

But Saetang seems content not to linger on the subject. "However you got here, I'm glad you're here." They look at Theren, their eyes lingering on his bruised jaw. "All of you. The attack we experienced weeks ago confused me, and I don't like to be confused by the Talusar. I hope you can help me make sense of it."

A soldier steps out of the building with a stack of umbrellas on his arms. Saetang thanks him, and distributes them to Elegy, Theren, Arias, and Parekh in turn. Then, shrouded by black fabric, they all walk across the rain-soaked landing pad to the barrier that stretches along the edge of the seawall. It's a safety barrier, not intended to keep out intruders. The seawall itself is sufficient for that, a sheer, smooth surface with waves battering it at the bottom.

They all stand at the barrier in a line, looking out at the storm-tossed sea. Rain sprays Elegy's cheeks even with the umbrella up.

"This is where they came in. They scaled the wall to get up here, which we didn't realize was possible," Saetang says. "You can see the anchor points."

They point down at the stone beneath them. Elegy squints through the rain to see a small hole in the stone beneath her, no bigger than a walnut. There are others beneath it, in a zigzag line down to the water.

Saetang turns, and points across the landing pad to the hangar, a huge white building with doors so large Elegy can't fathom them opening.

"Then they ran across the landing pad to the hangar, where our witness was working as a guard. He let them in, probably against his will. They used a candlesnuffer to knock out the hangar's electricity, so we don't have any footage of them inside the building. But we know they spent ten minutes there, then left."

"A candlesnuffer?" Theren asks.

"It's a Cedrae relic, from before the Empty Time," Elegy says. She has to raise her voice to be heard over the drumming rain. The hem of her pants is already soaked. "It emits a suppressive energy field, not unlike the one emitted by a large number of Fevered people, like in a Talusar city. It disables all electricity, all technology. I wonder how they got their hands on it to begin with—there aren't many."

"That's where my mind went first," Saetang says. "But we can only find out so much from our usual sources. I wondered if you could use more *unusual* ones."

"Scout sources, you mean," Elegy says. "So that's why you asked me here."

Saetang taps the side of their nose. "Exactly."

"I'll look into it." A piece of salvage as rare as a candlesnuffer would be memorable, but whoever sold it won't want to admit to making a deal with a Talusar. "And nothing was missing from the building? They didn't take anything?"

"I'll give you a copy of the inventories, if you like. Nothing missing, nothing strange."

"Please do. Did Julia Martin try to restore your witness's memory yet?"

"She did. I'm afraid it exhausted her; she's now resting." Saetang's umbrella bumps into Elegy's. "As we anticipated, the witness seems to be damaged beyond repair. He can't remember his own name, let alone what happened during the attack. Julia said his memory is like a paint-splattered canvas. No order, just colors. He's being transferred to a long-term-care facility this afternoon."

Elegy looks at Theren, remembering something he said to her about his own memory gap. She asked him if someone erased his memory, and he said, *No, that work is indelicate. I would show other signs of brain damage.* Now she understands what he meant.

"She didn't see anything interesting in his memory?" Elegy asks. "Even something that seemed like nothing?"

"She said she saw random images from throughout his life. Heard bits of phrases. 'Where we come from is where we belong,' that Restorationist motto. You can probably thank the Sword for that one, that speech she gave was broadcast in every news pavilion for days. A song quote, 'restless love guides my feet,' something like that. And a few words in Latin. 'Equo ne credite.' I had one of our linguists translate it earlier, it just means 'don't trust the horse.'"

"Don't trust the *horse*?" Arias says. "Oh, right. Equo, equine. Horse."

Saetang nods. "I told you, no order, just colors. Nonsense."

They all walk back toward the base. Elegy's hands are cold. She's desperate for more coffee, or for a hot shower. But there's a tugging feeling in her fingers that means there's a message waiting for her.

"Do you have a quill?" Elegy asks.

Saetang nods, and reaches into their sleeve. The feather is short and flared on one side, and the metal the quill is made of is tinted green. Elegy starts writing, and the quill takes over, turning her tidy handwriting loopy and loose. Hela's handwriting.

MEETING WITH K IS SET FOR TOMORROW. 1300 HOURS.

In all the chaos of rescuing Julia Martin, Elegy almost forgot about what she asked Hela to do: contact Kesia Forint to set up a meeting so they can ask her about the so-called "alien launch" she saw over twenty years ago. It doesn't feel as urgent as Primary Avka Becken waiting in an interrogation room, or even Julia Martin resting in the hospital ward before she can unearth Theren's hidden memory. But it's a reminder: Elegy is needed back at home.

"Unfortunately, I think this has to be a short trip," Elegy says to Saetang. "Mind if I interrogate your prisoner before I go?"

36

Theren stands outside the interrogation room with Elegy beside him, looking through the mirror glass at Avka Becken. Parekh and Saetang are leaning against the wall right next to the glass, talking about a recent change to Cedrae ship mechanics. Parekh is biting her nails.

"What does she feel like to you?" Elegy asks him.

Sometimes he forgets that Elegy being inside his memories in the erczet meant she was within *him*. That she knows to talk about his Fever gifts not as seeing or perceiving, but as physical sensations.

He touches his fingertips to the glass and leans closer.

Avka Becken sits in a bare room. It's small and square, with one window that looks out at the ocean, a table and chairs, a pitcher of water, and an orange. Cedre's laws are strict about the proper treatment of prisoners. The orange is a sign of compliance with those laws. He stares at it, a smear of color against the faultless white.

Avka's hair, too, looks almost garish. Orange-red and still wet from the shower she took that morning. Her febra armor and boots are gone, soft Cedre fabrics replacing them.

"She's brittle," he tells Elegy. "Hard and consistent. Easy to read."

Elegy frowns at the glass. She's wearing a loose gray sweatshirt that keeps slipping off one of her shoulders, baring the defined ridge of her clavicle.

"Will you help me?" she asks him.

He's put his abilities to use as a truthsayer countless times. Once Rava realized how deeply he could read people, she came to rely on him more than she had ever relied on Satka or even Nyx. But he's never been *asked* before. Never felt like he had the right to say no.

"Of course, Your Grace," he says.

The honorific chafes against her in the same way that the pronouns he selects in Talusar do. She doesn't like to acknowledge any status differences between her and anyone else. But Theren prefers to be honest with himself about them. If he isn't, he'll dwell on how it felt to touch her last night, the way she tasted and sounded and smelled—a momentary lapse, for her; and for him, something unexpected and stolen.

She flips the deadbolt on the interrogation room door and steps into the room. He follows her. Avka's eyes find him immediately, and there's something eager in her, almost gleeful.

"You," she says to him in Talusar, as if it's his name. And then, to Elegy: "And who are you, exactly?"

"No one in particular," Elegy replies. Theren pulls the empty chair across from Becken back from the table and offers it to Elegy. A moment too late, he realizes it was a mistake—Becken's eyes light up, like she's realized something.

Elegy sits. "Did you wake with a headache? The substance I drugged you with is known for that."

"I thought the Fever, in its wisdom, devoured all Cedrae substances," Becken says. "Or is it only your elixir that disintegrates at the touch of our God?"

"Before we restored all of Cedre's relics, we developed several powerful substances," Elegy says, sounding like a museum docent. "A sedative, a healing ointment, and a truth serum, among them. They don't require elixir, and they seem to stand up to your god just fine. Especially the truth serum."

Fear is an unsteady, fluttering sensation. Panic is electric. Theren searches Becken for either of them, and comes up empty. Which is strange, really, because she's a prisoner in Naarm Stronghold, with no reason to expect mercy. They could wrench the truth from her by force. They could execute her. They could keep her here for life.

But she's not afraid.

"I can imagine a truth serum would be effective." Avka crosses her legs, and leans back in her chair. "If a person actually knows anything of value."

"You're assuming, of course, that you're the only prisoner we have."

"It took a Talusar to bring me down, and I doubt there are many of *him* to go around." She gestures at Theren, carelessly.

"I'm Cedre-born, you know," he says, curious to know how she'll react. Not every Talusar feels this level of superiority over Cedre that Becken seems to; her confidence in Talusar supremacy seems to be accompanied by a borderline religious fervor. And perhaps it is religious. The Talusar are the chosen people of the Fever, after all.

What he feels, instead of the embarrassment he expects at the revelation that a Cedre-born man beat her in a fight, is a stab of insight, like a ray of light piercing the clouds.

"I forgot about that. You were a Knight, weren't you?" she says.

He leans back against the wall. Cold seeps through his shirt. "If you know me, then you know you can't lie to me."

"The only Knight left alive," she says, as if he never spoke. "I wonder why that is."

"You're not going to provoke me by reminding me of my dead companions."

"I'm shocked they're letting you attend this little interview." Her eyes are wide and wild. "Do they know who I am? Do they know what you spent the last few years doing?"

A cold weight settles on Theren's chest that has nothing to do with Avka.

"You're Primary Avka Becken, direct report of Ykev Talus," Theren says flatly. "They know who you are. And I haven't hidden anything from them."

"That can't be true. I'm sure you kept the most *salacious* details to yourself."

Theren hears ringing. Avka Becken has a clenched-teeth smile, like she's bracing against pain.

"Let's play a game," Elegy says to Becken, her voice colder than he's ever heard it, "where I tell you what I suspect, and he tells me if I'm right."

Becken says, "I'd rather not."

"You have no choice." Elegy sits back. "Recently, a group of Talusar soldiers invaded this base. They left behind a witness with a damaged memory. You kidnapped Julia Martin to keep her from restoring that man's memory."

Theren waits for a reaction—any reaction. But Elegy may as well have spoken to Becken in English. She's unaltered.

Becken presses her palms flat to the table. Her fingers are thicker at the knuckles and calloused, too, from splitting over and over. His own are the same. "Who's Julia Martin?" she asks.

"Julia Martin" isn't a Talusar name. It's the name Julia chose after she came to Cedre, to ease her transition into Cedrae society. Maeve told him the name she was born with, once. He can't remember it now.

Elegy sits forward, like she's going to argue with Becken, but Theren sets a hand on her shoulder, stalling her. Becken's eyes are steady on his. Her hands are steady on the table. The feeling of her is steady, too.

"She doesn't know anything," he says. "That's why she didn't refuse to drink the vial of sedative. Why she's not afraid of truth serum. She doesn't know anything, and it's by design. Ykev Talus intentionally kept information from you so that we couldn't force you to share it, didn't he?"

There's something there—a little leap in her chest, like he's wrong about something, but not completely wrong. He breathes in through his nose, and out. He has to stay calm. He has to *think*.

They all thought the Talusar attack and the kidnapping were planned by Rava Vidar. But Avka Becken doesn't report to Rava Vidar; she reports to Ykev Talus. He assumed that both of those things couldn't be true at the same time. But what if he was wrong?

His memory of the meeting between Ykev and Rava, of the rain-spattered windowsill and the warm air, flashes in his mind.

"Rava and Ykev have an alliance," he says, testing it out. "A temporary alliance to accomplish a particular purpose. That's what they were discussing the day you and I met."

He's still surprised, sometimes, by how obvious it is when the truth is revealed. Avka's expression is a study in control, mouth a flat line. But she can't hide the way the declaration slides into her mind without friction.

"But you don't know what that particular purpose is," he says.

"No, I don't." Becken smiles again, coldly this time. "But I know it will be *catastrophic*." And then she bends her head to Elegy, in a mockery of respect. "Your Grace."

Elegy's body jerks as if she's been slapped.

"The Hope of Cedre and her coward Knight." Becken touches a hand to her chest. "What an honor."

"I think we're finished here," Elegy says. She gets to her feet, the chair squealing on the tile. Parekh is already unlocking the door to the interrogation room and opening it, so that Elegy can walk right out.

He can't bear to feel whatever it is Elegy feels now, and he can't bear to look at her, either. It's one thing for her to know the truth about him and Rava, and another for her to hear someone degrade him for it. *I'm sure you kept the most salacious details to yourself.*

But all Elegy says is: "All right?"

He nods. Elegy steps closer, and takes his hand—not holding it, exactly, but gripping it to send warmth into his fingers.

"Eyes up," she says gently, in Talusar, and he forces himself to look at her.

"Parekh and Saetang don't speak Talusar," she says. "I'll only translate what's relevant. And her petty jabs at you aren't relevant." She releases his hand. "No matter what Larke says, I think you need to meet with Julia Martin as soon as we get home. Okay?"

He nods. She turns away to talk to Saetang.

The ringing in his ears is gone.

37

Isre is on the landing pad when Theren steps down from the hatch. He grins, wind from the engine blowing his dark hair back and forth, and throws his arms around Theren. The embrace, brief as it is, is like a warm meal.

"What are you doing here?" Theren says, as he pulls away.

"Her Grace invited me," Isre replies, and he bobs his head to Elegy. "She thought you might need a friendly face. You know, because of . . ."

Isre nods at something over Theren's shoulder. Like a fish on a line, his attention is tugged back to Julia Martin, descending the hatch steps with Arias at her side. She was exhausted from trying to heal the witness with the addled memories when they left, and she still looks pale.

Theren's mouth goes dry. He wants—no, he *needs*—this gap in his memory to be restored. But he's also afraid of what's in it.

"Right," he says.

Elegy hops down from the hatch without bothering with the stairs, and offers her hand for Isre to shake. "Thank you for coming on short notice." She turns to Theren. "Julia's going to rest for an hour or so. It was all the time I could give her—we have that meeting tomorrow afternoon."

Dread gnaws at Theren's stomach. The meeting with Kesia—how could he forget? It's the main reason they need to do this so soon. The last thing he remembers before the gap in his memories is Kesia coming to fetch him from Rava's chambers. Which means that whatever he was forced to forget, his mother was probably a witness to it.

He'll have plenty of questions for her.

Theren watches Julia and Arias walking slowly across the landing pad together. He says, "And Specialist Gylle? Didn't Larke say she needed to approve any meetings between me and Julia?"

There's something unsteady in Elegy today, a new current. She touches his shoulder. "I'll take care of it."

He wants to hold her hand there, again, the way he did after the fight with Becken. But he doesn't dare. He watches as she hoists her bag over one shoulder, nods to Isre, and walks across the landing pad.

The Sparrow's engines are powered down now, and silent. A pair of technicians descended as soon as they landed to replace fuel and check everything over; they're calling back and forth to each other from one wing to another, both in bright red jumpsuits.

"Want some coffee?" Isre says.

"If you want to call it that," Theren replies, and Isre laughs.

"Two days in Austra and you've become a snob?"

Together, they walk toward the cafeteria, on the far side of the barracks building. Unlike the other structures on Losan Stronghold, the cafeteria building is circular—it looks like an old-fashioned drawing of an alien ship, wider than it is tall with huge circular windows studded around its belly.

Theren isn't sure what prompts him to say it. Maybe he just knows that he can't go on this way, holding all these memories inside him, weighing him down. Or maybe he wants Isre to know him—actually know him. Regardless, he looks at Isre and says, "I lived in House Vidar."

Isre looks startled. His steps falter. "You did?"

Theren nods. "For two years." His throat hurts. "They had real coffee there. That's where I became a snob."

"Oh."

Theren can feel the pressure of Isre's questions building up at the back of his throat like a sob.

"They had good spices, too." He feels unbalanced, talking about this with Isre like it's normal, like any of it is normal. "Is it bad to admit that any of it was good?"

He chokes a little on the question. Isre's hand touches right between Theren's shoulders.

"Of course not," he says. "I'm glad some things were good, Theren."

They pass a prickly-pear cactus swollen with pink flower buds.

"You can tell me about them, if you want," Isre says, tentative.

Theren has spent so long refusing to think of House Vidar at all. When he does, these days, it's because he's trying to dig useful memories out of his mind to help Cedre, to help Elegy. House Vidar may have been his prison, but it was a grand one.

"The house is built into the side of a cliff, and in the winter, when it snows, all the mountains are white," Theren says. "It's blinding, when the sun shines. But there's real fire in the fireplaces."

He thinks of crouching in front of the fire in the kitchen, warming his hands.

"There was a library," Theren says.

"Oh?" Isre's smile is gentle. "Any poetry in there, nerd?"

They take their time walking to the cafeteria, Isre with his head bent, listening, and Theren with his hands in his pockets, talking.

✦ ✦ ✦

Theren is lining up books on the little desk in his quarters when the knock comes.

Isre brought the books. They belonged to Kesia—or to Theren himself, when he was younger—and Isre kept them. *I didn't know what to do with them*, he said, when he offered Theren the box. *They're written in Talusar, after all.* He thinks Isre just couldn't bear to get rid of them.

He's supposed to go to a meeting room in the library for his meeting with Julia Martin, the same one where they did the erczet ritual. But when he opens the door, he finds Julia standing in the hallway.

Someone must have retrieved her bag from the wreckage of the crash that set off her kidnapping, because she's wearing garments that fit her: a white dress with a belted waist, polished black shoes. Her wrist is in a brace, and a dark bruise stains her left eye. There are others peeking out from her sleeve or her starched collar.

For a moment they stand there staring at each other. He doesn't remember much about the end of the ritual, but he remembers the pressure of her hands on his head, and her shallow breaths as she touched a kiss to his crown. Despite her neutral expression, he feels grief wrenching her. Wrenching him.

"I'm sorry, was I wrong about the meeting place?" he says.

"No, I . . ." She clears her throat. "I decided it's better if we do this somewhere you feel comfortable. It can be—difficult. So I asked for your room number."

"Oh. Well—come in."

His room isn't fit for company like Julia Martin's. Kesia told him, when he was young, that when the exiles first set out from Valla, she laughed at them for their jewelry-laden wrists and necks and fingers—the journey was long and arduous, and they seemed so ridiculous to her. But once they were released from quarantine on Cedre Station and sold all of their finery to the highest bidder, she understood. Jewelry was wealth that could be worn on the body, and they came to Cedre with only the clothes on their backs. They wanted to come rich.

Though all their jewels weren't enough to guarantee *wealth*, exactly, Julia Martin is used to fine things, and he has none. At least the room is clean, the sheets tucked in at the corners and all his clothes put away. Apart from the books on his desk, the timeline of his years in Valla on the wall, and a small cactus in a pot on the windowsill—a gift from Arias—there's nothing of him in this place.

Julia moves toward the books.

"Alinus," she says, brushing the spine of an older volume with her fingers. "I always liked her work. Funny."

She's a Talusar author, and the book is written in Talusar. Theren is about to tell Julia that the book was Kesia's favorite when he realizes he shouldn't talk to her about Kesia, the woman who set off the chain of events that got her daughter killed.

"I prefer Volyn," he says.

"You would." She taps the spine of the collection of Volyn's poetry, cracked and worn. "He has more depth of feeling, as you do."

He stills. It's a more compassionate assessment of him than he expected. She considers him for a moment.

"Did you think, after that ritual, that I wouldn't know you?" she says, switching to Talusar. The pronouns she uses for him are authoritative, but warm. She speaks to him like an aunt.

"I . . . didn't really think about it."

She folds her hands over her ribs, as if covering a wound there. Her fingernails are painted pale pink.

"That's one of the ritual's purposes," she says. "It's for grief and mourning, yes, of course. But it's also intended to create a lasting connection between the one who had to witness the death firsthand, and the ones who bear the loss. It's impossible for me not to feel for you now."

"And you still did it?" he says. "Knowing it would . . . tie us together?"

"Child," she says, with a gentle laugh. "That's one of the reasons I asked for it."

He sits on the edge of his bed. She perches on his desk chair, her legs crossed at the ankle and her hands folded in her lap.

"You are one of ours," she says. "I know it doesn't seem this way to you, because we all grew distant from your mother in your adolescence, but that journey out of Valla, that harrowing flight to Cedre, that time we spent in quarantine afterward—we became like family. Your recent return should have been an occasion for joy. For one of our children to survive when we thought all five were lost is a miracle. But it was difficult to see that when I was trapped in my own grief."

Her eyes are Maeve's eyes, round and gray as stone.

"I wanted to make myself see it," she says softly.

His throat burns. He looks out the window, at the orchard, the hints of yellow between the branches. At the sky beyond it. Only when the burning starts to subside does he dare look back at her.

"Can I ask you about her?" Julia says.

"Of course."

"What could she do with the Fever?" Julia asks, and the construction of the sentence is backward, for a Talusar. They always phrase it as *What could the Fever do in her?* That she chooses otherwise says something about her beliefs, how they've changed, or perhaps how they always were.

"She could share her own memories," he says. "She used it to survive the Crucible. She would watch her opponents in advance, then share the memory with Fenn so they could talk strategy. Two minds were better than one."

"She didn't share with you?"

"For the first year, I wasn't in touch with them," he says. "I helped them at first, especially with the language, but then . . ." He shakes his head. "I was ashamed, I think."

"Of what your mother did?"

"That, and I was . . ." He shrugs. "I was excellent. Almost by accident."

He remembers the first time they met Orda, who had a month to get them all in fighting shape—*an impossible task*, he said, at the time. Orda invited Theren, who at that time looked like a newborn foal, still freshly Fevered, to spar. He intended it to be an exercise in humility. To show them all how far they had to go. But Theren, sharp with grief and tired of being mocked, had decked him right in the jaw. It got rougher from there.

He remembers how, after that, Maeve looked at him like he was a stranger.

He adds, "She was smart, though. A fast learner."

"She always was. If she hadn't been a Knight, I think she would have worked with numbers." A swell of pride—as if, for a moment, she's forgotten to grieve what Maeve would never become. "She liked for things to make sense."

Maeve was the only one who asked questions about the Talusar. Why they did this or that, what they meant by certain things. Curious, always curious.

"Was she a good fighter?" Julia says.

"She was competent," Theren replies. "Better to be competent than excellent, when it comes to violence, I think."

Lines frame Julia's mouth when she frowns—like parentheses, encasing her mouth.

"Are you a good dancer?" she says.

The question comes out of nowhere. Theren blinks at her. "I guess so."

"Then consider that it isn't violence you have a talent for, it's movement," she says. "You forget, I've been in your head. You're uniquely present in your own body. Perhaps that's why the Fever manifests in you this way."

He thinks she smiles. It could be a trick of the light. He fidgets, feeling uncomfortable. He's never thought of himself like this. It's easier to believe that he has a natural predilection for violence than to think that he could have become something more benign, if he hadn't been broken by Rava Vidar instead. He doesn't want to think of himself as that malleable.

"We should begin," she says.

"Are you sure you're recovered enough?" he says to her, his eyes lingering on her bruised wrists.

"Your mother may have given you the impression that all the exiles but her were weak," Julia says, with a small smile. "But I've endured worse than that sham of a kidnapping, Theren." She tugs her cuffs down over the bruises. "Her Grace told me you have a memory gap?"

"Yes," he says. "I think Rava brought someone in to bury a memory of mine. I'm not sure why, but it seems important that I know."

"This process can be unpleasant," Julia says. "I should be more specific: it will hurt. Like the worst headache you've ever had. And you'll need to maintain control of your mind."

He nods.

"What you need to do is focus on the very last thing you remember before the gap, and then the very first thing you remember afterward. Then I will try to . . . loosen, for lack of a better word . . . what's between them."

"And you'll be able to see all of it?" he asks.

"Yes," she replies. "But like I told you, Theren. You are one of ours. You can trust me."

It has the neat clarity of truth to it. She stands, carries the chair over to the bed, and sits right in front of him, knee to knee.

"Let's begin."

38

In the memory, he sits on the edge of Rava's bed, his heels propped on the frame. His back aches, and he still feels things crawling on him, as he does most mornings. On the bad days, he sits for an hour, waiting for the feeling to subside enough for him to take a shower. Today is one of the bad days.

He hears the door to the office open. He tenses, ready, but it's not Rava. Whoever it is feels too nervous, too eager. He forces himself to get up and grab his shirt from the window seat. It's only half-buttoned by the time he steps into the office.

The next room is colder, the fireplace dark and wind wheezing through the cracks between windows and wall. It chases the smell of paper away. There are so many books here. It would be his favorite room in House Vidar, if it didn't contain so many bad memories.

Kesia stands just a few feet from the doorway, in leather trousers, a white shirt, same old boots. There's a knife in a sheath at her hip. She stares at him, and her emotions crowd into him for a moment before he pushes them out, like he's slamming a door.

"What the fuck are you doing here?" he says to her.

"You've lost weight," she says.

He's surprised by how bitter he still feels toward her. How the sight of her is still poison. "And?"

"What are you . . ." She frowns at him. "Do you live here?"

"You haven't answered my question."

"Do you?"

It's her tone of voice, quiet and soft, that makes him answer her.

"Yes," he says. "What are you doing here?"

"I'm here to escort you to a meeting. Rava's orders."

"Fine. I'll get my shoes."

He turns away, about to walk through the door to the bedroom.

She says, "I thought you would be harder to persuade."

He pauses with his hand on the doorframe, and looks at the wrinkled sheets where he sat a few minutes ago, trying to get himself to move.

"She calls, I answer," he says. "Same as you."

+ + +

Julia Martin's hands are on his, cool and strict. There's a pounding behind one of his eyes.

"Good," she says. "Now take me to the next thing you remember."

+ + +

Rock scrapes the skin of his palms. He's standing in the hallway in House Vidar, braced against the wall. He's sweaty, like he was just running—only he can't remember where he came from, or where he was going. He wipes the back of his neck with his free hand, and then his forehead. He blinks tears from his eyes.

He recognizes the door he's standing near as Rava's office door. It has a brass handle, and there are scratches at the bottom from the cat that used to live here. He straightens, his hand slipping down as the door opens, and Rava stands in the doorway.

Her hair is loose over her shoulders, golden and wavy in places, straight in others. She's not wearing shoes.

"Forint?" she says.

He blinks at her. His throat is raw. He has questions, but the words feel out of reach to him. She stretches out a hand, and he tenses, but doesn't pull away as she lays her palm on his cheek. Checking his temperature, he thinks.

"You don't look well," she says. "Come."

He follows her into the office.

+ + +

"Prepare yourself," Julia Martin says.

But there's no preparing for this. He feels like someone put a chisel in his eye socket and pounded it deep into his brain. He screams into his teeth, unable to stop himself, and Julia's hands tighten over his.

"Focus," she says, and he hears Satka—

+ + +

"Focus, idiot."

Satka grabs him by the hair, and leans in close.

"As my teacher once said . . . let pain be the whetstone that sharpens the blade of you."

She slams his head back into the ground.

✦   ✦   ✦

"Focus!"

✦   ✦   ✦

A hand presses into his shoulder, forcing him to his knees. Dazed, he doesn't resist. The journey here, to Ileth Vidar's estate, passed in a blur of sound, Rava talking to Ranos and Satka about the Battle of Calgara where she made a name for herself as a butcher, and in their mouths it's just the reminiscence of soldiers, but he knows it was a slaughter.

But now he's here, Rava standing behind him, and she's *terrified*, something he would have sworn up until that moment was impossible. Could a woman like Rava fear anything? Apparently she could.

He sees Ileth's shoes, first, and they're black boots, unscuffed, polished to shine. She wears black fitted clothes. Her wrists and her throat are draped in stones—deep blue opals, left jagged and unpolished. Her hair is as pale as Rava's, and she has Rava's aquiline nose. But her eyes are brown, close-set, like a bird.

She looks down at him, and smiles. Her voice is pleasant, almost unctuous.

"At last we meet," she says. "I have heard so much about you, Mr. Forint."

✦   ✦   ✦

Theren tries to yank his hands away from Julia Martin, and she holds on tighter.

"Go back to the last thing you remember before the gap," she commands. "I will bring out the rest."

His head *burns*—

✦   ✦   ✦

"She calls, I answer," he says to Kesia. "Same as you."

He puts on his boots, changes his shirt into one that's not as creased, and checks his hair in the bathroom mirror. He catches Kesia peering through the crack in the door, trying to see into the bedroom. When he emerges, she looks startled by how close he is, or perhaps how big he is now, Fever-changed and far deadlier than the child she trained on Cedre Station.

"Lead the way." He gestures toward the door.

She tucks her hair behind both ears, and turns away from him. She used to make him feel like a slip of a person; now she looks spare to him, and small. He wonders if time has taken some of her sturdiness from her, if she's found a harder life here than she expected to, or if he's just changed that much. He tries not to give a damn either way, but it's a hard habit to break, caring about your own mother.

"I'm stationed at the monastery now," she says, as they climb the steps. They pass one of the cooks, who nods to Theren, and the sitting room with the blue rug that Ranos uses for his morning stretches. They walk beneath a portrait of the emperor, and Theren feels his eyes following them down the hallway.

"Sometimes I work with your friend Orda," she adds.

She's baiting him. Trying to pique his curiosity, make him ask a question. He's silent as they climb. She leads him down a short corridor where an unfamiliar soldier stands guard. He wears the seal of the Vidari on his sleeve, a halo of vines.

"He's unarmed?" the soldier says to Kesia.

"Yes," she replies, and the soldier opens the door for Theren.

He steps into one of the guest suites. This part of the house is on top of the peak, rather than built into the face of it, so it's all made of wood, polished and carved into organic shapes, leaves and flowers and branches. There's a low stove in the corner, and sitting in a chair beside it, her head turned toward the window, is an augur.

Not just an augur. *The* augur. The one he met at the Getty.

Rava isn't there. Not yet, anyway. Just the augur, and Kesia at Theren's back.

"Come here, boy," the augur says to him.

He's afraid to read her. He's never read anyone who could see the future before. But what he finds is nothing new. She's afraid. Angry. He suspects she's not here because she wants to be; this guest suite is an elegant prison for her.

He stayed upright when he met her before, in the Getty. This time when he draws closer to her, he bows with the reverence of the Talusar. She leans forward and studies his face, as he studies hers. She looks the same as he remembers, her nose dotted with freckles, her skin crinkled around the eyes but otherwise smooth.

"I saw this moment when we met before," she says. "It was fresh in my mind when I looked at your younger self. You've changed so much."

He knows he looks different now, but he can't imagine what it was like for her to see two versions of him layered over each other like a screen over a window.

"Why . . . why do you see me?" he says, not sure he wants the answer.

She tilts her head. "Some people I see once, and never again. Some people, though, keep showing up again and again, and it's hard to understand why. That was true of you, at first. As far as I could tell, the only remarkable thing about you was what the Fever did through you." Her voice lowers, softens. "And then I realized . . . that's exactly it. Nine people on this planet can do what I do, and that's rare enough. But only one person can do what you do."

The door opens behind him, and he turns to see Rava, her blond hair braided in its usual crown, her gray sweater neatly tucked, her worn boots tied tightly at her ankles.

"My lady," he says, and he inclines his head to her.

She pulls the door closed behind her, and stands with her back against it. Her eyes skirt his, and he realizes: she's *nervous*.

The augur folds her spotted hands over her belly and studies Rava. Theren has never seen someone look at her that way, with derision instead of fear. And he's never seen Rava tolerate it before, either.

"You haven't told him," the augur says.

"That's not your concern."

"It is if you want my help."

"You may be misunderstanding the situation you're in," Rava says.

"I assure you, I understand it perfectly," the augur replies. "This is a negotiation. You kidnapped me, and then offered me my release in exchange for my help. That was your initial offer. And now I'm telling you that I'll only accept that offer if you give me something else in return: you must face reality. I think you'll accept my terms because you want my assistance ever so slightly more than I want my freedom. So." The augur leans back in her chair. "Am I right, Rava?"

Rava's eyes are not cold, exactly, but flat. Fear prickles down his spine at the sight. It usually precedes violence, but he can't imagine even Rava Vidar, secret Talusar apostate, hurting an augur.

"Tell him, then," Rava says.

"Coward," the augur says, with a harsh laugh. The collective anger in the room is thick enough to choke on. The augur leans forward in her chair and looks up at him. When the sun hits her face directly, he sees little hints of the past everywhere: a pockmark in her cheek, a piercing in her earlobe, a scar beneath her chin.

"Three years ago the augurs offered Rava Vidar a path to Talusar victory," the augur says. "One of the signposts along that path was a man. When asked how she would be able to identify that man, we told her she would be in love with him." The augur's brow furrows. "By whatever definition of love makes sense to her, that is. We do not all love equally well."

At first, Theren only hears the words passing over him like a wind ruffling his hair. He wonders why she's telling him this, and he feels dread of the answer, almost in the same moment. But he can't stop his mind from piecing it together. Rava's averted eyes. The vine symbol inked on his hand.

He feels like he's going to vomit.

He thought his presence in Rava's house was mere happenstance. That her greed, her paranoia, had driven her to acquire him like a new weapon, eager to use his gift. But to hear that he's here because of her pursuit of destiny, that his presence is in any way fated—it makes him feel sick.

She's in love with him.

"I'm sorry to do this to you," the augur says to him. "But I wanted her to have to see your reaction to this, in the hope that it will help her come to terms with who she is and what she's done. A feeble hope, perhaps, but . . ."

"Stop," he says. "Stop, please."

He's hunched over a little, like an animal protecting its soft belly. He brings a hand up to his mouth—he can feel a scream rising in his throat, or maybe that's bile. Either way, he needs to keep it in, needs to stay contained, needs to—

"Have I met your requirements?" Rava says. "Can we stop wasting time?"

He doesn't want to read her. He can't. But even without the depth that the Fever gave to his perceptions, he knows her well enough to hear the unsteadiness in her voice.

Nothing has changed, he tells himself. However Rava feels, whatever reason she had for bringing him to House Vidar—the outcome is the same. He's here. He's enduring his time in this house the same way he was yesterday and the day before. *Nothing has changed, nothing has changed.*

"Very well," the augur says. "We can begin, then."

Rava nods, and pulls away from the door just enough to open it. "Bring him in," she says to the guard in the hallway.

"I told you all that was required for this was the meeting of past, present, and future," the augur says, sounding confused. "The three of us meet those requirements." The augur tilts her head. "Or are we still pretending that you're not an epocha?"

"I don't know what you mean," Rava says, and Theren expected no different. Rava Vidar knows better than most that the best way to pass off a lie is to never admit it's a lie, not even for a moment.

The augur sighs. Theren is too busy trying to breathe to react to this confirmation of what he's always suspected: that Rava's gifts aren't as singular as the Talusar think. That she belongs locked up in a monastery with all the other epocha, and only enjoys the freedom she now has because her mother is Ileth Vidar. It seems the least of the secrets she's kept.

"Kneel," Rava says to Theren, and in the last year, he's noticed that she gives this order when she's concerned that he'll react badly to something and she'll lose control over him, that his size and strength will suddenly become a problem. So he obeys, but with a hammer for a heart, anticipating what's coming.

A man walks into the room. He's wearing a blue robe embroidered, not with the interlinked circles of the Fever, as a priest's robe would be, but with the twin silver lines of an epocha.

Theren doesn't have the Talusar's reverence for the epocha, but he understands what's expected of him. He bows his head when the epocha lowers his hood, but not before he recognizes the epocha's face.

"Theren," the epocha says.

Theren closes his eyes.

It's Fenn.

The ache he feels is so intense he has to press a hand to his gut to steady himself. He feels the brush of Rava's fear against him, but she shouldn't have worried—lying to him about Fenn's death is just one in a long line of painful things she's done to him. It hardly registers.

What registers instead is Fenn himself. Fenn alive. Fenn, elated at the sight of him, even though Theren betrayed him to save his life. Fenn drops to his knees and puts his hands on Theren's shoulders.

"You're alive," Theren says weakly.

"I'm sorry," Fenn says. "I'm so sorry, I asked them to tell you I was dead in case I was the reason you hadn't run away yet."

Fenn looks older than he did the last time Theren saw him, thinner and sterner, his eyes carrying far too much history. Yet the way he talks, the way his smile looks hard-won, like it was carved from a frown—it's the same.

"It doesn't matter." And it doesn't, it can't matter, because Theren is sure they only have a few minutes with each other, because he can feel the thread of Rava's patience pulling taut. "I'm the one who's sorry, anyway."

Their dalliance was short-lived. Two Crucible fighters desperate for comfort, finding it where they could. It ended before Fenn's arrest, when Theren noticed, as only he could have, that Fenn's feelings were getting deeper and his own weren't. Fenn took the end of it in stride. *Ah, well. We'll be dead soon anyway.* A phrase that couldn't quite disguise his hurt—but it was a hurt that would pass.

But betraying him to Rava, telling everyone that he was an epocha? That was a hurt that would linger.

"I told you I've never hated you," Fenn says, with a breathy laugh. "I still mean it. I always will."

It's a kind of benediction. Something in Theren eases. Fenn doesn't hate him.

"How very touching," Rava says, the thread snapping. "Let's get on with it. Augur?"

Fenn's eyes search his, and Theren gets lost in the tangle of what he feels. Just as he used to, Fenn feels like wind that's blowing in all different directions, gentle but scattered.

"I was trying to explain to Mr. Forint before your arrival that his gift is what makes him exceptional," the augur says. "What we have in this room is a meeting of the past—" The augur nods to Fenn. "And the future." She touches her own chest.

Theren stares at Fenn. His serious expression. The silver embroidery along his collar. The lines at the corners of his eyes.

He shakes back his sleeve and holds his hand over Theren's cheek, without touching him.

"This would not be the first time an augur and an epocha have helped each other," the augur says. "An augur's vision is limited, you see, by what is available to us. But visions can be prompted. Encouraged. Unearthed. Sometimes a more profound knowledge of a person yields new revelations. New visions."

Fenn touches Theren's face, not gentle but firm, his thumb framing Theren's mouth. His eyes close. Theren tries to pull away, by instinct, but the augur's hand clamps over his shoulder and holds him in place.

"Tell me," the augur says.

"Down the line of his progenitor," Fenn says, voice low. "His father comes through a doorway."

"What kind of doorway?" the augur asks.

"One hidden among the stars," Fenn says. "Distant but not unreachable. He brings with him a seedling."

"A seedling."

"A creature. A plant. A destroyer," Fenn says. "He crashes, but he survives. His name is Sevik."

"Sevik." The word hisses between the augur's teeth. "I see Sevik now. I see the *Sundial* passing through the doorway. He waits on the other side for his son. He has waited a long time. Yes."

"What must I do?" Rava demands. "Should I facilitate this meeting?"

The augur looks down at Theren, and he gets the sudden urge to beg her not to say anything. To ask her for a strength she hasn't shown before, to make a choice she and the other augurs pretend never to make. He wants her to choose the Cedrae over the Talusar.

"*No*," the augur says, her voice flat. "There is no victory for you that results from his death, so you must keep him alive. But you must also keep him from passing through the doorway in the stars. You must keep him from meeting his father."

Fenn takes his hand from Theren's face. His eyes open. They're wet with tears.

"He waits for you," Fenn says softly.

The augur takes her hand from Theren's shoulder. He feels the same way he felt after fights in the Crucible, like something was taken from him, something big, and he can't get it back.

Fenn stands, shakes his sleeve back down over his hand, and steps back. Theren is trembling.

His father's name. Sevik. *His father* is waiting.

And Rava Vidar is standing in the way.

39

Elegy leaves General Thompson's office with fatigue settling deep into her body. *Don't trust the horse!* the general said to her by way of farewell, quoting the memory-addled witness to the Naarm attack, and Elegy suspects it will become a joke throughout the base by week's end. One thing she misses about living among soldiers is how they face the darkness: head-on, and with a laugh at the ready.

She wishes she had one at the ready now. She has a meeting with Larke in twenty minutes, and there's dread humming in her body. Right now, Julia Martin is with Theren, restoring his missing memory. Right now, they're all inching closer to whatever it is that Rava Vidar is planning.

On the way to the veil room, Elegy stops by Losan Stronghold's news pavilion. Early in Cedre's life, when resources were especially limited, the pavilions were the most important places in Cedre, the places where people could gather to ask for help, or to offer it, or find out about community events. They still serve that purpose, but now the national news dominates— especially if it's entertaining.

At Losan Stronghold, the pavilion is centered around an obsidian stone wide enough to park a Finch on top of it. The stone is surrounded by a wall just high enough for people to lean against as they watch the holograms move.

She slows her steps as she passes through. It's crowded here, the soldiers of Losan Stronghold gathered at the end of their day shift. She turns to the side to slip through the crowd, muttering "excuse me" as she pushes her way past people.

She's so busy navigating the sea of people that she doesn't even notice what they're all watching until she's close to the wall.

The images are grainy and a little blocky, but still, she recognizes the pale, glowing shape of Theren Forint with his sword held aloft. It's only after a few seconds that she identifies herself, bent low behind him, spear in hand. Across from them are the hulking man Arias stabbed from behind, and Avka Becken.

This is the surveillance footage from the rescue. She distantly remembers the Eye drifting around the forest, drawn there by the chaos.

Elegy has never watched herself fight before. She didn't feel graceful while doing it. She felt frantic, like a mouse scrambling to get out of a trap.

She leans forward, her elbows on the low wall, as the Elegy of two nights ago thrusts the spear, and it comes *so close* to Theren, finding the air right along his rib cage to force her opponent to dodge it. In the same moment, Theren slams his sword down hard on Becken's with brutal strength, making her visibly grunt with surprise.

She doesn't look elegant in the footage, exactly, but there's something about the way that she and Theren work together that looks almost choreographed. He moves, and she moves. He shifts one way, and she shifts the other way.

There's something about it that unmoors her.

"How long have they been training together? I thought she was recovering from a nervous breakdown the last few years, not learning how to fight," she hears someone near her ask, and Elegy twitches in response, but doesn't look their way. She doesn't want anyone to recognize her.

"I don't think they have trained together, is the thing," someone else replies. "I've got a cousin who works at the hospital. Said the Knight escaped Valla just a few weeks ago, turned up all covered in gore."

"Can't be true," the first voice says. "I mean, look at them."

Elegy watches the big soldier fall to Parekh's blade, and Theren turns on Becken to fight her alone. In the moment, Elegy considered helping him, but it only took a few seconds to abandon that idea. Theren fighting one-on-one is hard to look away from.

She steps back the second the fight is done. She doesn't need to see what comes next—her putting a hand on Theren's neck. She can still feel the ghost of that touch in her fingers, his hot skin, the prickle of his hair. And the way he held her there, a desperate clutch of his hand, like he couldn't bear for her to let go.

Uneasy, she continues on to the veil room.

✦ ✦ ✦

This veil room—the most secure one in Losan Stronghold—is bright and clean. Sunlight spills through the skylight overhead, making the veil's arch gleam. The veil itself scatters bright colors in every direction, like a prism.

Elegy steps through it, keeping her mouth closed so she doesn't breathe it in. The fabric brushes over her face like wind. Larke appears in front of her, gazing at something in the distance that Elegy can't see.

She looks exhausted. Even Elegy, unfamiliar with Larke's usual expressions, can see that. It's in the way she stands, in the half-focus of her eyes.

"Hello," she says to Elegy.

There's no "Your Grace" here, when it's just the two of them. No protocol. The last time they were alone together was right after Shir's death. Larke asked Elegy to come back to Cedre Station with her to put on a show—to inspire confidence in the new regime after their mother's death. Elegy, then barely able to think straight, just told her she didn't believe in prophecy, and she was leaving.

For once, Larke didn't argue. She just assured Elegy that she would take care of arranging her exit. Elegy thinks of that brisk but oddly compassionate reaction now. At the time, it was what she needed most, and Larke gave it to her without a second thought.

She wishes that was the Larke standing in front of her now. But Larke's jaw is even more set than usual. Not a good sign.

"Here she is," Larke says, her voice quiet. "The hero of the hour."

Elegy looks up at the skylight, searching for a reply that doesn't make things worse. The sky over Losan is a rich blue dotted with clouds. It'll probably be a beautiful sunset.

"Julia's safe. That's what matters."

Larke rolls her eyes. "Yes, Julia is safe. And currently disobeying one of my direct orders, I assume at your behest."

"I don't know what you mean."

"Did I or did I not tell you that Specialist Gylle needed to approve any further meetings between Julia Martin and Theren Forint?" Larke's voice is getting louder. "I believe I did. So then please explain why Ms. Martin appeared at Theren Forint's door a half hour ago."

Elegy keeps her expression passive. "I'm sure Julia just wants to talk to him about her daughter. He was close with her in Valla."

"Bullshit," Larke snaps. "Stop lying to me, Elegy. I know you didn't just happen to fly over that Talusar ship in Austra, I know you arranged for Julia Martin and Theren Forint to meet this afternoon so she could look into his mind, I know your sister is visiting Talusar sympathizers out in the desert. I'm far more observant than you suppose and far less stupid than you imagine."

"Fine." Elegy crosses her arms, and steps closer to Larke, stretching the limits of the veil. "I'll tell you the truth, then: you're trying to control what you don't understand, and if you could just stop focusing on the wrong things—"

"And you think you know what the 'wrong things' are?" Larke laughs. "You spend four years fucking around in the desert with Tausia Helasz, catching criminals and drinking whiskey, and then you come back and you know everything about our enemies? You know better than the person whose entire life has been preparing them for fighting the Talusar?"

"Your entire life has been about a political position," Elegy says. "Not about the Talusar. You've never fought a Talusar soldier, you've never gone to Talusar country, you don't know a goddamn thing about our enemy that you haven't read in a brief. I do. And instead of listening to me, you spend all your time playing these ridiculous political games—"

"Oh, sure. Elegy Ahn would never play games." Larke snorts. "You're the one who undermined me at Theren Forint's hearing. Who confirmed the rumors that you are the great, prophesied savior of Cedre only when it was most convenient for you. Who has been ignoring my orders, and lying to me, and scheming behind my back!"

Elegy says, "The one time I did what you said, you used me as a fucking puppet for your Restorationist agenda without my permission. Forgive me for not being eager to repeat the experience."

"I spent *four years* apologizing for your absence and your silence," Larke says. "And in return, I received blame from every direction. Larke Rosyk, who's keeping her poor bereaved sister in an attic somewhere. Larke Rosyk, who's lost control of Cedre's future. Larke Rosyk, who can't even get her sister's loyalty, so why should anyone else give it to her?"

"I'm sorry my grief was so inconvenient for you."

Larke doesn't respond right away. Instead, she shakes her head at Elegy like she's dealing with an incorrigible child or a puppy that just chewed her slippers. Elegy hates it far more than she has ever hated a word out of Larke's mouth.

"I know exactly what you're doing, and I won't allow it," Larke says. "I'm going to do what I should have done from the start. I'm going to approve the use of truth serum—"

Elegy imagines Theren Forint in an interrogation room, the serum forcing him to talk about Rava, about what happened to him in her house, about what he survived—

Her anger is sudden and intense. "No fucking way."

"—and *you*, meanwhile, will run everything you do past me first, including whatever it is you're doing through Tausia Helasz—"

"No."

Elegy's voice is louder now, deeper. She sounds both strange and familiar to herself. She sounds like their mother.

And it seems like Larke hears it, too, because she goes still.

"You," Elegy says, "are not going to add to his suffering."

Larke hesitates. There's a glint in her eyes that Elegy doesn't like.

"Oh." Larke laughs a little. "*Oh.*" She laughs again, full-bellied this time. "You think it's him, don't you."

Elegy feels like she's about to choke. "That's not what this is about."

"'I saw a man,'" Larke says, quoting the augurs. "'He will bring you death. You will fall—'"

Her eyes are burning. "Stop it."

"'—in love with him.'"

Larke is still smirking. In that moment, Elegy would do anything to wipe that look off her face.

"You think I'm playing a game, Larke? Fine. Then here are the new rules."

She steps closer. The veil pulls against her skin.

"You'll leave Theren Forint alone. You'll stop monitoring me. You'll stop tracking my sister. You'll stay out of my way as I do my best to stop Rava Vidar."

She watches the multicolored spots of light cast by the veil dance behind her sister's projection.

"I said I didn't want to take anything from you, and I meant it," she says. "But if you interfere with my work again . . . I really will come for your goddamn throne."

She waits for a moment to see if Larke will say anything back to her, but Larke is still just standing there, staring at her, spots of light on the wall behind her and her hands limp at her sides.

For the first time since Elegy has known her, Larke looks afraid.

Elegy steps backward through the archway.

✦ ✦ ✦

The building where Theren Forint lives is made of cement, like all the neo-Brutalist structures of Losan Stronghold. Orange light streams through the slanted windows in the ceiling, making it look like the hallway is on fire.

It's lonely here, and quiet. A good place for her to calm down after her meeting with Larke, only she doesn't think she'll be able to. She's never made things easy for Larke, but she's always preferred to sidestep her or manipulate her rather than stand up to her. She has no idea what she was thinking.

Actually, she does. But she doesn't want to look at it just yet.

She taps on Theren's door and hears, "Come in."

When she steps into his room, he's facing the cabinet where his clothes are stacked, tugging a shirt over his head. She sees just a flash of his scarred abdomen and the jut of his hips and her mouth goes dry.

He catches her eye in the mirror, and she realizes: he can *feel that*. He can feel whatever she feels when she looks at him.

No one surprises him.

She's been trying not to think about how he felt under her hands in that supply closet. Warm and strong and urgent. His arm across her back. The smell of him, like citrus. It's hard not to think about it now, with his hair wet from a shower, and the way he looks at her, so focused, like the rest of the world is irrelevant.

Thoughts of Larke, of how Elegy threatened her, of what happened with him and Julia Martin—they suddenly feel small by comparison to this, this desperate longing, this devouring guilt.

"This doesn't have to be anything other than what it is," he says.

Sometimes she wonders if he can read her thoughts as well as her feelings.

"And . . . what is it?" she asks.

"You want me." The boldness of it is almost embarrassing. But it's pointless to deny it. She knows how acute his sense of other people is.

She meets his eyes in the mirror and tries for the same boldness. "Yeah. I do."

"Well," he says. "You can have me."

The last knot of her control unravels. She moves closer, drawn like a moth to the fire of him, her footsteps soft on the concrete. He doesn't move, just watches her in the mirror until she's right behind him. She sets her hands on his hips, and hears Parekh telling her not to beat herself up about it, that it's biology, that it's all right. Then she slides her hands under his shirt.

He draws a sharp breath, almost like a gasp, as she slides her hands up, over the fresh scar on his side, over the ripple of muscle that covers his rib cage, over his chest. She leans in, and kisses the top of his spine, right above the collar of his shirt. Lemongrass—he smells like the lemongrass balm the army doctors give out for sore muscles.

It's hard to remember to feel guilty when she's touching him.

He turns toward her, and for a moment he just stands there, the barest sliver of space between them. Then he bends his head to kiss her throat. Her hands are still under his shirt, but she's less gentle after that first touch of his lips, holding on to him for stability as his mouth traces a line up to her ear—not quite kissing, more like he's deciding where to start. She can't bear it any longer; she turns her face into his and kisses him, hard, her lips parting.

Her body is hot, scorched by the contact. He puts his hands on her,

her hips, her waist, her chest, and she can't help the desperate sound she makes, can't help the way she grabs at him in response.

He backs up, still kissing her, and sits on the edge of the bed, so she has to trip after him. Breathless, heart racing, she lets him pull her to stand between his knees. She braces herself on his shoulders as he kisses her stomach, over her shirt—and then he lifts the hem just enough to kiss beneath it, right under her belly button.

She reaches down to undo the top button of her pants, and he kisses the skin she bares, right above the band of her underwear—

Then she puts her hands in his hair, and everything stops.

He freezes, breathing against her stomach, and his hands come up to her wrists. They're so gentle it startles her. He guides her hands away from his head, and looks up at her, apprehension in his eyes.

She doesn't need to ask about it. She already knows: grabbing his hair like that, it must be something Rava used to do.

She nods, and tries to steady herself. She should step back, button that button, sit in an actual chair for this adult conversation that she is definitely going to force herself to have, but she can't bring herself to move.

"You could ask me what I'm doing here," she says. "If you want."

He leans in, touching his mouth to her stomach again, and speaks against her. "I'd rather just take what's on offer."

His teeth graze her skin. She considers peeling her clothes away from her body, piece by piece, so he can do *that* to every inch of her.

She doesn't.

"What's on offer?" she asks quietly.

"You want me, and you trust me, I think," he says, raising his eyes to hers again. "Seems like plenty." At her dubious expression, he adds, "I so rarely get anything I want."

He makes it sound so simple. Like there really doesn't have to be more. He slips his hands under her shirt, just a little, just enough to brush his fingers over her sides—and she almost believes it. She believes it for now.

He says, "My hair's growing out. I'll cut it again."

She gets the feeling that's the most he'll say about his reaction to her hands in his hair, and she doesn't want to press him. The mood between them has shifted as a result, the desperation gone, so she doesn't mind, so much, when he slides his hands out from under her shirt and leans back.

"I liked it short," she says. "Your hair."

He smiles a little.

"You did come here for a reason," he says. "What happened? You feel—" He pauses. "Sorry. I know you don't like that."

"No, tell me."

"You feel . . . like you did something important."

It's hard, sometimes, not to marvel at him. The Fever reshapes everyone who survives it—she knows that. But the Fever in his blood only gives him more data than other people; it doesn't teach him what it means. That's all Theren.

"I might have. I'm not sure yet." She clears her throat, and puts a few steps between them, enough for her to regain her senses. "I'd like to know about Julia."

Elegy sits on his desk chair, just the edge of it. She watches his bare toes curling into the cement floor, then looks around the room—dim now, the sun almost set. There's a line of books on his desk that wasn't there before. The spines are creased and peeling. She recognizes some of the names, written in Talusar.

He looks out the window. "Fenn Kovek is alive."

Of all the things she expected him to say, that wasn't one of them. "You saw him?"

"Him, and an augur. They . . ." He sucks in a breath. "The augur said something about . . . past, present, and future. That the three of us would be sufficient. Actually, she said that to Rava, but—" He shakes his head. "Fenn touched me, and the augur asked him what he saw. He said he saw my father. He said he came from . . . a doorway. In the stars." He laughs a little. "Does that sound insane?"

Elegy thinks of the box of artifacts in the trailer in Twentynine, her father's conviction that there were otherworldly visitors on Earth. She thinks of the glowing plant that Hela almost died to protect, and the maybe-hallucination, maybe-visitation she experienced when she touched it.

She swallows hard. She promised herself she would never start to believe in wild things like secret aliens and . . . and *world-saving prophecies*, would keep her feet on firm ground. But what is she supposed to do when "firm ground" starts to feel like denial?

She who moves the fulcrum controls the outcome.

"I've heard quite a few ridiculous revelations in my time," Elegy says, trying to keep her voice level. "So, not really."

Softly, he replies, "Yes, you have, haven't you."

She clears her throat. "What happened next?"

"I don't know why, but I think hearing about my father triggered the augur to see something," he says. "Me, on the *Sundial*, going through that doorway."

Elegy grew up hearing about the voice beyond their solar system, beckoning them out to a much greater existence. Faith in it, in the *Sundial*, feels like faith in the Fever, in a god. The audacity of believing there could be something out there that was better than what they have. The absurdity of thinking there's meaning somewhere in the chaos of the endless universe.

The madness of believing in a prophecy that declares her to be the Hope of Cedre.

She spent most of her life believing in the *Sundial*, in the possibility of another world. What's one more impossible thing, really?

Her heart speeds up.

"The augur told Rava to keep me from going through that doorway. And she told me, at the beginning—that I was mentioned in a prophecy," he says, a kind of hysteria rising in his voice. "That I was a . . . signpost. On Rava's path to victory. And she would know me because she would be in—love with me."

He leans his face into his hands.

Elegy has wondered quite a few times what questions Rava Vidar asked the augurs, and what they said in response. She assumed that given how different she and Rava were, they would ask about different things, receive different guidance. How unsettling, then, to hear that they asked the same thing . . . and received the same answer.

"This is why—all of it," he says, his voice muffled. "This is why she . . . pursued me to begin with."

Elegy thinks this isn't quite what people imagine when they long for their suffering to mean something. There's something especially cruel about finding out that your tormentor isn't random, that they *selected* you, that they designed the shape of your pain in order to fit you into their destiny. Randomness, and chaos, and the indifferent universe . . . they would all be easier to bear.

Rava, the orchestrator of his fate.

Rava, chasing the destiny that Elegy refuses to acknowledge: *She who moves the fulcrum controls the outcome.*

Elegy feels like she's standing at the mouth of a cave. She doesn't know what she'll find if she walks into it. She only knows that if she stays where she is, life will be what it's always been. Elegy Ahn. The Sword's spare daughter, for emergencies only. A soldier with too much rage to get promoted, until Shir helped her heal from it. And even after—grieving, a haze of Scout missions, the struggle to put one foot in front of the other. It's familiar. It's safe.

But in this darkness, there's prophecy. A fate too huge to bear. The great lever with the Cedrae on one side and the Talusar on the other. And the problem from the start: that if she believed she was the Hope of Cedre, she had to also believe that she would love a man who wasn't Shir. She would have to accept her own inconstant heart.

And while she can't imagine being the person who *controls the outcome*—

When she looks into Theren Forint's dark, focused eyes, she realizes the alternative is handing that control over to Rava Vidar.

Is handing *him* over to Rava Vidar, in one way or another.

And she may not know what he is to her, not yet . . . but she knows she won't do that.

She stands, and moves toward Theren, careful of his bare feet. She covers his hands with hers, and tugs them away from his face.

"I need you to read me. Okay?" she says, bending closer.

He laces his fingers with hers, so their palms are pressed together. He looks up at her, waiting.

"When the augurs summoned me to the Cenobium, they also summoned Rava," she says. "They told us that one of us would triumph over the other. That the questions we asked them that day, and the answers we received, would set things in motion that couldn't be stopped."

She's only ever told Hela and Shir that Rava was there, at the Cenobium, when she heard the prophecy. Her mother insisted it would cause mass panic. It's making Elegy panic, now.

Elegy doesn't want her suffering to mean that much.

"The augurs . . . they told me what to look for, but I didn't want to hear it, and I didn't know what to do. And after Shir died, I stopped believing in purpose, in meaning, in prophecy," she says. "But Rava just made a huge mistake: she told you *exactly* what to do." Elegy thinks of the young augur touching the points of the triangle in the dirt. The trio of the fulcrum, the three voices in harmony. What did the augur say to Theren? Something about past, present, and future. About the three of them—augur, epocha, and Theren—being sufficient.

"She told us who we need," Elegy says, and she shivers with the awareness of it. *Past, present, and future. One will bear the Vidari name. One knows the taste of Cenobium salt. One . . .*

She forces herself to focus. "She gave us a clear mission. If that augur said she has to keep you from going through that doorway in the stars? Well, that's exactly where you're going to go."

She feels the memory of standing in the Cenobium on the scrying mirror close at hand, like if she just reaches out and touches it, it will come flooding back to her. But when she allows herself to brush against it, it's not the augurs' voices she hears.

It's the Sword's. *Trust that you will be what you're required to be, in this role you didn't choose.*

She leans in closer, speaking against his mouth in a harsh whisper.

"And I will get you there," she says. "Because I'm the goddamn Hope of Cedre."

His room is dark, now, the sun disappeared beneath the horizon. His eyes look black. Endless.

"Am I lying?" she asks him, and she's afraid to hear the answer.

He turns her hand, and kisses her knuckles, slowly, his eyes still on hers. She can't tell if he does it because he wants to touch her or if he does it like a vassal showing reverence for a queen.

Her hands are trembling. Her breaths are quaking, too.

"No, Elegy." She thinks it might be the first time he's ever called her by her name. "You're not lying."

She's relieved. She's horrified. Because the only thing worse than believing that Rava Vidar is fated to lead the Talusar to triumph . . . is believing that the faltering of her heart was written in the stars.

40

Theren watches Isre's hands on the navigation panel of the ship, their movements certain, almost automatic.

"Why did you decide against being a pilot?" Theren asks his brother. He's hesitant to interrupt someone whose consciousness is currently split in half, even though Isre told him when they set out that he could carry on a conversation just fine while flying.

They're on their way to the middle of nowhere. Right in the middle of a flat plain. Those were the coordinates of the meeting point Kesia set. There was obvious wisdom in it: there was no way for them to hide reinforcements. She could see for miles in every direction.

Her other demands were that no one be armed, and that Isre and Theren both attend. Elegy hadn't argued. They needed Kesia's answers too badly.

Isre shrugs. "I went where the need was. Everyone wants to be a pilot—even with only five percent of applicants being accepted into the program, they always have more than they need. It's a sexier job than 'technician,' I guess."

"And you had no desire to be sexy," Theren supplies, and he feels, for a moment, like he's his old self, teasing Isre across the dinner table about some new girlfriend. Once he sent a wax-sealed letter officially welcoming one of Isre's girlfriends to the family. It was his mission to make Isre's life a little harder, he used to say. That was an older brother's duty.

"No, I was already plenty sexy without it," Isre says, raising an eyebrow over the frames of his sunglasses.

Theren grins.

It's all wasteland beneath them. Crumbling settlements from a time long before Cedre existed—rubble in the shape of buildings, remnants of half-disintegrated roads. Theren is still amazed by how time eats buildings, how efficiently rust and rot devour.

"Did you ever think about what you would be if you weren't a Knight?" Isre asks. Theren feels a tremor of nervousness in him as he asks the question, like he isn't sure it's all right to talk about what might have been.

But that yearning for something else that he felt so acutely before he took his oath is gone. He shrugs, and says, "I don't ask for things I know I won't get."

"Oh, come on. You were so good at translation. Your old girlfriend even said so."

"My old girlfriend?"

"Zuzanna. She came to your funeral." Isre tries to keep his voice light, but Theren can still feel the hollowness in him at the memory. "She seemed nice. Said you had good . . . emotional intelligence."

Theren laughs a little. She had no way of knowing, of course, that the Fever would give him better "emotional intelligence" than she knew was possible.

Theren asks Isre about his coworkers, then, and Isre talks about his supervisor, who wants him to be more diligent in filling out forms, though he himself doesn't see the need. Theren lets Isre's voice wash over him as the land passes beneath the ship. They're going deeper into the desert, where no one ever bothered to build anything other than a road to cross from one side to the other.

It's not long before they start their descent. They fly over a small town, and then toward a glint of silver on the horizon that takes the shape of a chrome-plated structure—a trailer.

Isre lands smoothly, like it's one single motion. As Theren unbuckles his safety straps, the front door to the trailer opens, and a tall, white-haired woman steps out, her arms crossed.

"That's Hela," Isre says, before getting out of the ship.

Hela's face lights up. "Isre!" she says. "Long time no see. And you must be . . ."

Her focus shifts to Theren, and then . . . she goes still. She squints at him, and he feels a ripple of emotions from her—a prickle of shock, and the low simmer of recognition. As if she *knows* him.

"Have we met?" he says to her.

She seems frozen, for some reason, and he's not sure that she heard him. Then Elegy steps out onto the landing behind her, and pokes her in the back.

"Ready?" Elegy asks her.

"Yeah," Hela says, sounding distant. She clears her throat, and comes out of her daze. "Again, I have to ask—no weapons?"

"We won't need them," Theren says.

Hela gives him a stern look. "I know she's your mother, but—"

"I'm not saying that I trust her." Theren keeps his voice mild. "I'm saying I don't require a weapon to fight her, as I'm sure she's well aware."

Though he knows she can't read him like he can read her, he still feels exposed by the way Hela looks at him, like she's taking him apart and examining each piece. But she nods. "Fine. Here's your Ear, El."

She takes a small cloth bag out of her pocket and tips its contents into her palm. A metal bead about the size of a pea glints against her skin. Elegy pinches it between two fingers, then presses it behind her ear, where it sticks to her skin. Then she brings her hair forward to cover it.

It's illegal technology—all personal devices are, in Cedre—but he shouldn't be surprised. Scouts tend to walk on the line between legal and illegal.

Hela says, "I figured out how far away I need to be before she can spot me. So that's where I'll be parked. I'll follow you until we're in range, then let me do a sweep before you descend."

"Let's go, then."

They part ways, Hela going to one ship and Isre, Theren, and Elegy going to the other. As they approach the passenger door, Elegy says, "I'll take the back seat."

"That's not necessary."

Elegy looks him up and down in a way that makes his skin prickle. "You're taller. Stop arguing."

He flips the latch that folds the passenger seat forward, and by instinct, holds out a hand for her to take as she climbs into the back. Her fingers are cool against his. He can feel Isre noticing the contact with a little wriggle of curiosity, though he gives no sign of it.

They wait for Hela to take off before following her into the air.

+   +   +

Up ahead is the desert flat, empty earth and dry brush and boulder, the occasional Joshua tree tricking him into thinking he's seeing a person standing sentry. He has such strange memories of this landscape, panicked and exhausted with Maeve's back against his chest. He has to keep forcing his mind back to the present.

He's about to see Kesia again. He needs to focus.

He doesn't want to see her again. He never does. She came to watch him in the Crucible once, a year into his imprisonment when he had learned skill without finesse, and took care of his opponents too quickly to be of interest to spectators. She cornered him after the fight, and he felt how impressed she was with him for his brutality, for his survival. It made him sick, that what it took for her to feel proud of him was to watch him endure one of the darkest places on Earth. So even before she had the chance to speak to him, he summoned a guard, and had them escort her out.

He saw her again soon after his relocation to House Vidar. She brought a prisoner to the interrogation chamber there for Nyx to handle, and he passed her in the hallway. Her eyes went straight to the vine freshly tattooed on his hand. She stopped him and tried to ask him about it. He couldn't even speak, just pulled away and ducked into the kitchen to catch his breath.

And then there she was in his lost memory, asking him if he lived in Rava Vidar's chambers.

He sees her horse first, a gray-white smudge on the land. As they draw closer, he spots a piece of canvas stretched between a few poles, dug deep into the sand so the structure can withstand the wind. Kesia sits on a rock beneath it, dressed in pale Talusar linen. Waiting.

They wait for Hela to do her sweep of the area, and then Isre guides them down to the rocky earth. They park, and climb out of the ship, and Theren doesn't read Kesia—doesn't care to.

When she sees them, she stands up, her sand-colored clothes blown to the side by the strong desert wind, so they swell away from her body. Isre rushes toward her, and then stops when he's within reach, like he realizes that he shouldn't be so eager to embrace the woman who abandoned him.

She reaches for Isre, and he lets her take his hands and squeeze them.

"Look at you," she says, eyes sparkling.

"You all right?" he says.

"Never better." She looks over Isre's shoulder, and finally notices Elegy. Theren may not be reading Kesia, but he can't ignore the cold flare of Elegy's rage.

Kesia's hand goes to the knife in her sleeve. He can see the handle, dark against her skin.

"I thought we agreed no weapons," Elegy says.

"I requested that *you* have no weapons," Kesia says. "Since I'm outnumbered three to one, and one of you is *him*."

She meets Theren's eyes. For a moment he just stares back at her, his jaw set, and he's glad she can't read the chaos of contradictory emotions in him. She might believe it means more than it does, that he still loves her—but loving her is just an old habit he can't break.

"If I'd known I would be hosting the Hope of Cedre, I might have made my accommodations finer," Kesia says, gesturing to the canopy above her. "Please, come into the shade, Miss Rosyk."

"That's not my name, as you're well aware," Elegy says, but she does move closer, and Theren goes with her. Their eyes meet, and they can't speak Talusar here, with Kesia listening in, but he tilts his head, and she gives him what he assumes to be an encouraging nod. It's *his* memory Rava buried, it's *his* father Kesia lied about . . . so this has to be his conversation.

When Kesia sits back down on her rock, he sits on the one across from her.

"I hope you'll indulge me," Kesia says to Isre, smiling again. She pats the space beside her, and Isre sits, letting her hold his hand. "Do you still know your Talusar?"

"Enough. Don't speak English on my account."

"Very well." Kesia arranges the bottom of her robe around her legs. "You live in Losan now?"

"I share an apartment with two other technicians." He responds in English, though she spoke in Talusar. "Not far from the base."

"You like your work?"

Theren can't stop himself from making a strained, frustrated sound. Kesia frowns at him.

"I'm not allowed to care about my son?"

"You left him without a word, and for four years, you let him believe his brother was dead," Theren says. "So, no. You don't get to care."

Her hair, now threaded with gray, is pulled back in a tight knot. There's dust in the creases of her skin. He has the same brow as her, but otherwise, she always said, he's his father's son.

His father—who came through a doorway in the fucking stars.

"Theren." Theren doesn't need the Fever to hear the pleading in his brother's voice, but for once, he can't indulge it.

"No," Theren says. "I came here for a purpose. If you want to enjoy a charade of a family reunion, Kesia, you can do it when I'm finished."

Isre's hurt is a sudden twisting in his gut. He ignores it.

"Very well, let us accomplish your purpose, then," Kesia says.

"I recently recovered a memory. I have questions about it, and I know you have the answers."

"Recovered a memory."

"One that Rava had someone bury."

She doesn't seem surprised, and maybe that's the worst of what she's done to him—that she continues to witness the terrible things that have happened to him, and she acts like the fact that he can endure them means they aren't so terrible after all.

"What do you want to know?" she says.

"Tell me about Sevik."

The name, his father's name, rattles her. A gust of wind makes the canopy shudder and snap, and he closes his eyes against the dust. He thinks again of the days he spent crossing this desert with the grit of sand in every fold of skin.

Kesia tucks her hands into her sleeves, and squints at the horizon.

"Sevik." She speaks the name slowly. "If you know his name, then you know, I suppose, that he was from another place entirely."

Theren nods, though he still can't actually believe it.

"He asked me to keep the secret of him from you," she says. "Until you were *touched with Fever*—his phrase, not mine."

"I've been *touched with Fever* for four years."

"You would barely look at me. You were never alone. Guards in the Crucible, guards in House Vidar. This information is too important to risk revealing it to her."

"You could have arranged a meeting."

"You already hated me plenty. I couldn't bear to make you hate me more."

Theren squeezes his hands into fists, digging in his fingernails without thinking about it. Elegy reaches for him, her hand sliding just beneath the collar of his shirt to cover the top of his spine, her touch gentle and cool. Reassuring.

Kesia's eyes shift to Elegy's hand. She sets her jaw.

"Regardless of why you didn't tell me sooner," Theren says, "tell me now."

The horse, standing in the shadow of a nearby rock formation, tosses its head. It's a young animal, restless, white dappled with gray. Kesia watches it for a long time before she responds.

"Your father came from a distant place. He never gave me the name, and it would mean nothing to us anyway," she says. "He was a *man*, which is to say, he shared our biology, and told me that my people and his have a common origin. Not truly alien, though strange to me, in certain ways. I'm still not sure how he learned our language, or why he came here to begin with."

Her hand passes over her mouth, as if remembering some old tenderness.

"But he told me that after you survived the Fever, you would need to seek him," she says. "And that he would plant the coordinates in the past for you to find."

He waits on the other side for his son. He has been waiting a long time.

Isre frowns. "Plant coordinates in the *past*? What does that mean?"

"It means creating a memory in his own life, prior to Theren's birth, that can only be retrieved by an epocha looking into Theren's deep past," Elegy says. She's still standing at Theren's shoulder, like a sentry ready to defend him. "Right?"

Kesia nods. "He knew that the right person would be able to see down the line of your progenitor. Like the other Knight—"

"Fenn," Theren says roughly. *Down the line of your progenitor.* The same phrase Fenn said in the memory he retrieved. If the past was a string that Fenn could tug harder than other people, perhaps that was the "line" to which the phrase referred. And Theren's father was the fish hooked on the other end of it.

"Yes," Kesia says. "Fenn."

"Who is still alive."

"As far as I know."

"How long did you know he was alive before you came to House Vidar the last time?" Theren says. "How long did you know that I wasn't the sole survivor?"

Kesia doesn't answer. Theren's throat burns. His eyes burn.

"Is there anything else?" he says.

"Fenn was the one who ordered my silence," Kesia says. "And his orders must be obeyed."

Much as he would like to, Theren can't exactly blame her for that. He knows how epocha are treated in Valla. How severe the punishment is for disobeying them.

"Please look at me, Theren."

Her eyes are lighter than his own, an indeterminate hazel. Right now they look almost golden in color.

"It took me four years to realize how badly you needed help," she says. "I believed, when you were moved to House Vidar, that it was—a position of honor. Many Talusar would see it that way. But when I saw that you lived *there*, in those rooms; that it was all routine for you—"

"Is that what it was?" Theren chokes out. "Routine?"

"When I saw you there, I realized I had to do something—"

"Don't pretend you were in the dark," he says. "You *saw*—" He chokes again, but forces himself to go on: "You saw everything she did to me before then. And it was never enough for you to help me."

"I was a fool, but I didn't want *that*—"

"Enough." He shakes his head. "I have been telling you over and over again since the Getty, and each time you treat me like I'm an impetuous child throwing a tantrum. I'm not. So hear me now." He leans toward her, and says, in a quiet, level voice: "There is no way to repair what you broke, Kesia."

"Because you won't allow it," she says, her voice unsteady.

"That's true. I won't, and I don't want to."

He's shocked by how calm he feels, no ringing ears, no numb fingers, just a kind of weight—a weight like resignation, like loss, but also like stability.

He stands. Touches the place where Ranos stabbed him, though it's healed now and no longer tender to the touch. Kesia's eyes are bright with tears. He turns, and walks toward the Finch, the hot sun burning the back of his neck.

41

An hour or so later, Theren and Elegy are standing outside of the
trailer in the desert town of Twentynine, and Isre's ship is flying away
from them, toward Losan.

Theren has to duck to get into the trailer, which is narrow enough that he
couldn't extend his arms in both directions if he tried, and short enough to
keep him hunched even at its highest point. Hela arrived first, and she's already scrubbing out a mug with a sponge. She sets it on a drying rack beneath
a shelf of figurines—upon closer examination, he realizes they're all cats.

"Your brother isn't going to join us?" Hela says.

"No, Isre had to get back to base," Elegy says, in the kind of tone that
invites no further questions.

But when Hela glances at Theren, he adds, "He's angry with me."

It's true, though Isre didn't say it, and wouldn't have. He must know
he has no right to be angry with Theren for being so harsh with Kesia,
but the heart is often at odds with the mind, particularly where family is
concerned. So he gave Theren's shoulder a squeeze when he dropped him
off, and tried to be pleasant in his farewells, which is as much as Theren
could have asked for.

"I think we should drink," Hela says to him.

"Yes," he agrees.

Elegy busies herself at the little countertop, taking out a bottle marked
WHISKEY in her cramped handwriting, lining up three glasses of different
heights and shapes. He looks around at the trailer—at the corner of a mattress in the back, right up against the edge of a desk, where an array of tech
sits, dormant now. There's an odd shape on the desk, something covered
in burlap that he can't identify.

The kitchen is clean but cluttered with mismatched things, each plate
on the drying rack a different color, the two doilies nailed to the wall in
languages he doesn't speak.

Elegy offers him a blue glass, hexagonal, with a shot of whiskey in it,
neat. He runs his fingers over hers as he takes it, and suppresses a smile at
how that simple touch makes impatience flare to life inside her.

She sets another glass down in front of Hela, and then slides into the seat across from her. Theren leans against the counter, next to the cat shelf. He feels like he can't move without knocking something over.

"So," Elegy says, looking at him.

"I know I'm supposed to—to go looking for a doorway in the stars," he says. "Because if Rava doesn't want me to go somewhere, that's exactly where I need to go. But first I have to go get Fenn."

He's known it since he unearthed his hidden memory, since he realized Fenn was still alive. But he meant to hold it close for a while, to turn it over in his mind and let a plan take shape—not to throw it at Elegy Ahn Rosyk, Hope of Cedre, who has no obligation to help him rescue a friend from a Talusar monastery, whose very involvement could spark a huge conflict with the Talusar.

"*We* have to go get Fenn," Elegy corrects him.

He feels . . . well, he's not sure how he feels, exactly. Relieved. Grateful. He doesn't read Elegy intentionally anymore, not unless she orders him, as she did last night. But he's sure, now, that she's forgiven him.

"I'm sorry to say this," Hela says. "But . . . do we? Don't get me wrong, I feel for him, being a hostage of the Talusar and all. But shouldn't we be focused on Rava?"

Elegy is quiet for long enough that Hela starts fidgeting, impatient. Theren just lets the feeling of her take up space inside him until her eyes widen, and she looks up at him.

"Avka Becken didn't know Julia Martin's name because Julia changed her name when she came to Cedre," Elegy says. "Did Tor Kovek do that, too?"

"Of course," Theren says.

"Why 'of course'?" Elegy asks.

"Because he's Ileth's cousin," Theren says. "I thought you knew that—he's blond enough."

"He's Ileth's cousin. His name is 'Vidar,'" Elegy says.

Hela chokes on her whiskey.

"Yes," Theren says. "There are a lot of them. He's not an important one."

"*One will bear the Vidari name,*" Hela says, and it sounds like she's quoting something.

Elegy gives her a warning look. Theren is curious, but he's also used to not asking questions.

"Per the augur in Theren's recovered memory," Elegy says, "Rava

Vidar's triumph is assured by keeping Theren out of that doorway. And Fenn, an epocha, can help us find out where that doorway is."

Hela's jaw works. He can almost feel her sorting through all of it: the memory Rava buried, of a father who waits for him in the stars. The message his mother failed to tell him about, hidden in the past where only an epocha can reach it. Fenn resurfacing has the hum of inevitability in it, something he's destined for, something he can't avoid. And it sounds like he was mentioned in Elegy's prophecy.

"So he's in a monastery," Hela says. "Is he a priest of the Fever, too? I thought only priests lived in monasteries, and epocha lived in city strongholds."

He frowns at her, and after a moment of hesitation, he switches to Talusar to ask, "Are you from Vidara?"

Hela's eyes are hard.

"I was born in Silvis," she replies, and he can feel the certainty of a native speaker in the way she says it, every consonant and vowel falling together as they're supposed to.

There's a kinship between them, automatic and unspoken. Two people born to Talusar parents, living now in Cedre. Half of one thing, half of another. *Intere.*

Elegy is looking from Theren to Hela, her eyes thoughtful, as if she's just realizing this common ground they share, too.

"In the monastery just outside of Valla, priests and epocha share the same building, so it can be better protected," he says.

Hela laughs harshly. "'Protected.' So: contained. Because they're property of the Talusar state. Sounds miserable."

"Yes, but also no," he says. "They're treated like . . . royalty, almost. They're not free, but they're revered. If you touch one without their permission, you can be burned alive, which is the worst punishment the Talusar offer. Which speaks to the quality of soldiers assigned there. It's a position of honor. Only meant for the most trustworthy and the most loyal."

"Yet your mother is there," Elegy says.

"In the eyes of the Talusar, my mother delivered the Sword and her Knights to Rava," he says. "So yes."

Elegy's hands tighten around her glass.

"There's a problem," Theren says. "The monastery is where people on the west half of the continent go to infect their children with Fever, once they turn sixteen. All summer, there will be a huge influx of people—which means a huge influx of Talusar soldiers."

"When does that start?" Elegy says.

Theren hesitates. "By the next full moon. So . . . two weeks."

"So you're saying we have to do this before then," Elegy says. "Or wait until autumn. If whatever catastrophe Rava has planned hasn't hit us by then."

Theren nods.

"Hold on a second," Hela says, scowling. "We all know that even Cedre's best soldiers are outmatched by the Talusar on the ground. So how do we have even a shred of hope of getting into a place that well-guarded, even before summer hits?"

Theren considers this, the vanilla taste of whiskey on his tongue, the corner of the glass digging into his sternum. Hela is scrutinizing him, as she has been since he walked in, like she's trying to figure him out. He ignores her, thinking instead of Rava assuring him that Orda was released from the Crucible to guard the monastery, a place of honor.

"Someone on the inside will help us," Theren says, and at Elegy's confused expression, he adds, "Orda."

He can tell she remembers the name from his memories. His teacher, the one who told him how to kill Maeve with as much mercy as possible. "He'll help us?"

"Yes," Theren says.

"You're sure?"

"If he doesn't say yes to me, he'll say yes to you." He inclines his head to her, just a little, half joking and half not. "Your Grace."

Elegy's eyes glitter a little as they fix on his. She sips her whiskey, then sets the empty glass down on the table between her and Hela.

"What about you?" Elegy says to Hela. "Will you help me? Even if it means working with soldiers?"

Hela taps her glass against Elegy's empty one. "Obviously, *Your Grace*."

"Thank you." Elegy's voice is uncharacteristically soft.

"Don't say that shit to me," Hela says, and she comes to her feet, glass in hand. "We can't start thanking each other for stuff, or we'll never stop."

"Two weeks, then," Elegy says.

"Fantastic," Hela says.

Hela downs the rest of her whiskey and disappears into the bathroom, leaving Elegy and Theren alone.

Theren gathers up the glasses and hunches over the sink to wash them. Insects tap against the window in front of him, struggling toward the light. The desert is otherwise silent and dark. He can feel Elegy's eyes on him, can feel the tension between them like a guitar string, humming.

"What's with the cats?" he says, nodding toward the shelf of cat figurines.

"Oh, those?" She stands next to him at the counter, and picks up one of the figurines—this one a plastic cartoon cat with wide, white eyes. "Whenever my dad went out on jobs, if he found one, he would bring it back." She smiles a little. "I don't even like cats, really, but he liked the things that old cultures had in common. Dumplings. An obsession with cats."

He considers this for a moment.

"One of the only words that's the same in Talusar and English," he says, "is 'elegy.'"

"Yeah. I know," she says, her eyes dropping to his mouth as he says her name.

He can feel his pulse in his throat. He turns off the water, sets down the sponge, and kisses her. He doesn't try to read her, but it's hard to ignore the sudden rush of guilt she feels as he touches her, though it ebbs away quickly, replaced by something fiercer, hungrier.

She grabs the front of his shirt and pulls him in closer. He presses her to the counter, his hips and thighs against hers in a long line. His hands are still wet from washing the glasses as he touches the back of her neck, slides his fingers into her hair.

He's not used to this, just focusing on how *he* feels as he touches someone. With Fenn, he was unsure of himself; he read Fenn's reactions to make sure that everything he did was wanted. With Rava, he let what she felt crowd out everything else, because it made everything easier to bear. But here, with Elegy, he can pay attention to himself and what he wants, what he *needs*—because it feels like a need, the way he aches for her, the way every touch of her hands prompts the shock of desire. He relaxes into her, slowing down so he can savor the taste of whiskey on her tongue, the warmth of her body against his.

Hela clears her throat.

Elegy pulls away from the kiss first, her hand coming up to cover her mouth. Theren stays right where he is, catching his breath.

"I guess that answers a question I had," Hela says. "I'm afraid I have another one, though, before we call it a night."

"Sorry," Elegy says tersely, and she slides out from between Theren and the counter. It takes Theren a second to move, for the sake of . . . decency.

"What else?" Elegy says to Hela.

"I kept waiting for a good time for this, but turns out, there's no good time for a weird plant." Hela goes over to the desk at the back of the trailer and plucks the burlap from the object it covers, revealing a plant. "Touch one of the leaves, would you?"

It's unlike anything he's ever seen, veins of bright color striping each of its leaves, dense as a fern but firm as a prayer plant. Hela carries it over to the table and sets it down; as it enters the light of the kitchen, it starts to curl into itself. Hela turns off the overhead light, and it stops, its leaves spreading wide again.

He could swear that it's stretching toward him, and he stretches back, without thinking, running a fingertip down one of its leaves. The plant shudders a little, then creaks as something unfurls from its center.

A stalk sprouts from the middle of the plant. It's like watching a time-lapse video of growth, everything rapidly extending, shifting—then the end of the stalk bulges, swells—a flower bud appears and then bursts open. It's big and stiff, like an orchid, but it's symmetrical as a daisy, eight petals with a small, dark green labellum in the center.

"'To find the one who makes it bloom,'" Hela says. "'Seek the traitor's son.'"

And then he's in another place entirely.

+   +   +

When he opens his eyes, he's standing on soft earth, surrounded by growing things. The glowing plant is at his feet, bigger and lusher than the one in Hela and Elegy's kitchen, but hanging overhead are the coin-shaped leaves of a tree that otherwise reminds him of a willow, and beside him is a sharp, spiky bush that reminds him of a thistle. Yet these aren't plants he knows.

A dark shape catches his eye and he reacts immediately, bracing himself for an attack that doesn't come. Instead, the shape materializes into a woman. She wears a shift dress, black and simple, and her bare arms glow in moonlight that he soon realizes *isn't* moonlight. It comes from a line of light above them that splits the dark sky in half.

The woman, though. She moves toward him and that light stretches across her face, and he knows her like he knows his own reflection. Her nose, narrow at the bridge, is his nose. Her mouth, which gives her a look of resignation, is his mouth.

"Who are you?" he says, and it comes out almost as a gasp, in Talusar.

He can't feel her reaction to him, and he clings to that fact, because it means they aren't actually sharing the same space; wherever this is, he hasn't been transported there in truth, only in his mind. He wonders if this is how it feels to step through a veil.

But though he can't tell what she's feeling, he can see that she's as startled as he is; she wasn't expecting this, wasn't expecting *him*.

"It worked," she says. "She found you."

"Who," he repeats, more firmly this time, "are you."

"My name is Akara." Her voice is low and a little raspy, like she's recently strained it. "And you're Theren."

The way she says "Theren" is strange to him—instead of the *th*, it almost sounds like she's pronouncing an *s*. But it's still unmistakably his name. She knows his name.

"That's not an answer," he says, louder this time, frustrated.

"You *know* who I am. You can see it. Can't you?"

And he can—he doesn't know if she's a sister, or a cousin, or some other relative. But he knows that she's family.

"I can't tell you all the things you want to know," she says to him. "But I can tell you to come and find us. Come and find us, and do it soon."

He can feel the pull back to the trailer, can feel this strange place, this strange woman, disappearing. He tries to hold on to the sight of her, his *family*, as long as he can, but it's like trying to hold water in his fingers.

She's gone, and he's back in the kitchen, his breaths fast and shallow.

42

Elegy watches Theren pass through the gate to Losan Stronghold—the guard now recognizes him on sight—and disappear into the dark, his hands in his pockets. She sighs, and leans back against Hela's Finch, which is still hot from the sun. Hela leans next to her, her arms crossed.

Theren and Hela talked for a while about the strange, verdant room where the plant transported them both. For having solved a mystery, Hela said, she had more questions than she expected. Why Theren's touch had made the plant bloom, why the woman they both saw wanted him to find her without telling him how . . . they were bigger questions than any of the ones that preceded them.

There are those who see the future, and we don't want to reveal anything to them, the woman had said to Hela, and Elegy thought immediately of the augur and the epocha in Theren's lost memory—how Fenn saying the name "Sevik" had provoked a vision from the augur. Maybe Akara, whoever she is, has to break her message into pieces so that someone out there doesn't put them all together. But that doesn't make it any less frustrating.

Eventually, worn out by the day's events, Hela and Elegy took Theren back here. The moon is bright, so there's enough light to see by even outside the stronghold's limits. The distant glitter of Losan's downtown catches Elegy's eye; it's been a long time since she walked the streets of the city where she grew up, and she's not sure she even knows her way around anymore.

"So," Hela says, and Elegy knows her too well. This is her way of bringing up Elegy's stolen moment with Theren.

Elegy can't help but remember secondary school, after the annual school dance, wandering the market close to their apartment. Strings of light overhead, the smell of fried food in the air. Hela, trying not to cry over some girl, Elegy can't remember her name now. Elegy, trying to sound wise about matters of the heart, even though she'd only kissed one boy and he'd spent the whole time poking her closed lips with his tongue.

Not exactly what she's dealing with now.

She can still feel Theren's wet fingers curling over the nape of her neck. She can feel Shir's fingers brushing her spine as he zips up her dress, right before the ceremony at the Getty. She can feel the weight of her wedding ring on its chain around her neck. She can feel the weight of Shir's absence every single morning in the moments after she realizes he won't be lying next to her in bed when she opens her eyes.

She feels too much, all at once. She tips her head back against the Finch, and when she closes her eyes, tears run down her cheeks. They're hot on her skin, and then cold.

Hela moves to stand beside her, her foot up against the side of Elegy's foot, her arm bumping up against Elegy's shoulder, and then—her hand clasping Elegy's hand.

"So it's him, then," Hela says.

Elegy thinks of Theren's eyes on hers in the mirror, as focused as a thread passing through the eye of a needle.

She nods, her eyes still closed.

"It's all right, El."

"No." Elegy doesn't bother to wipe her cheeks. "It really isn't."

They stay there for a long time, listening to distant sirens and the faint music playing from the guard station.

✦   ✦   ✦

Two days later Elegy stands at the back door of the Octopus, peering out the back window to make sure the coast is clear. Aki, the bartender, agreed to let her use the space for the afternoon, and while she trusts him more than she trusts a lot of people, she still doesn't want him to overhear what they're doing here.

She spins the key ring around her finger, once, and walks back into the main room.

The Octopus gets its name from a mural on the back wall, a menacing tangle of suckered tentacles with light bulbs for eyes. But the rest of the place is like a tavern from a fairy tale, the main room framed by arches and columns that create shaded alcoves lit by lanterns—dim now, their flames not lit—and low stools and rickety wooden tables scattered throughout. Milky pale light comes in through the dusty windows around the front door, but otherwise the place is dark. The floor creaks with each step she takes.

Everyone she trusts with her life is in this room. Hela stands with her back against the bar. She's wearing one of Elegy's old Cedre army shirts with the sleeves sawed off, so red threads trail down her arms. Irreverent.

Across from her, sitting at one of the little tables, are Parekh, Arias, and Isre Din, dressed in their casual clothes but unmistakably military, thanks to their posture and the way they almost snap to attention when

Elegy walks back in, like she's their Primary and they're waiting for the next order.

And across from her, standing in a relaxed parade rest between the two groups, the weak light glowing all around his silhouette, is Theren.

She dragged a table out to the middle of the room before anyone got here, and slid an obsidian—an illegal one, naturally—on top of it, so she could transfer a map to it.

"Right," Elegy says, and she clears her throat, trying to remember how Shir would have done this. He was always better at rallying people than she was.

"Um . . . introductions first. Hela, this is Ciro Arias and Lydia Parekh, who both worked with me in search and rescue. You already know Isre, who's a technician." She gestures to Hela against the bar. "Arias and Parekh, this is my sister, Tausia Helasz. She's the one who sponsored me as a Scout. And . . . everyone knows Theren."

Her face heats. What a loaded phrase that is.

"I've talked to you all about our mission, which is to rescue a former Knight from a highly secure Talusar facility," she says.

"Also known as a monastery," Parekh supplies.

"Also known as a monastery," Elegy acknowledges with a nod. "I can't tell you why this Knight is so valuable, but suffice it to say that we need him in order to move forward in our fight against Rava Vidar. We only have two weeks until the monastery becomes impenetrable. Even in two weeks, we'll be outnumbered and outmatched, so we need to get creative. We're also working off-book here—Arias, Parekh, and Isre have taken temporary leave in order to complete this mission. General Thompson approved the leave, so he knows I'm up to something, but he wants to maintain plausible deniability."

"Neat-o. Where is this highly secure monastery?" Parekh says.

"Northwest of Valla." Lines of light spread down Elegy's hands as she steps up to the table with its obsidian stone. At her touch, a map unfolds across it, glowing with the topography of Valla. She taps something in the middle of it, a ridge she's memorized, and a red circle appears where she touched it.

Everyone comes to their feet and steps toward the obsidian to see the map, Hela on Elegy's right, soldiers on her left.

Theren, across from her, is lit from beneath by the obsidian map, so there are shadows in the hollows of his cheeks.

"We'll go to the Cenobium first, so Isre can run operations from there—insofar as that's possible, with the Valla energy field interfering," she says.

Small groups of Fevered people don't emit enough of an energy field to interfere with Cedre technology, but the population center that is Valla is downright impenetrable.

"Why the Cenobium?" Isre asks. "Isn't that a little close to Talusar territory?"

"It's the closest politically neutral spot to Valla, and we'll need you close so you can rescue us if something goes wrong," Elegy says. "Plus, I have some questions for the augurs. After that—"

Arias says hopefully: "Storm the castle?" He looks at Hela. "Sorry. That's S and R for—"

"A 'smash and grab,'" Hela says. "See? I can use jargon, too."

Arias only shrugs, good-natured as ever.

"Whatever term you use . . . not the right strategy." Elegy's shoulders ache with tension. She's not used to trying to combine worlds like this. "Theren, you've been there—you have a recommendation?"

Isre laughs a little and says to Theren, "You've been to their monastery?"

"I died there," Theren says, his voice unexpectedly gentle, like he's breaking hard news to his brother. And maybe he is, because the laugh dies on Isre's lips.

"If 'storming the castle' is what it sounds like," Theren says, "then no, if we try that we'll be ripped apart."

"Then what?" Parekh asks.

"Um . . ." Theren leans over the map and scratches behind one ear. "There's a guard who will help us. Selio Orda is his name; he's been stationed there for two years."

Theren looks up at her, his eyes black and gleaming. She thinks of Orda, graying and handsome, slamming a practice sword into Theren's.

"All our supplies need to be civilian. Unmarked, unregistered," Elegy says, looking at Hela. "Weapons, too. We can't signal that we're military in any way."

"I'm on it," Hela says.

Elegy speaks Talusar automatically when she addresses Theren, though she knows Hela and Isre can both understand it, too. "What else?"

"Training," he says. "We can't accomplish that much in the time we have, but we can get used to each other."

"Okay," she says. "Let's get started."

43

The next few days disappear into training and planning. Hela and Isre leave for hours at a time, hunting down supplies that can't be traced back to the Cedre military. Theren and Arias help Parekh with her hip exercises in the Octopus before training starts. Isre and Parekh fly back in an unmarked Sparrow one afternoon with sly looks and inside jokes.

The plan is to set out from the Cenobium and fly as close to the monastery as possible before the Talusar notice them. Once the Talusar spot them, they'll perform what Arias calls—and Elegy refuses to call—a "whoopsie daisy," which is disembarking from a ship while it's still in flight. They'll then approach Dexa, the outpost next to the monastery where its workers and guards live, on foot. Theren will find Orda in Dexa, and assuming he agrees to help, they'll plan the rest of the rescue mission from there.

To prepare, Elegy and Arias pore over satellite images of the monastery, the path of their approach, the land between the Cenobium and Dexa. Sometimes Theren joins them, leaning over Elegy's shoulder to look at the map, just close enough for her to feel his warmth, but never touching her. He gives details like how long it takes to walk from one place to another given the terrain, how loud a person's footsteps will be in the forests that surround the monastery, how bright it will be at night.

She tries to avoid him. She knows she can't do it forever, but she tells herself she needs more time. That before she can think about it, she needs to get through this day, then the next day, then the next. She can tell that Theren notices her distance, but he doesn't talk to her about it; he, too, seems eager to throw himself into the work they're doing.

There's one time she can't avoid him: training. It's likely they'll encounter isolated Talusar guards when they enter the monastery, and the only way for a Cedrae to beat a Talusar on foot is by outnumbering them. So they practice fighting in pairs. On the first day, he just had them do drills together, simple ones that helped them get to know each other. The next morning, he put them in different combinations, and they sparred, two-on-two. They train in the Octopus in the afternoon, and then again in the evening just outside the trailer in Twentynine, in the dirt.

Arias, meanwhile, has them practice moving in the dark, looking out for hand signals instead of verbal commands. Hela teaches them all how to scatter and how to look for exits.

By the time Elegy reaches the Octopus on the fourth day, she has sore muscles she forgot existed—the ones in her shins and forearms, in her hips and abdomen.

There are few residents in Twentynine, and most of them don't come out until nighttime. The ones who see them training here in the late-afternoon hours seem inclined to mind their own business.

When the others arrive, they all run together in a pack down Main Street. Elegy jogs alongside Parekh, and she's glad to see Hela and Arias together at the front—the first day, Hela and the soldiers kept apart, but now they seem willing to work as a group.

When they're done, they all duck into the Octopus, where Theren has pushed all the tables to the edges of the room and arranged practice weapons at his feet. Courtesy of Parekh.

Theren says, "I think I have everyone's preferred weapon—"

There's a spear for Elegy. She picks it up without having to ask if he intended it for her, and steps to the side to move through a few of the postures her father taught her. She fell into them naturally when fighting Avka Becken in Naarm; she falls into them a little less naturally now.

"Hela and Arias, you're up," Theren says.

He has an authority here that she wasn't expecting from him. Being good at fighting doesn't mean someone is good at teaching, but Theren is patient, never rising to their level of frustration.

"Two-on-one, really?" Hela says.

"Really," he replies, and he's more focused than Elegy has ever seen him, winnowed down to the bone. He moves around Hela to make her a barrier between him and Arias, and then he dances around them to reverse their positions, turning them both in a frantic circle.

Their confusion seems to give him clarity; he thrusts at Arias, the practice sword jabbing the other man in the rib cage. But Hela gets a cut in, too, prodding him in the leg.

He lowers his sword to acknowledge the hit, and then picks it up again, and they reset their positions. He prowls around them, and Elegy can hardly hear him move, just the faint sticking and unsticking of his bare feet on the floor. He attacks, and she can see every muscle in his body standing at attention. He occupies his body more fully than anyone she's ever seen, aware of every edge of it, every ending.

It's hot out, but that has nothing to do with the heat in Elegy's body, with the way her eyes cling to his muscled forearms, his heaving chest, the trickle of sweat that follows the line of his throat like a swallow.

A cold weight settles into Elegy's stomach as she watches a real, wide grin spread across Theren's face as he calls out encouragement to Hela. It's a brief thing, but Elegy wasn't expecting it—how joy makes him fierce as a wolf.

I saw a man, an augur says in her ear, in her memory.

Elegy walks out of the room and into the street.

+ + +

It's too cloudy in Twentynine to see Cedre Station. Elegy spends a few minutes staring up at the blank sky. There's something ominous about a desert storm.

It's a half hour until they're all supposed to meet again for their night-time planning session. Elegy showers and dresses, and then instead of combing her hair, she stands behind Hela's desk, dripping water on her father's box of supposedly alien artifacts.

Only she's not looking at them, this time. Instead, she looks at the small collection of objects behind the box. They're some of the only things Hela brought with her from Silvis, from her home. A journal small enough to fit in a palm. A trio of interlinked metal rings—an object used in Talusar prayer. A vial of her mother's perfume, now empty. And a tiny carved figurine of a horse.

Equo ne credite, she thinks. That phrase repeating in the memory of the witness to the Talusar attack. It keeps prodding at her.

"You're dripping everywhere," Hela says. "What is it?"

"Nothing." Elegy shakes her head. "I was just thinking of something we found out in Naarm. That the witness kept thinking of a phrase about a horse."

"About a *horse*?" Hela says. "He was Cedrae, though, right? What does he know about horses?"

"Yeah, I think that's why it's bothering me. Why would a Cedrae man know an obscure quote from an ancient text we don't even study in school here? It's not like he was a student; he was a guard."

"What's the quote?"

"'Don't trust the horse.'" Elegy snorts. "Don't ask me, I don't know."

Hela picks up the horse figurine, and turns it in her fingers. She taps its head.

"'Equo ne credite,'" she says, almost idly.

"Yeah. That," Elegy says. "How do you . . . ?"

"Ileth Vidar is obsessed with ancient warriors, you think she didn't insist on including old poems about them in the standard curriculum? Rava probably has that quote tattooed on her ass."

Elegy's heart leaps. "What does it mean?"

"It's about a clever trick that won a war," Hela says. "The Trojans presented their enemies with what appeared to be a gift—a big wooden horse. Their enemies brought it inside the city walls. But what they didn't know was that it was stuffed full of Trojan soldiers. *Don't trust the horse*, see? Don't trust a benign gesture from an enemy, basically."

Elegy rushes across the trailer to the bag she brought with her from Naarm. She takes out her clothes—still damp from all the rain—and her toothbrush to reach the slightly compressed sheets of recycled paper Saetang gave her before she left.

She sits on the kitchen floor and puts the sheets next to each other on the linoleum. On the left is the inventory of the hangar from before the strange Talusar attack. On the right is the inventory from after. Elegy touches an index finger to each item as she compares it. Ships. Tech kits. Fuel tanks. Down, down, down, each number the same. Engine parts, stands.

The bottom section of each inventory is the weekly list of supplies that will be shipped from Naarm to Cedre Station. Naarm may not supply as many goods to Cedre Station as Losan, but they still send a fair amount, especially fresh fruit and equipment. Elegy holds her finger over the number 7, for "equipment crates."

And on the other paper: *8.*

Elegy feels a stab of panic deep inside her rib cage.

"What is it?" Hela asks.

"The Talusar didn't steal anything," Elegy says, staring at the number *8.* "They left something behind. Another crate."

Hela's eyes widen. "Are you sure it's not just a clerical error, or something?"

"No, but think about it." Elegy sits back on her heels. "They used a candlesnuffer to knock out the power, so we couldn't see what they were doing. They went to all the effort of sneaking in. And then, they did *nothing* . . . but they still bothered to addle that poor man's memories so he wouldn't be a reliable witness. And one of the only things he remembers is 'don't trust the horse,' a phrase he has no reason to know."

She shakes her head.

"It makes no sense, unless it's this," she says, tapping the paper with her fingers. "Unless they were trying to sneak something *in* instead of out."

"How big are those crates?" Hela asks.

"Pretty big, I think. Sometimes they put a whole Sparrow engine in one. Why?"

"Because what if the phrase is even more literal than you're thinking?" Hela says. "What if they were sneaking in a bunch of soldiers? You know, to attack Cedre Station? Granted, the crate would only hold a few people—not much of an attack, really—"

Cold creeps down Elegy's spine. She rushes over to the dresser and starts opening drawers, pulling out clothing without looking at what she's grabbing.

"When the Talusar exiles came to Cedre Station in search of refuge, what did my mother think they were there for?" she says, and she doesn't wait for an answer. "She thought they were there to spread the Fever to Cedre Station. She assumed that the Fever was the greatest weapon the Talusar had. And she was right."

Hela makes a strangled noise. Elegy straightens, and meets her eyes.

"They don't need soldiers," Hela says. "All they need are priests. Priests of the Fever."

44

"Let me get this straight." Larke Rosyk stands across from Elegy in the veil room. The three generals flank her, luminous as specters.

She's still wearing her nightclothes: a silk robe crossed over her chest and belted. It looks fine and delicate—an expensive garment—but peeking out from the hem are the worn sweatpants Larke wears to sleep, fraying at the ankle.

"Based on the guard's memory of a line of ancient poetry . . ." Larke begins, and she pauses to laugh—a little forced, because she's practically trembling with rage—before continuing: "Based on that alone, you want me to alert the masses and lock down Cedre Station. Even though there've been no reported cases of Fever since the shipment was allegedly delivered."

Elegy glances at Saetang, standing beside Larke. They look composed, their hands over their abdomen and their dark eyes contemplative. But Elegy can see the pulse jumping in their throat.

On Larke's other side, Okoro bites down on her thumbnail. Usually, Okoro is focused and aware, but ever since this meeting started, she's been distant, like she's not even listening to what's being said. As if she feels Elegy's eyes on her, she looks up, then looks away an instant later.

"The shipment was delivered two days ago," Elegy says.

She doesn't add, *and the Fever takes two days at minimum to take hold.* Larke already knows.

"Your Highness, pardon me for saying so, but it's not just the poetry," Saetang says. "It's the way it fits into the rest. We already know Ykev Talus and Rava Vidar planned this attack together, and we know that whatever their objective was, it had to be mutually beneficial. Sending a biological weapon to Cedre Station would certainly be mutually beneficial for them, don't you think?"

Larke looks like she just tasted something sour. The Dreaded Crease is between her eyebrows.

"Yes," she says. "I will send people to look at the crates immediately. There are Eyes in the loading bay, so I'll have people comb through the footage, too. But until I find concrete proof that the Fever has breached

Cedre Station, I am not ordering a lockdown. I'm not going to cause another panic like the one after the *Hoatzin*."

Elegy winces at the reminder. When the *Hoatzin*—the ship where
Theren was born among Talusar exiles—first entered Cedre Station's orbit, her mother locked down the station. It caused such chaos that five
people died in the stampede for masks. When the fears about the *Hoatzin*
turned out to be unfounded, there were people—a lot of people—who
called for the Sword's removal. She understands why Larke doesn't want
the same thing to happen again.

But she has to insist. "Larke, we don't have time to be careful. If this is
about our argument . . ."

"This meeting is over," Larke snaps. "I have said what I intended to say,
and as you just acknowledged, we don't have time for this."

She turns, and Elegy half expects her to click her boots together—only
her feet are bare, so Elegy can see her short, squat toes, the nails painted
black, right before she walks out of the veil and disappears from the room.
The three generals, though, remain behind. They give each other uneasy
looks.

To Elegy's surprise, it's Okoro who speaks first. "She's not wrong, you
know. You didn't give her a lot to go on."

"I gave her everything I have," Elegy says.

"Then let's get more," Okoro says. "What else do you know?"

"The only lead I have is that the Talusar used a candlesnuffer to disable
the base's surveillance before they attacked. It was probably a Scout who
sold it to them." Elegy ignores the look of disgust on Okoro's face. "I can
find out who sold them the candlesnuffer, try to meet them. But it'll take
time."

"I've been pursuing this using our contacts in Naarm," Saetang says.
"I'll tell my people to get more aggressive with them."

"I would advise you both to take as little time as possible," Okoro says.
"I'm on Cedre Station now, so I'll warn the hospitals and ask if they've
seen any concerning symptoms. And I'll work on Her Highness. Maybe I
can get her to prepare for lockdown."

"You believe me?" Elegy says.

"I believe it's *possible* you're correct," Okoro says. "And as you are in
fact the Hope of Cedre, I suppose I believe your word should be heeded."

Without looking at Elegy, she gets up and walks out after Larke. Elegy,
stunned, turns to Saetang, who shrugs.

"That was almost a profession of undying love, coming from Okoro,"
Saetang says.

+ + +

A half hour later, Elegy is in the trailer in Twentynine, and Theren Forint is knocking on the door. Hela is at the Recordkeeper's, finding out who sold the candlesnuffer.

She sent a message to the others before she spoke to Larke, telling them tonight's planning session was canceled. But apparently Theren ignored that message.

He's been staying with Arias and the others in the inn, which is right next door to the Octopus. It's a dim, cramped space that used to be a single-family home, but the woman who runs it—Agatha, who delivers the water—knows how to keep her mouth shut, and she keeps a clean house, if not a particularly nice one. If he's here by himself, he must have walked, since he can't fly a ship.

She doesn't let him in. Instead, she steps outside. Theren leans against the trailer's chrome side.

He knows how to lean, she thinks. Long legs, crossed at the ankle, resolving into a trim torso, his sleeves pushed up to his elbows, his thumbs in his belt loops. His eyes are steady on hers.

"What is it?" she says. "Did something happen?"

"Should be asking you that. Arias filled me in. What did your sister say?"

"She told me to prove it."

"She's not wrong to want more concrete information than a quote." He shakes his head. "But people will die."

"I'm aware of that," she says. "That's why, once Hela finds that Scout job posting, we'll track whoever answered it and arrange a meeting. If Larke wants proof, I'll give it to her."

"Good."

She faces him, leaning one shoulder into the trailer to mirror him. "Did you *walk* here?"

"It's only a mile." He smiles.

"Still."

"Still." He tips his head back and looks up at the starless sky. "You know I've been confined all my life? The *Hoatzin*, then Cedre Station . . . then the Crucible, House Vidar, Losan Stronghold."

She hasn't thought of it that way before, but he's right. The empty desert must feel vast by comparison.

"I'm sorry," she says to him. "Even your oath was a kind of confinement, wasn't it?"

"I used to think so." He shakes his head a little. "Now I think what I called 'freedom' then would just have been a lack of obligation to other people . . . and that's not particularly appealing."

"No?"

"Caring about people makes you obligated to them," he says, his dark eyes glittering. "I tried not caring. Didn't take."

Elegy laughs a little. "So did I. Not fond of it, to be honest."

"Hard to believe. You seem to inspire loyalty."

"It's probably that whole world-saving-prophecy thing."

"No." He looks down at his shoes. "It's that whole 'walk into the fire for someone you hardly know' thing. You did that for all of them, in turn." And he looks up again. "For all of *us*, I mean."

She can't find the words to argue. Not because she agrees with what he said, but because she doesn't know what to make of him saying it.

"Did you come all the way here to give me a pep talk?" she says. "It's working, if so."

"Sadly, no." He pulls away from the wall and takes his hands out of his pockets. The moon, Cedre Station, and the white dot of the *Sundial* are all still hidden behind dark clouds. But she can see him by the light coming from the trailer as he says, "I came to find out why you're avoiding me."

"Not sure I know what you mean. There's a lot to do."

"You really shouldn't try to lie to a truthsayer." He steps closer to her, and she steps back, leaning into the trailer. The chrome is hot even through her shirt, warmed by sunlight. "I'm not asking for you to give me anything more than you have. I just want to know if I should let this go."

"I can't talk to you about this right now," she says, a little too harshly.

"If you won't give me an answer," he goes on, like she never said anything at all, "I'll find it for myself."

He puts his palm against the wall, right next to her face, and the other one comes up to mirror it. Despite that, there's still plenty of room for her to get away from him, if that's what she wants. But it isn't what she wants, is it? That's the whole problem.

He leans closer, his eyes fixed on hers, and she waits for the pressure and the heat of his body against hers, but it doesn't come. He still holds himself away from her, just a breath of distance between them.

She remembers the last time he kissed her, his wet fingers tugging the hair at the nape of her neck as he touched her, the way each movement of his mouth made her even more desperate for him. She wants, even now, for him to press her up against the warm chrome so she can wrap her legs around his waist; she wants to keep taking until there's nothing left.

He tilts his head, angling his mouth just over hers. She's aware of how fast she's breathing, how hard it is not to put her hands on him, how she can't quite think—

"I see," he says, and she can just feel his lips moving over hers, almost a kiss but not quite. "So it's not that you've stopped wanting me."

"No," she replies quietly.

"But something is—" He pauses, and frowns at her. "You're afraid."

"I told you, I can't talk about this right now." Her voice comes out softer than she'd like.

He ducks his head, and kisses her throat, so painfully slow she can feel his lips clinging to her skin as he pulls away.

"All right," he says against her jaw. "Good night, Elegy."

He drops his hands, and all at once, he's walking away, back toward Twentynine.

Elegy slides to the ground, and presses her hands to her cheeks to cool them.

✦ ✦ ✦

An hour later, a crack so loud it sends a shiver down her spine sounds outside, followed by a deep rumble. She pulls back the short curtains that cover the kitchen windows at the sheets of rain coming down outside, the Joshua trees swaying in the wind as if bowing to the distant hills.

She gets up and walks to the door, lured by the smell of petrichor. She opens it, though the air is rough and she shouldn't be outside. The stretch of land at the base of the trailer is already flooded with water.

She's never seen anything like this, in a lifetime of living in and around Losan. The wind blows the rain sideways, into her chest, and she's soaked already.

"'I saw,'" she says, to nothing and to no one, "'a great storm, quenching the thirst of the dusty streets of Losan, flooding its streets with water.'"

Rain rolls down her spine. She shivers.

45

Just hours after returning from the Recordkeeper, Hela finds herself strapped into a jump seat on a shuttle bound for Cedre Station.

The station glows like the moon. Drum-shaped, hanging in the air like a drop of water in low gravity. Red pinpricks of light trace its outline in the sky. It's massive, even from a distance, a marvel of engineering and an impossibility. It was constructed long before the Fever, and just how that came about—how the countries of Earth banded together to pour their resources into it, how they designed it to begin with—has been lost to time. She's been there only once, for a job, but she remembers how the metal walls always vibrated no matter where you went.

She doesn't mind the journey. She finds turbulence soothing, and there's something exciting about watching her planet get smaller and smaller. Strands of fine hair float around her face from where they escaped her braid; she watches them drift.

She was almost too frantic, too desperate, to find success with the Recordkeeper. She needed information about the Scout job involving the candlesnuffer, but she had nothing to offer in return. Eventually, she gave him her suspicions about the impending attack on Cedre Station. The Recordkeeper wasn't likely to spill secrets to just anyone, and even if he did, the situation wasn't likely to get worse than it already was.

It turned out the candlesnuffer job was filled by an old ex of Hela's. Code name Evenhanded. Not the most exciting news Hela ever heard.

"So, refresh my memory," Elegy says. "This is the ex-girlfriend who put all your old clothes into the compost bin, right?"

Across from her, Elegy is tense as a tightrope, her hands braced against her knees so all her muscles stand at attention. She keeps sneaking looks at Forint, like it's a secret. Like he doesn't notice—which he obviously does.

"It was a trash can," Hela says, "and she lit them on fire afterward. Vindictive."

"Did you do something to provoke her?" Theren asks.

Elegy snorts.

"I was nineteen!" Hela says.

"Nineteen is old enough to know that you shouldn't make out with one girl while you're dating another."

"She dazzled me with glitter."

By the time they drift close enough to Cedre Station to be drawn in by its gravity, they're all laughing, even Forint. The Grasslands Dock sucks them in like water through a straw. Her clothes fall against her body again, and she feels the landing gear engage. The dock doors rumble as they close, and as breathable air floods the dock again, the ship's hatch opens.

They get off the ship together. It's one of General Thompson's shuttles, so they're in the military loading dock, which is simple, industrial. There are ships of all kinds perched beyond the oxygen barrier, Sparrows and Crows and even one Eagle, huge and shiny in the back of the massive space.

"Why didn't we try to get a meeting room?" Theren asks Hela.

"Okoro offered, but I know Evenhanded. If there was even a whiff of military involvement, she'd be out of here." Hela points over her shoulder with her thumb. "We have to play it cool. Somehow."

An escort buggy arrives to take them to the tram, operated by a chatty technician named Haven who tells them all about her recent attempt at a blind date.

"I used to take this tram line to school," Forint says, when they board the tram. He brushes his fingers over the graffiti-etched wall, and they sit.

The tram looked sleek from a distance, but it's scuffed upon closer inspection, even aside from the graffiti: the screws holding the seats in place are rusted, the seats themselves are worn from the friction of too much fabric, too many people sitting and standing. It smells like fuel and old french fries and body odor.

There are markets all over Cedre Station, but none of them are as big and grand as the TM—the Tundra Market—which has its own tram stop. Anything a person could possibly want—anything from home-brewed cleaning vinegar to tiny wind-up car toys—is available there. The tram eases to a stop, and the three of them stand to exit. The doors open and the noise, the light, the crowd—they overwhelm her.

The market is arranged in a perfect grid, but she can't tell just by looking at it. In front of her is a wall of people. Framing those people on either side are awnings protruding from market stalls, most of them heavy with wires and lights. Above the crowd are projections of advertisements, each one a burst of movement that repeats every three or four seconds: a woman smiling; children playing; juice pouring into a glass.

They weave through the crowd on the right, past a flatbread stall that was, according to Theren, Isre's favorite, and around the corner to a place called Tube Bar. Whoever owns the place takes the name as literally as possible: decorating the ceiling are all manner of tubes, big and small, plastic and metal, bright and dull, functional and useless. There are little rickety tables arranged beneath them, too close together for Hela's comfort.

On the way here, she saw Elegy's face on the screens at the center of the market—a picture of her from her arrival at the Evacuation Day banquet. But today Elegy and Hela are both wearing filtration masks—not an uncommon sight on Cedre Station, given how careful the Cedrae are about viruses—so no one seems to recognize them.

She's glad. She feels jumpy even now, tucked away in Tube Bar. Exposed, like being here in full view of other people is a mistake. Hela stops outside the bar and takes an illicit Eye out of her pocket—sealed up, its eyelid shut. She rolls it between her hands, which light up with elixir, and the eyelid opens. The Eye rises into the air, and Hela ushers it forward, into the bar ahead of them.

Evenhanded, the Scout they're meeting—and the pyromaniac ex-girlfriend—sits at a table in the back. She's around forty, with long fingernails filed into points that light up when she drums them on the table. The right side of her body is inked with fluorescent tattoos that glitter through her shirt. Her left side is bare.

She gives Hela a sour smile when she surfaces.

"Just heard whispers that the Hope of Cedre was in the Tundra," Evenhanded says, ignoring Hela to focus on Elegy. "I confess it didn't occur to me that you were here to meet with me. Tausia failed to mention it."

"For security reasons, you understand," Hela says. "How are you, Eve?"

Evenhanded ignores Hela and looks at Theren, instead. "And who are you? The enforcer?"

"He's a friend," Hela says. "Are you going to just pretend I don't exist this whole time?"

"I'm considering it."

"Aha." Hela points at her. "I got you."

Elegy sits across from Evenhanded, and Theren takes the chair beside her, leaving Hela to sit at the next table over. She feels that uneasiness again, with her back to the rest of the market.

"You could take off your mask, you know," Evenhanded says to Elegy. "I've already recognized you."

"No, thanks." Elegy smiles, the corners of her eyes crinkling. "So. It's been a while."

"Two years, I think. I'd have been nicer to you if I knew who you really were back then."

"That's exactly why I didn't tell you."

Evenhanded snorts.

"Tausia said you wanted information." She has a gap between her front teeth wide enough to fit a straw through. Hela used to poke it with her pinkie finger, teasing. She has no desire to do so now. "But I'm feeling reluctant to give information to a political figure, even if she used to be a Scout."

"Eve, I'm not a political figure."

"A religious figure, then." Evenhanded smirks at that, amused by her own joke. "I have a neutrality policy. They don't call me 'Evenhanded' for no reason."

Elegy opens her mouth to argue. Probably that neutrality with the Talusar is impossible, since Evenhanded hasn't been infected with Fever, and the Talusar have a religious imperative to introduce people to their Fever god. Hela watches as Theren reaches for her under the table, and sets his hand on Elegy's leg. It's a presumptuous move, but it works—Elegy's eyes harden, but she doesn't say whatever she was about to say.

"Don't talk, then," Hela says to Evenhanded. "Just listen. Several months ago there was a Scout posting asking for a candlesnuffer. You remember it, I'm sure."

Hela doesn't need Theren's gift to read Eve—she wouldn't be giving Hela that sharp look if she didn't know what Hela was talking about. If she didn't remember doing a job for some Talusar army types.

Hela goes on: "You fulfilled the job, and you delivered the bounty to some Talusar."

"I didn't ask them who they were or where they were from," Evenhanded says. "And they didn't say."

"Come on, Eve, you still knew," Hela says. "And it doesn't matter, nobody's gonna do anything about it as long as you tell us what we want to know."

"Don't fucking threaten me, Tausia," Evenhanded says.

Hela scowls. "I'm not *threatening* you—"

"Everything's a power play with you. Always has been."

"As it happens . . ." Forint leans forward, his elbows on the table. "I am threatening you. Tell me about the Talusar who met with you, or I'll escort you to the police station myself."

"You'll *escort* me," Evenhanded says, and she draws a dagger from her sleeve, laying it flat on the table in front of her. "You say that like you think it would be easy."

In clear Talusar, he replies: "It would be."

Evenhanded stares at him. He stares back.

"I recognized something," she says. "A symbol on one of their blades. It was a circle of vines—Rava Vidar's symbol."

"The person carrying that blade—what did they look like?" Elegy says.

"Tall, dark brown skin, wore her hair all piled on top of her head," Evenhanded says.

"Nyx," Theren says to Elegy.

"Did they say anything about how they were going to use the candle-snuffer? Or for what purpose?" Elegy asks urgently.

Evenhanded looks out at the market, her pointed fingernails drumming on the table again. She sighs.

"Some of them didn't know I spoke Talusar. I heard them whispering," Evenhanded admits. "They were talking about whether there was breath-able air in the cargo hold. They seemed concerned."

Hela feels an interesting, nauseating mixture of dread and triumph.

They were right. Rava's big catastrophe, her alliance with Ykev, the dark cloud that's been hanging over them for weeks, has all amounted to this: there's a priest of the Fever on Cedre Station.

All they can do now is find them before the virus spreads.

"Got it?" Elegy asks Hela.

Hela holds out her hand, and her black-market Eye flies into her palm. She passes it to Elegy. Evenhanded glares at her.

"I'll go to the data pool and send it to Okoro." Elegy gets up. "She'll make sure the Sword gets it."

She rushes out of Tube Bar to the post office, which is right next door. Quill messages are just text, so they can be sent by anyone, from anywhere, but footage from an Eye is too "heavy" for quill transmission. Luckily, sending illegal data—like what the Eye just recorded—is as easy as paying off the postal worker and dropping the Eye in the well, which is right out-side. And nobody bribes like Elegy.

Once Elegy is gone, Eve says to Hela, "You were fucking recording me without my permission?"

"Sorry, babe," Hela says, blowing a kiss. "You look great, though. Whatever you're doing, keep it up."

Evenhanded stands, shaking the table with the force of it. Hela holds out a filtration mask, folded into a square.

"Trust me," Hela says. "You want this."

46

They leave Tube Bar and return to the grid of throughways that comprises the market. Theren remembers Isre begging him to go there after school at least twice a week. Isre liked to wander around and dream of all the things he could do when he was Imbued. The films he would watch, the games he would play, the pen pals he would write to in Austra, Nusanta, and Losan.

But this place was never for Theren—Kesia didn't want him to get Imbued, and for all that he considered Isre his family, Theren knew he didn't belong to his brother as much as he belonged to his mother.

Theren, Elegy, and Hela are stopping to let a line of children holding hands pass them when he feels it. The emotions of the crowd are just a distracting low-level hum to him. But in the midst of them is a pinching sharpness that can belong to one of two people: Ranos or Satka.

No, he thinks, as he reaches a little farther—too gentle for Satka. It can only be Ranos.

The last time he saw Ranos, he was holding a knife to the man's throat, trying to muster the will to kill him. *You know what she'll do to me.* Ranos had begged him for mercy, and he'd refused.

He stops short, so Elegy runs into him, but he can't even voice an apology; he's too busy scanning the crowd for *him*. He can't be far—his hate for Theren, his *rage*, is ringing in Theren's ears like he's in the center of a bell that has just been struck. Ranos must have been punished severely when Rava found him still alive on the ground outside of House Vidar, having allowed Theren and Elegy to escape.

Before Theren can locate him, though, the quarantine alarm sounds, filling the air with a pulsing shriek. Light, too, flashes above their heads, slow but impossible to ignore. All around them, the market erupts into chaos as everyone starts running in different directions.

He reaches for Elegy automatically, his fingers pinching her sleeve. He holds out his free arm like a barrier against the crowd. Elegy is reaching back, her hand fumbling for his.

The air is full of panic, crowding him on all sides. Hands and elbows and shoulders shove at him. He can still feel Ranos's acidic presence, but it's fading by the second. He's too focused on it to notice a man barreling right at the connection point between his hand and Elegy's.

He loses his grip on her, and can't find her in the crowd. The alarm is too loud for her to hear him shouting her name.

He picks a random direction and starts moving, taking in every feeling of every person he passes, careful not to linger on anyone. He gets impressions of them: determined to get home, afraid of what this means, annoyed about yet another quarantine drill—the array of emotions is dizzying. He keeps moving, keeps sorting and discarding each person he passes without really looking at them. The lights are still flashing, the alarm still blaring, and then—

He feels Ranos again. Prickling and stinging like lemon juice on a cut. He latches on to the feeling and moves toward it, running into a man and shoving him aside, ducking under the roof of a mechanized doll stand that's been abandoned by its owner. The stinging feeling gets stronger and stronger as he moves away from the center of the market to the edge. The market is empty of shopkeepers, now, but all the obsidians in the news pavilion are still on, lit up, showing the scroll of images. He sees Tube Bar up ahead, empty; he turns to the left, following the feeling of Ranos all the way to a hallway that leads to the maintenance tunnels.

There, Ranos stands with another Talusar soldier, his clothes simple and Cedrae. In Ranos's hand is a Vidari blade, the gold handle made of vine filigree. His companion is taller than he is, a single Crucible tattoo on the back of his hand, but Ranos is obviously the deadlier of the two, radiating capability like the hum of an engine.

Theren was never sure what to make of Ranos. Of all of Rava's lessers, he was the one who eased Theren's burdens the most. He took him for swims in the mountain lakes around House Vidar when the air was hot; he sparred with Theren so he wouldn't keep getting trounced by Rava and her practice sword; he sometimes smuggled food to Theren when the others were determined to deprive him of it. But he was unpredictable, sometimes lashing out even harder than Satka, greedy for other people's pain even when it seemed to serve no clear purpose.

Before either of them can prepare for it, Theren rushes at the Crucible fighter on Ranos's left and shoves him up against the wall. The man brings an elbow down hard on Theren's arms, breaking his grip but dropping his sword in the process. Ranos is on top of Theren by the time he can reach for it; Theren grabs the blade by mistake, and his hand lights up with pain. Still, he swings it, beating Ranos back just long enough to get his hand on the sword's handle.

It's two against one, and Ranos alone is more than enough opponent for one man. Theren counters Ranos's blow from the side, leaving his right ribs exposed; the Crucible fighter punches Theren so hard he can't breathe, and he stumbles back toward the market, leading them away from the maintenance hallway.

"Forint!" Hela runs toward them, then rushes at the Crucible fighter, ramming her shoulder low into his belly. Caught off guard, the man goes down.

Ranos advances on Theren. Theren wants to look out for Hela, but then Ranos is on top of him, his movements quick and unpredictable, and it's all Theren can do to keep him at bay. He's far better than Avka Becken. If he were faster, he might rival Nyx.

Ranos parries with his sword, and Theren has to counter with his forearm. The blade cuts deep, and blood spatters on the ground, but there's no time to dwell on the pain—he has to block again, with the sword this time. The ache in his arm drives him deeper into his focus.

Ranos's blade catches the light and scatters it, dizzying Theren. He trips away from Ranos, and the spark he feels before each of Ranos's movements means nothing, the attention he pays to Ranos's footwork means nothing. He's fought Ranos so many times; he knows what it is to lose to him.

But he also knows how to beat him. Ranos only wins when he's steady, when he's enjoying himself. Theren has to destabilize him.

"How did Rava punish you, after you let me escape?" Theren says. "Or is *this* your punishment—being sent here to die?"

Rage chokes Theren—Ranos's, not his own—and he moves faster, fiercer. He swings at Ranos, and Ranos laughs a little, dancing back, his teeth bared. He thrusts his sword and Theren arches away.

The hallway—Hela, the lights, the alarm—disappears. There's only darkness and Ranos at the center of it. He cuts at Theren, never enough to be debilitating, but messy, frustrated chaos.

"Rava knew what you felt for her," Theren says. "And it disgusted her. Did I ever tell you that?"

Ranos screams into his teeth and attacks Theren harder—too hard, his finesse faltering. He leaves his left side exposed, and Theren is already swinging, but the angle is wrong. He hits Ranos with the flat of his blade, square in the rib cage.

Ranos stumbles into the wall, and Theren follows, pressing the other man into it, the blade against Ranos's throat, Theren's bloodied arms pinning him.

Their eyes lock. Theren jerks the handle sharply upward and to the right, cutting Ranos's throat.

He pulls away all at once, so Ranos slides to the ground with a sickening gurgle. Gasping, he stares at Ranos until the light leaves the other man's eyes. Only then does the alarm come flooding back in, and the lights, and Hela, shoving her incongruously large ring into the Crucible fighter's face. The man slumps to the ground. She's panting.

"I put sopora in the ring in case I need to knock someone out. It's a little Scout trick," she explains. "Let's go find Elegy."

Theren nods, and wipes his forehead with the back of his hand, trying not to disappear into panic. His ears are ringing, but he hands the short-sword he's holding to Hela, and pries the gold filigree handle from Ranos's limp fingers.

47

Elegy's father always told her that if they were ever separated, she should return to the last safe place they were together. So when the alarms go off, and the press of the crowd separates her from Hela and Theren, Elegy fights against the flow of bodies to get to Tube Bar.

It's empty, now, abandoned in a hurry by its manager—there's a half-poured beer under the tap. All the strings of light woven between the tubes are set to blink at random intervals; the effect is dizzying. She walks around the bar top, and hunts under the counter for a weapon, certain there has to be one stashed there.

Possession of a gun is harshly punished on Cedre Station, thanks to the catastrophic danger of a bullet hole, so when her fingers find the flat of a blade, she's not surprised. She detaches a simple shortsword from the underside of the bar top.

Which is lucky, because when she straightens, there's a man standing in the entrance.

He would look like an ordinary Cedrae, if she wasn't attentive to details. He wears blue jeans and a gray T-shirt, Cedre-made. But the ring on his right hand is copper, a Talusar color, and there's a black tattoo on the side of his neck. The mark of the priest.

He catches her looking at it, and lifts his hands to tie his straight black hair back, as if to show it off.

"Hello, Elegy Rosyk," he says, in precise English.

The bar is between them; she's trapped with a man who breathes Fever. The mask will protect her to an extent, but the longer she spends with him, the more likely an infectious particle is to penetrate the barrier. And it only takes one.

"Do you have a name?" She speaks in Talusar. "Or should I just call you 'priest'?"

"I heard you were fluent in our language, but I confess I thought the reports were exaggerated," he says. "My name is Nisov. We actually have a mutual friend in common. One of my flock, so to speak. Theren Forint."

"Your *flock*." Then it dawns on her. "Oh. You mean you infected him."

"Such a crass way to describe the encounter with God, but I suppose you have been raised to that belief." He pulls out a chair from a table near the door, and sits in it. "Please, sit with me. You're masked, and I mean you no harm."

"Masks aren't perfect, as you well know."

"Then sit at a safe distance." He gestures to the table on the other side of the entryway.

Holding the shortsword in front of her, she inches around the bar top and backs up toward the table he indicates. She pulls the chair away from it, so her path to the market is unobstructed, and sits.

"So paranoid. I'm not a soldier, you know."

"I'd be a fool to think every Talusar who wasn't a soldier couldn't fight."

"I suppose that's true." He folds his hands on the table in front of him. His fingernails are trimmed and buffed, a sign of a softer life. "This place—this station—is a marvel. I didn't think I would ever get to see it, for obvious reasons."

"Well, they keep you locked in a monastery like a very fancy prisoner."

"That's why I volunteered for this mission. A one-way mission, in all likelihood, alongside one of Rava Vidar's lessers. The one who failed to catch the so-called Hope of Cedre when she was escaping House Vidar," he says. "Ranos Kavad."

Elegy straightens. Ranos, who attended her interrogation in House Vidar, who Theren almost—but not quite—killed, is *here* on Cedre Station?

"I thought this place was worth seeing." Nisov gestures to the market, now eerie and empty, its stalls toppled, its colorful wares broken and spilled over the throughways. "My task was to simply be among your people and give the gift of the Fever to them—"

"You can't possibly believe you were sent here to give Cedre a gift."

"—but I had another task, one that would be more difficult to complete. I was to deliver a message to Larke Rosyk." He smiles a little. "But then I saw your face in the market, and I thought, 'even better.'"

"Why?" Elegy snaps. "You think I'm more merciful than my sister?"

"I think you know more about the Talusar, because your sister's experience of us has been more . . . intellectual. There's no education like a Scout's education." His eyes are cold. "Which means you will understand the consequences if I am killed."

"You came here as a biological weapon."

"That's not how the Talusar will see it. If you arrest me and punish me for my supposed crimes, my people will see only that the Cedrae executed one of their holiest people. Someone it's illegal to even *touch* without their permission. And for those Talusar citizens who are tired of conflict with Cedre—and there are many—the death of a priest will galvanize them to support open war against your people."

Elegy's jaw aches from clenching it. She stares at the tattoo on the side of his throat. It's the Talusar character for "breath," an elegant tangle of lines.

"You and I both know," Nisov says softly, "that you won't be able to persuade the Sword of this. She will have me publicly executed in the aftermath of this quarantine, for her own political gain."

"You know what?" Elegy says. "Fuck you."

Nisov smiles. "I assume that means you know I'm right. So here's what I propose: I'll deliver my message to you, instead of your sister. Then you will peacefully escort me to an escape shuttle, and send me on my way unharmed. I will return to Valla with your response, as well as with a tale of the compassion and understanding I found at the hands of our enemies."

The alarm, so piercing when it first went off, has faded to the background.

The Fever is on Cedre Station. No matter how stringent the quarantine protocols, it will still spread. It will decimate—or worse—the population of this station. They won't be in a position to defend against the full might of the Talusar military. They can't afford to invite Talusar wrath.

She swallows hard. And nods. "But you have to wear a filtration mask on your way to the escape shuttle."

Nisov's smile widens. "A lovely compromise."

"What's your message?" Elegy says. "We don't have a lot of time."

Nisov crosses his legs at the ankle. He doesn't look like someone who's been hiding for two days. He's clean and well-kept. Someone here must have hosted him. Which means there's at least one traitor on Cedre Station.

"Rava Vidar has made you a generous offer," he says. "An offer of permanent peace between your people and mine, which she will present to Emperor Talus when you agree to it. With her mother's support *and* Ykev Talus's support behind her, she believes he will be easily persuaded to accept it."

Elegy has never been more aware of her heartbeat.

"After this crisis on Cedre Station is dealt with, you will relocate your Earthbound population to the continent of Austra," he says. "You will be permitted to maintain your quarantine in peace. But you will submit to the authority of the Talusar empire." Nisov's eyes soften. "There will be no more war. No compulsory 'infection,' as you call it."

The offer brings a sour taste to Elegy's mouth. Cedre has already surrendered the vast majority of the globe. Now Rava Vidar asks them to surrender more? To give up their autonomy, their freedom?

But she's been staring down the point of a sword for her entire life, knowing that if the Talusar wanted to obliterate Cedre, they were more than capable. This offer is generous, for Rava.

It's also utter bullshit. The Cedrae and the Talusar have had treaties before. They brought a decade of peace, maybe more, before the fighting began again.

"What's the catch?" she says. "What does Rava want in return, apart from the ceding of Losan and Nusanta, which we both know she could simply *take* if she really had that much support?"

"She wants you to return something to her. Something you stole." Nisov uncrosses his legs, and leans toward her. "Theren Forint."

Elegy is tempted to laugh. The idea of Rava allowing a treaty to hinge on one person, *any* person, is so absurd it doesn't seem real. But she knows it's not just whatever twisted affection Rava feels for Theren that drives her to make this deal. It's the promise of the augurs, that if Rava can stop Theren from boarding the *Sundial*, she can stop Cedre's victory.

She who moves the fulcrum—

Suddenly Elegy feels like an augur herself, seeing down a potential path. If Elegy was the sort of person who would hand Theren Forint over in exchange for peace—peace without freedom, but still peace—then she would be helping Rava Vidar fulfill her prophecy. By moving Theren, Rava would be moving the fulcrum. Controlling the outcome.

But Elegy is not that sort of person.

"I'm supposed to give you a return message, right?" Elegy says.

Nisov nods. Elegy sees movement in the market beyond—two people walking around the corner. Two familiar people, bloody and disheveled, but unharmed. She meets Theren's gaze across the space that separates them.

"Please tell your commander only this," she says, without looking away from him. "She will never lay a hand on him again."

Hela rushes toward her, slowing only when she realizes Nisov is there. Her eyes catch on the symbol on the side of his throat. She whips her head around to stare at Elegy.

"What's going on?" she says.

Nisov has come to his feet, too, and he's approaching Theren, whose hand tightens around the sword he's carrying—oddly delicate, for a Talusar sword, and recognizably a Vidari artifact, thanks to the decorative vines that make up the foil. But he doesn't move, not even when Nisov brings a hand up to touch his face.

"Look at you," she hears Nisov say. "So strong with the Fever."

"Stop touching me," Theren says.

"Make me." Nisov's eyes twinkle with amusement.

Theren steps back, out of reach. He looks at Elegy.

"Again," Hela says. "What's going on?"

"We're escorting this man to an escape shuttle unharmed—and untouched," Elegy says.

"Um . . . what? He's a fucking priest of the Fever, and you want to just let him go?"

Elegy closes her eyes, briefly. Just to gather herself.

"Yes," she says.

Hela looks confused. She glances at Nisov, at the bright green shoelaces he wears and the tattoo on his skin and the smug expression on his face. And then at Theren, tense but unsurprised.

"After you, Your Grace," she says to Elegy.

✦   ✦   ✦

They go through the maintenance tunnels to avoid the crowds of frantic people trying to obey the quarantine orders by returning home. In the tunnels, maintenance staff are still working to keep the station's systems running, masked and sweating. Everyone is too busy to pay attention to them, despite Elegy's famous face and Theren's bloody arms.

The shortsword is against the small of Elegy's back, the handle tucked beneath her belt. Theren got rid of his—too flashy. Elegy hopes they won't need a weapon at all.

Nisov's now-unbound hair covers the mark on his neck. Not many Cedrae know the Talusar custom of marking priests of the Fever, but she didn't want to risk panicking anyone, so she told him to cover it. The filtration mask is now sealed over his mouth, shimmering as it catches the orange emergency lights.

Most civilians don't know about the shuttles at the Tundra Dock, so when their party emerges from the tunnels, they're surrounded by soldiers. This part of the station is dark and cold, the ceiling full of ducts and pipes.

Elegy looks back at Theren, alarmed by the crowd; they need to move Nisov through this space as quickly as possible. Theren turns to Nisov.

"May I take your arm?" He says it with such disdain, Elegy almost expects Nisov to refuse.

Nisov smiles, instead. "Who could say no to such a request?"

Theren takes Nisov's arm without meeting his eyes. It would have looked like a guard escorting a prisoner if Nisov hadn't bent his elbow and covered Theren's hand with his own, so instead it appears as if they're on some kind of lovers' stroll. Elegy has the sudden urge to slap Nisov's hand away.

They make it a long way unnoticed—everyone on Cedre Station has a job to do, and they each seem to be intent on doing it. But the closer they get to the shuttles that can take them to Earth, the sparser the crowd, and soldiers' eyes start to linger on her.

She opens the door to the docking bay, and on the other side of it is Frederick Green, his shaved head reflecting the fluorescent light. Frederick Green was her mother's Knight before the exiles' children came of age to swear their oaths, but she only ever knew him as the captain of the Army of the Sword, where he still serves.

Gathered around him are four others, wearing identical black uniforms. Over their shoulders she can see the lines of spacefaring Finches behind the glass barrier, waiting for emergency takeoff. They're small, and preprogrammed to go only to Losan, Austra, and Nusanta without having to be operated by a pilot. Lights flash around the docking bay doors as they open to let another row of crafts escape the station.

"Freddie," Elegy says, with a tentative smile.

She saw Frederick every summer when she visited her mother and Larke for lessons. He taught her the right forks to use when she was a child, and when she was a teenager, he helped her sneak back in after a night of harmless adventure in Cedre Station. She's hoping those fond memories help her now.

"Your Grace," Green says, with obvious relief. "I'm so glad to see you alive and well. I'm sure the Sword will feel the same."

"She's all right?"

"Yes, she's currently under quarantine nearby. There are a lot of people looking for you, Your Grace. I was ordered to escort you directly to the Sword if I found you."

"That won't be necessary," Elegy says. "I have to get back to Losan. Now."

Theren's fingers brush her elbow.

"He's not going to let you," Theren says, in Talusar, in her ear.

Elegy feels like she should have anticipated that. Of course Larke doesn't want to let her go. She wants Elegy right here, so she can present her to the public and declare that she personally ensured the safety of the Hope of Cedre. She wants Elegy as a political pawn, as usual.

Theren steps closer to her, a solid wall of heat at her back. His fingers brush against her spine as he wraps his hand around the hilt of the short-sword at her back. He draws it, but holds it low, where Frederick can see it.

All at once, Frederick and the four soldiers behind him draw their own weapons. She can see Hela in her periphery. All around them, people have stopped to watch.

Elegy's heart races. This isn't good.

"Your Grace," Frederick says. "Tell your Knight to stand down."

Theren doesn't move.

"Only one card left to play, El," Hela says to her.

Elegy knows it, even as she resists it. She reaches back and touches Theren's wrist. His response is automatic, as she knew it would be—he shifts his grip on the sword so that he's offering her the hilt. She takes it from him, and sets it on the ground in front of her. Frederick relaxes by a fraction.

"Freddie," Elegy says. "I'm the Hope of Cedre. What I need to do is very important. And if you help me now, I won't forget it."

General Thompson told her to make use of her status even if she had no faith in it. But she can't lie to herself anymore: she's starting to believe it. She has ever since she felt a flutter in her stomach at the sight of Theren Forint. She wonders if she did from the start, standing under the skylight in the Cenobium as an augur told her there was hope for Cedre. The memory is so vivid now, the broken reflections in the mirror, the feeling of destiny strangling her.

Claiming her fate now means asking Frederick Green, captain of the Army of the Sword, to defy Larke. He could be fired for this. He could be arrested for it. So she's a little surprised when Theren steps back, just an instant before Green moves aside. All around him, the other guards follow suit.

"Your Grace," Frederick says, inclining his head to her.

Elegy feels like a boulder rolling downhill. She knows what she'll find at the bottom, and she can't stop now until she reaches it. She just refused an offering of peace from Nisov, acting as an envoy of Rava Vidar, and then commanded a member of Larke's personal guard.

She's doing exactly what she told Theren she had no interest in doing: seizing power from the Sword of Cedre.

48

When Theren steps out of the Sparrow onto the salt flat that surrounds the Cenobium, everything is so bright he can hardly see.

The salt flat is wet now and still, reflecting the sky like a mirror. The Cenobium itself is like a mirage up ahead, rippling.

They couldn't take Nisov back to Losan, so Hela reprogrammed the Sparrow once they got Nisov into quarantine at the back of the ship. It was Theren's idea to go straight to the Cenobium, to ask Parekh, Arias, and Isre to meet them here for their mission to rescue Fenn. They can't delay it until autumn now, not with Cedre Station vulnerable to the Fever. Cedre might not last until autumn.

The Cenobium is grand in the way that sparse things can be grand. Though there are two long, low buildings on either side of it, the sanctuary is all he can look at; it towers over them, casting a long shadow on the ground.

As Nisov approaches the doors, they open, and an old woman steps out barefoot on the salt.

"What an interesting day this is turning out to be." Her eyes skip right over Nisov, Hela, and Theren, and land on Elegy. "Elegy. Welcome back."

"Nerina. Seems like you were expecting me."

"I was told the odds of your arrival were good," Nerina says mildly. "Priest and Knight will come with me, since they're permitted in the consecrated space. Scion and Scout will remain in the antechamber until the augurs make their summons."

"I'm not going to leave her," Theren says.

"This is a sacred space. No violence will come to Miss Rosyk here. And you need to clean up if you're going to stand before the augurs, child," Nerina says, making a show of looking at his arms. He cleaned and sealed his cuts on the journey over, but his shirt is still stained, and there's blood smeared on his skin.

"Stand before the augurs?" he says. "I wasn't aware I would be doing that."

"Oh, certainly." Nerina turns and walks through the open doorway, Nisov at her back.

Theren hooks his fingers around Elegy's for just a moment, then he follows.

The antechamber is dark and cool, lit by lanterns. They pass through it, into a brighter hallway that follows the curve of the sanctuary, its windows showing the salt flat and the mountains beyond; at the end of it is another hallway, this one straight and airy, with rooms jutting off to either side.

"This is the living space for augurs and attendants," Nerina says. "As a priest of the Fever, you are our honored guest."

"Thank you." Nisov smiles. "It's a pleasure to be here. I never thought I would see the Cenobium."

"The circumstances of your arrival are something I'm ignoring in favor of diplomacy." Nerina stops beside the first room on the left, and gestures to the open doorway. "I may be required to welcome you, priest, but I know how you find yourself here, and I am not kind to those who wield our holy instrument against the innocent as if it's a blade. You will remain in these quarters for the duration of your stay, which I hope will be short."

Nisov's smile remains fixed, but Theren feels him deflate. Nerina gestures for Theren to follow her to the next room down, which is a communal bathroom.

It's bright, with a row of sinks down the middle and tubs for bathing along the edges. The windows are rippled glass, letting in light but not shapes.

"I'll bring you clothes," Nerina says, and then she's gone, and he's alone.

He stoppers one of the sinks and fills it. He can hear the water pump running in the walls. There is no Fever field here that makes electricity impossible—there are too few augurs to emit that much disruptive energy. The Cenobium has a closed power system, probably running on solar panels. Still, there are some Talusar customs that hold—no electric lights, for example.

He strips to the waist and washes with the soap they provided, a colorless lump with lavender and mint pressed into it. It smells like Valla, like washing up with Orda after Crucible training sessions.

He rinses the dried blood from his arms, from his hands. The sweat from his brow. The dust from his hair. He's just drying off when Nerina walks back in with a stack of fabric in hand, all black.

"Have you heard any news about Cedre Station?" he asks her.

"Only what the augurs saw in advance."

"How good of them to warn us," he says, though there's no real point in offering that criticism. The augurs don't take sides in the conflict between the Cedrae and the Talusar. At least, that's what they claim.

He can feel a question in her, tickling at his mind, and he says, "Just ask."

She looks startled, but says, "I've heard you perceive the present."

"That's one way of putting it." He finishes drying off and takes the shirt from the stack she brought him. The material is soft from repeated washings. A little smaller than he likes to wear things, stretched over his arms and shoulders. Or maybe he's just filled out a little after weeks of full meals and plenty of sleep in Cedre. He rolls the sleeves up to his elbows.

"In the life I had before, I studied the Fever," she says. "There's a kind of . . . monastery, on the eastern coast. For priests and those who study them, near Ileth Vidar's home. I was half a monk, half a scientist."

"I wasn't aware there were any Talusar scientists."

"The Talusar empire spans a planet. You have had a very particular experience of us."

He can't argue with that.

"In my monastery," she goes on, "we identified the gene that makes a person a priest. Some of our number perceived this knowledge as too close to heresy, and they had sway with Ileth. She shut us down, and I came here to serve instead." She tilts her head. "I have long thought that if we could have continued, we might have identified the gene for augurs and epocha, as well. And, perhaps, for whatever you are."

He pulls the stopper from the sink drain, and watches the water disappear. "You think I'm a genetic anomaly."

"Maybe." She beckons. "Follow me. The augurs would like to speak to you."

When they reach the sanctuary, Nerina tells him to remove his shoes, and he does, lining them up next to another pair of boots near the door, with his socks folded inside.

The sanctuary reminds him of the room where he was infected with the Fever. Round and cavernous, like the inside of a barrel. But he's never seen anything like the huge, multifaceted mirror in the center of it, glittering like a diamond.

Elegy stands in the center of the mirror, her fingers twisted together over her stomach. He lets the feeling of her in, just enough, like their fingers brushing together as they walk. What comes back to him is dread. Elegy isn't eager to hear what the augurs have to say. He can't blame her.

Nerina stops him. She carries a copper dish full of ash paste, for the blessing that only the Fevered receive. He bends his head to her automatically, letting her brush an ashen fingertip over his forehead. She says the prayer, and though Theren has only heard it once, he knows the words.

"The Fever is change. To change is to die. To die is to experience annihilation. To be reborn is to conquer it. May it be so, may it be so."

Theren lifts his head.

"Join her," Nerina says, gesturing to Elegy.

His mother was the first person to teach him about the augurs. Though apparently loyal to Cedre then—if she ever was—she still performed the sign of the Fever over her mouth when she spoke of them. *They have no names*, she said. *And who they were before the Fever, or where they were from, it doesn't matter.*

He stops next to Elegy on the mirror. He can see the side of her face in one of the mirror's facets, the curve of her cheek and her furrowed brow.

"I asked about Cedre Station. No one seems to know anything yet," Elegy says. "They just told me they wanted to speak to me and my Knight at the same time."

"But I'm not your Knight," he says.

Before she can respond, the door across from them opens, and four augurs file into the room. Each one is an identical gray robe with a white band at the throat, salt-stained at the bottom as if they walk the salt flats each morning.

He's known people like this before. People with too many things buzzing inside them, people of machinations and schemes and games. He can feel the gears clicking away inside them, their certainty, the *inevitability* they feel.

"Hello again," an augur with pink cheeks says to Elegy.

"She's very annoyed," one of the others says. They're smaller than the rest, and lean the way a child is lean, like their body hasn't become something yet.

"Or afraid," the pink-cheeked one replies.

"I'm standing right here," Elegy says. "This is Theren Forint, not that you asked."

Theren feels the sudden urge to laugh. Only Elegy would speak to an augur that way, with obvious antipathy. He allows the augurs' feelings in, for a moment, to find out if it bothers them. He feels tickles of amusement, twinges of irritation. And boiling beneath it: fear.

Fear of what?

"Oh, we'll get to him in a moment," the pink-cheeked augur replies. "You must know why we wish to speak with you."

Elegy says, "Actually, I don't. You all seem to have trouble with specificity. Where's the eldest of your number?"

That fear again.

"We will get to that as well," the pink-cheeked augur replies. "If you had to guess why you were here, what would you say?"

"Either you want to stop me from doing something, based on some outcome you'd like me to avoid," she says, "or you want to pressure me into doing something based on some outcome you'd prefer."

"Outcome," says the augur with the shaved head, "requires an end point, which is of course nonsense."

"Not nonsense to those who only see *then*," the smallest augur replies.

"In any case," the pink-cheeked augur says, "we are not here to stop you from doing anything. We are here to arm you with purpose, as we did with limited success the last time you stood before us."

In his periphery, he sees Elegy's hands tighten into fists at her sides.

"You wish to fly the *Sundial* to a doorway in the stars," the augur says. "You must do this in order to walk the path we laid out for you."

Theren hasn't spoken to many augurs, but he thinks this is the most specific he's ever heard one get. It's unsettling.

The augur goes on: "You seek an epocha in order to do it. You seek the one who bears the Vidari name. Yes?"

"Yes," Elegy says.

"It will not be enough," the smallest augur says, their voice high and feather-light. "You must build a fulcrum of past, present, and future, as Rava Vidar did."

"I'm not sure what that means," Elegy admits.

"What did we tell you about the fulcrum?" the pink-cheeked augur says. "Surely you remember our words."

"You said it was three voices in harmony." Elegy sighs a little. "One who bears the Vidari name. One who knows the taste of Cenobium salt. And . . . another." She pauses. "And you told Rava Vidar to look for past, present, and future, I hear."

"Yes," the augur replies. "You seek the one who bears the Vidari name— the epocha, the past. And you have the other." He gestures to Theren with an open hand. "The Knight who reads hearts—who reads the present. But you must also bring with you the future. The one who has tasted Cenobium salt. Or you will not be able to navigate the doorway."

"So I need an augur." Elegy claps her hands together in front of her. "Any volunteers?"

Unexpectedly, the smallest augur smiles.

"You have two options," she says. "One of our number has been taken captive by Rava Vidar. You have spoken of her already, our oldest member.

She is being held under heavy guard at the monastery where you are already headed." She looks to Theren, and her voice softens. "*You* remember her, my dear."

She must be talking about the augur in his restored memory.

"Rava promised to return her here," Theren says.

"Rava Vidar doesn't return what she borrows if she can still make use of it," the smallest augur replies.

"You want us to rescue your augur," Elegy says.

"We want you to know that she *can* be rescued, in some futures," the augur with the shaved head replies. "But there is another option."

"Oh yes," the pink-cheeked augur says. "You can also replace her."

"Replace her?"

Fear creeps in at the edges of Elegy. Theren feels it, too.

"You can meet our God," the pink-cheeked augur replies.

In unison, all the augurs make the sign of the Fever over their mouths.

"If you survive the encounter, Elegy Rosyk," the pink-cheeked augur says, "then you will be an augur."

In the silence, he hears the distant echo of footsteps in other parts of the Cenobium. But this room is silent and still as the sunlight fades.

Elegy laughs. It sounds strained.

"To be clear," she says, "you're saying that if I get infected, I'll be able to see the future."

"To be *clear*, you may not survive it," the pink-cheeked augur replies. "Sometimes you do, and sometimes you don't. But when you do, yes, that is how the Fever works in you."

He thinks of Nerina's study of genes. The complex pattern layered through Elegy that the Fever would first kill, and then revive so that she can encounter, not the past, but the future. There's something fitting about this, that a woman destined for something great would meet the Fever with greatness.

"No offense," Elegy says, "but I have no fucking interest in being one of you."

"Then you must choose the other path," the pink-cheeked augur says. "But you must not board the *Sundial* without the fulcrum in place, or it will mean death for everyone on board."

"Though death among the stars is not the worst form of death," the smallest augur muses.

"I could just take one of you with me right now," Elegy says.

"You could," the pink-cheeked augur acknowledges with a nod. "But those paths inevitably lead to capture and death."

"Or you're just telling me that so I won't kidnap you."

The pink-cheeked augur smiles. "I suppose you'll have to trust us."

Elegy snorts.

"The difference between you and Rava Vidar," the smallest augur says, "is that she would use force to take one of us somewhere we didn't want to go, and you will not. You must hold fast to the differences between you, Elegy Rosyk." She pauses a moment. "Elegy *Ahn*."

It's a small concession, saying Elegy's real name. Theren knows it might be a manipulation intended to soften Elegy, but he thinks it works anyway.

"Why are you helping me?" Elegy demands. "You could have told me this—you could have told me a lot more than this—at any time. Why now?"

"We have particular priorities," the pink-cheeked augur says. "It would be impossible not to."

"Does the tree resent the gardener who prunes it into a desirable shape?" the smallest augur says.

"Does the field resent the farmer for planting his crops in perfect rows?" the augur with the shaved head chimes in.

"We have particular priorities," the pink-cheeked augur says again. "And our priority now is you."

"And the others?" Elegy says. "The augurs who threw their weight behind Rava? What do they say about this?"

"They can no longer perceive you unless you are with Rava Vidar," the pink-cheeked augur replies. "Just as we can no longer perceive Rava Vidar unless she is with you. That is the cost of our choices. Some are pleased with it, some are not. But time cannot run backward for any of us."

The sun is done setting. At the edge of the sanctuary, Nerina moves from lantern to lantern to light the wicks with a sturdy flame. She's quiet and practiced in her movements. Soon the room flickers with unsteady light.

The augur with the long, black hair, who has stood silent at the end of the row since the start, finally speaks up.

"My turn now," she says.

She steps onto the mirror without raising her robes, inelegant, letting them trip her a little until she stands in front of Theren. She smiles, wide, a row of slightly crooked teeth showing for just a moment.

She feels . . . warm. Fond. Like someone who knows him.

"It is so wonderful to meet you at last," she says. "These other augurs see Elegy Rosyk, and not Rava Vidar. The remaining four see Rava Vidar, but not Elegy Rosyk. But I . . ." She steps toward him, her voice gentling. "I see only you."

Her features are elongated and narrow. Her hair is long enough to brush her rib cage, parted down the middle and graying at the temples. She's not quite beautiful, but it's difficult not to look at her. She's close, within arm's reach, and he resists the urge to back away from her.

She sees *only him*.

"Why?" he says weakly.

Instead of answering him, she looks to Elegy.

"You already know what he is," the augur says. "But you haven't told him, and that is why I must do it now."

Elegy's next swallow is labored.

"He deserves to have choices," Elegy says. "What you're about to tell him takes them away."

"My dear, we are not granted endless choices," the augur replies sadly. "Any decisions we make are within the confines of what we did not—could not—decide. We have run out of time, and now he must know."

Theren has no room for frustration, or anger, or even apprehension. He's still stuck on the idea that this woman, this *augur*, only sees him.

"You are the apex of two potential destinies," the augur says to him. Her voice is low and clear. The room shrinks around her. "Two women with equal claim to the future of this world, and the other thing they have in common is *you*."

Her eyes are as gray as her robes, a maudlin color.

"When we called Rava Vidar and Elegy Rosyk here, years ago, we told them each about a man who would precede the fulfillment of their opposing fates." Lantern light flickers on the surface of the mirror, scattered by its facets. "This man, we told them, would be a signpost on the way to their twin destinies. And they would each be in love with him."

Theren goes still.

He remembers kissing Elegy outside the trailer in Twentynine, his palms on the hot metal, asking her why she was avoiding him. The fear in her voice as she replied, *I told you, I can't talk about this right now.*

This is why she was afraid. Because the prophecy that ruined her life was coming true. Through *him*.

"To the extent that each of them understands love, which in Rava's case is . . . variable," the augur says, "they have met this criteria."

Theren feels something deep and aching in Elegy, painful enough for him to bring his hand up to his sternum automatically; he feels the tumult of panic; he feels something else, too, something wild and weightless. It's too much, all of it.

And then there's the grief tearing through her. It's familiar. It's the feeling of Shir Alexios, only stronger than Theren's felt before, like a wail. He looks at her, alarmed, but she's very still, now more than ever resembling the statue of Cassandra the Seer that stands two stories high in the Getty.

"I don't know why you are resisting this so strongly—" the augur begins, frowning at Elegy, and he cuts off whatever she's about to say. He's not going to let her make it worse. The augurs have brought Elegy nothing but grief.

"Enough," he says. "Is that all? You just wanted to tell me this?"

"Well . . ." The augur looks confused. "Yes, but—"

He reaches for Elegy's hand, and tugs her back across the mirror, down the aisle, and through the doors.

49

Theren leads Elegy out of the sanctuary, past his boots and her boots, past the flames that flicker against the antechamber walls, and she lets herself be led. She sees black robes in front of them; Nerina, walking them to wherever they'll be staying that night.

She can't think about Cedre Station, about Nisov and the Fever and "equo ne credite." All she can think about, in this moment, is Shir. He was with her the first time she came here. Hair flopping over his forehead, his smile wide and eager. And after, how he spoke to her. *If saving Cedre means you'll love two men at once . . . well, it'll be worth it.* Like Elegy being destined to betray him by loving another man changed nothing between them. Like everything was still normal.

That isn't how Theren Forint talks to her. With him, everything is its proper size, everything has its proper weight, even if it's far too big and far too heavy. For better or worse, he lives in reality. He's *here.*

He's *now.*

They're in a cool stone room. Someone has already been there to light the lanterns. She's standing on a rug, cream-colored and soft. There are plants everywhere, vines, their leaves tumbling down to the floor from the bookcase, tilted toward the windows. The air smells like citrus and smoke.

She knows there are things she has to say. Apologies she has to make— that she let him find out about the prophecy this way, that yet again, some- one has made him no more than a pawn in a game augurs play, that she's sorry he's trapped between her and Rava—

"I'm—" she starts.

He cuts her off. "Don't."

He doesn't look angry. Only . . . curious. It's an expression she's not sure she's seen him wear before. Not because he isn't interested in people, but because curiosity requires, among other things, a hesitation between not knowing and knowing—and he always knows too much.

"I'm not waiting for an apology. Or an explanation," he says.

"Okay." Her voice sounds rough.

"I'm waiting . . ." He reaches out, and hooks his fingers in her belt loops, drawing her closer. She's too startled to do anything other than let him. He bends his head so he can speak close to her ear. "For you to take what's on offer."

She doesn't even need to ask what exactly that is. He offers *himself*, and he always has. He's never asked for her to be rid of her grief. Never asked for any promises, any declarations, or any answers she wasn't ready to give. He's never even asked for her forgiveness, though he got it a long time ago.

He's only ever asked her what she wants.

He holds himself apart from her, just a breath of space between them. So she has to move; she has to choose.

And she does.

She backs him up against the wall and kisses him, clutching at his shirt—and then shoving it *up* so she can bend down, almost kneeling, to get her mouth on his stomach, his chest. He touches her hair, her shoulders, like he's tracing the outline of her body, then he raises his arms as she pushes the fabric up and over his head. The shirt falls on the ground next to them, and she smells the Cenobium soap, lavender and mint. In the unsteady light she sees that he's not as spare as he was when she first saw him again in House Vidar; life in Cedre has made him thicker, stronger.

She feels frantic with the need to get closer to him, her hands trembling with it, her breaths fast and unsteady. She touches him, palms flat against his arms, which are muscled from the longsword, and she gives up on patience, gives up on savoring this. She fumbles with his belt; he covers her hands, and she thinks he's pushing her away, slowing her down—but all he does is take his pants off for her. His eyes stay locked on hers, black and focused.

God, she thinks, because there's nothing else to think, with all that bare skin in front of her, asking to be touched; scars begging to be traced, maybe with her fingers, maybe with her tongue. She swallows a curse at the thought. The world has done a number on him, and he wears it on his skin. She's dizzy with the sight of him, drunk on it, but she still hesitates with her hands on the hem of her own shirt.

"The last person who touched me," she says, breathless, "was him."

He runs his calloused fingers along her jaw and behind her ear, tenderly.

"The last person who touched me was her," he replies.

Elegy pauses for a moment as the weight of those twin statements settles between them. Sometimes she forgets that she's not the only one who brings grief here. He does, too, though a different kind.

She nods, as if deciding something, though she already decided it a long time ago, when she pushed him up against a shelf in Naarm Stronghold. She lifts her shirt away from her body and drops it at her feet.

He bends to kiss her—her shoulder, her breast, and then, dropping to

his knees, he kisses her stomach, right under her belly button. He unbuttons her pants, and she thinks of the last time they did this, the way his
teeth scraped her skin and she put her hands in his hair—only this time she
doesn't intend to stop and have a mature conversation instead; she intends
to take whatever he'll give her, and offer whatever she has.

She plants her hands on his shoulders to steady herself as he takes her
pants off, slowly, his lips following every inch of skin he exposes in a line
of heat—her belly, her thigh, her knee. She's so alive with sensation she
doesn't think about how bare she is, how vulnerable. His mouth is on
her, and she arcs forward like a plucked harp string, gasping. She steadies
herself on the wall.

But she wants—

"Up, get up," she says, breathless.

He stands, and she guides his hand, lightly, to the hard line of the con-
traceptive implant in her arm. Then she backs up toward the bed, pulling
him with her. She marvels at the lantern light flickering over his skin, at
how long his legs are, at every line of tension in his body. She pulls him
down to the bed with her.

She laces her fingers with his, and almost laughs at how much smaller
her hands are. It would be so easy for him to overpower her, but he seems
content to let her take the lead, instead, with the same patience he's showed
in every training session, every *conversation* they've ever had.

She brings his arms above his head, pressing him into the mattress as
she leans down to taste the salty skin of his shoulder, to close her teeth
lightly over his clavicle. She wrenches desperate sounds from him, and a
part of her can't believe that she can make someone sound like this, can
make someone *want her* like this.

When she runs her fingers over his lower lip, he kisses at her fingertips.
His gaze moves over her body, slow. She's never liked to be stared at, never
enjoyed eyes on her. But his eyes, dark and attentive, feel just like his touch.
They erase everything else. They wake every nerve. And the same attune-
ment that he has to her in the training room, or in the heat of combat, is
here, too, as he moves with her. Easy. Present. Focused.

She doesn't need to speak—as usual, he already knows what she needs;
he already *knows her*. He touches her, his fingers gentle but certain. Release
hits her so hard that her body shudders and she lets out a wordless, sharp
sound.

In the breathless aftermath, she tries on the truth like a new garment:
She loves him.

Yes, she thinks. That fits.

+   +   +

She steps out of the bathroom after washing, later, to find him standing by the bed, buckling his belt. As he picks up his shirt, she puts her arms around him and stills his hands, her face pressed to his spine.

"I do have to get dressed sometime," he says, obviously amused, and she likes him this way, loose and laughing. This version of Theren Forint that few people ever get to see.

She says, "Is that a rule, or something?"

He tugs her hand up to his mouth and kisses her fingers. "I think there are laws against public indecency, yes."

"Not all laws are just." She smiles into his skin, and wonders if he can feel it. "I like looking at you."

"I like looking at you, too. I'm sure you've noticed."

She hasn't, exactly, but she does remember Parekh telling her, *He's gorgeous, and he barely looks at anyone who isn't you.* Elegy wonders how much she's missed because she was too afraid to look for it. She intends to make up for that now.

He turns, and sits on the edge of the bed, so they're almost at eye level. "I suspect you have things to do right now."

She runs her thumb along the underside of his jaw, slowly.

Guilt pinches at the edges of her, the parts of her that feel like moving forward is a betrayal of Shir and everything they had. But she's discovering that there's a lot more space inside her than she thought there was—that she can grieve for Shir and still feel *this*, this giddy possibility, this scorching desire, unabated even now.

Only—she wants other things, too. To find out how Theren likes to be touched, and how she likes to touch him. To find out what he looks like when he does ordinary things, like wash his face, or put on his clothes.

"Things to do," she repeats, and she traces the line of his neck with her finger. His eyes close, and she can't read him, but she thinks that's a good sign. "But I'm already doing something."

He rests his hands on her waist, and his thumbs find the points of her hips. He squeezes, gently.

"Trust me," he says. "There are things I'd rather do than whatever is waiting for us out there."

She tilts her head. "Oh?"

"Would you like me to enumerate them for you?" he asks, laughing a little.

Elegy grins, but she knows he's right, knows they can't ignore everything for any longer than they already have.

She's hungry, for one thing. But for another: the attack on Cedre Station. Her grin fades as she considers her next move.

"I think I have to do something that I really don't want to do," she says.

He nods, and picks up his shirt, breaking the spell between them. "What do you need?"

"From you?" She sighs a little. "A Knight, I think."

He raises his eyebrows, and she covers his mouth with her fingers to stop whatever response he was about to give.

"I don't need you to swear an oath again," she says. "I just need you to say yes, for as long as it suits you."

He closes his hand around her wrist, and lifts her fingers from his lips.

"May I speak now?" he says.

She rolls her eyes.

"My answer is yes," he says. "Go have your meeting. I'll find Hela and get the update about the others joining us."

"Don't believe I mentioned a meeting," she says.

He tips his head up and kisses her.

"I'm very good," he says, against her mouth, "at reading people."

50

The Cenobium doesn't have a veil, obviously, so Elegy flies the Sparrow—parked on the salt flat—to the nearest one, in a so-called neutral settlement west of the Cenobium known as Laketa.

Before she set out, she took a quill from the Sparrow's emergency kit and scribbled a message:

> *General,*
> *Requesting an emergency meeting.*
> —*Elegy*

She only hopes the general is quick to receive it.

Laketa is nestled up against a huge lake, bright blue and dazzling in the daylight, but at night, dark as a hole in the ground. The buildings crawl along the coast, some lit by their own closed power systems, some by the flickering lanterns. It looks like a piece of Cedrae country spliced together with a Talusar city.

The trees are dense at the edge of the settlement, but she lands the ship in a clearing and secures it.

She looks like a Scout, and looking like a Scout is like wearing armor, in a place like this. People in Laketa don't want to catch the attention of a bounty hunter.

The veil she knows about is in the back room of an old inn. It's a building made to look older than it is, with huge stones stacked into a tower and grand arches above each doorway and window. Walking up to it, she feels like she's from a time of princesses and bards and horse-drawn carriages.

There's an older woman behind the front desk, tongue sticking out of her mouth as she pokes at a piece of embroidery. She glances up at Elegy. "No Scouts allowed."

"Not here to find anyone," Elegy replies. "I just want to use your veil."

"Owning a strictly regulated Cedrae relic would be illegal."

"So I guess I just hallucinated using one here a couple years ago?"

The woman pulls the needle through her embroidery again. Then she sets it down and beckons for Elegy to follow her.

The lobby is warm and creaky with a fire burning in the fireplace. None of the inn's guests—if there are any—are awake at this hour. The woman leads Elegy through a hidden door in the wood paneling and into the veil room.

It's small, just large enough for the veil apparatus itself, with a threadbare red rug on the floor. The woman holds out her hand for her payment, and Elegy presses a gold coin into it. Gold is useful everywhere, no matter what country you're in, and this meeting is important enough that Elegy doesn't mind parting with it.

She steps through the veil and speaks the general's name into the iridescence. There's nothing to do after that but wait for the general to arrive. She had three to choose from: Thompson, who's fond of her but still sees her as the near-child she was when she first met him; Saetang, who also likes her, but breaks rules too easily; and Okoro, who seems to hate her, but who has the most sway with Larke and the Quorum that rules Cedre in all matters except military. She knows that if she can get Okoro to listen to her, the others—and crucially, the Quorum—will follow.

It doesn't take Okoro long to arrive. Her hair is black now, no trace of blue, and she's dressed all in white. She squints at Elegy when she arrives, and demands, "You couldn't find somewhere safer to call me from?"

"Actually, no," Elegy says.

Okoro seems to reflect on this. "Fine, then. You're safe? You didn't get exposed to Fever?"

"I'm fine," Elegy says. "You? Are you on Cedre Station?"

Okoro nods. "I was cleared. I return to Nusanta tomorrow."

"What's happening there?"

"Surely you didn't bring me here to *deliver news* to you." She scowls at Elegy, and Elegy scowls back.

"Obviously not. But I'd still like to know."

"Cedre Station is under lockdown. Testing everyone. Those who get cleared move to the Grasslands District until everything is sorted. But the Fever is spreading rapidly, even with the quarantine in place. It is difficult to contain, as you know."

Elegy does know.

"I saw footage of you escorting a man off-station," Okoro says, and she paces a few steps before turning back to Elegy. "A man with a tattoo on his throat that signifies he's a priest of the Fever."

"Yes." There's no point in pretending it didn't happen.

"Would you care to explain why you saved the life of the man responsible for thousands of Cedrae deaths?"

"You know he's a priest," Elegy says, "so you already know why. If you lay a hand on one without their permission, the Talusar will cut it off. Imagine what they would do if we held, tried, and executed one."

Okoro snorts, and the sound, her posture, her demeanor—they remind Elegy that the general is young. She likely ascended to her position because of some valorous act in battle. That's how succession works in Nusanta. Leaders are battle-proven, which means their path is cleared by loss. She wonders what losses Okoro endured to get where she is.

"You're planning something," Okoro says. "And you need my help."

It's as clear an opening as Elegy could have hoped for, but she isn't sure where to begin. There are so many threads to weave together. Theren's missing memory. The plant from another world. The prophecy that focused Rava's attention on Theren. Elegy clears her throat, and starts where instinct tells her to start.

"Do you think someone from outside our solar system has ever landed here?"

Okoro is still facing out, arms crossed. Her eyes slide to Elegy's.

"Given how dire our situation is, I'm going to assume you're asking because you already know someone has," she says. "So tell me what you found out."

"I know that the invitation this planet once received was not the only time we've had outside contact," Elegy says. "I know that just before either of us was born, someone from another world landed here and left a message for us. What do *you* know?"

"I know . . ." Okoro sighs. "I know that Kesia Forint had contact with a man whose origins she couldn't identify. And I know that your father had a collection of fragments from that man's ship."

"How . . . what?"

"Your father wasn't just some *Scout*, or even just the father of the Sword's second child," Okoro says, looking frustrated. "After the Talusar exiles from the *Hoatzin* were questioned under truth serum, and Kesia Forint revealed her connection to an otherworldly visitor, your mother tasked your father with finding out whatever he could about him. Most of what he gathered, he sent along to her; some of it he kept for himself—probably not legal, but your mother only cared about certain rules, not all rules." Okoro sniffs disapprovingly. "The Sword then shared her findings with Larke as a matter of state security. And whatever she shared with Larke, she also shared with her generals."

Elegy suppresses a flare of anger. She knew Larke had secrets—that Cedre had secrets. But information about her father? Relevant intelligence from the woman who betrayed their mother? She can't believe Larke kept that knowledge from her.

"You say that this man from another world, he left us a message?" Okoro says. "How? Is he still among us?"

"No." Elegy forces herself to focus on the present rather than her anger. "The man—Sevik is his name—left a message in the past. It was something only an epocha could find. He told Theren Forint to come and find him . . . through a doorway in the stars. And he buried the coordinates for that doorway in the past, where we can't currently access them."

"Forint? Why *Forint*?"

Elegy just waits for her to piece it together.

"Oh." Okoro sighs. "He's the man's son, obviously. Interesting. So now—you're on your way to find an epocha of your own to retrieve the coordinates this otherworldly paramour of Kesia Forint left behind."

"Not just any epocha. Fenn Kovek, who is currently imprisoned in a monastery outside of Valla," Elegy says. "It's a dangerous mission, one I recognize I might not come back from. But if I do come back from it . . ."

Okoro laughs. She stops, and then laughs again.

"You'll need the *Sundial*," she supplies. "So that you can make your Pilgrimage dreams come true."

"I don't give a shit about the Pilgrimage or the Restorationists or any of it," Elegy says. "I tried so hard not to walk a path where I'd have to make big decisions like this, but I can't avoid it anymore. This is what I have to do now. And I need your help."

"You may be overestimating my influence in government," Okoro says. "Not even I can persuade Larke and the Quorum to agree to let you take the *Sundial* out for a spin like it's a damn Hummingbird. It's an ancient, extremely valuable piece of equipment, and that's not even factoring in its symbolic value—"

"The *Sundial* is rebuilt and ready to fly. It's staffed with a small crew of volunteers ready and eager to go on a one-way mission—a minimal risk to Cedre's overall well-being," Elegy says. "And I don't think you can persuade Larke. At this point, she's so afraid of me trying to take power from her that she won't listen to a word I say."

"The Sword has authority over the *Sundial*," Okoro points out.

"Unless two of three generals and the Quorum vote to overrule her," Elegy replies.

"Ah. So you propose mutiny."

"She won't listen to me," Elegy says. "I tried to warn her about this attack, and she didn't listen—"

"Because the only evidence you had was *a quote about horses*—"

"She tried to compromise the integrity of a valuable asset with the threat of truth serum—"

"His mother was a traitor!"

"Do you believe I'm the Hope of Cedre?" Elegy says, suddenly, louder than she meant to.

Okoro seems startled by the question.

"I believe . . . that the Fever produces effects we don't currently understand with our limited scientific knowledge," she says. "I believe those effects pertain to the past and to the future. I believe the augurs have reliably communicated their perception of the future to Cedre before, and it's reasonable to assume they're being honest with us now. So yes, I suppose I do believe you are the Hope of Cedre. What does that have to do with anything?"

"Did you really think that a single individual would be able to *triumph over the Talusar* without doing something out of the ordinary? Without making extreme demands? Without ignoring protocol?" Elegy says. "Did you imagine I would singlehandedly defeat our enemies without needing allies or any kind of assistance? Why is it that people are content to know that a huge, terrifying fate has been dumped in my lap by a bunch of people who see the fucking future, but when it comes down to seeing that fate realized, they're suddenly too spooked to do anything to bring it about?"

Elegy leans toward her.

"After this attack on Cedre Station, we'll be weaker than ever before," Elegy says. "Outnumbered and outmatched in every way possible. If this feels like a dramatic move with little chance of success, that's because it is. But if I fail, it won't matter, because Cedre will be dead anyway. Surely you realize that."

And she knows that Okoro does. Maybe that's why she chose to meet with her, of all the generals—not just because she's known for being reasonable and politic. But because she's realistic to the point of seeming cynical.

"Okay," Okoro says.

"Okay?"

"*Okay*, I'll convene the other generals immediately, and tomorrow we'll call for an emergency Quorum meeting," she says. "No guarantees, but I promise you that . . ." She sighs. "I promise you that I will fight as hard as I can to get this done."

Elegy is so relieved she almost bursts into tears. She reaches across the gap that separates them and touches Okoro's arm. She can't feel it, and neither can Okoro, but she can see it, the place where the sheen covering her body intersects with the illuminated projection of Okoro's. Okoro stares at her arm in obvious surprise.

"Thank you," Elegy says.

51

The unconsecrated wing of the Cenobium is empty, though the lanterns are lit and Hela can hear the hum of the water heater in the bathroom. The wing is made up of four bedrooms, a communal bathroom, and a small library packed with old works translated into Talusar. That's where Hela waits for either Forint or Elegy—preferably both—to tell her what the hell is going on.

The augur attendants bring food, at least—on huge wooden trays that overestimate Hela's appetite. They also bring bottles of alcohol that, one of the attendants informed her, is made here in the Cenobium from the lemon trees that grow in its greenhouse.

She's sipping lemon liquor from a small stone cup when the door to the library opens and Forint walks in, looking a little disheveled.

"Thank God, I've been so bored," Hela says. "I was even starting to consider reading a book that isn't a romance novel."

Forint smiles a little in response, which she thinks is probably the best reaction she's going to get from him. He moves toward one of the shelves, and Hela reads the spines. They're religious texts, some from before the Empty Time, when Earth's religions were plentiful and varied, and some from after, when the Talusar united behind one single faith wrapped around the Fever.

"While you guys were in with the augurs, I traded messages with Arias. Everyone will be here in the morning with all our supplies." She's come to like Arias, with his even temper and his willingness to throw protocol out the window. "Where's Elegy?"

"At a meeting with a general."

"Ah."

Forint moves on to another shelf, which Hela notes is full of poetry. Volyn and Alinus are among the most famous, but also Zhao, Boadu, and Fox, all names she recognizes from her childhood, like remembering something from a dream.

She doesn't like to think about her parents. They were well-off, which is how they were able to afford to hire Keen Ahn to get her out of Vidara territory to begin with. Their house was full of books, though as a child Hela had trouble sitting still, and preferred to run through the fields that surrounded their estate, pretending to hunt for large game. Her childhood was full of frustration, having to stay clean when she hated to pay attention to the state of her clothes, having to keep her elbows off the table at breakfast even though it was easier to eat with them on it, having to scrub her face every night even though she was tired and wanted to sleep. But she recognizes, now, that it was also warm and comfortable—and that her parents loved her enough to spare her from the Fever, which for two Talusar seems like the deepest love of all.

She picks up a piece of bread and smears it with some kind of beige paste—it tastes like beans, but she's not sure—and watches as Forint's fingers flutter over the spines of the books until she feels like she's about to explode.

"Oh my God, Forint, you're killing me," she says. "What happened with the augurs?"

He sits down across from her. On the table is an assortment of food: cheese and bread and fruit, a vegetable spread made from something green, steamed dumplings. She's tried it all, and it's all delicious—the problem with the Talusar was never their food.

"The augurs want us to rescue one of their number. Rava is holding her captive in the monastery," he says. "Apparently an augur is necessary for the journey on the *Sundial*."

"Hmm," Hela says, humming around her mouthful of bread. She swallows. "Seems like combining an epocha and an augur accomplishes a lot, doesn't it?"

He nods, and she can tell there's something he's not saying—possibly half a dozen somethings, since Forint seems to have trouble saying much of anything.

"Another impossible errand," she remarks. "Add it to the list, I guess."

Forint picks up one of the dumplings and eats it. It's one of the ones stuffed with fermented cabbage.

"Why did *you* get summoned?" she asks, since she's pretty sure he's not going to volunteer the information on his own.

He looks at her, as if weighing and measuring her, and she wonders if he knows. She sits back, her arms crossed.

"How much has Elegy told you?" he says.

"All of it," Hela replies.

He reaches for the bottle in the middle of the table, and pours a splash of the lemon liquor into a cup.

"A fulcrum of three people, one of whom is a man she'll fall in love with," she adds. "And the man is you. Obviously."

His next breath is unsteady, though his expression stays neutral. He sips from his cup.

"How long have you known?" he says.

"Since she started talking about you too much," Hela says. "I think she knew, too, before she even felt it. Four years of nothing and then suddenly . . . there you were. She couldn't admit it to herself without feeling like she was doing something wrong."

She watches as he drains the cup. He's handsome—she knows that, even though she experiences it as a fact rather than anything of particular interest to her. But there are a lot of handsome men in Elegy's life. Shir was one of them, and he was lively and opinionated and eager to drink from the world and have it fill him up. He was a good match for the Elegy who was, the Elegy who needed to see how good things could be.

But she's not that person anymore. Now she's the Elegy who lost everything, and she needs someone who understands what that means.

"I'm sure it's a lot to take in," Hela says. "Probably not the way you imagined hearing a profession of love, either."

Forint shrugs. "I didn't actually hear one."

"She didn't *say* it?"

He shakes his head.

"You didn't ask?" Hela demands, incredulous.

Forint props his elbows on the table and looks at her. She feels something creeping down her spine. She's pretty sure he's reading her, the way he reads everyone, and she has no idea what he sees. Feels. However it works.

"No," he says, finally. "Regardless of how she feels, I think she might only ever say those words to Shir Alexios."

"And that doesn't bother you?"

"Why should it? I know what's between us. Isn't that enough?"

She picks up her cup and drinks from it, contemplating him.

She's been thinking about the conversation she had with Elegy about Forint—the one where Elegy burst into tears—often. She thinks of things she didn't say, but should have. Namely, that the human heart isn't a drinking glass, with only so much room for love at any given time. That it's more like the void of space, infinitely expanding and endlessly strange.

Forint may be a little too perceptive and so reserved it's hard to talk to him. But he seems to understand how hearts work.

"I think I like you," she says to him, and she touches her cup to his.

52

Later that night, after Elegy returned and ate; after Hela made half a dozen sly jokes about their augur revelations; after they drank the rest of the liquor in the jug on the study table, they all go into the communal bathroom to get ready for sleep.

It's intimate to brush your teeth in front of someone for the first time. Theren watches Elegy rise up onto her toes to poke at a spot on her face, and braid her hair over one shoulder, and their eyes meet in her mirror.

Hela disappears into one of the rooms, and before Theren can go into the third, Elegy catches his hand.

"If you want to join me, you're welcome to," she says. "Just—for sleep, I mean."

Their fingers twist together and he lets her pull him toward her room, where the blankets are still creased from before. More intimacies: the choreography of pouring water for each bedside table, the negotiation of who gets what side of the bed, and the shy unlacing of boots.

He hesitates before climbing in next to her, and Elegy, already buried in blankets and pillows, sits up to look at him.

"What is it?" she says.

As with so many things in his past, it's difficult to give words to. He and Fenn were together for only a short time, and the Crucible was no place for bed-sharing, only for quick fumbles in the dark. And with Rava, there was only ever vigilant half sleep, and shame that locked up his insides every morning.

"I've just . . . never done this before." At her confused look, he adds: "Not when I wanted to."

It's a heavier admission than he was expecting it to be.

She reaches for him, twisting her fingers around his. She doesn't say anything—maybe there's nothing to say. But many people in his life, even the ones who were kind to him, have been uncomfortable around his pain. All he feels in her is a sympathetic ache.

They sleep curled away from each other, their backs touching.

In the morning, he sits on the edge of the bed a little too long, his body rigid with tension, trying to come back to himself. And without needing to be asked, she just holds out a shirt for him to slide his arms into, and waits for him to surface.

✦ ✦ ✦

The others arrive just after breakfast the next morning, when the sun is still coming up. The Sparrow winks in the sun as it lands, kicking up a cloud of salt. Elegy, Theren, and Hela board as soon as the hatch opens. Now that Cedre Station is vulnerable, there's no time to waste.

Once aboard the Sparrow, Theren moves to the back of the ship to greet Isre with a tousle of his hair. Isre is behind the nav panel, guiding them from landing to takeoff; he slaps Theren's hand away from his head.

"Glad you're all right," Isre says.

"And you," Theren says.

They all brace for takeoff, though Isre's flying is smoother than Parekh's, and once they're at a comfortable drift—low to the ground and slow, as Theren instructed, to better avoid attracting Valla's attention—he opens the bag Arias packed for him to change his clothes.

Elegy is already in a state of undress, uncaring as she strips off her pants to replace them with darker, sturdier ones. He guides his eyes away from her bare legs, and sorts through the shirts Arias packed for him to find the right one. The goal is to look passably Talusar from a distance, which means plain fabric, not skintight, easy to move in.

The others are busy distributing sheaths and holsters and all the other gear they'll likely need for their journey through the forest—and for infiltrating the monastery.

"Arias, did you bring that package I asked you about?" Elegy says, and Arias points just above Elegy's head, at a black box roughly the size of a toolbox strapped down to one of the shelves. She reaches for it and, finding it a little too high for her, nudges Theren with her elbow to help her.

He undoes the straps and takes the box down. It's much lighter than he expected it to be.

"Open it," Elegy says, with a quirk of her mouth.

He sets it down on one of the jump seats, and unlatches it. Nestled in a bed of foam inside are two vambraces made of polished febra—simple sheaths with faint, delicate etching. On the left is the symbol of the Fever, which is the symbol of the Talusar—three interlinked circles—with part of a quote beneath it.

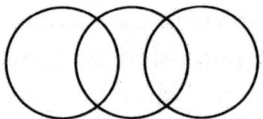

Do not ask how many times he falls

On the right is the symbol of Cedre: the planet below, the station above, and a line connecting them. And beneath it, the end of the quote.

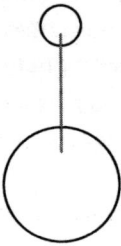

But how many times he rises.

He runs his fingers over the words.

"Volyn," he says, a little weakly.

"Your favorite, I hear," Elegy says. "The quote made me think of you."

"You had these made?"

Her expression is guarded, almost defensive. As if it reveals too much about her that she would do something so thoughtful.

"From that armor you wore during the Naarm attack. It was too small for you, so I thought you could use these instead. You said you trained with vambraces." She clears her throat, her green eyes skipping away from his. "Let's make sure they fit."

He rolls up his sleeve, and offers his left forearm to her. She loosens the straps on the underside of the vambrace, slides it over his arm, and tightens it. It's the right length for his forearm; he wonders how she guessed it so well. He holds out his right arm for the other one, and he feels the febra hum all the way down his fingers.

"Seems right," Elegy says.

He reaches for her, laying his hands on her cheeks, lightly, and drawing his forehead down to touch hers. He notices the others have gone quiet around them, but it's too late to take it back. Her fingers slide around his wrists, but she doesn't push him away, holding his gaze instead.

"Don't thank me," she says, in Talusar.

Their noses brush together.

"Yes, Your Grace," he says.

He doesn't kiss her, just pulls back, his cheeks warm.

It's as good as a profession of love.

✦ ✦ ✦

"We've caught their attention," Isre announces, an hour later. "Ship incoming, but we're not in view of them yet."

He sounds strained, like he's trying to disguise his panic. Theren can feel it in the sudden uptick of his own heartbeat, like Isre's body has temporarily taken control of his own.

Elegy unbuckles herself, and staggers across the ship to stand behind the captain's seat.

"It's all right," she says. "We're going to do exactly what we practiced."

"The whoopsie daisy," Arias says, with a grin.

Elegy makes a face. "Isre. Go low, hover for two minutes as we disembark, and then fly as high as you can, as fast as you can. Okay?"

Isre nods.

Above the nav panel, Theren can see rippling green land resolving into sharp white peaks. The monastery is in the valley just beneath them, and they'll approach from the north, moving through forest cover around the base of the mountain.

"Everybody get ready. We need to descend fast," Elegy says. "Gloves on. Arias first; I'm last."

Theren takes his gloves out of his pocket and pulls them on. They're too small for his hands, but they'll protect his palms from the rope. Across from him, Arias unbuckles and crouches next to the hatch door with the coiled rope in his hands.

"Why do you call it that, anyway?" Hela asks Arias. "'Whoopsie daisy,' I mean."

"Because it scares the shit out of me," Arias says. "And I find it a lot less intimidating when it's called a 'whoopsie daisy.'"

They drop so low Theren's ears pop, and all he can see out of the windshield is green. Hela moves to stand behind the hatch door, and when Elegy shouts, "Now!" Parekh slams her fist into the emergency eject button. The hatch door opens, and Arias throws the rope out. Almost in the same movement, he grabs it in both hands, swings his body over the edge, and disappears.

Hela goes next, her face so pale her lips are colorless, followed by Parekh, who lets out a "whoop!" as she goes down. It's Theren's turn.

He sits on the edge of the open hatch, and before he can think about it, lets himself fall. He catches the rope between his feet and drops—he barely registers the weightless feeling before his boots are on the dirt.

He steps away to watch Elegy descend. She slides down fast, her face placid as she lands. She tugs sharply on the rope, twice, and it retracts into the ship just as Isre pulls away from the ground. Together, they watch the Sparrow climb, fast, and disappear.

"Tree cover," Elegy says.

She leads the way into the dense forest, where the Talusar won't be able to see them from above. Theren ducks under a branch, and draws a deep breath of cedar and wet earth and pollen. He lays a hand on the trunk of a tree. They all crouch, and wait, and though he's supposed to be listening for Talusar patrol ships, instead he listens to the sounds of the birds and the wind through the trees.

The Talusar patrol ship emits a low hum even from far off. He tenses as it grows louder and louder, and then it's on top of them, the engines creating wind even at a distance. He resists the urge to look up. Then the humming gets quieter, and quieter, until it disappears.

"Will they double back?" Elegy asks him.

"Not likely. They would land right here, right now, if they saw something."

"Good. Then let's get moving."

They move in pairs, Arias and Hela at the front, since they're both good navigators, Parekh in the middle, and Elegy and Theren at the back. There are no paths in this forest, so their pace is slow, with Hela cutting through undergrowth when it's too dense and Theren always turning, looking, listening.

They don't talk except to point out hazards—a stream, a ridge, a stretch of mud. But when they stop for water, Parekh looks up at the tree canopy and sighs.

"They've taken so much of this planet from us," she says.

For a long time, no one responds.

"So let's take some of it back," Elegy says, and she passes Parekh her canteen.

"A rousing speech from the Hope of Cedre," Parekh replies, laughing. "You really think we can do that?"

Elegy looks pensive. Above them, a squirrel leaps from branch to branch.

"I'm starting to," she says.

53

An hour later, they wait at the edge of the tree line, the outpost of Dexa below them.

The monastery is visible from here, high on an overlook, an elegant sprawl of wood with a small pond behind it. The others were impressed by its size and its detail, but for Theren, it will always be the place where he died.

"Are you ready?" Elegy says to him.

Theren's job is to go into Dexa alone, find Orda, and secure his help. He'll return to the others after nightfall and escort them into the settlement in the dark.

He checks his things: the pack on his back, the sword at his side, the vambraces protecting his forearms. He looks like a Talusar on a journey into neutral territory, unsure of what he'll find there.

He glances back only once when he moves out of the tree line and into the open field beyond it. Elegy waves him on.

Dexa is too small to be called a town, so the Talusar refer to it as an outpost, but there are still people other than soldiers living here. He passes a woman unloading apples into a market stall, and a blacksmith hammering a sword into shape, and it feels like stepping back in time again. A child leads a horse to water on a side street; a shop sign advertises high-quality salvage, with a display of metal filing cabinets out front.

He turns to the woman at the market stall.

"Excuse me," he says, and as in all Talusar interactions, he has to decide who he thinks he is, and what status. He decides it's safe to address her as somewhat inferior to him, as if he's an army officer. "Do you know where I can find Selio Orda?"

"Soldier?" the woman says, and at Theren's nod, she waves her hand at the buildings closer to the monastery. "Don't know that name, but they mostly live over that way."

"Thank you."

He keeps walking, ignoring the voices that implore him to buy. He's never handled Talusar coin. Crucible fighters weren't paid, and he certainly never received money in House Vidar. He tucks his left hand into his pocket to disguise the symbol tattooed there.

He moves closer to the buildings the woman pointed out, and then circles them, trying to find the route that the soldiers will take when they walk home from the monastery after their shifts are done. He has to ask a child to confirm it, and she does, pointing out the deep footprints the soldiers leave there with their heavy boots.

Theren waits in an alley, watching passersby. He hasn't had much opportunity to observe the Talusar in their everyday lives, and it's a good reminder that they aren't all Rava Vidar. He sees a group of children chasing a ball, a pair of older women exchanging onions for potatoes from their shopping bags, an old man stopping to roll a cigarette against his own leg. When the first cluster of soldiers ambles down the road, laughing at some shared joke, he straightens. If it's time for a shift change, he'll either see Orda walking toward the monastery or away from it.

For a soldier to be assigned to the monastery, they have to either be well-connected, wealthy, or have earned their position through loyalty and service. So many of the soldiers that pass him, moving in both directions, have soft hands and unburdened smiles. Their uniforms are tidy and they don't wear febra armor. There's no point; no one ever attacks the monastery. So though they're required to be proficient in the sword, they've undoubtedly gotten lax and comfortable. They aren't ready for action.

He spots Orda when it's just starting to get dark, and the chill is settling over his shoulders like a cloak. Theren knows him by his stride, loping like a wolf, from an old injury in the Crucible that makes him favor his left side. His smile, bright against the gathering dusk, is a little wolfish, too. Not mischievous, exactly, but a little wicked. He's walking with three other soldiers, one of whom peels away with a friendly wave before she passes Theren's alley.

Theren pulls away from the wall as Orda passes, and then he falls into step a few paces behind him. He can't exactly call out to him with the other two soldiers still flanking him, so he follows all three to one of the buildings the shopkeeper pointed out, and waits at a distance, leaning against a wall with affected casualness.

He slips into the building and listens as they all unlock and open their doors, keys jingling, conversation still continuing though they're separated by one story—the two soldiers seem to live together on the second floor, but Orda is on the third.

Theren creeps up the stairs, his footsteps as silent as he can make them. When he gets to the second-floor landing, he sees Orda pause with his key in the lock. He turns, and looks at Theren.

His expression doesn't change, but Theren can feel how his heart leaps, and he grins.

"Well," Orda says neutrally. "You'd better come in, I suppose."

Theren climbs the stairs that separate them, and follows Orda into his apartment.

The place looks just like he expected it to. The apartment is a single room, small but pleasant. Orda's guitar hangs on the right wall, and his shoes—salvaged sneakers, red with fraying laces—are next to the door. In the center of the kitchen is a woven rug made of grass. The dishes are drying next to the sink, heavy earthenware on a threadbare towel. It's not a proper kitchen—just a burner and a sink the size of a bucket, a table big enough for two people to eat.

Theren turns back to Orda, who's shut the door and is now leaning back against it, trapping his hands behind him.

It's been two years since they saw each other last. Theren won the Tournament and stood before Rava Vidar as the untriumphant victor. It was his right to ask for a reward for his victory, and most fighters asked for their own freedom. But Theren asked for Selio Orda's, instead. The last thing he remembers of that moment is Orda staring at him from the first row of seats in the amphitheater, his eyes blank, too far away for Theren to read him.

Orda is unchanged. Shorter than Theren, but still tall and lanky, his straight hair now long enough to sweep away from his forehead, and grayer than it used to be. His nose is crooked from breaking more than once in the Crucible, and there's a scar through his lip, but the combination works for him.

"Teacher," Theren says, in greeting.

"Aren't we past that nickname now?"

"I thought it might amuse you."

Orda smiles, and pulls away from the door to wrap his arms around Theren. Theren returns the embrace, and for a long moment they hold on to each other with obvious relief radiating between them like two tuning forks resonating at the same frequency.

"You look better. Cedre must be treating you well," Orda says. As he pulls away, Orda's hand comes up to the back of Theren's neck, light and brief. "I see you have someone in your life."

"I asked you not to do that." Theren doesn't know which of his memories Orda saw, but he knows Orda's usual time frame—he reaches back only a few days, so he can only have seen Elegy.

"And if I asked you not to read me in return, that would be easy for you?" Orda's smile fades a little. "I assume you're not here for a social visit."

"Fenn is alive."

Orda trained Fenn just as he trained Theren—to survive the Crucible. But they were always at odds, and Orda was never charmed by Fenn's combativeness the way Theren ultimately was.

Sighing, Orda turns away from Theren to unbuckle his sword from his waist, to untie his shoes and line them up next to his sneakers. He goes into the kitchen to pour himself a drink, a glass of something cloudy from an unmarked bottle. Brandy, Theren assumes, because that's what people drink outside of Valla. He pours some for Theren, too, and they sit across from each other at the kitchen table.

The sun is setting. A grid of bars protects the space from intruders, and through them, Theren can see soldiers walking to the monastery in a pack, the new shift on its way. Theren touches his glass to Orda's before sipping. The brandy burns his lips, but it's sweet—made from apples, maybe, or pears.

"I knew that Fenn was alive, of course," Orda says. "Since he's in the monastery. But there was no way to tell you, and—"

"I don't blame you," Theren says. "But surely you understand that I can't just leave him here when I'm the reason he's a captive to begin with."

Orda presses his mouth into a line.

"You saved his life. If you hadn't told them he was an epocha, they would have executed him. And you would have had to carry it out."

"He preferred death to captivity. I knew that, and I still chose for him."

"You gave him a life as a holy man instead of death. It wasn't just the best choice; it was the only choice."

"Don't try to tell me that you think life as a 'holy man' is some kind of universal reward."

Orda shakes his head. His sister was an epocha. She was infected a few years after him, and sent to the monastery. But the Fever tormented her with visions of the beginning of the world, and the horror of it was too much for her. She took her life a few years after.

A few years her family would have liked to spend with her, Orda said, when he told Theren the story.

"You came here for my help," Orda says.

"I just need to know where in the building he is."

"For a truthsayer you're a miserable liar," Orda says. "You need far more than that from me, if you want to get him out of that monastery."

Orda was a hard man when they met. He'd been assigned the three coltish Cedrae, the most useless fighters in the Crucible, in retaliation for some past slight, and he made sure they knew it. But he'd still taught them, made it possible for them to survive their first few months. His kindness didn't come in the form of gentle words but in *doing*.

"I'm sorry to ask this of you," Theren says.

"*Theren*," Orda says, and he reaches across the table to touch Theren's arm. Theren stares at the black bars tattooed between each of Orda's knuckles, markers of time spent in the Crucible. Too much time.

"If you need my help, you'll get it," Orda says, as if it's a simple fact. He releases Theren and sits back in his chair. "I assume you didn't come alone. You wouldn't be that foolish."

Theren drinks the rest of his moonshine, and doesn't answer.

"That woman I saw in your memory," Orda says. "You referred to her in a particular way. As if she's much higher status than you are. Can I ask how high?"

"Why does that matter?"

"Because. If she's important enough to get me into Losan . . . maybe even get me citizenship papers . . ." He sits back in his chair. "Then you don't need to feel so bad about asking for my help."

Theren runs his finger along the edge of the glass, and tries not to give away too much in his expression.

"As it happens, that woman you saw is certainly important enough to get you into Cedre."

54

Though she knows she's in Talusar territory, Elegy still finds herself waiting for street lights to turn on in Dexa, for the whole place to awaken after nightfall. Instead, of course, everything stays dark, except the inconstant glow of firelight behind closed curtains.

Theren leads them on a winding path through the streets without incident. At one point he ushers them all into an alley and waits as a group of soldiers passes, but he timed their journey so they wouldn't encounter any shift changes going to or from the monastery. When they reach a narrow wooden building near the edge of the outpost, he pushes through the door and leads them up two flights of creaking steps to the third-floor apartment.

There, Elegy encounters a man she's seen only in Theren's memories. Tall and striking, his skin bathed in the warm light of a lantern, Orda looks just as he did when he was teaching Theren how to mercifully kill Maeve. Handsome in a worn way. His eyes sleepy and his mouth clever.

Parekh stays in the hall to keep watch, but Arias moves toward the guitar hanging on Orda's wall automatically, and Hela examines the low bookshelf near the foot of his bed.

Orda asks Theren, "Do any of them speak Talusar?"

"I do," Elegy says.

Orda's eyes glint as they settle on her. "Of course you do. I'm Selio Orda." He comes to his feet, and offers her his hand.

"Elegy Ahn," she says, shaking it.

His hand goes slack in hers, and slips free. But he recovers well, bowing his head, and gesturing to the chair across from his.

"Please. You should sit," he says, and his address is formal now, respectful.

There are no other chairs, so Theren leans against the kitchen counter instead. Elegy thinks this must be strange for him—two people from his past and his present, sitting across a table from each other.

"I'm surprised to see you here, Your Grace," Orda says to Elegy. "Surprised you are permitted to put yourself at risk in this way."

"I'm not so easily restricted. Theren tells me you're willing to help us in return for a place in Cedre."

"That's right."

"That won't be a problem."

"I'm pleased to hear that." Orda looks up at Theren. "There's paper and pen in my bedside table."

Theren pulls away from the counter to fetch them. Hela and Arias are standing off to the side, with Hela translating for Arias in a low murmur.

Theren sets pen and paper in front of Orda. There's still ease between them, she notices. No please or thank you. No formality.

"Our mission is twofold," Elegy says. "We came to retrieve Fenn Kovek, but the augurs told us to rescue one of their own who is apparently being held in the same building."

"An augur, in the monastery?" Orda frowns. "That explains the presence of Rava's guards in the north wing. We've been barred from the area for the last day or so. I thought it meant she was there herself, but . . ."

"Rava's guards." Elegy sighs. "Great."

"You'll need to split up, of course." Orda bends over the paper and starts to sketch, in neat, straight lines, the outline of the monastery. She recognizes the shape of it from the surveillance images they analyzed before their departure: like a neuron, with a circular room at one end buried in a tangle of short corridors serving as the cell body and dendrites; a smaller tangle of rooms at the other end standing in as the axon terminals; and a long hallway connecting the two ends, like the axon itself. "One group can't possibly attack one end and make it all the way down that hallway to the other without encountering Talusar guards at some point along the way."

"We need speed and surprise on our side, since we don't have might." She pauses, and asks Theren, "What do you suggest?"

Theren watches Orda marking the augur's probable location on the larger half of the neuron, the north side of the building. Fenn's location, meanwhile, is on the left half of the neuron, the south side of the building.

"Arias and Parekh will go to Fenn," Theren says. "They'll encounter less resistance that way. But if they can create a disturbance on their way in, that would draw some of the soldiers guarding the augur away, which would help Hela, Elegy, and me." He pauses a moment, then looks at Orda. "Feels like you don't like it."

"It's not that." This, too, is casual—that he's not fazed by Theren reading him even for a moment. "I'm just surprised you would send someone else to retrieve Fenn, that's all."

Elegy feels the slightest flutter of worry. She doesn't know how long

Theren's relationship with Fenn lasted—or even if they called it a relationship. She was so afraid of loving him that she never stopped to wonder if he loved someone else.

Theren just shrugs. "I trust them."

"Well, if you trust *me* to lead your friends to Fenn, I can join them to even out the groups."

"That's more than we agreed to."

"Don't be an idiot," Orda says, taking his time with each word.

He reaches out, as if for a handshake. Theren clasps his hand around the thumb, and brings it to his sternum.

"If we're agreed, I'll brief the others in English."

"Please do," Orda says. "I'll take the Hope of Cedre to the roof and show her our entry points."

Roof access, as it turns out, is as easy as Orda poking a door in his ceiling with the handle of a broom, and bringing over a ladder from the hall closet. He climbs up first, and Elegy follows, only a little alarmed by how the ladder creaks with each step.

The roof is almost flat, pitched toward the front so rain rolls into the gutters. The view of the monastery is clearer than she expected—it looms over them on the hill, lit in the same halting, dim way as the rest of Dexa.

Orda points at one of the distant flames.

"That's your entry point." He shifts his hand over to the left. "And the others."

"The odds of them seeing us coming?"

"Your group will have to find your own way, but I think I can pick a path that disguises us, for the most part. We'll need to move fast and hit hard at the guards by the door."

She nods. Silence falls between them, and she thinks there's no reason for them to be out here, discussing entry points—not really. So he must have suggested this to get her alone for some other reason.

"Something else you'd like to say?" she says.

He looks at her out of the corner of his eye. "Only that there's nothing for you to worry about."

"I beg your pardon?"

"I may not be able to read you like he can, but I saw the look on your face when I mentioned Fenn," Orda says. "He's made his feelings for you quite clear, hasn't he?"

She feels like she's missing something. "Has he?"

"In the way he addresses you," Orda says, as if it's obvious.

"My Talusar is good, but I don't understand all the nuances," she admits. "Status indicators in particular."

"Ah." Orda smiles a little. "Well, you should ask him sometime."

She hears voices in the street outside, and footsteps. Orda ducks down, and Elegy imitates him.

"Changing of the guard," Orda says. He turns back to the ladder. "Time to go."

✦　✦　✦

The path to the monastery leads them down the main thoroughfare of Dexa—uneven packed earth, riddled with rocks the size of her fist—which narrows into a worn path at the foot of the hill. The path splits in two, one leading up to the south wing of the monastery, and the other leading along the foot of the hill until it climbs to the north wing.

At the split, Elegy reaches for Parekh's hand and squeezes it. Orda is already walking, his sword tapping his thigh as he moves, but the others turn toward her, and she considers that all these people have supported her at different points in her life, and she's given them so little in return.

"Thank you," she says to them. Hela rolls her eyes, and Arias blows her a kiss, and Parekh squeezes her hand again.

"Shut up," Parekh says warmly, and a moment later, she and Arias are gone, following Orda up the southern path.

Elegy turns to Theren. "Lead the way."

She thinks he has better night vision than she does, though they hardly need it on a night this clear. She *knows* he has better footing on this type of ground. She watches his feet, and tries to copy his movements as much as possible, moving in his shadow. With Hela at her back, she walks the winding path through calf-high grass, steering around dry bushes and boulders. She hears an owl hooting somewhere in the distance.

She's not used to climbing, and by the time they make it to the top of the hill, she's winded. So is Hela, though she does a better job of hiding it. Theren leads them to a cluster of trees near the outer wall of the monastery, and together they crouch down there to wait for the others to do their work in the south wing. Theren and Elegy are in one cluster of greenery, and Hela is a few feet away, in another.

The moon—or Cedre Station, it's hard to say which—brightens his face. He's focused on the monastery, likely tracking the movements of the guards. She can't see far enough to even attempt that, so she watches him, instead. His furrowed brow, drawn low over his eyes. His hands twitching at his sides.

Ready. *Present.*

"What is it?" he says to her, in a quiet voice.

"Nothing," she says, just as softly. "Orda said I should ask you what the pronouns you use for me mean. I didn't learn many, since I prefer the ones for equals. But . . . now's not the time."

She feels Hela's eyes on her, and ignores them as she searches for the outer door, the one they'll need to pass through. It will be flanked by two guards. They need to disable both without making too much noise. She touches the spear strapped to her back, though she can already feel it against her spine.

"I'm still not speaking to you as an equal, if that's what you're wondering," Theren says.

She rolls her eyes.

"It's not *accurate*," he says, defensive.

"You've seen me naked, you think I want you to call me 'Your Grace'?" She says it quietly enough that Hela won't hear her—she hopes not, anyway.

Theren surprises her by grinning. "You don't?"

She jabs him in the ribs with her fingers.

"I don't speak to you like a *subject*, either," he says. "The term I use is intimate. The connotation isn't subservience, it's . . . devotion."

For a moment, he looks almost . . . bashful.

"Oh," she says. Orda's sly smile on the rooftop makes more sense now.

Then Theren frowns, shifting forward onto his toes as he tips his head toward the monastery. He touches a finger to his lips, and closes his eyes as he listens. A moment later she hears it: a bell.

"That's the alarm." He nods to Hela. "Let's go."

They break away from the tree line and sprint toward the door. Theren reaches it yards ahead of them, the butt of his sword colliding with the side of one guard's head. The man stumbles back, and the second guard draws his weapon on Theren.

Elegy doesn't slow down. She throws her body at the man as hard as she can, sending him face-first into the monastery wall. Before he can recover his senses, Hela lunges and hits him hard in the jaw. His head snaps back, and he, too, goes limp.

Theren adjusts his grip on his sword, and opens the door. Before they left, they all memorized the map Orda drew for them. They have to go to the end of this hallway, up a flight of stairs, and then travel east until they reach a blue door on the right.

The interior looks different than she expected. She thinks of the Talusar as spare and practical, because that's how the people of Valla are, living at the edge of Vidara territory. But she forgot that most of the Talusar occupy the best spaces that remain of pre-Fever civilization, repurposing all its beauty for their own.

The monastery is no exception. Every surface is intricately carved, here in a leafy, florid pattern. The fixtures on the walls—lit with flames, like lanterns—are made of bright copper. There's a plush runner down the center of the hallway, muffling their footsteps.

Theren moves fast, sword in hand, and she's still impressed by how silent his footsteps are for a man of his size—for a man of any size, really. He reaches the foot of the stairwell and collides with a guard. She can hardly see; his sword catches the light, and there's the sound of metal against metal, a grunt of effort. She steps aside as Theren stumbles back into the hallway, parrying with a woman in febra armor. Elegy slams her spear into the soldier's legs, and the woman goes down with a grunt. Hela is ready with the butt of her sword; neither of them wants to kill when they don't have to, though the blow Hela delivers to the woman's head may be hard enough to cause damage she doesn't intend.

Together they climb the stairs to the second floor. Hela runs her fingers along the wood paneling, over the triple circles beneath each light fixture. There are no guards ahead.

Elegy frowns at Hela. That's strange.

They creep toward the next hallway, and turn the corner, weapons ready. But there are no guards there, either.

Theren holds up a hand to stop them. He looks over his shoulder at Elegy.

"Something's wrong," Elegy says, and Theren nods.

"I don't hear anyone. Feel anyone," he says. "I think . . . Hela should go find the others."

"I'm not leaving her," Hela argues, her hand coming up automatically to grip Elegy's elbow.

"One of us has to go," he says gently. "And I'm her Knight."

The flame in a nearby lamp lights Hela's cheek unsteadily. Elegy and Hela have been going on missions together for four years now, though none of them were as important as this one, and Elegy knows it's not easy for Hela to yield her place at Elegy's side. But there's nothing to be done about it. Elegy can't go alone, and Theren is the best person to stay with her.

"Take weapons and armor from some of the guards we already knocked out so you can pass as Talusar," Elegy says. "But go. Now."

She braces for Hela to argue with her again, but all she does is squeeze Elegy's shoulder and nod.

"Be careful," she says, and then she turns and runs back the way they came.

Elegy doesn't like to watch her go, but at least if Hela, Talusar-born, is caught . . . they'll probably send her to the Crucible rather than kill her.

She can't think about that now. They still have to find out if the augur is here. Elegy nods to Theren, and they continue down the hallway toward the blue door. It's been painted so many times the blue is shiny as plastic, peeling in places to reveal a lighter shade beneath.

Dread gnaws in her stomach, but there's nothing to be gained from standing still. Elegy reaches for the knob, and opens the door.

Behind it is a woman with her hair in a high knot. Elegy recognizes her: One of Rava's lessers. Nyx.

55

Nyx is the one who taught Theren the finer points of the sword.

He'd been trained before that—by his mother, and then by Orda, and then by the Crucible itself. But even after all that, the sword was still a blunt instrument in his hand, no more than a hammer or an axe. Effective enough to beat roughened Crucible fighters in the Tournament, but not any kind of art form.

It was Nyx's idea to train him, nonsensical to him at first—they were keeping him captive, so why would they bother making him a good fighter? But he had been so deeply mired in misery since Maeve's death that he wandered the halls of House Vidar like the walking dead, doing only what was required, and Nyx had suggested that he needed *purpose*. Rava, who was determined to learn to beat opponents both larger and stronger than she was, agreed, telling her to "make him worth my time," which he now realized meant "make him worth falling in love with," per the requirements of her fate. As much as Rava *could* fall in love, anyway.

In contrast to Satka, who seemed to delight in hurting him as much as possible, Nyx was forbearing, though she didn't tolerate laziness or complaining. She taught him to be lighter on his feet and to hold his weapons gently and to be patient in pursuit of victory.

So when he opens the door and sees her standing in the room where he was supposed to find an augur, he doesn't think of beating her—only of surviving. He raises his weapon as she raises hers; their swords collide and they both turn, in the same moment, to lay their blades against each other's throats, their arms crossed.

Both left-handed.

He stares at her, and she stares back at him.

The room is fit for an augur, even an augur being held prisoner. The windows are wide and framed by heavy blue curtains. A canopy bed with a carved wooden frame stands between them. The mantel of the fireplace—unlit now, because of the season—is all tiles the size of his fingernails, a mosaic in the shape of a sunburst. Its yellow rays frame Nyx's shoulders.

"Where's the augur?" he demands.

"We haven't had the augur for months, you fool," Nyx snaps. "She was returned to the Cenobium right after she met with you and the epocha."

Nyx's feelings are always strong, as rigid as bone. Not complicated, the way some people's are, or difficult to interpret. She's being sincere. As far as she knows, the augur was returned to the Cenobium.

Theren feels the beginnings of a suspicion too dark to name.

"I was just at the Cenobium," Theren says. "The augurs are the ones who sent us here. She's still missing."

Nyx's blade pulls away from his throat just slightly. She glances over his shoulder at Elegy.

"I don't believe you," she says.

"Why the hell else would we be here?" Elegy says, her spear held defensively across her chest. He has no doubt that if he pulled away from Nyx, Elegy would strike, but for now she seems to be honoring their stalemate.

He knows a lot about Nyx. That she won't kill him unless she has to, for one thing—she doesn't relish cruelty the way some of Rava's officers do. That she's perhaps the one person in Rava's employ who sincerely worships the Fever and honors the augurs. Finding out that Rava did something to one of them . . . it would devastate her.

"The commander leaked intelligence to Cedre that the augur was here," Nyx says. "You fell for it."

"Cedre is a bit distracted at the moment by Talusar biological warfare," Elegy snaps. "They have no time to send the sister of the Sword on a mission to Talusar territory because of a rumor."

He feels Nyx's confidence wavering.

"You're thinking Rava wouldn't do anything to harm an augur, if not out of her own reverence for them, then out of respect for her family's—or yours," Theren says. "But we both know what kind of woman she is. We both know that's *exactly* something she would do."

He pushed too hard. Nyx grits her teeth and moves the sword right up against his throat again, so he can feel the sharpness of the blade.

"What I *know* is that the family Vidar is both devout and reverent. Don't play with my mind, truthsayer," she says. "We have you pinned down on all sides and you're just trying to get out of it."

He glances at Elegy.

"What do you mean, 'all sides'?" she asks.

"I was told to lie in wait for Cedre soldiers," Nyx says. "But Rava is across the monastery with your friend Fenn. She thought you would go directly to him." A fleeting smile passes over Nyx's mouth. "Guess she overestimated your affection for him."

By now, after Lisia, and Furik, and Maeve; after he thought Fenn died the first time; after finding out about Kesia's betrayal—after all that, he thinks he should be used to this feeling, this yawning hole inside him that opens up when he loses people. But it's new every time, somehow. Big and heavy and yet also empty, an impossible feeling.

Rava is here. Rava has Fenn.

"I can knock her out," Elegy offers.

Theren shakes his head, not trusting himself to speak. If they knock Nyx out, they still don't know where Fenn and Rava are—or the others, who have no doubt run into her by now, and may all be dead. They'll waste time wandering the monastery and they may never come out of it.

He has to *think*. Think about what he knows about Nyx, about Rava, about all of this.

"No," Theren says.

Nyx's eyes dart back and forth between him and Elegy, wary.

Before Theren arrived in House Vidar, each of Rava's lessers served as interrogators, depending on what information Rava needed—and depending on how far back in a person's memory that information was. Satka could see hours back. Ranos could see days. And Nyx could see months.

"I'll make you an offer," Theren says.

"Absolutely not," Elegy says, in English, her voice sharper than he's ever heard it.

"If you let Elegy go—"

"I said *no*—"

"Then I'll come quietly to wherever Rava and Fenn are, and we can both find out the truth about what happened to the augur."

Elegy raises her voice: "You are not going back to her. Not after everything—!"

She cuts herself off. He doesn't need her to finish the sentence, he can already do it for her: after everything they've been through. After everything she's done for him. After all of it.

She touches his arm. Her green eyes are bright. He feels the weight of the vambraces around his wrists, suddenly, each of them a reminder of her concern for him.

"*Trust me*," he says to her. "Please, Elegy."

Elegy's hand tightens for a moment, and then releases him.

"How do you intend to verify 'the truth' of what happened to the augur?" Nyx asks, her jaw tight.

"If I'm remembering right, you don't need to touch her to see her memories, right?" he says. "So I'll prompt the memory so it's easier to read. And you'll read it."

Memory reading isn't exactly like mind reading, as far as he understands it—a memory can be retrieved even if the person isn't thinking of it. But just as Fenn reading Theren's past prompted the right vision from the augur, the right information can bring a particular memory forward, whether the subject likes it or not.

"And if the truth is exactly what I expect?"

"That will be very bad news for me," he says.

He lifts his sword, and holds it by the blade to offer it to her by the handle. She grabs it, and looks expectantly at Elegy.

"And her?" Nyx asks.

"She'll go," Theren says, "and Rava will never know she was here."

Elegy, pale and frowning, slides her spear into its holster on her back.

"I hope you know what you're doing," she says to him, in English.

So does he.

56

As a general rule, Hela doesn't mind robbing the dead. They're gone, after all, and it's a hard world—no sense in making it even harder for yourself because you can't let a dead person be dead. It's one of the reasons people don't like Scouts, but she's never much cared about that.

But there's something downright spooky about robbing a body in a Talusar monastery. Maybe it's the light, and the way it flutters as the air moves; maybe it's the way everything echoes and whistles in this place; maybe it's the knowledge that somewhere underground are a bunch of Talusar with tattooed throats who could give her the Fever by breathing on her. Whatever the reason, as she strips the jacket from one of the guards Theren killed on the way in, she has the chills.

She puts the jacket on, picks up a fallen longsword, and moves as fast as she can toward the central hallway. The axon, Elegy called it, when she was describing the layout of the place.

But the little sketch Orda gave them didn't capture how beautiful the monastery was. The hallway is full of stained-glass windows. The first one she sees is a huge rendering of the planet Earth. Sometimes she forgets how big their planet is, and how small Losan is, just a speck on the green glass. Her steps falter for a moment as she gazes up at the intricate glass panes. Then she pulls herself together and keeps walking.

She spots two guards stationed at the very end of the hallway, on either side of the double doors that open up to the other section of the building, the one that Arias, Parekh, and Orda are in. She swallows hard, and makes a decision.

An ironclad Scout rule: when you get into a bind, lie your ass off.

She runs, passing more stained-glass windows: a detailed rendering of the Cenobium, perched alone on the salt flat; the great palace of the emperor standing on its hill across the border from Nusanta; the mysterious shrouded febra mine of Euroa, with amber glass glinting here and there. By the time she reaches the end of the hallway, she's out of breath, which gives her a second to assess the guards on either side of the door. One of them is big, with a longsword as heavy as hers; the other is smaller and slim, with a rapier at her hip.

Hela points over her shoulder with her thumb.

"Intruders," she says. "North door—"

"We already got the alert for intruders at the south door," the small, slim guard says, their voice high and irritated. "That's why we're locked down."

Hela plays up her breathlessness, shaking her head. "*More* intruders. Let me in, I have to warn them, we need to redistribute—"

The big guard frowns at her. "There's blood on your jacket."

"You're damn right there's blood on my jacket!" Hela snaps. "Why do you think I'm running through this building like a damn idiot trying to warn everyone? *We're under attack.*"

She's ready to kill them. That's what she tells herself, anyway. She's ready to kill them, even though she really hopes she won't have to. She's never killed anyone before, after all, and it would be really nice not to start right now, with this mountain of a guard who has freckles on his nose—

But the smaller guard just tugs open one of the doors, and Hela rushes through it with a grateful smile in their direction.

She feels like she's sneaking into the world's fanciest dormitory. Everything is the same carved-wood, copper-trimmed, needlessly decorative bullshit, and she tries not to touch any of it, because it feels wrong to mark it up with her greasy fingerprints. She tries to think of Orda's sketch, but she only memorized the route that she would need to get to the augur.

She turns down another hallway, this one finishing in a dead end that she thinks she heard Orda mention to Arias earlier. She rushes toward the door and opens it. Inside it is a lavish bedroom, with a lump under the blankets—no, two lumps, Hela realizes, as one of them sits up, her bedraggled hair hanging across her face.

"What the *hell*—" the woman says, and Hela is about to apologize when she hears a scream.

She takes off running. Her lungs burn, begging her to slow down, but she can't slow down. She sprints past the top of the stairwell and down the next hallway where Parekh, Arias, and Orda must have gone. She turns the next corner and finds herself face-to-face with a Talusar soldier in febra armor, holding a shortsword up to her throat. His hair is shaved brutally short, a nick around his ear still bright red.

Over his shoulder, she sees Parekh lying on the ground in a pool of blood. Arias is on his knees next to her, his hands in the air. And standing above him is a woman, even taller than Hela herself, her fair hair braided in a crown around her face.

She's beautiful, and Hela thinks of the religious texts she had to read for that one history class in high school, where the angels would appear to mortals and immediately tell them not to be afraid. Angels, Hela decided then, must look scary as fuck.

This woman's no angel, of course. She's Rava Vidar.

And the sight of her sends electric terror through Hela's entire body. This woman massacred the Cedrae in Calgara. She killed the Sword of Cedre. She wreaked God knows *what* havoc on Theren Forint—

"Drop your weapon," Rava says, in English. "Or get a blade through your jugular. Your choice."

Hela is a little impressed that Rava knows English well enough to use official anatomical terms like "jugular." But there's no choice involved in this: Hela drops her sword.

Parekh isn't moving. Arias looks up, hesitant, his eyes bright with tears. She wishes there was something she could say to him to make this better— she wishes she could go back in time and find a way to keep this from happening altogether.

But wishes are bullshit, as her mother was fond of saying.

"What's your name?" Rava asks her, and it takes Hela a moment to figure out she's actually expecting a response.

"Tausia Helasz," Hela replies, too wrecked by everything around her to come up with a clever response.

"Helasz," Rava repeats. Her mouth quirks into a smile. "Interesting. Well, Tausia—*cousin*—I'm afraid you're going to die today. But not quite yet."

57

Go to the pickup point," Theren tells Elegy, and though it's stated as an order, it comes out sounding like a request anyway. He feels Nyx's eyes on him, probably as she takes in his choice of pronouns and registers their meaning.

And that's why he feels like it reveals nothing more, to bend his head and touch a kiss to Elegy's lips in farewell.

She kisses him back, and says, "I will."

And she's not quite lying to him, he decides, but she's not telling him the truth, either. If Elegy reminds him of clear, still water, her deceptions are little ripples on the surface of her.

He opens his mouth to demand an explanation, or a promise. But he hesitates. She's letting *him* go, trusting that he knows what he's doing. The least he can do is extend that same trust to her.

So he turns away from her, and follows Nyx through the monastery.

Nyx leads him down the hallways he already knows, where he left guards unconscious or dead by their posts. Then she takes him into the central hallway, where the moon glows through stained-glass windows.

"You have a knack for getting into the beds of important women," Nyx says to him as they walk.

He's too worried about what's ahead to respond. He looks at the sword in Nyx's left hand, and considers taking it from her and running—back toward Elegy, so he can make sure she's safe. But he forces one foot in front of the other on the color-dappled stones.

He remembers the last time Nyx walked him through these hallways, taking him down to the basement so he could be scrubbed clean—and drugged—and then letting him lean on her as she guided him up the stairs. His memories of that time are hazy, but he recalls her being reassuring. He clings to that memory now—of her kindness.

When they walk through the doors to the sanctuary, he remembers that, too. Round and bare, with a square oculus in the ceiling, letting in moonlight. All the lanterns are lit, and in the shifting glow he sees two disparate parts of his life spliced together—people from his time in Valla, and people from his time in Losan, taking up the same space.

Arias and Hela kneel on the stone floor, unarmed and roughened up. Orda is with them, his shirt bloody and ripped, braced against the ground like he can hardly keep himself upright. Standing guard over all three of them are Satka and a soldier he doesn't recognize. Parekh is nowhere to be found.

On the other side of the room is Fenn Kovek, who meets his eyes with the same fervent relief Theren saw in his recovered memory, as if Theren is the only thing that matters to him.

And standing guard next to Fenn is Kesia.

It's absurd, really, that Kesia can still disappoint Theren after everything she's done. Days ago she told him she only ever wanted to help him; now she's here, guarding the same man Theren came here to rescue.

And in the center of it all, of course, is Rava Vidar, standing in a shaft of moonlight. She looks like a soldier, and she always has, her shoulders back, her feet apart, her hands behind her, ready to draw the weapon at the small of her back. There's a bruise under her jaw, faded and old, likely from sparring. She's never bothered to cover bruises or scars, as if she likes the way they look on her.

He's surprised by how familiar it feels to stand in front of her, despite all that's happened since the last time he saw her. He was in her bedroom, then, after Elegy's interrogation, tense to the point of trembling at the thought of what he was about to do—what he had already done. He'd waited, tension humming in his body, for Rava to fall asleep, then got the key to the interrogation room from where it was hidden: inside one of the books on her bookcase. He doubled back to grab the boots she left by the door, too, remembering Elegy's bare feet. And then he left.

But now he's different. Well-rested and well-fed; no longer in constant pain; given respect and purpose. It should feel different to face her now. When her pale eyes lock on his, though, he's exactly the man he was a few months ago, and exactly as terrified.

Rava steps over Orda's quivering form as if he's a stone in her path. Her pale eyes glint as they meet his.

"You're here," she says, and he's struck for the hundredth time by how curious she is—always interested even in the midst of her cruelty, like a child who pulls the wings off a fly just to see what it will do.

"I knew that you would come," she says, "but I confess that I thought you would go to the epocha first, and not the augur."

Fenn looks like he just tumbled out of bed, his feet bare and his linen pants rumpled from sleep, a silk robe askew across his shoulders.

"You don't know me that well," Theren says to Rava. Out of habit, he addresses her the same way he used to, as if he's still a captive and she's still the master of his fate. Perhaps she is.

"I know you enough." She smiles a little. "Still so respectful, even though you've clearly forgotten our rules of engagement."

"If I kneel now, will you spare them?"

"If I told you I would spare one of them, which one would you choose?" That curiosity again. "One of the Cedrae soldiers? The Talusar Scout? Your former lover?"

He can't help the way his eyes widen at that last one.

"I'm amazed you managed to keep the exact nature of your relationship with him from me for so long," she says. "I might have sent him to a monastery farther away if I'd known."

"No. You would have killed him."

She smiles.

"I almost forgot," she says softly, "how much you know. Tell me . . ." She reaches out, and clamps her hand around his jaw, squeezing so tightly he winces. Then she leans in close to his face. "What's in my heart now, truthsayer?"

"What did you do with the augur, Rava?" he says, and he doesn't think he's referred to her by her name, in her presence, ever before. He flinches a little at the sound of it, expecting retaliation.

She releases him, but doesn't back away.

"Your little tricks aren't going to work on me," she says. "I know what happens when people answer your questions."

"I don't need to ask questions. You killed an augur."

Rava gives him what appears to be an indulgent smile. "That would be sacrilege."

"You *killed an augur*," he says. "And you know that if anyone finds out, not even Ileth will be able to save you; you'll be burned alive. You told your people the augur was back at the Cenobium. You told the augurs she was here. But she's dead, isn't she?"

Rava looks for all the world like she's just unimpressed with a particularly bad performance. But he can feel the truth, the rabbit heartbeat that tells him he's getting close to something real.

"That is a ridiculous accusation," she says evenly, "designed to turn my people against me—"

He has to push harder. "Did you plan it? Or did you lose control? You never liked the way she talked to you, like she was better than you—"

"Fortunately my people know better than to take you at your word, Forint—"

"Maybe she said something to set you off—"

Rava brings the back of her hand down hard against Theren's face. His cheek stings. Beside him, Nyx draws a sharp, rattling breath.

Then without a word, she tosses Theren's sword to him.

He catches it in his right hand and draws with his left. Everything erupts into chaos.

58

Elegy isn't sure when, exactly, she realized what she has to do. Maybe it was right when she walked into the room and realized that if the augur wasn't here, and she wasn't in the Cenobium, she was probably dead. Or maybe it was when Theren successfully negotiated for Elegy to go free while he walked right back into his own personal hell.

Or when she remembered, like it was something out of a dream, biting her fingernails the day after she first went to the Cenobium. The taste on her tongue.

One who has tasted Cenobium salt. Those fucking augurs.

Either way, when she parts ways with Theren and Nyx, a promise to meet him at the pickup point on her lips, she's sure he knew she was lying. He always does, doesn't he? But he lets her go. He trusts her.

She watches him walk away, his shoulders back, his posture so straight it almost looks painful. Trying to steel himself to face Rava, and Elegy has never hated anything more. She has to grip the stone wall to keep herself from going after him. To remind herself that for all the pain she might cause him, Rava Vidar won't kill Theren. She can't.

Elegy pauses at the end of an empty hallway to gather herself, and to try to remember Orda's map. His hand moved in quick, confident strokes as he sketched it, and then the map spread wide on the kitchen table as he pointed out significant points on it: the south entrance, the north entrance, the probable location of the augur, Fenn's sleeping quarters, the central hallway, the temple.

The temple, she said to him, as if it was a question, and he told her that was where people were infected with Fever. From ritual bath to exposure in a room made to look like a church, and Orda's long, scarred finger traced the path, careless, as she thought about the fact that he and Theren had both passed through those hallways days before they died.

She starts to walk. Her footsteps are quiet and quick. And as she goes, she remembers the day her father was killed. Tax Day. Their next-door neighbor grumbling about the government as she swept the hallway with her old broom, the strawberry yogurt Elegy ate for breakfast, the way she ran out of faux coffee grounds and her mug was still half-full when she got the news that his body was found. He was killed trying to help a Talusar child flee Vidara so she wouldn't have to be exposed to Fever. A child just like Hela, in desperate need of help.

Sometimes there are no choices—one of her father's favorite phrases. She never understood why he said it to himself like a pep talk.

She understands now.

She goes down the steps to the first floor, and then around the corner to a small corridor with a vaulted ceiling. One of the stained-glass windows depicts a woman in a blue robe, her hand over her mouth and a mark on her throat—a priest. Beneath her is a set of stone steps leading down into the basement.

At the bottom of the steps is a heavy wooden door. At eye level is a little window the size of her palm, covered by a decorative screen.

She pounds on the door and waits. This part of the monastery is silent as a tomb. Which seems fitting, given what she's about to do.

There's a scraping sound as someone on the other side of the door slides back a shade. She meets the creased eyes of an older woman.

"My name is Elegy Ahn," Elegy says. "I'm here to meet your god."

59

Theren almost forgot how impossible it feels to fight Rava Vidar. Her eyes fix on his, and she pokes her tongue into her cheek, the way she does when she plays chess, and steps into a thrust that's actually a feint. He blocks the slash that follows with his vambrace, but only barely; he still feels the tip of her sword catch on his shirt as she withdraws, pivots, and advances again.

She turns him in tight circles, overwhelming him with speed. She may be smaller and weaker than he is, but in every other respect she has the advantage—speed, experience, technique, strategy.

She cuts again, quick, and he feels blood running down his arm. The pain is lost in the frantic need to press her back again.

She takes apart his skill like she's disassembling a weapon, making his feet falter and then unbalancing him, so he can't even muster enough power to threaten her. She cuts him again, this time in the leg, and deeper, so blood runs hot down his calf. He gets lucky and ducks under a blow to get away from the wall—if he lets her corner him, he's done for.

The only thing he manages to think, as he parries again and again and *again*, is that she could have won half a dozen times already. But she hasn't.

"You're not going to kill me, are you?" he says to her, and maybe he means it as a taunt, but it comes out like a revelation.

"I don't need to kill you to beat you," Rava says.

She grits her teeth, and swings so hard that catching the blow against his vambrace sends a painful vibration all the way to his shoulder. She's warmed up now, ready to batter him into submission, and so he does the thing that feels almost unbearable to him: he buries himself in the feeling of her.

Her vigor fills his chest, her fear gnaws in his stomach, her rage lights up his nerves. And only when he does that, when he loses himself completely in her, can he feel the little flash of insight that precedes every one of her movements.

He steps in time with her, their feet shuffling in unison like they're partners in a dance. They move through the motions his mother taught him, high guard and low, swords clattering together and pulling apart.

He moves *like her*, for the first time.

He swings his sword as she withdraws hers, and he can see it, the wide-open stance she just presented to him, as if offering her death to him.

He swings.

60

In the moments just before Theren Forint catches a sword in his out-stretched hand, Hela considers her situation. She's kneeling on the dirt under the watchful eye of two guards: one is the soldier from the hallway with the shaved head and a bleeding ear, and the other is a ragged-looking woman with dirt under her fingernails. Hela is pretty sure that one is Satka—she matches Elegy's description of the woman who once dislocated her arm.

Hela knows she's no match for either of them. Scouts aren't fighters, and she only has enough sopora in her ring to take out one of them . . . and that's only if she can get her hands free. Someone told her, once, that if your hands are bound behind you, the trick is to get your feet over them so you can shimmy your arms to the front of your body—but with two guards watching her, there's no way she can do that.

At least, not until they're distracted.

Then the sword is in the air, and Theren is catching it with his right hand, and both of Hela's guards are looking the other direction. She leans back to put her bound hands on the ground, then pulls them under her feet. At the same time Arias—either because he sees what she's doing, or because he's a real goddamn idiot—gets to his feet and rams his body into Satka, even though his hands are still tied. Hela scrapes her fingers against the stone as she drags her wrists under her ankles, her shins, and finally, her knees.

"Stop them!" Arias screams, and Hela looks up to see Kesia dragging Fenn out of the room with a knife at his throat.

Hela is pretty sure that manhandling an epocha is a good way to get yourself executed by Talusar authorities, but Kesia must have decided that Rava's wrath is worse than that potentiality.

Behind her, Arias is still trying to fight Satka with his hands tied, and she wants to help him. But this is her window. If Hela loses sight of Kesia and Fenn, they'll be gone for good.

So she sprints after them.

The hallway beyond the sanctuary is lined with blue stained-glass win-dows, so the light feels gloomy and unreal. Kesia is moving fast, and the blade is too close to Fenn's neck for him to do much to fight back. So Hela grabs one of the lanterns hanging from a hook on the wall and hurls it in Kesia's direction.

The lantern hits Kesia in the back, but instead of basking in her triumph, Hela feels a hand on her shoulder, shoving her hard against the stone wall. The guard with the nicked ear has caught up with her. He grabs her by the hair and slams her head into the wall. Hela's vision goes black for a second, and a warm trickle of blood runs down the side of her face as she tries to elbow the guard in the—well, *wherever.*

She hits him, but there's not much force behind the blow. His hand is on her arm, gripping so tightly she wants to scream. Instead, she turns toward him, leaning into him instead of away—and punches both hands into his chest at the same time.

It feels stupid, and she's pretty sure it looks stupid, too, but she doesn't care about finesse. All she cares about is cracking the shield of her ring, the one that contains the puff of sopora that can knock this idiot off his feet.

The shield breaks, and she thrusts her hands into the guard's face. He staggers back, and topples to the stone right in front of the door to the sanctuary. Behind Hela, Fenn has slipped Kesia's grasp and he's holding the lantern like a weapon.

Hela pursues the fallen guard, thinking only of the sword he was holding when she drugged him. She gets both of her hands—still bound—around the sword's grip, and looks up to see, inside the sanctuary:

Nyx, bleeding from the eyebrow and parrying with another guard.

Arias on the ground, his hands somehow free, about to take a kick to the chest from Satka.

And aglow with moonlight and febra, Theren Forint sparring with Rava Vidar.

People talk about Rava Vidar's brutality all the time, but they never mention how beautifully she moves, with all the controlled strength of a dancer. For just a moment, Hela is spellbound. She realizes that Theren isn't just Rava's captive, or her truthsayer, but her *student.* Even now, as they're fighting, he's imitating her, his movements becoming more fluid, his footfalls more graceful.

The sound of a lantern hitting the floor, its glass shattering, brings Hela back to herself. Kesia has Fenn crowded up against the wall, and she obviously sliced at his arm to get him to release the lantern, because he's bleeding now. Hela charges at her, sword held high, and swings.

She remembers, too late, that Kesia may be a coward and a traitor, but she's also a Talusar soldier. Kesia's hand clamps around Hela's wrist, so strong Hela has no hope whatsoever of breaking her grip. Kesia wrenches Hela's arm to the side, straining her shoulder, and punches her hard in the gut.

It knocks the wind out of Hela, and she stumbles back. Kesia pursues, her hand still tight on Hela's wrist, and pries the sword out of Hela's grasp.

Fenn swings the broken remnants of the lantern at Kesia from behind, but she's too quick for him; she turns to hit the lantern with her sword, sending it spinning toward the wall. Then she bashes the side of Fenn's head with the pommel of the sword.

All Hela can think to do, while she's unarmed and gasping and desperate, is to hurl her body at Kesia's as hard as she can.

The two women fall hard.

Out of the corner of Hela's eye, she sees a blur of blue as Fenn rushes back toward the sanctuary, back toward danger. But then Kesia is hooking a leg over Hela's to destabilize her, and shoving her to the side so Kesia is on top of her, pinning her to the stone.

Her hands close around Hela's throat, and she tries to scream, but a strangled sound is all that escapes her. Fenn is gone; she's alone in the hallway, and this is where she's going to die. Panic floods her system like electricity. She flails and thrashes beneath Kesia, but Kesia keeps her hold, pressing harder against Hela's windpipe.

Everything starts to go black at the edges, and all she can think is that it's not right, it's not right that Kesia gets to take so much and there are never any consequences—

And then Kesia screams—not a scream of rage, but a scream from deep inside her body, almost unearthly. Her hands slacken around Hela's throat, and Hela gasps. She feels warm blood gushing over her from a wound in Kesia's gut, and she sees the blue glint of a blade.

Kesia slumps to the side, and standing over her, face battered and body hunched and bloody sword in hand, is Arias.

61

Elegy waits with held breath for the priest's response.

The priest's eyes tighten, as if she's frowning. There's a patch of hazel on one of her otherwise-dark irises.

"We are not in the habit of performing this ritual on demand in the middle of the night," the woman says. "Particularly when the demand is made by one of our enemies."

"I thought it was your policy to pass the Fever on to the willing," Elegy says. "That Cedrae are considered untested and unrefined thanks to our avoidance of Fever, a weakness your people seek to correct."

"Political rhetoric has no place here."

"Yet you still referred to me as your enemy. Is that not a political distinction? Certainly you don't think I, personally, mean you any harm."

"You haven't been cleansed," the woman says firmly. "You can't enter if you haven't been cleansed."

Elegy doesn't have time for this. She needs to persuade this woman, and she needs to do it now.

"I spared a friend of yours," Elegy says. "Nisov was his name. I escorted him off Cedre Station and delivered him safely to the Cenobium. If you won't do this simply because I ask it, maybe you'll do it to repay me for that act of mercy."

The woman stares. Elegy considers removing the pins from the door's hinges.

"We received word of his arrival at the Cenobium just this morning," the woman says. "We didn't think he would survive the attack."

The woman slides the panel across the window again, and just as Elegy returns to contemplating the hinges, the door opens.

Elegy walks into a dim basement chamber. The air is moist, so dense she feels like she could take a bite out of it. The woman takes down her hood to reveal stark white hair that reminds Elegy painfully of Hela, in danger somewhere upstairs. The priest mark on her throat is distorted by her creased skin, but still distinct enough to see in this lighting.

"I take it you don't have time for the ritual bath," the woman says, a little wry.

Elegy can't quite tell if the woman is kidding. But then she sees lantern lights reflected in the faint ripples of a pool, and she realizes why the air is so moist. The woman takes her hand, and leads her past the pool and into the room beyond it, which is smaller, some kind of utility room. There are robes and towels piled high in the corner, spare lanterns, boxes of matches, bars of soap.

The woman drags a stool from the corner, sets it down in front of a low wooden crate, and points at it. "Sit. I must prepare."

Elegy sits on the stool and watches as the woman busies herself at a low counter. She picks up a small vial of something Elegy doesn't recognize, and holds it up.

"This will calm you, if you'd like," the priest says. "We offer it to everyone. It can produce a more . . . pleasant experience, for those who fear death."

"Doesn't everyone fear death?" Elegy asks, and the priest shrugs.

"Not to an equal degree." She sets the vial in Elegy's outstretched palm so Elegy can consider it.

The substance is dark red, like a Cedrae military uniform. She might have mistaken it for blood if she hadn't been told otherwise. She feels afraid enough to take it, eager for the peace it might offer her, but she needs her wits about her for what comes next. But she doesn't give it back to the priest—one thing she learned from her four years as a Scout is that you never give back a potentially useful object if you don't have to. She tucks it in her pocket, instead. The priest doesn't seem to care.

"Who may I credit for winning you over to the Fever?" the woman asks.

"The augurs," Elegy says.

The woman performs the sign of the Fever over her lips, and then turns to Elegy with a small bowl in hand. She sits down on the wooden crate across from Elegy, and sets the bowl in her lap. There's a slice of lemon in it. It's a beautiful object, Elegy thinks, the instrument of her death. Gleaming with delicate filigree. Blue and copper.

"Some of my younger brothers and sisters are more *romantic* about this process," the woman says. "They offer the Fever in a kiss, or they disguise what they're doing to make it more comfortable. I think it's better that you prove your commitment."

She holds the bowl up to her mouth and spits into it. Then she squeezes the lemon over it. Which is how Elegy realizes she's about to drink this woman's saliva.

"Elegy Rosyk," the woman says. "Until this day you were a child, untested by the world. After this day you will be an adult, or you will cease to be."

Elegy chafes at this, but doesn't comment. She's aware that her entire body is shaking, but her mind is clear and steady. *Sometimes there are no choices.*

"Do you know the words of our blessing?" the woman says.

Elegy shakes her head.

"The Fever, we say, is change. To face change is to die." The woman licks her lips, and continues. "The past self must die for the new self to be born, you see, and the Fever facilitates that birth."

She holds the bowl up to her mouth again, and spits again. Elegy's stomach turns.

"To die, we say, is to experience annihilation—just as the caterpillar dissembles itself in the chrysalis and reassembles in a new body. To be reborn, we say, is to conquer it. May it be so. May it be so."

She holds out the bowl.

"Are you certain?" the woman says.

It's probably too late regardless, Elegy thinks. She's been breathing the same air as this woman for several minutes now, which is enough to spread the Fever. But when she drinks this mixture, there will be no uncertainty: she *will* contract the Fever, and she *will* die.

Whether she comes back or not . . . well, even the augurs weren't sure.

But they also told her she would need to see the future to navigate the doorway in the stars. And it's not like she can kidnap an augur for her journey without starting an all-out war with the Talusar.

Elegy nods. She holds the bowl up to her lips.

The woman reaches for her, cradling her head as she drinks.

"I am eager to meet the real you," the woman says.

62

Theren sees a smear of blue in the doorway as Fenn rushes back into the sanctuary. Theren blocks Rava's next blow, and her next, but he can't find the focus he had before, he can't think of anything but Fenn too close to Rava for comfort.

And then there's a scream. A deep, horrible scream.

He knows that voice. It's his mother's.

"That sounded serious. My condolences," Rava says, as their blades cross again, pressing into him.

Theren lets out a wounded noise, and trips backward. She pursues him, fast, pulling back her sword long enough to sweep his legs from under him with a well-placed kick. He lands hard on his back, and scrambles away from her, his vision blurred.

Fenn's blue robes snap as he steps in front of Theren, his arms spread wide. Rava halts in her pursuit, her sword high. Theren thinks it's instinct for her not to attack Fenn, rather than intention—she has spent her life forbidden from doing violence to epocha, even though she likely is one herself.

Theren takes advantage of her hesitation and stands, chest heaving. He sidesteps Fenn to attack her again. This time he bears down on the blow with all of his strength, and she twists away, her stance collapsing. No matter how fast she is, she still can't out-muscle him.

He pursues. He blocks with one arm and swings his sword with the other, hard, his shoulder aching with the impact. Rava screams into her teeth as she counters it. He backs her toward the wall, moving fast and predatory, all hesitance lost.

Then he shoves her against the wall, pushing his blade up and into her throat, only to find that her sword is between them, holding him back. Their faces are so close together he can see the freckles at the corners of her eyes, the deepening furrows in her forehead.

All the times he thought about killing her, and here it is, her life in his hands, her pulse quick in her throat—

"You're done," he says roughly.

"I don't think so," she says, with a tight laugh. "To build a fulcrum, you need an epocha."

Rava Vidar's body suddenly loses all its tension, and he loses his grip on her. She slips down to the ground, like she's made of water. Then she lunges up, and away from him, thrusting her sword up—

And into the belly of Fenn Kovek.

Rava yanks the sword out right away, her eyes wide and mad, and Fenn falls to his knees on the stone. Theren can't think—he can't breathe. He's aware that Nyx and Satka have stopped fighting, that his mother might be dead, that Elegy is still gone, but he sees dark blood spilling over Fenn's hands and it's all he can think about.

He throws himself at Rava without remembering that he's even holding a sword, his teeth so tightly clenched they feel like they might crack under the strain. He can hardly see; he can hardly *think*, all he can do is lunge at her. He grabs her right hand, and she's not expecting it—reflexively, she releases the weapon stained with Fenn's blood, and he brings his blade up to her throat.

He feels—relief. As if something he's been waiting for, *longing* for, is finally in his hands.

"Careful," she says to him. "You need me alive."

"There are plenty of epocha in this building," he says. But even as he says it, he remembers: the fulcrum requires "one who bears the Vidari name."

"What will you do?" Her eyes are bright with moonlight. "Kill Ileth Vidar's daughter and then steal a holy epocha from a monastery? Do you believe that the entire nation of Cedre will not suffer the repercussions of such an act?"

He wants to spit in her face. He pushes the blade closer to her skin, so it bites her, and a drop of blood trails down to her collarbone.

"Cedre will suffer either way," he says. "I may as well take my revenge."

He feels a hand on his shoulder and almost lets go of Rava's wrist to elbow whoever is touching him, a reflex. It's Nyx, her grip firm.

"She won't be spared our justice," Nyx says coolly. "She'll be tried, and she'll be burned. Release her."

"I find it amusing that you believe the child of Ileth Vidar will be given a fair trial," Theren snaps. "Her mother has spent a lifetime covering up anything she doesn't want people to see."

He's so close. One moment of misjudged pressure, one push, and he'll do the thing he always planned to do—the thing Maeve died to do—the thing that will release him from the fear of Rava forever. The legendary soldier, the Butcher of Calgara, rendered small and fragile by the press of his knife.

"Theren," Elegy's voice says.

She feels cool and clear, as always. He feels her drawing closer, hears her scuffing footsteps. He still hasn't managed to teach her to walk quietly. She doesn't touch him, but steps into his line of vision. He doesn't know where she's been, but she looks pale and shaken. Vulnerable in a way he's never seen her before.

Arias is walking behind her, bloody and limping but still intact. He points his own weapon at Rava's back. They have her surrounded.

"Say your goodbyes to Fenn, while you still can," Elegy says. "Let me take care of this."

She covers his hand with her own, as if to take the sword from him. Her fingers are cool. He releases it almost without thinking, to let her take his place. There's no question of disobeying her. His loyalty to her is stronger than his thirst for Rava's blood.

Rava's lip curls, and he turns away before she can say anything that will make him regret it.

He crouches in front of Fenn and puts his hands on his friend's shoulders to keep him from pitching forward. Fenn's eyes find his, and for once they aren't distant, staring into a past that the rest of them can't even remember. He looks like the man who swore his oath, the man Theren knew before.

"My parents already think I'm gone?" Fenn says to Theren, in a low, weak voice.

Theren nods. Fenn's mother died last year, but there's no reason to tell him that now.

"That's good," Fenn says. "That's good."

Fenn tips his forehead onto Theren's shoulder, and Theren puts his arms around him.

"I'll stay right here until you go," Theren says softly, into his ear.

He can feel it, the moment Fenn loses consciousness. It's like a fishing line that's been cut, the tension suddenly gone. Theren smooths his hair behind his ear, and lowers him to the floor.

63

Elegy knows there's a deadly substance working its way through her body, and she almost expects to feel it, like a poison burning through every cell. But she feels the same. It will take hours for the Fever to grip her. She needs to make sure everything is in order before it does.

Fenn is almost gone. Fenn Kovek, whose real name is Fenn Vidar, like his father. One of the members of her fulcrum.

Only . . . obviously he's not. Because Rava Vidar is standing right in front of her. *One who bears the Vidari name*, indeed. Another clever bait-and-switch from the augurs.

Holding the sword right where Theren put it—right up against Rava Vidar's throat—Elegy reaches into her back pocket to take out the vial of the drug the priest gave her.

"Hello again," Elegy says to Rava, her voice quiet.

"Cedre swine," Rava says, like it's a greeting.

"You're going to drink this," Elegy says, holding up the vial. "Or one of my friends is going to hold you down while another one pours it down your throat. Which do you prefer?"

Rava sneers at her over the blade held to her throat, but she slowly raises her hand, palm up, to take the vial. Elegy gives it to her, and their fingers brush in the exchange, hers cool and Rava's warm.

Rava unscrews the top of the vial and pours its contents into her mouth.

"I don't know why you're still trying," Rava says, "when half your population is currently dying of Fever. There's no way you can hold off a Talusar attack now."

"I'm aware of that. That's why I'm taking a very important hostage."

She smiles at Rava. Rava's eyes roll back into her head, and Nyx surges forward to catch her by the arms. Elegy lowers Theren's sword, which is heavier than she expected it to be. Her hand is shaking.

"You're not taking her," Nyx says. She touches her fingers to Rava's throat almost tenderly, feeling for a pulse. But when she looks up at Elegy, her eyes are hard with anger. "She has committed the highest possible crimes against my people—"

"You're severely outnumbered," Elegy says to Nyx. "If you think you can stop us from leaving with her—"

"I'm outnumbered in this room, but you're outnumbered in this building," Nyx says, and she comes to her feet, her sword still clutched in her hand. "I can get you through it unharmed, but not if you kill me first."

"I suggest a compromise," Elegy says. "I'll appoint you as Rava Vidar's warden, with protected status among the Cedrae. You'll come with us on our journey on the *Sundial*. When we return to Earth, you can take Rava into Talusar custody, no questions asked."

Nyx narrows her eyes at Elegy.

"You want me to board a Cedrae spaceship on a journey you've never made before," Nyx says. "And just . . . trust that you won't kill me?"

"I'm offering you shelter after you turned against Ileth Vidar's daughter, something I think you'll find it difficult to hide when she sends her truthsayers to determine what happened here," Elegy says sharply. "In addition to the free pursuit of the justice you say is important to you. And the fact that I'm not ordering my friends to kill you right now, while you're outnumbered and alone, should earn me some trust."

Nyx's hand is tight around her sword hilt. Her eyes skip around the room, taking in Hela and Arias, Theren and Elegy, the limp form of Rava Vidar on the stone. Elegy has a feeling Nyx could take a few of them down with her, if she chose—she's one of Rava Vidar's lessers, after all. But she's unmoored, her faith in her commander broken and the cost of her decisions hanging over her head.

"You aren't worried about Talusar retaliation against Cedre if you remove its favored daughter from here?" Nyx says.

"Not when I inform your emperor that I've taken her alive," Elegy says. "I expect an armistice until our return, in fact."

"Your return will be bloody, if so."

"At this point, that's inevitable." Elegy holds out her hand. "I give you my word, you'll be returned here safely, with Rava Vidar's life in your hands, and yours alone."

Nyx considers Elegy for a long moment. She swallows hard. Then carefully, deliberately, she puts her hand in Elegy's and shakes.

+   +   +

Several minutes later, they all stand on the roof of the monastery, watching the Sparrow descend.

Scattered among them are four bodies.

In the aftermath of Fenn's death, it wasn't the Knight's body that

Theren wanted to take with them, but Kesia's. *He'll be honored here*, he said, of Fenn. The "and she's still my mother" went unspoken. Arias, who struck the killing blow, didn't argue, just heaved Kesia's body over his shoulders and carried her from the room.

Hela had already gone back for Parekh.

Elegy blinks tears from her eyes as the ship draws near and lowers its hatch. She remembers crouching next to the climbing wall during basic training, making her interlaced fingers into a cradle for Parekh's foot. She remembers how proud Parekh was when she told a long-estranged Elegy that she was now a Tertiary. Now blood stains her lips and hands, and the color has drained from her skin, leaving her ashen.

Elegy boards the ship first, then stands by the door to usher the rest in: Nyx and Theren, with Rava's sagging, half-conscious body stumbling between them; Arias, who lays Kesia Forint's body down on the floor next to the jump seats; Orda, now conscious but barely upright, his wounds temporarily sealed so they can get him to a hospital; and finally, Hela, carrying Parekh.

"Go," Elegy says to Isre, and he pulls away fast and sharp, because Valla's ships will find them any minute now. "Let's head straight for the *Sundial* before anyone can ask questions."

Air rushes through the cabin, the hatch still closing as they lurch away. She stands behind the seat and watches as the gentle lights of Dexa fade beneath them. All around the outpost is wilderness, dark and formless.

And the Fever is still crawling through her.

Come and meet our God, they said, and their god
was death.

—ZANNA HAVEN,
"THE FALL OF CALGARA"

BEFORE

Though he tries to delay it, the man knows it's time to leave.

He did what he came to the Cloistered Planet to do. He brought the plant to a safe place where no one from outside the Quarantine Zone will find it, and none of the native population will disturb it. He took his time building a launch platform for his ship, with the help of the strange doctor who still hasn't given him a name.

And he got to know the soldier. The woman.

Kesia, she said to him, when she'd finally given up on the idea of him being a spy for her emperor or for her enemies. And it was hard to persuade her of what he really was: an outsider, like the ones who once invited this planet out of their containment field to join the greater society outside of it.

She said her name with a *z*, like the buzz of an insect, but he can't help but soften it to the whisper of a bedsheet against a bare leg, or the distant drum of rain on leaves.

Kess-ee-ah. A name of relief, and that's what she was to him, a relief. A hard woman, as hard on herself as she is on him, at times.

He isn't expecting anything to develop between them, though the air seems to crackle every time they're together, and though he can't stop watching her face move as she talks. But she tells him that her people require every able-bodied person to bear at least one child, to further the goals of their empire—and she tells him the man she's been assigned is repulsive to her, but the only way out of it is to find another.

He almost sighs at the pieces coming together, as he always does. The exarch didn't tell him what else he would be doing here, on this Cloistered Planet, only that his mission was twofold and its second part would present itself in due time. And it's no hardship, to put an arm around Kesia's waist and draw her close and kiss her. To let it all unfold from there.

But now he has to leave.

He spends the night with her in her favorite place: in the desert, under the stars. She points out constellations to him that he won't remember, and he points to dark spaces that look indistinguishable from the rest, to tell her where he's going. It's too cold for them to strip down, so they bare only what they need to, to come together one last time. And in the morning, as the sun rises, he kisses her sleepily and walks a few yards away, to a patch of bare land.

With a twig, he scratches a long line of numbers into the sandy soil, one by one. He memorized them a long time ago, before his child ever existed, before he knew there might be a need for one. When he finishes, he presses his palm to the ground, and tries, insofar as it's possible, to imbue this moment with significance, so it will be easier for the seer of the deep past to find.

When he returns to Kesia's side, she's awake, the blanket wrapped around her shoulders. She looks up at him.

"You should name it," she says. "Since it's the most you can give the child of yourself."

"Apart from whatever genes I pass on," he points out, as he kneels in front of her.

"Let's hope they get your face." She smiles, but he knows she means it, too; she describes herself as plain, and perhaps she is, but he still can't stop looking at her.

"My sister passed a long time ago. Her name was Akara," he says. "So if it's a girl, Akara. And for a boy . . . you can give him an old family name. Traditional for my people."

"You're hesitating, which means it must be silly," Kesia says. "I reserve the right to refuse a silly name for my son."

"No, no." He looks down at their hands, tangled together between them. "It's not silly. It's just that I have a feeling it will be a son, so it feels . . . significant."

"Spit it out, Sevik."

"Theren," he says. "Name him Theren."

64

It's the day of the *Sundial*'s launch, and Hela is dreaming about a conversation that already happened.

She's sitting in a teahouse. Its support beams are painted bright red and the walls are lined with low benches, each one upholstered in colorful patterns. The room is packed with couples leaning over small tables, their feet and hands brushing. Hela and Parin look out of place only because they aren't gazing lovingly at each other.

"You ever take a date here?" Hela says.

"No. Too cheesy."

"Some people like a little cheesiness," Hela points out.

"Some people like you?" He picks up the glass teapot on the table between them. Inside it is a single orange goldfish swimming around. Dream logic.

"I wish you'd come with us on the *Sundial*," she says.

"I would, but my uncle . . ." Parin shrugs. Parin's uncle has what he likes to call a "delicate constitution." "Besides, there's no room for me anyway. Tight crew."

"I know."

"Be safe, okay?" he says, and she understands, just for a moment, how he manages to win over so many paramours. Soulful eyes. Soft voice.

"Yeah," she says, and both of them look toward the door, where Rava Vidar is charging in with her sword held high.

"Time to go, I think," Parin says, and Hela nods. And wakes.

When she opens her eyes, her blankets are bunched up at the foot of her slim cot on the *Sundial*.

The ship is already launching, and has been for at least twenty-four hours—a vessel large enough to sustain a journey this long takes a long time to get moving. The only sign that anything's changed is a faint hum in the walls and the urgent feet of the engineering staff in the hallways.

She checked the news pavilion before she spoke to Parin yesterday. There are still no hints anywhere about Elegy's coup with the *Sundial*. No one has reported that the ship was cleared for launch by two generals and the Quorum instead of the Sword herself. Larke seems content to pretend that it was her plan all along—to announce that the *Sundial* would be converted into a museum as a cover for finally launching it with her sister on board—which is just fine, as far as Hela is concerned.

A tapping sound makes Hela straighten. She drops the blanket and looks up to see Forint in her doorway, looking even more worn than the last time she saw him.

"She's asking for you," he says.

Hela gets to her feet and follows him into the hallway. She's been hearing about the *Sundial* all her life. A little ship that would seek out strangers in another solar system—Elegy spoke of it like a beautiful dream. The reality, though, is a tight space built with ruthless efficiency. She's in the women's barracks, in a five-high stack of beds.

"Arias's with her now?" Hela says, as she falls into step beside him.

He walks like a soldier, she notices, with his hands clasped behind him and his shoulders back.

"He just left, had to report in for the launch," he says. "Did you check in with the security team about Nyx?"

"She's fine. They're giving her a wide berth."

Rava is imprisoned across the ship, locked in a storage room converted to a cell, with a rotating security detail. Nyx is right beside her. General Thompson was kind enough to start drafting the contract guaranteeing her protected status as soon as they arrived. Not that a Cedrae contract means much to a Talusar soldier, but it will mean something to the people on the *Sundial*.

They turn the corner and step into the Priory—the quiet part of the *Sundial* where the essential crew live. She walks back and forth down this hallway twenty times a day now.

Theren, Arias, and Hela have been taking turns staying with Elegy as the Fever progresses. There were some arguments in the beginning about whether she should eat—Theren said no, Hela said yes—and how they should handle the flow of information outside of this hallway—Arias advocated for informing the ship's commander that she was sick, Hela said absolutely not—but they've ironed most of those things out.

Now all that's left to do is wait for her to die.

She's right outside Elegy's door when Theren stops her with a gentle touch to the elbow. He's gentle in general, Hela has realized. Quiet and careful. She isn't sure what to do with someone like that. She can't needle him like she does everyone else.

"You should know," Theren says, "she's seeing things."

"Seeing things."

"People." Theren tilts his head a little. "Shir, mostly."

She finds herself wishing, as she has a few times the last few days, that he was easier to read.

"Is that normal?" she says.

"Happened to me."

She thinks of asking him who he saw. But then she thinks better of it, and opens the door to Elegy's room.

It's one of the bigger living spaces on the *Sundial*, which isn't saying much. The walls are gray, but warm light seems to emanate from them, so she feels like she's standing inside a lantern. A screen along one wall—made to look like a window, just like the ones that are so common on Cedre Station—shows footage of a forest during a rainstorm. The sound of the droplets against the leaves plays gently in the background. Elegy sits on a cushion, her knees bent and her arms wrapped loosely around them, staring up at the trees.

Hela goes to sit next to her. This close to the screen, the trees are the only thing she can see.

Elegy looks like she's dying. There's no other way for Hela to think of it. She's paler than she's ever been, and sweaty. The skin under her eyes is purple. Her lips are almost colorless. She blinks at Hela for a few seconds before recognizing her.

"Hela," she says, and she smiles. "You came."

"Of course I came, El," Hela says. "I heard you wanted to see me."

"Shir wanted to meet you," Elegy says, and she bumps her shoulder to the right, like there's someone sitting on her other side. "He wants to hear all the embarrassing childhood stories."

Hela's chest aches.

"Oh boy," Hela says. "Buckle up, Shir, you're in for quite a ride."

Elegy laughs, and Hela begins.

65

Theren is sitting with his back against the wall the next morning when Arias comes in to relieve him. Elegy's sleeping, the heat of the Fever having passed and the chills only just beginning. It went against his instincts to give her a blanket, knowing it would only make her body hotter, but they're all waiting for her to die, including Elegy herself. So when she asked for a blanket, he got her one.

Arias steps into the room, holding a cup of coffee. He looks down at Theren with a frown.

"Have you slept at all since we boarded?" he says.

Theren shakes his head. "I'll sleep when she's gone."

"No, you'll spend three days worrying she won't come back," Arias says. "Come on, man. Get some rest. I've got the next few hours."

Theren sighs, and pushes against the fabric wall to get to his feet. Arias has a point. Elegy's death, which will come sometime later today if his own Fever timeline is accurate, doesn't offer any relief. Even the augurs weren't sure if she would survive this.

He can't quite meet Arias's eyes when he moves toward the door. Arias holds out a hand, touches it to Theren's chest to keep him from leaving just yet. He wears his trademark expression of deep concern. Theren doesn't think he can bear the sight of it for more than a few seconds.

"You ever going to be able to look at me again?" Arias says.

Theren meets his gaze. "I don't blame you. Kesia was about to kill Hela. I'm glad you didn't let that happen."

"Sure." Arias takes his hand away, but the look of concern remains. "She was still your mom, though."

"Not really. Not by the end."

The worst part was watching Isre cry over her body in the back of the Sparrow, after they linked up with the *Sundial*. Theren couldn't watch for long. He was too busy making sure Orda was being cared for. He left his brother alone to grieve as he argued about the necessity of hazmat suits with some of the paramedics, and then pestered one of the aides General Thompson sent about providing Orda with a pardon. Elegy helped with that, in the end.

It was hours before she told him she was infected.

I had to get some things in order first, she said. *We don't have much time.*

There was never any goddamn time.

"I'm sorry," Arias says, and he's sincere, and that's worse.

"I'm not," Theren snaps, and he leaves the room in pursuit of a few hours of sleep.

+ + +

He falls asleep on a hospital bed in med bay, waiting for an update on Orda's condition. He wakes an hour later to a cleared throat. A nurse stands above him, her surgical mask tucked under her chin, still wearing the full-body smock they all put on as a precaution when they learned Orda was Fevered. It floats around her like gossamer.

"We're putting your friend in the healing tank to make his recovery less painful," she says to him. "Thought you might want to say goodnight before we sedate him."

Theren nods, and gets up. The nurse looks alarmed.

"Careful there," she says. "You don't look so good yourself."

He blinks at her, still half-asleep. He's bruised, and he has some gashes that are now glued shut, but he's otherwise unharmed. Nothing like Orda, beaten bloody, or Elegy, dying of Fever.

She leads him down a short hallway to a room that almost looks like a boiler room. He's used to the hospital nearest him on Cedre Station, stark and white and clean, but this one's all pipes and ductwork and wire, less inviting than the imitation stone walls in the rest of the ship. There are three healing tanks in the room, each one a glass coffin. Two are dark now, empty, but the one on the end is glowing like an aquarium, ready to be filled with solution.

Orda is lying down on a metal tray extending from the foot of the tank, wearing skintight shorts, an IV in his arm. His body is mottled with bruises and streaked with cuts. The nurse loops a plastic tube over her elbow; at the end of it is a mask that she'll attach to his face, so they can pump oxygen into the tank. They'll sedate him first, though.

Orda sees him, and flips his hand over, reaching. Just that small movement makes him stifle a moan of pain. Theren hooks his fingers around Orda's, and stands over him.

"I hear you get to dream through your recovery," he says.

"Lucky me," Orda replies weakly. "How is she?"

Dying, Theren thinks, but he can't bear to say it out loud. "You know how she is. But it can't be helped."

"She'll make it." Orda squeezes his hand. "When she wakes up, tell her thank you for the pardon, okay?"

"A pardon's just paper; you should thank her for sneaking you on this ship like an adolescent hookup." Theren grins.

"Not enough climbing the drainpipe for that. So we're going to the great beyond?"

Theren nods.

"You should say the prayer," Orda says.

"I'm not going to pray for you like you're dying, Selio."

"Not for me." His fingers squeeze again. "For your mother."

"She was Rava's, in the end," Theren spits, before he can stop himself. "Just as she probably was the entire time."

"Come on, Theren. She only ever served herself, and you know it." Orda closes his eyes. "Put her to rest anyway."

Theren is quiet just long enough for Orda to look at him again.

"Do as I say," he says.

"Yes, Teacher."

Orda's lips quirk into a smile. The nurse holds up the syringe she'll use to inject the sedative, like she's not sure either of them can understand English. Theren releases Orda's hand.

He steps back as the nurse injects Orda, staying in the other man's eye-line until he drifts off. Then he steps back again, giving her space as she attaches the mask to Orda's face, secures it, and slides the metal tray back into the healing tank. She seals that, too, and flips the switch to start the flow of solution.

"It'll take a half hour to fill up," she says to him. "You should go lie down. You look dead on your feet."

"I can spare a half hour," he says.

He stays until the tank is full, watching Orda's now-weightless body drift in the blueish fluid like a child in a swimming pool, practicing a dead float.

✦ ✦ ✦

Later, when Hela is finished telling stories to an imaginary Shir Alexios, and Elegy has fallen asleep again, Theren returns to Elegy's room. He lies on his side in front of the big screen at the back of the room, face-to-face with her, the same way Kesia did when he was dying at the monastery.

Elegy surfaces, blinking at him slowly. Their hands are centimeters apart on the cushion. She kicked off the blanket at some point in the last hour, and her feet are bare. She puts one foot over another, letting her toes knit together.

He was worried, when they first boarded the *Sundial*, that there was nothing they could do to help her with the pain of the elixir in her blood coming into contact with the Fever. But Isre went to a friend, who raided the hospital's supply of elixir purge—used for allergic reactions to Imbuing—and they gave Elegy a dose right away, before the Fever could boil her from the inside out. It was a small mercy, but he's grateful for it now, that she doesn't have to spend her last hours screaming in agony or drugged into a stupor.

"Do you remember it?" she says to him, in a whisper. "Dying?"

He wonders if she recognizes him. The last time he was here, she didn't.

"Sort of," he says.

"What was it like?"

"Did you ever go swimming as a kid?" he says. "And sit at the bottom of the pool to see how long you could hold your breath?"

She nods.

"It's like that," he says.

"That doesn't sound so bad."

He brushes her hair behind her ear. "It's not."

She curls her arm beneath her head, and leans in close to him. "Oh, you shouldn't do that. I don't think my husband likes you very much."

Her eyes skip over to a space somewhere behind him, where the specter of Shir Alexios no doubt waits. Theren smiles at her.

"Sorry," he says. "I keep forgetting you're married."

"He's just jealous because you're sort of devastating."

His smile turns into a grin. "If I recall correctly, he's not so bad himself."

She gives him a sleepy wink.

"Tell him I mean no disrespect," he says.

"Tell him yourself."

"We're speaking Talusar," he says. "Does he speak Talusar?"

"He knows the dirty words."

She reaches out and presses her palm to his forehead, like she's checking his temperature. Her perpetually frowning mouth frowns, if possible, even further.

"You don't feel so hot," she says. "I thought Talusar were supposed to run hot."

"I don't feel hot to you because you have a high fever."

"Do I?" She yawns. "I think I'd like to sleep now."

He leans in, and touches his forehead to hers. From here, all he can see is her freckles.

"Good night, Elegy."

He's not sure how long he stays there, breathing the same air as her, before her heart stops beating. But he doesn't move until her skin cools.

+   +   +

The *Sundial* is in motion.

There are no windows on board. They would only be points of vulnerability in a craft that can't afford any. But there's a screen in the navigation deck that shows Earth and Cedre Station behind them, so that's where the crowd gathers to watch their planet shrink by fractions of fractions.

He stands near the back of the room with Isre at his left. Isre is still glassy-eyed with grief, wearing the red jumpsuit that signals his work as a technician. They crane their necks to look through the crowd at the space station that was, at one time, the only home they'd ever known.

"How long do we wait?" Isre says to Theren. "Before she wakes up?"

"No more than three days."

His fingers are still pruned from caring for Elegy's body. Hela helped him with the ritual, once he explained its purpose. To clean the dirt from her skin, from between her teeth, from her scalp—so that when she wakes up, it's with less horror at the state of her own body. After, they dressed her in clean clothes, and covered her with a blanket, as if she was just sleeping.

Even he was surprised by how obvious it was that she *wasn't* just sleeping, though he'd been through it himself. There was no mistaking her stiffness, her coldness. She was gone. It seemed impossible that her hollow lungs could ever draw air again, that her quiet heart could ever beat again.

He's spent a lifetime not understanding why the Talusar worship the Fever. But for something to bring life back to that empty body does seem . . . otherworldly.

Isre puts an arm around him. Theren drapes his arm across Isre's shoulders, in turn.

"So we sail for a doorway," Isre says to Theren, and though he doesn't ask it like it's a question, Theren can feel that it is.

Theren nods.

"Do we . . . know where it is?" Isre says.

He's not sure how to answer that question. The coordinates are buried in the past, and only Rava Vidar—an epocha just like Fenn, no matter what she claims—can access them. He has no idea how to get her to do that, or how to pry the information out of her mind once she does. He doesn't want to admit how little he knows. But this is Isre. He has to be honest with his brother.

"No," Theren admits. "But Rava can find out. So I just have to get her to tell us."

Isre's response is hesitant: "Not to be a pessimist, here, but . . ."

"But why would she ever do that?" Theren supplies. He looks at Cedre Station, now noticeably smaller than the last time he focused on it, and his jaw tightens.

"I'm going to make her," he says.

66

Elegy dreams of the void.

She dreams of darkness unfolding infinitely, like a skein of black yarn with no ends.

She dreams of pinprick stars and distant, glowing nebulae and planets swollen with gas and ice and rock.

She dreams of twin moons and fields of broken asteroids; of the poison brightness of the sun as it inches inexorably toward supernova.

She dreams of the end of Earth, coming by—

fire and

winter and

radiation and

its core petering out like a spent coal.

She dreams of the *Sundial*, sun sail unfurling to deflect rays too bright and too potent for its inhabitants to bear; and the numbers of coordinates sealed behind Rava Vidar's knife-slice mouth; and catapulting around the edge of the galaxy to return, a failure, to the planet from which they came.

She dreams of a fleet of ships far too vast to comprehend

and a throat so dry the air tastes like ash

and a man with honey-colored eyes spitting blood.

She dreams—

—of a dark doorway

—and beyond it, a swirl of color

—and a sequence of words like a knot of syllables that she can't tease apart.

She dreams of what might come next—of what may and what does and what doesn't.

She opens her eyes.

ACKNOWLEDGMENTS

I started writing this book almost six years ago with no intention of publishing it. I had it in my head that a book that made all the pleasure centers of my brain fire at once just couldn't be a serious project. But when I told two of my friends about it, Courtney Summers and Somaya, they pointed out that there was no reason that should be the case. The world is too dark and life is too short to spend it resisting things that bring you joy. So why not write a big, romantic, indulgent, genre-straddling story? So thank you to S and C for that pep talk, without which this book would still be a (giant) pile of words on my computer.

Thank you also to:

Joanna Volpe and Jordan Hill, for hopping right on board, as always, and for being so diligent in helping me with a project that was a little closer to my heart than usual.

Lindsey Hall for being up for the big chonky duology challenge, and for helping me find clarity. Aislyn Fredsall and Hannah Smoot, for all your hard work and for keeping the train on its track.

The team at New Leaf Literary, my home since its founding: Lindsay Howard, for the support without which we would all collapse; Katherine Curtis, Eileen Lalley, Kwali Liggons, Keifer Ludwig, Alaina Mauro, Hilary Pecheone, Kim Rogers, Joe Volpe, Tracy Williams, and Donna Yee.

The team at Tor Books, the best possible home for a genre book that's hard to describe: Megan Barnard, Andrew Beasley, Alexa Best, Harper Bullard, Alex Cameron, Claire Eddy, Michelle Foytek, Rafal Gibek, Dakota Griffin, Will Hinton, Emily Honer, Lizzy Hosty, Catherine Hui, Audrey Iorio, Jim Kapp, Katie Klimowicz, Eileen Lawrence, Christina MacDonald, Emily Mlynek, Devi Pillai, Sarah Reidy, Lucille Rettino, Erin Robinson, Heather Saunders, Stephanie Sirabian, Tiana Tolbert, Becky Yeager, Yvonne Ye, Jaime Herbeck, and Katy Miller—this book would also still be a pile of words if not for you all; thank you for working so hard on it at every stage. Elishia Merrick, at Macmillan Audio, for giving this book life in audio.

Kristin Dwyer, for strategizing, cheerleading, and sending me a heap of GIFs when you finished this book. Adele Gregory-Yao, for keeping me organized, and for our various design chats.

Most of the writers who have been kind enough to give me their friendship over the years write contemporary fiction (i.e., no futuristic cities, no spaceships, no magical resurrecting viruses). They have nonetheless been the most supportive and sympathetic friends a gal could ask for. Thank you especially to Kaitlin Ward, who read an earlier draft of this book and gave valuable feedback. And Maurene Goo, Morgan Matson, Sarah Enni, Zan Romanoff, Diya Mishra, Jennifer E. Smith, Kate Hart, Amy Lukavics, Kara Thomas, Michelle Krys, and Laurie Devore.

My family, both the Ross/Roth/Rydz/Rockoviches and the Fitches/Gerlichers/Johnsons, for your continued support and care. Please, for the love of God, skip chapter forty-nine.

My non-writer friends in Chicago and Los Angeles, for giving me a life outside of work, full of laughter, understanding for my deep introversion, and also wine.

And of course, Nelson and Avi, my dearest friends.

ABOUT THE AUTHOR

Veronica Roth is the *Sunday Times* bestselling author of the Divergent series (*Divergent, Insurgent, Allegiant* and *Four: A Divergent Collection*), the Carve the Mark duology (*Carve the Mark, The Fates Divide*), *The End and Other Beginnings* collection of short fiction, *Chosen Ones, Poster Girl, Arch-Conspirator, When Among Crows, To Clutch a Razor* and many short stories and essays. She lives in Chicago.